THE C

The human race has [...]
for millennia. Certainly t[...]
the generations whose g[...]
from the norm. Most di[...]
be born. Those who did, often had only a very brief
existence.

But once in a great while genetic mutations may
not only survive but prosper. Have the next steps in
human evolution already been created? If so, what
forms have they taken?

Now sixteen talents take us on exploratory journeys
into the nature of humankind's future, in such memo-
able tales are:

"Freak"—Most people couldn't stand to be around
[hi]m. Some pitied him, others ignored him, but Jenny
[...]d offered him nothing but kindness. So how could
[...] turn away when he was the only one who could
[...] her from a terrible fate?

"The Great Deep"—Father and son, they'd come
back to the shore and the house that had brought
them so much happiness before death had stolen the
most precious member of their family. They'd hoped
to find healing here, but neither had ever anticipated
seeing a family legend come to life. . . .

"Paint Box"—They were art students, here for a
week's study. And though they'd been warned to
watch out for ghosts, no one had told them that the
living could be far more frightening. . . .

THE MUTANT FILES

THE
MUTANT
FILES

Edited by

Martin H. Greenberg

and

John Helfers

ELIZABETH R. WOLLHEIM
SHEILA E. GILBERT
PUBLISHERS
www.dawbooks.com

CONTENTS

INTRODUCTION
by John Helfers

The word mutant carries different connotations depending upon the point of view of the person who hears it. For scientists, it represents a creature marked by a basic hereditary change that is fundamentally different from its parents, and is sometimes better adapted to live in its natural environment. Natural selection ensures that these advanced creatures are the ones to survive, thereby making what was once a mutation the accepted norm. In this way, we have evolution.

However, say the same word to any twelve-year-old boy during the summer of the year 2000, and chances are all you would hear about for the next few minutes was the movie *X-Men*, in which mutants with superhuman powers battled other mutants in order to protect the rest of us puny normal humans. The same word, but two very different definitions.

Of course, when we think about and discuss mutation today, we usually prefer to think about the positive aspects of it. Physical deformity, increased susceptibility to disease, and mental deficiency are all hallmarks of mutation as well, nature's failed attempts at creating a superior human being. But once in a great while, the scale tips the other way, and there are people born into this world with strange and unexplained powers.

People who can see through space to locate missing persons. People such as Uri Geller, who claims he has telekinetic powers. Even today, there is a man on television named John Edwards who claims he can speak with the dead. Many people would call these examples of psychics—others, excellent con artists. But who's to say that they don't represent the next step in the human evolutionary chain?

Ultimately, what makes mutants fascinating is that they know, on a basic level, that they are different from everyone else around them. They may not be able to put a finger on why they feel this way, they just know it is true. It makes for a hard life, for if mutants truly existed, as in movies and literature, they would be unable to confide in others for fear of ridicule or scorn or fear. They would be destined to walk a different path, hiding whatever it is that makes them different and unique from everyone else.

Of course, the idea that powerful mutants are living among us right now is speculative nonsense, fodder for comic books and special-effects-laden movies. But if mutants did exist, then they would keep their powers secret from the rest of the world for obvious reasons. Which doesn't mean that they aren't out there. . . .

The following sixteen stories celebrate the idea that there are those men and women in this world with powers unexplainable to normal humans. Charles de Lint takes us inside the mind of a boy who knows your every thought, and the ultimate sacrifice he makes to protect his only friend from that knowledge. Tanya Huff tells of a very special little girl who fights for her freedom the only way she knows how. Jody Lynn Nye takes us to a dark future where mutants are outcasts exiled from Earth, and a group of them prove that they are just like any other human. And Michelle West drops in on a girl living on the streets of a city, perhaps the same city you live in, doing whatever it takes to survive on her own. These and other tales await you, stories of men and women who may look just like us, but most assuredly are very different. But rather than fear them, try to understand them instead, and realize that, no matter what powers others may have or what they may look like, in the end, we are all just human.

FREAK

by Charles de Lint

Charles de Lint is a full-time writer and musician who presently makes his home in Ottawa, Canada, with his wife MaryAnn Harris, an artist and musician. His latest novel is *Forests of the Heart.* He has a new collection out called *Triskell Tales,* and his classic novel *Svaha* will once again be available. Other recent publications include mass market editions of *Moonlight and Vines,* a third collection of *Newford* stories, and his novel *Someplace to Be Flying.* For more information about his work, visit his website at www.charlesdelint.com

1

"Do you understand the charges as they've been read to you?"

"Yes, sir. I do."

"How do you plead?"

"Guilty, your honor."

2

"Get your head outta them comic books." Daddy'd say. "They're gonna rot your brain."

And I guess they did.

Or something happened to me that don't have any kind of an explanation that makes a lick of sense 'cause there's a mess inside the bones of my head that's been giving me a world of grief pretty much ever since I can remember.

I hear voices, see. Sometimes they're only pictures, or a mix of the two, but mostly it's them voices. Words. People talking. The voices show up inside my head with no never you mind from me, and I can't shut 'em out.

They come to me about the same time I learned how playing with my pee-stick could be a whole lot of fun. I never knew it was good for anything but peeing until I woke up one night with it grown all big in my hand and I never felt anything near as good as when out comes this big gush of white, creamy pee. I felt bad after—like I was doing something dirty—but I couldn't seem to stop.

But when I finally did, the voices didn't.

For the longest time, I thought I was imagining them. I didn't have me a whole lot of friends, living out by the junkyard like we did, so it makes sense how maybe I'd get me an imaginary friend. But they was just voices. They didn't talk to me; they talked at me. Sometimes them voices used words I couldn't tell what they meant—they'd be too big or in some foreign language. And sometimes the pictures that come to me were of things that I'd never seen before—hell, stuff that I couldn't even start to imagine on my own—and sometimes they were of things I didn't *want* to imagine. People doing things to each other. Mean, terrible things.

I figured maybe the voices were punishment for all that playing I done with my pee-stick. You know, instead of growing hair on my palms, I got all this noise in my head.

But because they wasn't telling me nothing personal—they wasn't talking *to* me, I mean, like telling me I'd been bad or something—I come to realize that maybe I got something broke in my head. It was just something that happened, no accounting for it. Like I'd become a kind of radio, tuned to a station only I could hear, and these voices was just coming to me outta the air.

I can't remember when I finally worked out that

they was other people thinking, but that's what they are, sure enough.

Funny thing about 'em is how they come with a smell. Like, take Blind Henry, lives on the street, same as me. His thinking's like the tobacco juice usta build up in the spit pot in Daddy's office. It was my job to dump it. I'd take it out to that cinder-block building at the back of the junkyard where we been dumping all manner of things. Oil and dirty gas, yeah, but other stuff, too. You'd go into that building and your eyes'd start to sting something fierce and the taste of puke'd rise up in your throat.

I remember the first time I saw the pirates come— I knew they was pirates because they had the Jolly Roger on the side of the barrels they brought in that big truck of theirs and they come late at night, secret-like. I looked hard, but I never saw no one with a peg leg or a parrot. Still, they had the skull and crossbones, so I knew 'em for what they was. That first night I snuck outta the trailer and followed Daddy and them pirates to the cinder-block building and stared in at 'em through the window. But they wasn't hiding any treasure. Them barrels with the Jolly Roger on 'em only had some kind of watery goo that Daddy dumped into the pit.

Anywise, I was telling you how every voice's got its own smell. Daddy's was sweaty leather, like that old belt of his he used to whup me whenever he got in a mood. Mama's was like fruit, rotting on the ground. Kinda sweet, but not right.

The best voice is Jenny Winston's. It smells just like she looks, fresh and kind, like apple blossoms and lilacs when the scent of them comes to you from a few backyards over. Not too strong, but you can't mistake it.

I learned pretty damn quick to hide the fact I could hear what a body was thinking. People don't like it. It don't make no never mind that I can't stop from hearing it. They just assume you're a-doing it on purpose.

But I'd give anything to make it stop.

I can't never make 'em go away completely, I guess, not unless I went to live on some desert island where there was nobody else to do any thinking, but how would I live in a place like that? I can't do much for myself 'cept look for handouts as it is.

But I can tune 'em down some by listening to music. I don't know why it works, it just does. That's why I always had me spare batteries for this little transistor radio of mine—I'd make sure I got batteries afore I saw to getting me enough to eat.

It's hard in here without that radio. The voices that fill my head are cold and mean and hurting.

But better'n the radio was live music.

Sometimes, afore they put me in here, I'd go in back of The Rhatigan, that little jazz club over on Palm Street. I'd sit in the alley by the back door and listen to the house bands play. It was best in the summer when they got the door propped open and them cool, moody sounds come floating out—they don't just take the voices away; that music makes me feel good, even when the band's playing a sad song, or the blues.

3

"Bernie—can I call you Bernie?"

"Sure. That's my name."

"You know I'm here to help you."

"Sure."

"The court may have appointed me to represent you, but that doesn't mean I don't care about winning this case."

"Sure."

"I think we need to send you in for psychiatric evaluation."

"I'm not crazy."

"Bernie, copping an insanity plea is the only chance we're going to have to save you from long-term incarceration or worse."

"I'm not crazy."

"This state still has a death penalty."

"I know that."

"If we don't do something, Bernie, you could end up on death row."

"Maybe that's the best place for something like me."

4

Daddy died first of the cancer. It just started growing in him one day and afore you'd know it, it was spread all through him. He was in a lot of pain by the time it finally took him, which made him real hard to be around. My head was filled with the screaming of his thoughts the whole time. That was an ugly time.

Mama died not long after—cancer took her, too— but she went quietly. Like a long, drawn-out whimper.

Cousin Henry took possession of the junkyard and become my guardian until I turned sixteen. Then he sent me packing with hard words and meaner thoughts.

That's how I come to be living on the street this past couple of years. I tried to find work, but nobody wants something as ugly as me to look at, day after day.

See, I never had no chance at a normal life. It's not my hearing the voices—I learned pretty damn quick to keep that to my own self. It's that I look like a freak. Got no meat on my bones, but I got a head big and round as a damn pumpkin, and my skin's all splotchy with big red marks like I got me freckles on steroids. It made the kids laugh afore I dropped out of school, but now people just stare, then look away, like I turn their stomach or something.

I always had that big head and I never did grow into it. There's times I wish it was even bigger so that I could get a steady gig in a sideshow or something. People'd still make fun of me, but it wouldn't be the same, would it? It'd be like my job. I'd be getting paid for being a freak.

In them comic books I used to read, I'd've been a hero, what with being able to read people's minds and all. I woulda got myself some fancy clothes and a mask and I'd go out and save people's lives 'n stuff. It wouldn't matter if I looked like a freak 'cause I'd be part of some gang of superheroes, saving the world 'n stuff and people'd admire us and like us, even me. In the comic books, a freak like me can still live a good life. Hell, sometimes they even get them a girl.

But I don't live in no comic book, and the only time I'd tried to be a hero is what put me in here.

I ain't saying I didn't mean to do what I done. Hell, I'd do it again if the situation come 'round same as it done before.

How it happened was I was panhandling outside the gates of Fitzhenry Park. It's mostly women give me money. I guess, ugly as I am, they still want to mama me. Or maybe they're mamas themselves, thanking God their own kids didn't turn out like me and they drop a couple of bills in my cap like they would an offering of thanks in church.

I don't ask. I just keep my head down and say, "Thank you, ma'am," earphones in my ears and the music from my radio keeping me from hearing too much of what anybody's thinking.

The day it all went down, Jenny Winston comes by like she often does. She's one of Angel's people, them sorta social workers who help street people 'cause they care, not 'cause it's some job.

Jenny's good on the inside and out. I should know. She's the prettiest woman I ever saw, but anybody can see that. But I hear her thinking and there's not a bad thought in her head. She can look at me and all she sees is a person, not some freak with an oversized head.

This day she gives me a sandwich and a little carton of milk, asks me if I need anything, so I take the 'phones outta my ears to answer her properly. That's when I hear the thinking of the guy standing behind her.

The look of me turns his stomach, but that's no big surprise. It's what he's thinking 'bout Jenny that makes my blood run cold.

Lotsa people think bad things. The difference between bad people and good is that good people don't act on 'em. If you didn't know better, you might get confused as to which a fella might be, but I've got so's I can tell the difference.

And I can see in his head, he's done this afore. Courted a pretty gal and then done away with her. He's got him a whole set of graves, laid out in a nice little row, way back up in the mountains.

How come he never got caught? You'd think somebody'd have figured out he's got all these girlfriends disappearing on him. But there he is, standing behind Jenny, not a care in the world, just kinda daydreaming of the day he's gonna do her in, too, so I guess he's got something working for him.

There's folks like that. There's folks get away with pretty much anything. It's like common sense just turns its head away from them, don't ask me why. And the more I listen to him, the more I see he's a sly one. Not many folks know how serious him and the gal's getting. Usually he pretends he's getting a divorce so they can't let on how it is between 'em until the paperwork's done. So this gal, she's got herself a true love, they're gonna get married and all, but she can't tell anyone just yet.

I see all that in his head. It's something he thinks 'bout all the time—these are the things that make him feel good.

And this time he's gonna do it to my Jenny.

I don't mean I ever thought she'd be interested in the likes of me. Hell, I'm just an ugly freak; I ain't stupid. But she's been kind to me. She's kind to everyone. She's not like some of the others who work with Angel to help us street people. Most of the others come up offa the streets and it's their chance to give something back. But Jenny wasn't like that. She's helping 'cause she's got her too big a heart. She wasn't hurt as a kid. She didn't live on the streets. The thing is, she just can't stand by when others are in need. It's as simple as that.

So she's ripe for the plucking of a man like the one standing behind her now, accompanying her on their rounds afore they go to dinner, pretending to care so much for her. She don't see through him 'cause she can't read what's inside another's head like I can. 'Cause she only sees the good in people. While he, oh, he's a-glorying in what's to come.

How come somebody as good as her attracts that kind of person?

I don't know. Same reason that people like my parents are allowed to have them kids, I guess. There's no sense to it, not unless we were really bad people in some other life and this is payback time. But I don't buy that. Life's just the way it is. Kids get born into families that don't even want 'em, never you mind love 'em. And good always attracts evil. The strong feed on the weak. Guess if there's any rule to living, that's what it is, and it's up to each of us to put what charity and kindness we can muster back into the world.

So I get up off my feet and I walk over to him. I reach under my coat to where I got me a sheath hanging under my armpit and pull out that old Randall knife I stole from my Daddy's office afore Cousin Henry sent me packing. It's got an edge sharp enough to shave with, which I've done a time or two. I don't say a word. I just whip the blade across his throat and cut him deep.

People mistake me. They think 'cause I'm so skinny, got this big head, that I can't move fast. But it ain't like that at all.

It's over and done afore anybody can make a move. Then he's falling, blood spurting outta his neck. Jenny's screaming—oh, what she thinks of me hurts something fierce. There's other people on the sidewalk screaming and rushing around.

I try to tell Jenny what he was thinking, how I can read what's in people's heads, but she won't listen. She can't hear me. And I realize it don't make a whole lot of difference anywise.

I just drop the knife on the pavement and stand there, watching the real freak die while I wait for the cops to come and take me away.

5

"Do you have any last words?"

I look through the plate glass window to where the witnesses are sitting, staring back at me, all strapped down and waiting to die. There's a lot of dark thoughts coming my way, but I can pick out Jenny's real easy. I just follow the scent of apple blossoms and lilacs. She's sad, but there's a hardness in her, too. She's looking at me, thinking there's the man who killed the fella I loved. He deserves to die for what he done. But she's not easy about this business of a death penalty. It feels too much like revenge to her. And though there's a part of her wants revenge, she knows it's not right. Trouble is, she's not strong enough to stand up and say it's wrong neither.

Do I have any last words?

I could tell back what Jenny's thinking right now so that she'd know I was telling the truth. I could go right into her head and pull the thoughts out, word for word. But then she'd have to live with her part in putting to death the man who up and saved her—and I can't let that happen.

She's safe now. That's all that matters.

"Yes, sir," I say. "I ain't sorry for what I done. Best you give me that injection now."

And they do.

SUGAR AND SPICE
AND EVERYTHING NICE
by Tanya Huff

Tanya Huff lives and writes in rural Ontario with her partner, four cats, and an unintentional chihuahua. After sixteen fantasies, she's written her first space opera, *Valor's Choice* (DAW April 2000) and her sequel to *Summon The Keeper,* called *The Second Summoning,* is a DAW March 2001 release. In her spare time she gardens and complains about the weather.

Dr. Philips is an idiot. Oh, she's nice enough in that too-smiley, "I want us to be friends" kind of way, but I've been seeing her for almost two years now, ever since the tests showed I'd turned four, and she still hasn't caught on. The thing about child psychologists is that they don't observe you in order to learn about your behavior. See, they've already made up their minds about how you should be acting, so they're actually observing to see that your actions agree with their theories. Once you know what their theories are—piece of cake.

One afternoon, when she was paying less attention than she should have been, I gave myself a nasty paper cut during the building of a large papier-mâché T-Rex. In spite of anti-cuddling rules, there's really only one way a caring person can respond to a four-year-old who refuses to stop crying. With my face pressed damply into the curve of Dr. Philips' neck, I think I learned as much about her as I could about her thoughts on me. And you know what? By the time you can put a doctor in front of your name, you're way too old to be dotting your i's with little hearts.

Anyway, as long as I answer her questions within the parameters she's established, she's happy.

"I assure you, Mr. and Mrs. Howard, Danielle tests well within the parameters for a gifted child of her age—an exceptionally gifted child of her age."

See what I mean?

"Yeah, well, her age."

A quick glance showed Dad slumped in his chair staring at the scuffed suede toes of his dress shoes. He sounded tired and confused. I didn't blame him; neither of my parents were very bright. Considering they were chickens trying to raise a duck pretending to be a chicken they were doing a pretty good job and I loved them a lot, but, bottom line, anyone with half a brain would never have accepted procreative help from the Benjamin Avob Basic Biology of Aging Center in the first place. Dad wasn't even my biological father—but since neither of them knew that the other half of my chromosomal mix had come out of a seven-year-old sperm deposit, I kept the discovery to myself. It wouldn't have made any difference and, besides, they'd have asked how I knew.

From the change in her tone, Dr. Philips had re-arranged her smile into its almost patronizing but ever so supportive curve. "I understand that it's been challenging, which is why the Center feels it's time Danielle begins attending that play group we spoke of earlier."

"One of the main tasks of childhood is to establish friendships with other children both in one-to-one situations and in group situations. Peers play an essential role in the socialization of interpersonal competence and skill acquired in this manner affects the child's long-term development."

Mom does that, parrots back information the doctors have told her, or that she's read online, or clipped from one of the half-dozen parenting magazines she subscribes to. It's her way of letting them know that she's paying attention.

It always annoys Dr. Philips when she does it. Sometimes, I think that's *why* she does it. I mean, Mom got screwed by this almost as much as I did although I'm pretty sure I've fixed most of the early, accidental damage.

I couldn't quite suppress a heavy sigh, but by the time the doctor turned to look at me, I was crouched over a model of the International Space Station, rubbing my right ear reflectively against my knee, stretching out the top of one pale pink ankle sock and trying to place a bright blue rectangle intended to represent one of the solar cells on the body of the station. Given the visual evidence, she could only conclude that the noise had come from some sort of construction frustration.

When she closed the file and stood, my parents—trained through dozens of similar meetings—stood as well. "Bring Danielle in on Monday, then, at one PM."

"She has French on Monday afternoons," Mom reminded her.

"I think Danielle is as fluent as she's going to get right now. It's not unusual for children to plateau in their language development for a time," Dr. Philips added quickly, "particularly as other areas of growth are occurring." From the way her voice trailed off, she'd just realized she'd given Mom another quote. Unable to do anything about it, she continued. "The play group is where Danielle needs to be at this time. If you want to be there for the first introductions, Mr. Howard, I'm sure I can arrange it."

"No. Thank you."

My dad works as a janitor at the Center. After eighteen years, they call him a Custodial Supervisor but he's really just head janitor. Good thing he likes the job because he'll never be able to leave it.

"Dani."

Leaving the Space Station half completed, I crossed to Mom's side and wrapped my hand around hers in a practiced, protective gesture. It was perfectly normal for small children to be overprotective of their mothers. I could almost see the warm glow of satisfaction radiating from Dr. Philips. She just loved the fact that, in spite of everything, I was so normal.

We met Dr. Thorton in the hall. Mom's fingers twitched, and I tightened my grip.

"Mr. and Mrs. Howard, how are you this afternoon?" Dr. Thorton's voice filled the broad hall outside Dr. Philips' office and would have been enough to stop progress even if his bulk wasn't blocking the way.

"We're all fine, Dr. Thorton."

"Good. Good. And, Danielle, how are you?" The broad smile under the button nose folded swooping curves into the generous cheeks.

I muttered something that might have been, "Okay" and then buried my face against the warm curve of Mom's hip.

The doctor leaned closer and I wondered why he didn't tip over with all that weight balanced so precariously on tiny feet. "Aren't you a little old to be making strange, sweetie? You know me."

Oh, I knew him all right, the sadistic s.o.b.

"She's four." Dad gripped my shoulder protectively.

"Yes. Of course she is." Dr. Thorton's voice rang with fake jolly tones that would have embarrassed a shopping mall Santa. Dr. Thorton sucked at doing jolly. "I'll bet she's really looking forward to play group."

"Children ages three to six require opportunities to learn cooperation, helping, and sharing," Mom told him, and we shuffled past.

I had a feeling his mouth was open, but I didn't dare check his expression.

Dr. Thorton is a megalomaniacal fool, but he's not an idiot. As Director of Research at the Center, he's one of the few with all the pieces of the puzzle. This is all his fault. I'm *his* failed experiment. I hate him more than you can possibly understand, and I'm going to do him if it takes the rest of my life.

Which is a joke.

With any luck, it's going to take about six months.

Am I looking forward to play group? He can bet his double doctorate I am.

"Danielle, this is Julie Natoobo, Franklin Chin, Sean O'Mara, and Betsy Wojtowicz."

Dr. Philips' cheery political correctness was evident in the racial mix. It was like being on the bridge of the original *Enterprise* without the cheesy special effects. If she hadn't needed an odd number to better study group dynamics, I'm sure there'd have been gender equality as well.

I flashed the quartet of children a brilliant smile and let go of Mom's hand. "Race you to the top of the monkey bars," I called and took off across the grass at top speed. Franklin reached the painted steel a moment after I did, the other three about two paces behind. I won, but by a very small margin. The moment all four were on board, I started talking.

Did you know that conversational skills increase the likelihood that children will become friends with a peer?

I laid it on with a shovel. Wow, could they ever run fast! Gee, look at them climb! I did a little playful teasing. I threw in some interesting gossip—although it was tricky figuring out what gossip even smart four-year-olds would find interesting.

Children sustain and feel satisfied in friendships where the ratio of positive to negative processes is maximized.

Mom isn't the only one who reads those magazines.

Human beings are hierarchical by nature. Toss a group of them together and one of them will end up the leader, the rest followers. It was essential I become the leader of this particular group. Fortunately, four-year-olds are fairly easy to impress because no matter how smart they are—and this lot was at least as smart as Dr. Philips thought I was—they're still four years old.

And I'm not.

Physically, I'm no different than my companions. Looking at me, you'd see a normal, healthy, four-year-old girl—essentially blonde hair, more-or-less blue eyes, dirty knees, the whole package. But according to the experimental data I uncovered by hacking into Dr. Thorton's files through his laughingly inadequate encryption, I'm about fifteen. An exceptionally intelligent fifteen.

Next year, I should be getting my driver's license. I should be starting to date. I should have breasts. I should be menstruating. My incipient womanhood should be making my father nervous.

Given my intellect, I should be at the stage where I've gained power over my own life—an early high-school graduation, the beginning of advanced degrees, a few inventions, a couple of discoveries, my picture in the papers.

Next year, I'll still be four.

And I'm pretty pissed about it.

Way back when, Dr. Thorton did a little illegal mucking about on the genetic level, re-creating a mutated copy of a gene found in nematode worms that controls aging. Of course it wouldn't have been illegal if he'd stuck with worms, but he overheard my Dad telling a fellow custodian how he and Mom were having trouble getting pregnant. Taking advantage of their desperate desire to breed, he offered to help, pumped Mom full of fertility drugs, and scrambled her eggs.

His intent was to slow aging *after* maturity.

Oops.

Failures don't get the kind of publicity success does, so I'm the Center's dirty little secret. Mom and Dad were convinced if they told anyone I'd be taken away and dissected. I'm not sure why Dr. Thorton's never gone the "accidental death" and dissection route, but I suspect it's because I'm the closest thing to a success he's ever had. Of the hundreds of other mutated zygotes mentioned in the early files only three of us attached ourselves to the uterine wall and only I was carried to term. The other two were selectively terminated when it became clear things were going very wrong. I liked to tell myself that I was going to do Dr. Thorton for my siblings' sakes as well, but—bottom line—it was all about me.

By the time I grew out of the eggplant stage, I'd been tested in every way known to science and in a few ways they'd created specially for me. Over time, Dr. Thorton's various reactions taught me what to shut down to make the test results conform to a normal profile. Every anomaly meant more tests. More hours spent strapped down like a large lab mouse.

The more normal I appeared, the more he left me alone.

Most babies wouldn't remember the pain and the terror.

I did.

I needed to get Dr. Thorton alone in a place with no surveillance cameras, and I needed some help getting us both in there at the same time.

Not exactly easy for a four-year-old.

Thus my manipulation of Dr. Philips, who continued to think that the play group had been her idea.

We met three times a week for ninety minutes— Monday, Wednesday, and Friday—playing outside in the enclosed playground when the weather was good and inside in a redecorated conference room when it wasn't. After the first three weeks—having survived a challenge by Betsy in week two when it was discovered she had twenty-seven teenie babies to my twenty-two—I was the undisputed leader of the group. By week four, I could get them to do anything I wanted.

"I'm bored," Franklin announced, hanging upside down from the top of the monkey bars. He made a grab for Julie's Mr. Sparky and missed. "Bored. Bored. Bored. Stupid. Bored."

I leaned into the tiny triangle uncovered by the

cameras—the reason we spent so much time on the monkey bars, well, that and because I was sick of being thirty-seven centimeters tall—and said, "Let go."

You'd be amazed at how high something as essentially fragile as a child can bounce without damage. When, during the hysteria that followed, Franklin never once said, "Dani told me to," I knew it was time to move on.

That afternoon, I started a new game based on a lame Saturday morning cartoon that involved a secret society of dogs saving the world—usually against cats. We did a lot of barking and burying things in the sandbox and arguing over who had to pretend to be the cats. The cats were the bad guys and no one wanted to play them—especially after what we found in the sandbox. We called it Spy Game and the whole thing was pretty much inexplicable to adults which was exactly how I wanted it.

Two days later, when the rain had moved us indoors, I tried to move Spy Game inside. Sean stared at me like I was out of my mind.

"Not *now,* Dani! We *always* play hide-and-seek before snack!"

Four-year-olds, even smart ones, like schedules. It helps them make sense of a confusing and ever changing world. Don't think for a moment I didn't know that.

There were lots of places to hide in the conference room, thanks to Julie. After an early and unsuccessful game, she'd planted herself in front of Dr. Philips, crossed dimpled arms, and announced indignantly, "We need more stuff. We can't hide without stuff."

"Why don't you play something else?" Dr. Philips had asked in her most condescending way.

Smiling broadly, Julie locked eyes with the child psychologist and said, "Let's spend the afternoon watching Barney!"

We got more stuff so fast it made skid marks on the carpeting; big foam shapes, a tent with a tunnel, child-sized beanbag chairs, plastic shelves, multi-colored boxes, and all the mess that five active children trapped inside on a rainy day can make.

And we *always* played hide-and-seek before snack.

Snacks came up from the cafeteria kitchen on the same kind of carts they used in the laboratories—stainless steep top and an enclosed bottom with enough space under it for a four year old to hide. After Sean made it all the way down to the kitchens and was returned by a snickering security guard with stories of enough fish sticks to reach the moon, the Snack Lady kept the lower doors open and checked the compartment before she left the room.

Adults essentially keep to schedules for the same reason as children. You could set your watch by Snack Lady.

We played Spy Game after hide-and-seek and, with pointed looks at Dr. Philips, developed a secret language capable of expressing astoundingly complex thoughts using bits of four other languages, funny gestures, giggling, and rude noises. Adults didn't get it. Not even when we tried to explain.

"So, Danielle, I hear you kids have a secret language."

The straps kept me from turning my head but, as usual, I could see the reflection of the monitor in Dr. Thorton's glasses. Brain wave activity was textbook normal. "Uh-huh."

"Tell me about it."

"Can't."

"Why not?"

I rearranged my face into the easily recognizable *grown-ups are so stupid* expression. " 'Cause it's a secret."

Okay, I, personally, didn't try very hard.

Spy Game held everyone's attention for two more play groups and then blew up when Betsy vehemently and vocally protested the unfairness of a game where she *always* had to play cats. Then she pushed Franklin over and sat on him. This was exactly the opening I'd been waiting for.

"I know, I know! We make grown-ups the bad guys."

Well, that's how it translated—I actually hit my forehead twice while spinning around, used the French word for "we," played patty-cake with myself, stood on my head, coughed up a little German, and meowed. If it's all the same with you, I'll stick with the translation from now on.

The others were intrigued, especially by the idea of keeping it a secret. Children love secrets. They give the powerless a sense of power. We wouldn't let the "cats" know we were on to them.

The groundwork had been laid, and Dr. Thorton still had no idea I was coming for him.

Part two was going to be trickier, but by the next rainy Wednesday, everyone knew the parts they were to play in the Case of the Big Red Cat with the Neutron Ray Who Was Trying to Rule the World. Franklin made up the name. Julie was so excited she began wetting the bed again.

It all started with Sean. Usually, Sean's nanny picked Franklin up at his mother's condo, drove to the Center, walked both boys up to the conference room, and handed them over to Dr. Philips. On this particular Wednesday, Sean was going to take one for the team. Halfway up the stairs, he'd pull free of his nanny's hand, miss the next step, and bounce back to the bottom before she could say, "The rain in Spain falls mainly on the upper Pyrenees."

Franklin had been upset that he wasn't going to be the one falling, but then Franklin had been upset when he hadn't been the one to get the eraser stuck in his ear.

It had to be Sean.

Sean's father was an actual practicing MD rather than a research scientist. He worked for the Center as the doctor in residence, and I strongly suspected that Dr. Singh's sabbatical and Dr. O'Mara's hiring had been so that Sean could join me in play group. Because it had been a temporary situation from the beginning, the O'Maras wouldn't be around long enough to notice anything unusual about the way I aged. Or rather, didn't.

Sean would fall, scream, and be taken to see Daddy. Franklin would tag along because, well, he was there.

Dr. O'Mara was a bit of an overprotective father or possibly an all inclusive hypochondriac—the number of preventive supplements Sean took daily lent either conclusion equal weight. With his only son shrieking in his office, neither he nor the woman being accused of allowing the accident to happen would be keeping much of an eye on Franklin.

Benjamin Avob Basic Biology of Aging Center worked with a number of research subjects in their eighth and ninth decades. If we ignored the way they'd given their permission for the wires and the probing and the tests and I hadn't, the only real difference between us was that my bowels worked fine, thank you very much. In Dr. O'Mara's office, in a cabinet kept unlocked due to frequency of use, were some of the strongest laxatives known to science.

It's amazing what people will repeat in front of a four year old. Maybe they think we're too short to hear them.

Franklin's mission: while Sean's daddy's distracted, grab one of the capsules that looks like a big root beer jelly bean.

"And I'll hide it in my belly button!"
"Okay." Who was I to discourage initiative?

Sean won't actually be hurt. Once Dr. O'Mara and the nanny are convinced of this, both boys will continue on to play group.

Next up, Betsy.

Dr. Wojtowicz was the Center's Chief Administrator, and on Dr. Philips' recommendation, Betsy had lunch with her mother every day we had play group.

Professional parents feel extremely guilty about the time they spend away from their kids, and since they were both at the Center, they might as well put in some quality parental bonding, right?

That bit fell into place without any help from me.

Dr. Wojtowicz's office was down the hall from the conference room we used when the weather was bad.

Usually, when Sean and Franklin passed Dr. Wojtowicz's office, Betsy would join them. On this particular day, there'd be a certain amount of shoving and, during this childish give and take, Franklin would pass Betsy the capsule. Betsy would then run back to kiss her mother and drop the laxative in the coffeepot.

Betsy almost refused to cooperate.

"My mama's not a cat!"

When Franklin sniggered, "Betsy said snot!" she pushed him down and sat on him again. Classic displacement of immature affection into violence according to Dr. Philips who is, as I may have mentioned, an idiot.

"We're protecting your mama from grown-ups who *are* bad guys," Julie explained, glancing over at me for approval.

When I nodded, Betsy reluctantly agreed to do her bit.

Every Wednesday afternoon, Dr. Thorton went to Dr. Wojtowicz's office where they spent approximately ninety minutes arguing about the business of science. They managed to run the Center in only ninety minutes a week by having agreed not to bog each other down with minutia. For example, Dr. Wojtowicz didn't bother telling Dr. Thorton about how she'd saved hundreds of dollars by ordering food for the lab animals in bulk from a Brazilian supplier and Dr. Thorton didn't bother telling Dr. Wojtowicz about me.

I was just the janitor's unexpectedly smart daughter who went to play group with her Betsy. When Betsy moved on at the end of the year, it wouldn't occur to Betsy's Mommy that I'd be staying behind. She didn't move in the same social set as my parents, and it wouldn't be long before she forgot me entirely.

Dr. Wojtowicz drank only herbal tea. Dr. Thorton drank the coffee.

By the time Sean, Franklin, and Betsy joined me in the conference room, I'd nervously chewed the antenna of a plush Teletubby into purple polyester pulp. Waiting to discover if the first part of the plan had been successfully executed had been the longest twenty-seven minutes of an already chronically skewed life.

With all three of them talking at once, high-pitched voices raised to maximum volume as they tried to outshout each other, there was almost no need for a secret language. Dr. Philips, the only adult present, all but covered her ears and I imagined the audio portion of the surveillance tapes would be unintelligible without some high-tech adjusting.

But why would anyone bother? Of course my friends had exciting things to tell me; Sean had just fallen down the stairs.

When Julie showed up with Mr. Sparky, we synchronized our watches. Winnie the Pooh, a Power Ranger, Barney, and two Blues of Blue's Clues all showed essentially the same time—given the various objects rotating as second hands, an exact match wasn't possible.

As usual, we started playing hide-and-seek just before the Snack Lady was due to arrive. I watched the cart pull up in front of my hiding place and, while the Snack Lady unloaded juice boxes, carrot sticks, and animal crackers, I slid carefully onto the bottom shelf.

The Snack Lady never turned the cart to leave the room, she walked around it and pushed it straight back out. She'd notice the extra weight at the first turn, but I wouldn't be with her that long. As we drew near the bathroom door, Franklin announced he had to pee and everyone had to stay hidden until he got back. When he opened the door, I rolled off the shelf and, hidden from the cameras by the cart, crawled into the bathroom.

Franklin was tall for his age. By placing the rubber stool we used to reach the taps onto the toilet seat and then standing on it, he could just reach the cover of the ceiling vent with the plastic screwdriver from the Big Guy Handyman set. One twist pried the cover off, and then he boosted me up.

"Find the others really, really slowly," I reminded him as he shoved the vent cover back in place.

Even for a four-year-old, the air duct was a tight squeeze. I dragged myself along by my elbows following the building plans I'd pulled up out of the maintenance files while a loop of Smileyland music had convinced my parents I'd been enthralled by dancing happy faces.

Dr. Wojtowicz's bathroom was exactly like ours. A quick look through the vent determined it was empty. That wasn't good. There was a limit to how badly even Franklin could play hide and seek. Fortunately, as I was securing my hair ribbon, the door opened.

Dr. Thorton.

I watched enthralled as he hurriedly lowered his trousers but the rolls of fat blocked my view. He dropped to the toilet, it groaned in protest, and I stopped paying attention to exactly what he was doing.

With one hard push, I shoved the vent out. Held by one end of the ribbon, it swung down and hit the wall. Dr. Thorton looked up. Eyes wide, he managed half a sound as I emerged from the duct. Hanging by my knees, a move practiced over and over again on the monkey bars, I grabbed his cheeks.

During the first two years of a child's life, most of the growth of the brain occurs accompanied by the structuring of neural connections. The first "two" years of my life went on for a very long time.

I always knew how much my mother loved me. As long as we were in physical contact, I could hear her thoughts. *Love. Comfort. Safety.* When I got a little older, I could hear the words that went with them. Technically, I was receiving and translating the electric impulses of her brain. Colloquially, I could read minds.

Certain childish desires, vehemently expressed, led to the discovery I could also edit minds.

Like I said earlier, I was mostly able to fix my mother.

No one was going to be able to fix Dr. Thorton

Trouble was, I needed physical contact, skin on skin, and I needed to get that physical contact in such a way that no suspicion would fall on me. I had no intention of losing even the limited rights childhood allowed.

I got back to the play group bathroom just before Winnie the Pooh's right hand—or possibly paw—pointed to the three. Elapsed time, six minutes, most of that spent crawling through ductwork. Dangling from the vent, I dropped down onto the toilet and slid off the edge, one of my feet plunging into the bowl ankle-deep. Way gross. Fortunately, my shoes and socks were dark and the soaking didn't show.

I shook off as much water as I could and waited just inside the door.

Julie never went anywhere without Mr. Sparky, a ten-centimeter-tall metal robot her dad had made her out of an antique building set he'd had since he was a boy. At quarter after, safely hidden behind a bean-bag chair, holding Mr. Sparky between Snuffy and Bots, my two least favorite teenie babies, she was to stuff his conveniently sized arms into a wall plug.

Winnie the Pooh said quarter after. The lights went out.

I slipped through the smallest opening possible and, by the time the lights came back on not even a moment later, was crawling out from under the computer desk to see what Sean was screaming about. Turns out Sean's afraid of the dark.

I'd have fixed it for him, but he wasn't the only one screaming.

For a woman her age, Betsy's mother managed impressive volume.

It seemed that Dr. Thorton had taken two nice, new number two pencils out of his pocket protector, put the pointed end in each eye and, holding them steady, had taken a hard run, face first into the bathroom wall.

Let's see how *he* likes having things poked into his brain.

No one told the play group that, of course. Not the sort of thing you'd want four-year-olds to hear about. I don't know what Betsy's mother told her to explain the screaming, but no one told the rest of us anything.

A nearly hysterical lab tech filled Dr. Philips in on the gory details as she stood in the open door, staring down the hall toward the commotion but unable to leave her charges. She was obviously shaken as she closed the door and sank down into the nearest chair.

Sucking a tiny burn on one thumb, Julie walked over and patted her hand. "Are you okay, Doctor?"

"I'm fine," she said, catching up Julie's hand in hers and smiling weakly around at the rest of us. The smile froze as it reached me, and I realized that the pale gray carpet under my wet sneaker had darkened. Dr. Philips looked from the carpet to my face, holding my gaze for a long moment before continuing to smile at each of us. "I'm fine," she repeated with even less conviction.

Maybe Dr. Philips isn't as much of an idiot as I thought.

Not a problem.

I have plenty of time to deal with it.

THE GREAT DEEP

by Sophie Masson

Born in Jakarta, Indonesia, in 1959 of French parents who are themselves of mixed ethnicity—Basque, Portuguese, Spanish, and Canadian as well as French—Sophie Masson lived with her grandmother in France when she was a baby. She went with her parents to Australia at the age of five, and lived there for the next twenty years, with visits to France every two or three years. It is this growing up between different worlds, languages, and cultures, that is reflected in her work. Her first two books, the adult novel *The House in the Rainforest* and the children's novel *Fire in the Sky,* were published almost simultaneously in 1990. Since then, she has had more than twenty-five novels published in Australia, for adults, young adults, and children. Several of her novels are now being released in the U.S.A., and she has also had many short stories published in anthologies, magazines and newspapers in Australia, the U.K., the U.S., and Italy, as well as essays in journals and magazines all over the world, including online. Her books have been shortlisted for many awards, including for the Aurealis Award for Science Fiction and Fantasy (for *Cold Iron,* published as *Malkin* in the U.S.). Some of her novels have also been optioned by film producers, and her stories broadcast on radio and released on audio books.

> *"Full fathom five thy father lies;*
> *Of his bones are coral made;*
> *Those are pearls that were his eyes;*
> *Nothing of him that does fade*

But doth suffer a sea-change
Into something rich and strange."
—William Shakespeare, *The Tempest*

If it had not been for his son Henry's broken heart, the Reverend Doctor William Featherstone would never have been on the remote little Welsh beach on that bright, fateful summer morning in the year 1712. If poor, naive Henry had understood the nature of the light-footed, light-headed Imogen he had set his heart and soul on, Dr. Featherstone would have been comfortably ensconced that day in his lodgings in Oxford, working busily on the notes for the latest chapter of his vast compendium of natural and unnatural history.

Now, a broken heart, despite the sufferer's perception of it, is not usually fatal. But in Henry's case, it very nearly was. The night after Imogen had laughed his love to scorn, Henry's manservant Roley had found his young master insensible in his room, having taken what he presumed to be a lethal dose of laudanum—which, fortunately, it had not been, only enough to make him very ill indeed.

Henry had shown little gratitude at being pushed back into the world. "Why didn't you leave me to die?" he had cried out to his father from his sickbed.

"You could hardly expect me to do that," his father pointed out reasonably. "You are my only child, after all."

Henry sighed bitterly. "Nothing in life has any savor anymore, for Imogen will never love me; worse, she despises me."

"Well, then, return the compliment with interest," said Dr. Featherstone briskly.

"Oh, Father, how can you speak thus! But then, you don't understand about love, at your age," said his son, closing his eyes. Foolish, commonplace words, but they had stung Dr. Featherstone deep inside a place he had thought carapaced long ago. He looked at his son's face—the skin very pale, the dark, soft, cropped hair, the long, dark eyelashes curving on the hollow cheeks—and for one terrible moment, saw the face of his beloved wife Cristin, Henry's mother, lying there in her last illness. *Water on the lungs,* some quack doctor had called the strange illness that had made her waste away so quickly. He had not thought of her for years; had blocked her picture away from his mind. But now he spoke quickly, sharply, words he had not thought through, that he had no idea had been in his mind at all.

"As soon as you are quite well, we will leave for Wales," he had said to Henry, making the young man's eyes fly open again, and dispelling the grievous illusion, for Henry's eyes were blue where Cristin's had been dark brown, and combative where hers had been gentle.

"Wales! Why, Father . . ." Henry stopped, confused. Perhaps he regretted the words he'd uttered, or perhaps he merely thought his father was acting as fathers do, according to their sons: in the way of another alien kind, another mutant race.

"I intended to go there this summer, in any case," said Dr. Featherstone, in a willed return of his earlier briskness. "And now is as good a time as any."

"We will stay at the Red House, like in the old days?" Henry's sudden smile was as sweet as Cristin's had been, and Dr. Featherstone's heart turned over most painfully.

"Of course." Fussily, to hide his feelings, he went on, "And I hope that Mistress Llewellyn will have aired it well this spring, or we may look forward to some rather damp evenings."

"I am sure she will have done so," said his son listlessly, closing his eyes again, and Dr. Featherstone saw that though Henry had him fixed again as an old fusspot, at least now the danger—to both of them—was past. Henry had not forgotten Imogen, of course; but he had something to look forward to again. The Welsh coast, the Red House, and the smells and sights and sounds of a happy childhood. *The young can easily start again,* thought Dr. Featherstone, rather bitterly, as he tiptoed out of the sickroom, leaving the rest of Henry's recovery in Roley's capable hands. Not so easy for us older folks, who must forget, for sheer survival's sake, what it was *really* like to live for love.

And so it was that both Featherstones, senior and junior, found themselves back in the cliff-top Red House, on the remote southwest coast of Wales, facing the Irish Sea. The house had reputedly been built some two hundred and fifty years previously by Cristin's legendary ancestor, Morgan Meredith. Sealmen and -women, strange and wondrous mutants of the deep, were not unknown on that coast of marvels, and all who knew Morgan had no doubt he was one of them. As a baby, he had been recovered from the sea by the fisherman who became his adoptive father. More, he swam just like a sea creature, and was always to be found in or near that element.

When he reached manhood, Morgan had taken employ in the King's navy; and the stories of his bold exploits at sea came home to his own place, filling the people there with pride. When he returned home, he took a bride from amongst the villagers, and built the Red House on the cliff overlooking the great green deep. None knew exactly when he had died; for one day, in old age, he had simply disappeared, never to be seen again. It was said by all that he had returned to the sea from whence he had come.

Despite—or perhaps because of—the strange stories about their legendary ancestor, the Merediths were well-liked and respected in the area. Cristin, last of the Meredith line, had been loved, too, and her English husband accepted, for her sake at first; and later for his own.

The Red House, Morgan's creation, was set at a considerable distance from the village. In structure, it was similar to many of the larger cottages in the area. But instead of being washed with the usual caustic white paste, it had been painted bright red, and the red silk banner of the Meredith family flew proudly from its roof ridge. Red was a most auspicious color in Wales; it protected a house and its inhabitants from demons and evil spirits and any other ill-intentioned supernatural things that should come nosing at the corners of the mortal world. Red also contrasted with the dominant green of the world around the house: the green of the hissing, whispering sea, deep-colored and clear as ancient Roman glass, and the wild-scented dark green of the heather, splashed with white and pink and yellow flowers, that surrounded the house like a secondary tide.

Though most years the winds howled and wailed around the Welsh cliffs, that year, by a most fortunate chance, their fury was stilled. Such a beautiful summer, it was said, had not been seen since the Red House itself was built. Henry spent his days rediscovering the little beaches and coves and secret caves that honeycombed the cliffs, while Dr. Featherstone either worked on his book, or discussed the world's affairs with his good friend in the village, Cristin's cousin Dafydd ap Rhys, who had once traveled all over Europe in his capacity as surgeon-infirmer in the Army.

As a man of both science and religion, whose double degree had been in divinity and natural history, Dr. Featherstone had a great deal of interest in the places, such as this one, where the physical and the metaphysical met. He did not, of course, believe literally in stories such as that of Morgan Meredith's origin, but wanted to express the poetry of them nevertheless. So far, the fullness of what he sought had eluded him. But he was content enough for the moment with writing copious notes, and puzzling over ideas, and reveling in nature.

And if the kindly ghost of Cristin and the petulant shade of Imogen stalked with the Featherstones at times that summer, they did not allow themselves to be unduly troubled. For Cristin walked often enough with her husband, while in Henry's heart Imogen's memory was being steadily bleached away by the summer days, and the ghost of her voice blown away by the sound of Welsh laughter. All about them seemed stilled, peaceful, timeless in harmony.

It was on one of those bright, peaceful days that the sealmen came. They came unannounced and unexpected, breaking out of the calm water of the rocky little cove below the Red House, where Dr. Featherstone had been spending a happy morning exploring rock pools. That was the first thing that was extraordinary about the whole event: there had been no change in the day's placid tempo, no strange lights, no trumpet of judgment, nothing to warn an unwary world—or at least, as the world was represented by that solitary gentleman, the Reverend Doctor William Featherstone. No; one minute the sea was empty, innocent of anything other than heaving waves, and the next, two black dots had broken the cold green surface and come gasping up into what for them must have been a brave new world.

At first, because of their sleek and shiny dark skin, Dr. Featherstone thought they were indeed common seals. An interesting enough sight, to be sure, and Dr. Featherstone watched them happily for a moment or two, until it became quite clear that they were unlike any seals he had ever heard of, for one of them was shouting to the other as they bobbed about. The words were carried loudly, but totally unintelligibly, over the water. It was not English, or Welsh, or French, or German, or any of the other languages Dr. Featherstone had ever heard. Even as his sensible mind tried to categorize and search for vocabulary lists, his wild fancy took an instant leap into fairy tale, and the strange story of Morgan Meredith. These were creatures from the green underworld of the sea, he thought, dazedly. And that was the second strange thing about the coming of the sealmen. For Dr. Featherstone, the sudden disarranging of the sensible world he had believed in for so long was not wholly frightening. No; there was excitement and glee and a kind of weird, remote wonder, too, mixed in with the disbelieving fear. "Such things are not meant to happen," he told himself, very quietly. "One does not go down to the beach and see mutant creatures of dream and legend bob up from a perfectly innocent and sensible sea!" But as he spoke the words, he hugged himself for glee that it was so; that such things did happen, and always had done, for as long as the world was the strange, strange world; and he watched carefully, not revealing himself for the moment.

The sealmen—for thus the thought of them swam up into his mind as well as his heart—came closer to shore, their sleek dark bodies now breaking the surface, now submerged in the green. They were quiet at present; their movements strange, both natural and not, both graceful and clumsy. Now Dr. Featherstone saw that their faces were not seals' faces, but humanlike, and of the greenish pallor of things that have long been in the sea. One of them sported a pair of yellowy-green whiskers as finely sodden as some old grampus', but the other's face looked very young and hairless indeed. Their heads were round and dark, like seals' heads, and Dr. Featherstone could see no fish's tail, though once or twice he caught a glimpse of thrashing feet flippered like those of seals.

Closer they came, closer; and now it became apparently to Dr. Featherstone that the sealmen were not playing, as he had assumed them to be. One of them, the young one, seemed to be in some kind of trouble, for he—it?—was flopping around like a dying fish, supported by its—his?—whiskery friend, who was swimming along, with a black upper limb supporting the other under what looked like its shoulders. Dr. Featherstone saw that the whiskered one was having difficulty; and then, all at once, he realized that blood red as any human's was pouring out of the young sealman's mouth.

Dr. Featherstone did not stop to hear the urgings of his sane mind. From his earliest childhood, he had hated seeing any creature in trouble. He came out of hiding, calling out in firm, clear tones, "Do not be afraid! I only wish to help you. You have come to

Meredith country here, where sealmen are not reviled."

The sealmen froze—or at least, the healthy one did. The wounded one flopped about, and rolled its eyes. Dr. Featherstone took off his buckled shoes and silk stockings and rolled up his breeches, and came toward the sealmen. They did not move, but stared at him as if it was he, not they, who was the weird mutant. The water—even in summer cold as the glass whose color it imitated so well—gripped painfully at Dr. Featherstone's calves and thighs, but he ignored the discomfort. "Allow me to carry your friend, too," he said, and helpfully mimed the action.

After a wary instant, the whiskered one nodded. Together, very gently, they heaved the wounded sealman up out of the water. Carefully, they carried him— *it?*—up onto the sand. It was a very odd experience, and Dr. Featherstone would never forget it for as long as he lived: the thick, slippery touch of the wounded sealman's sleek skin, the deepwater smell coming from his—yes, his, Dr. Featherstone had definitely decided—body, the strangely human yet weirdly remote gaze of his gray-green eyes, the flopping flippered feet . . . And the other one, the whiskered one, working in silence, grunting very humanly, yet once on the sand, hampered and awkward as a seal is on land.

Once the wounded sealman was on the beach. Dr. Featherstone looked closely at him. His skin was gray from loss of blood now, his eyes closed, a trail of blood still oozing from the side of his mouth. Dr. Featherstone wondered how long the creature had to live. He could see the mark of death on his features, just as he had seen it on Cristin's face in her last days. It did not seem wrong, somehow, to think of Cristin and the sealman in the same breath, not with the knowledge of her ancestor Morgan Meredith.

All at once, the whiskered one said something incomprehensible but unmistakably urgent. William looked at him and tried to smile reassuringly. "I will go and get help," he said, and pointed up to the cliff.

The sealman's eyes followed the direction of his gesture, toward the Red House on the cliff, its silk banner fluttering bravely in the breeze, then looked down at his friend. With a kind of stricken astonishment, Dr. Featherstone saw that the older sealman was weeping, tears rolling out of his dark eyes, and into the already-sodden depths of his whiskers. Dr. Featherstone swallowed at the sudden fiercely-hot lump that had come into his own throat, and the turmoil that surged up from the deepest part of him. He put a timid hand briefly on the sealman's shining dark shoulder. "A doctor—I have a friend," he stammered. He mimed the administering of medicine. "I will be back. I promise."

The whiskered sealman stared at him, his dark eyes fathomless; then he got to his knees beside his friend and took the wounded man's head in his lap. It was clear he was going to wait. Without stopping to put on his shoes or stockings, Dr. Featherstone hurried away up the beach toward the cliff path. His thumping heart and whirling mind throbbed with strange questions; he felt like weeping and screaming and laughing aloud, all at once, while the back of his neck prickled with an odd kind of fear. Out of the old stories those sealmen had stepped: submarine legends, swimming out of the ocean of mystery, the fathomless depths of the great green deep, they had come to break the surface of the ordinary. And he, William Featherstone, would never be the same again. The world would never look the same again to him.

Panting and gasping, he reached the top of the cliff, and stood for a moment to catch his breath. The whiskery sealman was still sitting motionless on the sand, his companion's head cradled in his lap. There was something both piteous and noble about his posture, something stilled and fated, too, and it made Dr. Featherstone shiver a little. Some said the first sealmen had been humans who had somehow mutated, grown flippers, and slipped into the sea. How different did that make them from ordinary humans? How far apart from humans were they? Not so far that they could not mate with them—like Morgan Meredith had; but far enough perhaps for their feelings to be truly strange and maybe forever incomprehensible to us.

He hurried on, down the hill, and into the village, where people stared curiously at him. In a mixture of glee and wryness, he thought that he must indeed look a weird sight, wild-eyed, disheveled, wigless, barefoot, his breeches rolled up over his salt-encrusted bare legs like some tinker. The gossips would have a field day about the metamorphosis of Dr. William Featherstone. But that was the third strange thing about that strange day: he did not care about what any of them might think, or say. For the wild, ardent young man who had been William, who had wooed and won Cristin, and had seemingly died with her years ago, had stirred into life again.

There was Dafydd's house. William knocked at he door, and Dafydd opened it at once. "Gwilym!" he exclaimed, using the Welsh form of William. "What ails thee, friend?"

"Sealmen," gasped William. "On the beach . . . wounded . . . come . . . quick . . . please . . ."

Dafydd's eyes widened, but all he said was, "Just let me get my instruments. See thee; it will take me a little time to gather everything, but I will be as quick as I can be."

All the way back to the cliff, the two men barely spoke. After a few words of explanation, William had fallen silent, unable to put into proper words the emotions of the morning. Dafydd did not question him; he seemed quite calm, as if it was some simple shipwrecked sailor they were going to tend, and not some fabulous creature from the green deep. But William felt anything but calm. Waiting for Dafydd to gather his instruments had seemed an agony to him; and he wished wildly that they could have mutated themselves, grown wings, and flown back to the cove. In the time from seeing the sealmen to fetching Dafydd, he had changed, and the whole world seemed bright and mad and strange and marvelous to him. Cristin's ghost no longer walked with him; her presence seemed instead to fill the air, so that he felt as if he could smell the nightsea darkness of her hair, as if he could hear the very words she used to speak to him in her love. She was of the sea, he thought wildly, like her ancestor Morgan Meredith, like the sealmen; and surging out of the great deep, her people, her kin had somehow reawakened his soul.

Presently, they reached the Red House, and the clifftop, "See," said William, pointing down, "there they are, and—" He stopped suddenly.

"Why, Gwilym," said Dafydd, "whatever is the matter?"

Then he saw. He looked at the beach, then back at William. He opened his mouth. "My friend, I . . ."

But whatever he had been about to say was never spoken, for William gave an inarticulate cry and tore off down the path, so that all Dafydd could do was hurry after him.

"Gwilym," he panted, when they stood on the sand near the rocks where William had left the two sealmen, "there is no one here, thou can see that."

William did not answer. He swung his head from side to side, looking, looking, wildly, almost desperately; Dafydd, distressed and a little frightened by the expression on his friend's face, said, softly, "They're gone, Gwilym. Gone back to the sea. To their own kind."

"You believe me, then," said William, swinging his gaze—a stormy, stormy gaze such as had never been seen on the face of Dr. Featherstone—back to Dafydd.

"Ie, Gwilym bach," whispered Dafydd, forgetting to speak English in his agitation. "Yes, William, friend."

William gave a great sigh. His face, Dafydd saw, was strained and tight as a mask. He began to say, "He was terribly hurt, somehow, probably dying. He could not possibly . . ." and stopped speaking, for Dafydd had silently pointed out a red trail, faint but definite, on the wet sand at some distance away. They followed the trail to where it stopped, at the edge of the water, and for a long while said nothing, looking out to sea, trying desperately to see signs of life out there, to catch a glimpse of two black dots, at the very least. But there was nothing. Nothing except the small glassy-green waves, and the ragged-lace foam, and nothing to be heard but the seabirds crying over the water.

"His friend carried him back to the sea," said William dully, at last. "Why? He couldn't have survived it. Why didn't they wait for me? Oh, why, why did I leave them? They were afraid and alone, you could see that—in great trouble, and landed on a strange shore, with a stranger gobbling foolishly at them." The deep black sorrow in him was almost too great to be borne. He did not know why he felt like this over the fate of two mutant strangers who had barely touched his life except in that odd, glancing way, but he knew the sorrow was a real, real thing, bitter and strong as the ocean itself.

Very quietly, Dafydd said, "You did all that you *could* do, Gwilym. We, on land, we can only offer our trust and our friendship—and if they will not take it, why, there is nothing to be done."

William opened his mouth, then closed it again, for he could not explain all the emotions he had been drowned in today, not to Dafydd, not to anyone. To no one—except for Cristin. And she was dead. Dead forever, returned to the great dark ocean whence we all emerged and all vanished, and he would never, never see her again. At this thought, new-minted it seemed, this ferocious feeling bloodily burst from under the shattered carapace of his carefully manufactured middle-aged calm, he gave a great cry, and flung away from the beach, and the shore, and up the cliff path toward the Red House, the house that had once been hers.

The door was open. He noticed that, even through the fog of long-suppressed grief that overwhelmed him. He did not remember having left it open, when he had left that morning. But what did it matter? He stumbled into the house, and cried aloud to the walls. They caught his cries and swallowed them, as they had caught the cries of so many Merediths over two hundred and fifty years. He sank to his knees, the tears pouring down his face, crying as he had not done since he was a child, seeing in his mind's eye the whiskered sealman, with the tears pouring down his face, and rolling into his already-sodden yellowing mustache, the sand graining on his flipper-feet and . . .

Sand. There was sand here, at the corner of the table, a little pile of it . . . and there wet patches . . . wet patches . . . where he had not stepped himself. William rose abruptly, almost hitting his head on the table in his haste. He looked around wildly. Suddenly, the familiar house looked strange to him, subtly different. Someone had been here. He did not stop to speculate, but went quickly around the room, looking for what was missing, what was changed, what was, perhaps, added. Nothing—nothing that he could put his finger on. Yet he could see, in his mind's eye, a dark seal-shape moving restlessly, awkwardly, perhaps fearfully through the house, looking at this, looking at that, looking for something. . . .

He moved from the main room into the little room at the back, which he used as a study, and where indeed his manuscript was still sitting on the desk. He gave an exclamation, and started forward.

He had begun on a new page only this morning, before going down to the beach. As was his custom, he had headed it with the date: Midsummer Eve, June 22, 1712. He had begun writing about the cloud formations he could see from the window, before abandoning his task, lured by the wild brightness of the air outside.

But now, under the entry in his own hand, he saw that someone had written something else, something that made no sense: HET, it looked like, repeated over and over, as if for practice, three jumbled letters, not even properly written, but scrawled, tentative at first, then deeper, darker, frenzied, the quill wielded by someone with no skill in penmanship: HET, HET, HET HET . . .

He was still looking at it when Dafydd burst in through the door. "Gwilym, I . . ." he began, then stopped when he saw William's expression, and then the manuscript

"I think," said William, haltingly, "I think he came here . . . perhaps looking for me. I'd pointed up at the cliff, you see . . . he saw the house . . . perhaps he thought I was here."

"But why . . ." asked Dafydd, pointing at the manuscript.

William shook his head, very slowly. "I do not know," he said. "I have no idea at all."

"HET," said Dafydd, frowning. "HET. That means *hat*, in our language. But why would he write that? It makes no sense."

"I am sure he did not mean hat," said William, smiling a little. "You are right—it makes no sense. It's curious, Dafydd, how letters together may mean everything, or nothing. If they'd been changed around, we could have THE, for instance."

"If you look at it a certain way," Dafydd said, peering at the letters with one eye closed, "awkwardly written as it is, it looks a little like that Cyrillic script I saw in the lands of the Slavs, when I was in the Army . . . like the Russian word for No. Yet of course it cannot mean that at all, any more than it means HAT, or THE wrong way around."

"I had no notion sealmen could write," William said. "The old stories do not say so, do they, Dafydd?"

"They do not . . ." began Dafydd, when all at once Henry's fresh young voice came floating in from outside.

"Father! Father! Are you there, Father?"

"Yes, Henry, I am here," said William patiently; and in the next moment Henry came breezing into the room, his face all flushed with excitement. Behind him, shyly smiling, followed Dafydd's own pretty niece, Rhiannon.

"Father, I am so glad you are here!" said Henry, and William saw with a jolt of tender surprise that his son's summersea eyes were sparkling with genuine pleasure. "Rhiannon and I, we have seen such a sight, Father!"

"Really, Henry?" His son looked happy, William thought; *truly* happy, for the first time in weeks.

"Yes, Father—we were looking for shells on the next cove round and we . . . well, we had . . . er . . . stopped for a moment to rest on the sand when all at once, we heard the strangest sound, far out at sea . . . like insistent bells pealing underwater, or a kind of weird, weird siren song. Then, on the water, came two black things, which looked like . . ."

"Morlo," said Rhiannon quietly.

"Seals," translated her uncle, just as quietly.

"There was a brightness around them, a kind of wild brightness. They seemed to be following the sound . . . and then . . . they just reached a spot on the sea, and disappeared, completely," said Henry. Suddenly, his clear young face was clouded with bewilderment. "I did not even see them go," he murmured. "One minute they were there—the next, gone, as if the sea, or time itself had swallowed them."

William thought, two sealmen, one either dying or already dead, the other paddling away with a desperate kind of courage. Yet there was no pain in the thought, not anymore, just a kind of pity, and a sad admiration for the courage of the other, who had tried so hard to take the young sealman home to the great deep. Perhaps, he thought, with a jolt, they were father and son. And perhaps not. All that was sure was that they had not been at home, here in this place; and could not stay. Something had frightened them, perhaps; something had told them they would never belong here. William might never know exactly what that had been. But he thought that now he might find the clear, beautiful way of writing he had sought for so long: for the sealmen had brought it with them, from the great deep, and he would never, ever forget them.

"Henry, my dear son," he said, putting an arm around the boy's shoulders. "Do not be afraid— for you have seen a wonder, true enough."

"True enough," echoed Henry, and smiled into his father's eyes. Then he colored. "Father— Master Dafydd—Rhiannon and I, there is something else . . . you see . . . we . . . we wish to be engaged . . . and we wish for your blessing."

And in the explanations and exclamations that followed, the thought that had so suddenly flashed into Dafydd's mind, about how the strange letters scrawled over and over on the clean sheet of manuscript looked almost like the Russian word for "no," was forever forgotten.

PAINT BOX
by Lisanne Norman

Born in Glasgow, Scotland, Lisanne Norman started writing at the age of eight in order to find more of the books she liked to read. In 1980, two years after joining The Vikings!, the largest British reenactment society in Britain, she moved to Norfolk, England. There she ran her own specialist archery display team. Now a full-time author, in her *Sholan Alliance* series she has created worlds where warriors, magic, and science all coexist. Her latest novel from DAW in the series is *Stronghold Rising,* and the next novel in the series, *Between Darkness and Light,* will be released in 2002.

T he fingers that protruded from the tips of Anne's gloves were stiff and blue with cold. With a sigh, she laid her paints and sketch pad down on the ground and reached for her flask of coffee. Steam rose from both flask and cup as she poured herself a drink. Gratefully she cupped her hands around the warmth.

Glen glanced at her from his perch on an upturned waste bin filched from the studio a quarter of a mile away.

"Giving in already?" he asked teasingly.

Anne took a drink before answering him.

"Too right," she replied. "We've been sitting here freezing our bums off for the last three hours. I, for one, want a break."

"You have a point," admitted Glen, rubbing his hands together briefly. "It's far from warm today."

"I can't see why Frazer put the studio out of limits, especially in this weather," Anne grumbled.

Heather looked up from her work. "Probably to stop us getting into bad habits on the first day," she said mildly. "This is supposed to be a field trip, after all."

"Well, I think it's cruel. I can easily do my plant study inside, and Glen can see his trees from the window, can't you?" she asked, turning toward him.

Glen opened his mouth to answer, but Heather forestalled him.

"You just aren't dedicated enough," she said, shaking her head. "It isn't as if we were sitting exposed to the elements on the end of the pier. We're sheltered among the trees here."

"We would have been on the pier if it had been up to you," pointed out Glen, putting away his things. "It was only because the others went there that we came in this direction."

"That's beside the point," replied Heather archly. "The weather isn't as bad as you make out. At least we're here in May and not January like the other first year section."

Glen grunted and turned to Anne. "You don't happen to have another coffee in there, do you? I could do with a drink to warm me up. I wish I'd thought of bringing a flask."

Anne grinned and reached for the thermos. "I looked at the weather forecast on Sunday, which is why I also brought my gloves," she said, wiggling her fingers at him before pouring a second cup and handing it over. "My older bones feel the cold more acutely than yours do."

Heather sniffed audibly. "Just no dedication to your craft," she repeated.

"The day of the artist starving and freezing in his garret is long gone, Heather," said Glen, warming his nose in the steam before taking his first sip. "There's no reason why we shouldn't enjoy our creature comforts, too."

As Anne put her cup down, she heard a twig snap.

Looking up, she caught sight of a movement in the bushes.

"There's someone there," she hissed at Glen.

"Rubbish," he said. "Unless you believe all that nonsense about the Culzean Castle ghosts."

"Don't be ridiculous," she whispered. "Ghosts don't snap twigs! There's someone there, I tell you."

She got to her feet and moved silently forward, motioning Glen to go around the other side of the small thicket ahead of them.

Amused, he got to his feet.

There was the rustle of leaves as something moved its feet.

Anne saw a flash of black at the heart of a rhododendron bush and pounced.

There was a sharp squeal, and a female voice said, "Don't touch me! I didn't mean any harm. I was only watching you."

A small figure, followed by Anne, backed defensively out of the bushes.

"It's all right," Anne assured her, "we won't hurt you. We just wondered who it was."

The girl was slightly built, with elfin features set in a pale face topped by a mass of long ginger curls. Probably about sixteen at a rough guess, gauged Anne.

"This is Glen, Heather, and I'm Anne," she said, pointing to the other two in turn. "Are you a local, or a visitor like us?"

"I live over there. My name is Cassandra," she said quietly, her voice almost a whisper. She pointed through the bushes to the headland beyond. "You're art students, aren't you?"

Anne nodded. "We're here for a week's study."

"My family don't like me mixing with strangers, so I don't get to meet many people. Can I see what you're doing?" she asked, some of the tension leaving her face.

"Of course," said Anne, warming to the girl. "Come

and have a look." She led the way over to where her sketch pad lay propped against the tree stump.

"I've been doing some plant studies in watercolors," she said, picking up the pad. "That's the fern over there."

Cassandra gazed at the sketch, a look of rapture on her face. She reached her hand out and then stopped, fingers hovering just above the paper.

"Can I touch it?" she asked. "It looks so real, and the colors are beautiful."

"Yes, of course you can," mumbled Anne, embarrassed. "It isn't really that good."

"Oh, it's lovely," she said, turning an intense look on her. "I've never seen anything like it before. How do you do it? What makes the colors?"

"The paints," said Anne, confused. Surely Cassandra knew what paints were?

The girl answered Anne's unspoken question. "What are paints?"

Baffled, Anne picked up her paint box and showed it to her. "These are. It's a colored paste that comes in tubes, and I squeeze a little of each color into my box."

The girl pointed to the paintbrush. "You use that to put the colors on the paper?"

Anne nodded.

Cassandra touched the crimson carefully with one finger, then rubbed it onto the back of her other hand. "I love bright colors, but Mother won't let me wear them." She looked down at the long black skirt that she wore and smiled wryly, an oddly adult expression. "She says it would only make people notice me."

"Why can't they notice you?" asked Glen, intrigued by the image of seclusion she was painting.

Cassandra shrugged. "They just mustn't," she said. "I shouldn't be talking to you now. If my brother catches me, I'll be in trouble."

"Just for talking to us?" exclaimed Anne.

"Yes," she said simply. "Can I look at what you're doing?" she asked Glen.

He showed her his sketches of the trees, and after admiring them, Cassandra was about to move over to Heather when the other girl closed her pad and stood up.

"I don't like people looking at my unfinished work," she said coldly, bending down to pack away her things. "May I remind you that we were told to stay away from the families living on the estate. It's nearly tea-time. I'll see you two back at the hostel when you're finished with your captive audience." With that, she strolled off.

"Did I upset her?" asked Cassandra, a worried frown on her face.

"No," said Glen. "She's always like that—arrogant about her work, and short on manners."

"Forget her," said Anne, dismissing Heather with an airy wave of her hand. "You don't seem to know much about art. Didn't you do any painting or drawing at school?"

"I never went to school," Cassandra said. "My brother did, though, and he says I didn't miss much."

"How come you didn't go to school?" asked Glen, sitting down on his bin again.

"I told you, I'm not allowed to meet people," she said, frowning. "Mother says it isn't safe."

"Isn't safe for whom?" asked Anne. "The world isn't that bad a place."

"I wouldn't know," she said sadly. "You're the first strangers I've spoken to in years. If I get the chance, can I come over and talk to you again?"

"Of course you can," said Anne, reaching out to touch her. "I just don't see . . ."

"Hush!" said Cassandra suddenly, ducking the gesture and tilting her head to one side. "I hear someone coming. It has to be my brother." She looked around frantically. "I'm not supposed to be out at all! I must go." The girl left so quickly she seemed to melt into the bushes.

Anne and Glen looked at one another in bewilderment.

"What do you make of that?" he asked.

Anne shook her head. "I just don't know," she said. "She seems so naive, yet . . ."

Glen nodded. "I know what you mean."

They heard footsteps nearby and looked up. A dark-haired youth in his early twenties dressed in a green waxed jacket and jeans stepped into the clearing and glanced around. Slung over his shoulder, he carried the bloodstained bodies of two rabbits. In his other hand, he held a shotgun, broken open to show it was unloaded.

Anne blinked. His features were perfect—he looked like one of the old classical statues come to life.

As he caught sight of them, he stopped, his face creasing into a scowl. "You're trespassing," he said shortly. "This is private land here. You students have been told to stay inland, not come wandering in the woods."

"We're allowed here," said Glen, getting up. "I made a point of checking the map of the estate. So long as we stay off the headland, we can go where we want."

He continued to stare at them. "Have you seen anyone else today?" he asked abruptly. "A girl, ginger-haired?"

"No," Anne said quickly before Glen could answer. "We've seen no one."

He nodded, the frown easing slightly. "You see her, you stay away from her. She's my sister. I don't want her mixing with the likes of you."

Once the sound of his footsteps had faded, Glen let out his breath. "If that's the brother, I don't blame her for being nervous of him. Did you see what he was carrying?"

"The rabbits? Yes," she said.

"The shotgun, actually. I didn't like the look of him, Anne. I think we'd better head back to the hostel, too."

Anne glanced at her watch. "It is teatime," she agreed readily, bending down to pick up her things.

*   *   *

The next morning dawned bright and warm. Heather and Anne had drawn the short straw to make breakfast that morning, and the prospect of good weather had made everyone anxious to get an early start. The kitchen, roomy enough for three, was totally inadequate for the twenty students each trying to "help" by fixing their own meal. By dint of shouting, pushing, and outright threats of violence, Anne finally managed to chase them out into the common room to wait their turn. Heather, nose in an art book, stood guarding the small oven's grill.

Several minutes later, Glen stuck his nose cautiously round the door.

"Can I help?" he inquired. "I'll take the milk and cereals through for you if you want."

"You just want to get fed first like the rest," muttered Anne, banging the offending packets onto a tray alongside the bowls and milk.

"Yes," he agreed complacently, venturing into the kitchen. "But unlike the others, I'm genuinely offering to help."

"Take them!" Anne said, amused and exasperated at the same time.

Glen lifted up the tray and headed back out. He paused at the door.

"I should have a look at the toast if I were you, Heather. I don't think it's supposed to be served flambé."

Glancing up from her book, Heather pulled the grill tray out and surveyed the ruined toast critically.

"He's right," she announced after a moment. "It shouldn't be that shade of burnt umber, more a sort of yellow ocher."

"It's a piece of bloody toast," exclaimed Anne, snatching up the pieces of smoking bread and hurling them in the direction of the bin. "Not a work of art! Just don't burn the next lot or we'll never get finished!"

Breakfast finally over, everyone made their way into the great outdoors to start sketching. Anne declined the invitation to join Glen and Heather on the beach. She'd had enough of the younger girl to last her the week, let alone the rest of the day.

"I want to have a look around before I settle down to paint today," she said by way of an excuse.

"Don't take too long," warned Glen. "Frazer missed us yesterday, and you can guarantee he'll make a point of seeing our work today."

"I won't," she assured him, setting off along the path to the woods.

She strolled leisurely along, in no particular hurry despite Glen's warning, reveling in the solitude after the hubbub of breakfast. Presently she came to the little clearing near the studio where they had worked the day before. She stopped, surprised to find herself there when she hadn't intended to return to the same spot. Coincidence? She'd been thinking about Cassandra; perhaps subconsciously she'd taken the same route. Well, now she was here, she might as well indulge her curiosity and see if she could find out where the girl lived.

Looking carefully around, Anne finally spotted the path—more of a rabbit track—that Cassandra had taken when she left. Pushing through the bushes, she followed it until the trees thinned out, giving way to a grassy slope. Over to the left some distance away was a small croft.

Now what? she wondered. She couldn't exactly go and knock on the door and ask if a girl called Cassandra lived there, especially if her family did dislike strangers. She shrugged. Still, she could always walk nearby and see if Cassandra was about.

Anne was only a few hundred yards from the cottage when a slight figure came out of the door. Recognizing the girl, she opened her mouth to call out just as Cassandra spotted her.

The girl's hand flew to her mouth in a silencing gesture and Anne stifled her greeting.

Warily, Cassandra looked around before running over.

"You shouldn't have come here," she said breathlessly, coming to a stop beside her. "We'll both get into trouble if I'm caught talking to you."

"How can I get into trouble?" asked Anne indignantly. "I'm doing nothing wrong. This land belongs to the Castle, doesn't it?"

Cassandra sighed. "Just believe me, please. If my brother finds you here, then he'll make sure I have no chance of getting out on my own before you leave, and I do want to talk to you again."

"You make it sound as if he keeps you virtually a prisoner here. Why can't you mix with other people? What about your parents? I don't understand. The whole thing sounds cruel and pointless."

"They're only trying to protect me," said Cassandra defensively. "Last time there was an accident and someone got . . . hurt," she faltered.

"Hurt?" queried Anne. "What happened?"

"Never mind," she said hurriedly. "I can hear Mother calling me. You must go."

In the distance, Anne could hear someone shouting.

"Please. Just leave," she begged when Anne hesitated.

"Very well," Anne agreed reluctantly when she heard the voice getting closer. She turned and began to walk away, wondering about the family's paranoia, and how on earth someone could have got hurt. Perhaps she was exaggerating. Girls of her age often did to make themselves appear more intriguing. Well, if she was, Anne thought wryly, it was certainly working!

When she reached the edge of the trees, she glanced back toward the croft and saw Cassandra standing with the dark young man of the day before. They were moving back in the direction of the cottage.

"Ah, Anne!" she heard a voice hail her from across the other side of the headland. "I've been looking for you. Haven't you found somewhere to work yet?"

"Oh, no," she muttered to herself. "Hello, Mr. Frazer," she called, walking toward him. "I was just having a look around before deciding where to settle."

"In that case, I suggest the pier," he said decisively,

pointing out toward the sea. "There's a path leading down to the harbor over there. On the shingle you'll find a lovely collection of lobster creels beside a beached dinghy. Lots of mussel colonies to draw, too. Not the sort of thing you see much of in the city."

"No, Mr. Frazer," said Anne obediently.

"Off you go, then. I'll be by again in an hour or so to see how you're doing." He nodded to her, then set off briskly toward the woods.

Anne watched his retreating figure with a grimace. Damn! She would have to bump into him. She didn't like harbors or piers, and seafood made her throw up. The thought of spending a day sketching the blessed things did not appeal to her in the least. She heaved a deep sigh and set off in the direction he'd indicated.

By Wednesday morning, it looked as if the good weather would last out the week. Anne decided to get off immediately after breakfast so as to make sure she didn't meet Frazer until she was firmly ensconced in the day's work. She couldn't face another session at the smelly little harbor.

Glen and Heather were returning to the beach to continue their paint studies and this time Anne decided to join them. They made their way along the drive toward the Castle, cutting off down the small track that led to the beach. It was a pleasant walk, leading through a lightly wooded area. As they approached the sands, they saw a familiar figure bending over a group of rocks near the path. She looked up as they approached.

"Hello," said Cassandra, smiling shyly. "I hoped you might come this way."

"I see you managed to escape again," said Anne.

"Yes," said Cassandra, totally serious. "My brother has gone into town today, so I have some time to myself. Mother doesn't watch me as closely as he does."

"Hmm," grunted Heather disbelievingly.

"I've been trying to paint," Cassandra went on,

standing back a little from the rock. "Would you have a look at it and tell me what you think? I've never tried before," she confided to Anne.

On the rocks she had attempted to draw a group of figures, but they were naive representations of the human form, almost childlike in their simplicity of structure.

"It's supposed to be you," she said, indicating all three of them. "I tried to get the colors right, but it wasn't as easy as I thought it would be." She waited, obviously anxious for their approval.

Heather was the first to speak. "Are we going to stand here all day admiring this child's primitive daubs, or are we going to get on with some work?" she demanded. "You can waste your time with her if you like, but I've more important things to do," she said, sweeping off down the path without a backward glance.

Anne looked at Glen, trying not to see Cassandra's stricken face as the girl gazed at Heather's retreating figure. He raised his eyebrows questioningly at her.

She turned back to Cassandra. "They aren't bad for a first attempt," she temporized, "but you've a lot to learn. You can't become an artist overnight, you know."

"The colors are very good," added Glen lamely, shifting his bag from one hand to the other. "I don't think my first picture was as good as that."

"It's terrible, that's what you're saying, isn't it?" Cassandra said, looking as if her world had just collapsed. "I'm no good at painting, am I?"

"I didn't say that," said Anne hurriedly. "We're not great artists either. That's why we go to art school, to learn more."

Glen began to fidget. "Look, Anne, I've got to go after Heather. You know what she's like if she gets into a mood. I'll see you down there, okay?"

Anne nodded. "Go on," she replied shortly. Kneeling, she put down her bag and folio and got out a soft dark pencil.

"Let me show you," she said, beginning to sketch around the outline of one of Cassandra's figures. She looked up at the girl, seeing her dash tears from her eyes with the back of her hand. "Come and watch," she said softly. "Some of your mistakes are fairly easy to correct."

"No," Cassandra gulped, rubbing furiously at eyes that wouldn't stop overflowing. "It's just another thing I'm useless at. For once, I'd like to find something I can do well."

Anne sat back on her heels. "You can't expect to paint a masterpiece first time, you know," she said kindly. "It takes years of hard work, and even then very few people become great painters. Don't take what Heather said to heart. She's no authority, you know, just another student like me."

"Forget that I mentioned it," said Cassandra, pulling herself together with a visible effort and giving a final dab at her tear-stained face. "I have to go now, and you've got your painting to do." She began to back away up the path. "Maybe I'll see you again before you leave."

"Don't go," called Anne, but she had already left in a flurry of black skirts.

Anne sighed, looking again at the rock painting. She frowned and leaned closer, reaching out to touch it. The paintings were very immature, having more in common with a bad copy of Lowrie's matchstick men than any realistic representation of people. Her use of color, however, was another matter. She seemed to have a natural appreciation of tonal relationships. There was a vibrancy about the colors which was unique.

How had she done it? Anne couldn't remember Cassandra having a paint box or any colored pens with her. What had she used? She began to scrape at the figure depicting herself, but the paint seemed to have sunk into the surface of the stone. Wetting her finger, she rubbed at it, but again none of it came off. She looked more closely, then on an impulse pulled out the small knife she carried and began scraping, then digging, at the surface of the rock. The paint seemed to be embedded into the actual fabric of the stone.

"That's impossible," she murmured, sitting back to think for a moment. She leaned forward again and began to dig more deeply this time. Stopping momentarily, she prodded an unpainted piece beside the figure. The stone was definitely softer under the paint, and the color seemed to go deep down into the rock. She tested several other areas and found that everywhere Cassandra had painted, the pigment had changed the actual substance of the stone and become an integral part of it.

"How the hell did she do that?" she wondered aloud. This time, Cassandra didn't need to try to be intriguing, she genuinely was. How could she possibly have altered the rock and put colors into it? Anne shook her head in bewilderment as she put away her pencil and knife again. Maybe she had a strange talent, like the chap who could bend spoons. Well, at least rock paintings, even if they were this simplistic, were more interesting to look at than a pile of bent spoons.

She got to her feet and picked up her bag and folio. Tomorrow she would try to pin the girl down long enough to ask her about the paintings. A talent like that would be wasted if it wasn't used and developed.

Cassandra did not reappear that day, nor did Anne see her the next day until late afternoon when she was making her way back to the hostel. The meeting was a chance one. Anne had struck out on her own to sketch by the inappropriately named Swan Lake, and was cutting back through the woods when she came across her in the clearing near the studio.

"Cassandra," she called, "just the person I wanted to see. Don't run off, I've got something for you," she said, digging into her bag with one hand as she hurried over to her.

Cassandra hesitated, a sullen, unhappy look on her face.

"I had another look at your paintings, and your use of color is lovely. You do have a talent. Don't worry about the drawing, that will come with time and practice. I wish you'd tell me how you got the paintings into the rock the way you did. That's a rare gift." She came to a halt beside the girl and held out a small box.

"Here, take it," she urged. "It's a paint box." She gestured with the box. "Please take it. I thought you could use the paints when you aren't able to get out." Anne let her voice trail off. It was obvious that Cassandra was upset and had been before Anne arrived.

"Look, I can see something's wrong. Is there anything I can do to help?" she asked.

Cassandra's face changed to become a mask of fury. She lashed out at the paint box, knocking it from Anne's hand and sending it flying.

"I don't have a gift, I have a curse!" she said harshly, her voice low with barely controlled fury.

Anne stepped back, shocked and frightened at the change in this quiet girl.

"I don't want your or anyone's help. No one can help me anyway, so just leave me alone—pretend you never met me," she said. "It would have been safer for you if you hadn't."

Anne watched, stunned, as Cassandra stalked off into the trees. She had never expected an outburst like this from her. What had happened to upset her so? She walked over to where the paints had fallen and bent to pick them up. As she touched them, the box seemed to collapse in on itself, settling into a little pile of dust. Horrified, she drew her hand back. A shiver went down her spine, and she looked up sharply expecting to see someone. There was no one there. Straightening up, she backed away from the clearing. Something told her to run, and without questioning the impulse, she turned and fled. Short of breath and shaking, she eventually arrived at the hostel.

Glen looked up from where he was sitting as she entered the common room.

"You look as if you've seen a ghost," he said, noticing her pallor.

Anne's legs refused to hold her up any longer and, helpless, she slid to the floor.

Leaping to his feet, Glen rushed over to her. "Are you all right?" he asked, feeling her forehead.

Anne nodded weakly. "I am now."

"What happened?"

"You wouldn't believe me if I told you," she said. "Let's say I had a fright."

Glen hauled her to her feet. "Then what you need is a cup of hot, sweet tea," he said, conducting her to the kitchen.

"Not tea, coffee," she protested. "And not here!"

"There's still half an hour before our amateur chefs take over. You've plenty of time to tell me what's happened," he said, pushing her onto the stool and plugging in the kettle. "Now talk."

"It'll just sound as if I'm being foolish and irrational," she objected.

"Never mind, just tell me," he ordered, leaning her back against the work surface and folding his arms.

Anne told him what she'd discovered about the rock paintings, and of her meeting with Cassandra in the clearing a quarter of an hour before.

"That damned paint box just disintegrated before my eyes, Glen! That sort of thing just can't happen, can it?"

"I don't know, Anne. I'll tell you what we can do, though. We can go back and have another look at those rock paintings. Now finish your coffee like a good girl," he said grinning at her.

"Don't patronize me," Anne grumbled, draining her cup before getting up.

"Are you sure these were the rocks?" Glen asked after half an hour of fruitless searching.

"Can you see any others beside the path?" demanded Anne, scrutinizing the boulders yet again. "You know as well as I do that yesterday there were paintings on them, and now they're blank! And the marks I made with my knife have vanished, too."

"I know I saw the paintings, and I'd swear these are the rocks, but the fact remains that if you did scrape away at the stones, it couldn't have been these," Glen replied patiently.

"Then where are the paintings?" Anne demanded in exasperation.

"There's any number of rational explanations for the lack of the paintings," he said.

"Give me one!"

"The rain washed them away."

"It hasn't rained in the last two days."

"The dampness and the salt air, then," he said promptly. "It really doesn't matter why they're not here. The fact is they aren't. Are you absolutely positive that you did stick your knife into them?"

"Absolutely!" snapped Anne. "You don't imagine things like that, unless you're having a breakdown," she glared, daring him to say anything.

Glen sighed. "Shall we go and have a look at the clearing?"

"What for?" she asked, suddenly weary. She started back up the path. "All you'll see is a pile of dust that could have been anything. Let's get back for tea."

Glen came up beside her and wrapped his arm around her shoulders. "I'm not suggesting you imagined it all," he said. "Let's go and have a look by the studio. It's my bet that you'll find your paint box lying on the ground in one piece. Did it occur to you that these two incidents happened when Cassandra was upset, and that perhaps you saw what she wanted you to see?"

Anne frowned. "What do you mean?"

"The power of suggestion. She's a young teenager, and they're capable of all sorts of strange things. Maybe you saw what she wanted you to see rather than what really happened."

Anne considered it for a moment. "Impossible," she said. "The nature of both the rock and the paint box was changed. They had become . . ." she searched for the right word but couldn't find it. ". . . different," she ended lamely. "No, I don't want to go and look for the box. We're leaving tomorrow, and as far as I'm concerned, Cassandra can keep her secret, whatever it is."

"I think you're wise," he said. "Let's get back and eat. We need to line our stomachs if we're going to do some serious drinking on our last night."

"I don't know if I feel up to walking to the pub."

"It's not far."

"Not far! It's a four-mile walk there, never mind back."

"Just a brisk stroll," he said airily. "As for the walk back, you'll never notice it with a wee dram inside you to keep out the cold."

The pub in Kirkoswald was warm and comfortable. High-backed wooden settles kept out all but imagined draughts, and the log fire burning quietly in the grate complemented the subdued lighting, lending an old world charm to the place. The publican and the locals were a friendly lot, used to the weekly turnover of students. All too soon, last orders were called, but the little group they had joined round the fire didn't move and shortly the publican brought his own drink over and sat down with them.

"Now yon ghosties," said one old boy, puffing mightily on his pipe till a cloud of dense smoke all but obscured him. "Yon ghosties up at the Castle. Ye must 'a seen them, have ye no?"

"Ghosts?" queried Glen, feigning innocence. "What ghosts are those, Mr. McNabb?"

"Ye mean ye've no seen them? Och, come on, laddie," he said, poking him in the arm with an authoritative pipe stem. "Ye canna get me to believe that ye havna seen one of the Culzean ghosts!"

"One of them!" exclaimed Heather, rising to the bait. "How many are there?"

Satisfied, Mr. McNabb sat back, puffing once more on his pipe.

"Oh, a great many if truth were known," he nodded sagely.

"Aye," echoed one of his cronies, "there's a fair few up there."

"Tell us about them," said Glen, taking a mouthful of his beer.

"Aye, and so I would," said McNabb, lifting his empty glass sorrowfully, "if my throat werena' so dry."

Glen laughed and raised an eyebrow at the publican.

A few minutes later they returned to their nook with recharged glasses. McNabb took a long draught and smacked his lips appreciatively.

"The ghosts," prompted Glen gently.

"Ah, the ghosties. Now ye'll have heard of the Kennedys, I'll be bound. The American family that was big in politics twenty or so years past? Well, they left Ireland, making their way o'er here first. They bided here for a couple o' hundred years, then went on to America."

Anne groaned. "Don't tell me there's a ghostly piper!" she said.

"Dinna ye laugh, lassie," said McNabb tartly, stabbing the air with his pipe. "It's no joke in the dead o' night to hear their bagpipes skirlin' and know no mortal man is playin' them!"

"I don't believe it," said Heather firmly.

"Ah, well, you'd be wrong, then," said the publican seriously. "He's been heard the night before any of the Kennedys have died. We heard him back in '63."

"Aye," nodded McNabb. "The night before he was shot. You could hear the lament o' the pipes for miles."

Glen shifted uncomfortably. He had been hoping

for ghost tales, but this was getting just a touch too heavy.

"What about other ghosts?" he asked.

McNabb broke out of his reverie. "Tam, you used tae work at the restaurant in the summer season. Where was yon one you told me about?'

Tam began to grin. "Ach, they willna' want to ken about that one," he said.

"It's their last day the morn," said McNabb. "They're no' likely to meet it now, if they havna already."

"Ben the Ladies'," he grinned.

"The Ladies'?" said Anne. "In the Ladies' toilet? You're joking!"

He shook his head. "It doesna happen a' the time, just now and then."

"What does happen?" asked Heather, her face beginning to turn a little pale.

Tam shrugged. "Things get flung about. We had some students here havin' photos taken. The lassies, they didna half start a song and dance when their bits of makeup went flyin' round the room."

"I'm not surprised," murmured Anne, taking a sip of her lager.

"Is that all?" asked Glen.

McNabb gave him a long look.

"What more d'you be wantin', laddie?"

"I meant, did the ghost do anything else?" explained Glen.

"Well, now, I'd have said by looking at yon two lassies, that was enough, but I'm no judge o' things like that," McNabb replied, indicating Anne and Heather, who were definitely looking a little uneasy.

"You forgot the ghostly walker," said the publican. "You know, the one who walks beside folks out for early morning strolls."

"Where does he walk?" asked Glen.

"On the path down to the beach. You can hear his footsteps stirring the fallen leaves at the side of the path, even if there are no leaves on the ground."

"What about the one in the hostel?" put in Tam.

"Ah, now that's a sad one," nodded McNabb, sucking on the pipe stem. "Story goes that last century, the daughter of the Laird had an illegitimate child. The parents took the bairn away as soon as it was born and she never saw it again. She died young, o' a broken heart, they said, and her ghost still searches for the lost bairn."

Glen looked surreptitiously at his watch.

"Remember last night I told you I thought I saw a dark figure by the dorm door?" said Heather, turning to Anne. "It must have been her," she ended in hushed tones.

"You were half asleep at the time," said Anne, "and when I looked, I couldn't see anything. There's no reason to believe it was a ghost."

"Maybe it was, maybe it wasn't," said McNabb wisely.

"We'll have to go, I'm afraid," said Glen, finishing his beer. "It's twelve-thirty, girls, and we've a four-mile walk home."

Anne and Heather downed their drinks and grabbed their coats.

"Thanks for a great evening," said Anne, stopping at the door.

"Pleasure t'meet you, lassie. You watch out for yon ghosties on your way back, ye hear?" said McNabb with a wave of his pipe.

The cold air hit them like a slap in the face. As they walked away from the comforting lights of the pub, they could hear the sound of uproarious laughter.

"They were just winding us up," said Glen, linking an arm with each girl.

"I don't think so," said Heather. "I got the feeling he believed his own stories."

"He's probably told them so often, he's forgotten he made them up," Glen retorted, leading them onto the roadway. "Come on now, best foot forward. We've got a full moon and a nice clear sky. We should be home in no time."

"It's Beltane tonight," observed Heather, glancing at the silvery disk of the moon.

"So what?'

"It's a pagan festival," she murmured, stumbling over a stone on the road. "Strange things happen at this time of year."

"You don't believe in that rubbish, do you? Those old codgers in there have really got you going, haven't they?" laughed Glen. "Come on, there's nothing magical or mystical about a full moon, except that on a clear night you can see for miles, which means we can't lose our way."

"You mentioned the ghosts to me once before, Glen," said Anne. "Remember? When I said I heard someone in the bushes by the studio?"

"When you found Cassandra?" he asked. "Yes, I remember."

"How come you knew about them then?"

"One of the third year students told me about them when he heard we were coming down here this week."

"If they knew about them, then the stories they told tonight must be true.'

"Not necessarily. They'll tell the same stories to every section, and I haven't yet met anyone who has personally experienced one of the ghosts. Plenty of people who know someone who . . . but no one who has actually met them. I really wouldn't think about it anymore," he advised, setting an even smarter pace so that they were almost trotting to keep up with him. "You'll get yourselves so spooked that the first owl that flies near us will have you shrieking as if all the devils in hell were after us."

They walked, or trotted, in silence for a while until Glen suddenly veered off the road toward a field.

"There's the stile," he said. "Over you go." He helped Heather up and then went over himself, waiting on the middle to help Anne. "Nearly home," he said, looking over at the trees. "The path leads through the woods and brings us out at the bottom of the drive beside the hostel."

"Is this the way you came back last night?" asked Anne, jumping down.

"Yes. I thought we'd take the pretty way there, but the shortcut back."

"I won't go through the woods," said Heather, obstinately refusing to go any farther.

"What?" said Glen incredulously.

"I refuse to go through the woods," Heather repeated firmly.

"Why?"

"They're haunted, McNabb said so, and I won't go through haunted woods on Beltane Eve."

"I don't believe this," exclaimed Glen. "Do you seriously expect us to go all the way down the main road, not to mention the drive—which incidentally is wooded, too—just because of the tales of a couple of old men in a pub?"

"Yes," she said firmly.

"Get a grip on yourself, girl! Where's this much vaunted impartiality of yours? There is no way I am making a four-mile walk into a six-mile one just because you choose to believe the ramblings of a bunch of old drunks," he snapped. "You want to take the long way, fine, but I'm going through the woods. Are you coming, Anne?" he demanded.

Anne looked from Heather's stubborn face to Glen's angry one.

"I think we should all go the same way," she said, moving toward Glen.

"You can't leave me!" exclaimed Heather.

"We aren't leaving you. It's you who is staying behind," said Anne peaceably. She felt no sympathy for Heather. Living with her this last week had made her intolerant of the other's continual moods and demands.

The light began to fade, and Anne looked up. Clouds had formed and were drifting across the face of the moon.

"Looks like the weather might be breaking," she said, following Glen across the grass.

"At least we had the best of it," he replied. In a

whisper he added, "Don't worry, she'll catch up with us in a minute. Less, now the light's going."

Sure enough, a few minutes later they heard Heather yelling.

"Wait for me!"

As they reached the trees, the cloud bank totally obscured the moon and they were plunged into darkness.

"Damn!" swore Glen, stumbling into a tree. "Here, take my hands, you two. We don't want to get separated. I think we go this way."

Anne stumbled along through the undergrowth, trying to keep up with Glen. Her foot caught in a root and down she went, falling heavily on her knees and ripping her hand free.

"Ow!" she yelled. "Hold on, wait a minute!"

Glen bent down and lifted her to her feet. "You all right?" he asked.

"I think so," she replied, rubbing her bruised kneecaps. "Do you have to go so fast?" she complained.

"I'm not sure where we are," he said. "I want to find some recognizable landmarks."

Gradually it began to grow lighter again, and Anne squinted up through the trees. "The moon's back. We should be able to orient ourselves now."

Glen looked around for a moment, then pointed off to his right. "Over there, I think."

They started off again, making slightly better progress now that they could see. Suddenly Heather stopped.

Anne bumped into her. "What're you stopping for?" she demanded.

"I can see something in front of us," she whispered, trying to hide behind the nearest bush.

Glen peered over their shoulders. "There's nothing there," he said.

"There is," Heather insisted, keeping her voice low. "I'm not moving until you find out what it is."

Glen made an exasperated noise. "I'm getting fed up with you ordering me about, Heather." Unceremoniously he pushed her aside and moved forward a couple of steps. "I can't see anything."

"The moon's gone behind another cloud now, but I saw a patch of black by that tree over there," she insisted, her voice beginning to quaver.

"There's nothing there."

"There is!" she insisted.

Glen grabbed her by the hand and hauled her toward the tree.

"Now you show me . . ."

Heather's terrified shriek split the air. A shaft of moonlight picked out the frozen tableau at the foot of the tree just as surely as if it were a spotlight. Something was hanging from a branch above their heads.

As Anne looked up, she felt everything around her begin to take on a slowness, as if time itself had become stretched. The scream seemed to go on and on forever. There was the sound of a sharp slap, but it was she who put her hand up to a smarting cheek and found Glen shaking her violently.

"Snap out of it, Anne," he said urgently. "You can't help her now, she's beyond it." He stopped shaking her and held her close for a moment, releasing her when she feebly pushed him away.

"Cassandra?" she asked.

He nodded. "She's dead."

Like a sleepwalker, Anne moved toward the body, but Glen held her back.

"I wouldn't," he said.

"I have to see!" she insisted, pushing his restraining hand away.

She walked over, gazing up at Cassandra's body. The girl hardly seemed dead unless you looked closely. Her feet were only a few centimeters off the ground—it was as if she was standing waiting for them.

A faint breeze seemed to catch the body, and it began to rotate slowly at the end of the creaking rope. Anne frowned. There was something wrong, something that didn't fit, if only she could see what it was.

A hand clutched at her arm. "Don't look, Anne," urged Glen, pulling her away.

She turned to face him, seeing for the first time that he was ashen and sweat was beading his forehead. From nearby came the sound of Heather retching.

"Let's leave. We need to tell the police and there's no point in staying here. We can't do anything for her now," he said.

"Her family, they'll have to be told," Anne said abruptly. "I know where she lives. I'll get them. You wait here with her."

She could hear Glen calling for her to stop, but she ignored him in her need to do something positive. If she did something—anything—then she wouldn't have to think. She wouldn't have to face the reality that perhaps they had contributed something to Cassandra's despair, perhaps the final straw.

It was a mad race through the trees. She had no real idea of where she was, let alone in which direction the headland lay. Instinct must have guided her, for eventually she ran free of the brambles and thorns and found herself at the edge of the woods with the lights of the croft ahead of her.

Up the slope she ran, panting now, to collapse against the doorframe with barely enough strength left to knock. The door was flung wide, almost catapulting her into the light and warmth of the main room.

She looked up into the face of the brother, dark and angry with her for not being his sister.

"Cassandra," she blurted out. "You must come. She's .... hurt." She steadied herself against the doorframe and made to move away.

The brother's arm snaked out, catching hold of her.

"Hurt, is she?" he said harshly. "What've you done to her?"

"Nothing," said Anne. "She did it herself."

The grip tightened. "How hurt?"

Anne looked away. "Dead. She hanged herself," she said, her voice devoid of emotion.

"Where?" he demanded. "Show me."

"Have they found Cassandra?" asked an older female voice from inside.

"They found her," affirmed the youth over his shoulder. "She's gone and hanged herself. I'm going to get her now." He turned back to Anne. "Where is she?"

"We came over the fields from Kirkoswald and cut through the woods. We found her in a tree beside the path."

"It's your meddling that brought her to this," he snarled, his face twisting in anger as he shook Anne. "If you'd left her alone . . ."

"Paris! Enough!" said the preemptory voice from inside. "It's no one's fault. Fetch a torch; you'll be needing one."

He let her go and with a look of pure hate, stormed from the room. Anne heard the distant sound of raised voices, then Paris returned with the torch and a blanket.

"Let's be going," he said, shutting the door.

"Shouldn't we phone the police or something?" faltered Anne, backing away from him.

"Mother'll see to that," he answered shortly, setting off across the headland.

It was a silent journey. There was nothing really to say. When they reached the spot where Cassandra was hanging, Heather was still lying in a heap on the ground sobbing while Glen sat beside her.

He looked up as they arrived. "You found the house safely, then," was all he said.

She nodded.

The youth spread the blanket down at the foot of the tree and reached for his belt knife. Clasping Cassandra's body around the waist, he began to saw through the loop of the rope where it extended above her head.

Glen got to his feet. "Can I help?" he asked.

"We look after our own," was the short reply. "My

thanks for telling us," he grunted, "but you see to your own women and get them home."

The rope parted finally, making him stagger briefly as he took the full weight of his sister's body. Laying her down on the rug, he wrapped her in the blanket before putting his knife away. Silently, he lifted Cassandra's body up and vanished into the night, leaving them alone.

"I think we'd better get back," said Glen lamely. "There's nothing we can do now."

Anne nodded.

"Get up, Heather," he said, giving her a nudge with his foot.

She didn't move.

"For God's sake, girl, get up!" he said, leaning down and pulling her to her feet. "And stop that awful whimpering. If anyone has a right to be upset, it's Anne, not you. You didn't give a damn about the girl, and made it obvious to everyone."

Glen turned his back on her to put an arm around Anne.

"Are you all right?" he asked, drawing her along the path with him.

"I'm fine," said Anne quietly. Her grief was a cold knot inside her that wouldn't dissolve.

"Follow when you're ready, Heather," said Glen. "We're leaving now."

"Just a minute, there's something I want to check," said Anne, ducking out from under him and going over to the tree. She took hold of the end of the rope. She'd noticed something strange about it when Cassandra's brother had been cutting the girl's body down. She teased at the loose fibers on the cut end. They looked different from the rest of the rope. There was a strange elasticity to them. She pulled, feeling them stretch slightly. There was a resilience where the rope had been in contact with Cassandra's neck. Thoughtfully, she felt above the loop, but it was just a piece of hemp. Once again, something the girl had touched had been altered.

"Anne, come away," urged Glen. "Whatever you've found, it doesn't matter now. All I'm concerned about now is getting you back to the hostel."

Anne released the rope reluctantly, letting it swing back against the tree. She turned and walked back to him, feeling her legs begin to wobble slightly. He was right, if they didn't get back soon, she was likely to collapse on them.

It was a bleary-eyed face she presented to the world late the next morning. She had lain awake for several hours puzzling over Cassandra and her strange talent, replaying all their meetings with her and worrying that they might have been the cause of her suicide. She hadn't come to any conclusions; eventually, sheer exhaustion had taken over and she had slept.

Most of her section had left to get in a last few hours' work before the bus came after lunch to take them home, so she was spared the necessity of telling anyone what had happened. Those who had demanded the grisly details had got them from Glen the night before or over breakfast. In fact, the hostel was empty except for the three of them.

After a meager breakfast, Anne announced that she was going for a walk.

Glen looked at her with concern. "Would you like me to come with you?" he asked.

Anne shook her head, smiling. "No, thanks, I'm fine. I just want some fresh air to clear my head, and to do a bit of thinking."

"Take care, then," he said, reaching out to touch her cheek gently, and intimately. "I'd hate anything to happen to you."

"I don't believe it!" said Heather indignantly. "Now's not the time for a testosterone high! How can you be so insensitive when we've all been through such a trauma?"

"Can it, Heather," said Glen, letting his hand drop. "Anne's been through more than us. She lost a friend. I want her to know I care about her, that's all."

Embarrassed, Anne nodded and headed for the door, but Glen followed her.

"Stay away from the woods where we were last night, Anne," he said quietly, taking her jacket off the peg and holding it out to her. "I don't trust that brother of Cassandra's. Head for the beach. If you're not back in an hour, I'll come looking for you."

"There's no need," she protested.

He held onto her jacket as she tried to take it from him. "I meant what I said in there." His voice had deepened, become more intense as he leaned toward her. He hesitated, taking a step back and letting her jacket go as he realized now was not the time for more. "Please don't take any risks. I don't want anything to happen to you."

"I'll take care," she promised.

The day was gray and overcast, and a fine drizzle had begun to fall. As she headed out of the courtyard for the shelter of the trees, she smiled gently to herself, Glen's obvious interest in her lightening her somber mood.

Once under the canopy of leaves she slowed down, content just to amble where her feet took her. For once, Frazer had shown some humanity and had given the three of them the morning to themselves. She aimed to take advantage of it.

The path forked in two, one branch leading to the studio, the other toward Kirkoswald and the route they'd taken home last night. With a shudder, Anne took the lower path down to the studio.

Her thoughts returned to Cassandra, trying to make some sense of the past week. Cassandra had been brought up isolated from everyone except her family. Not only that, but she had been constantly watched by her brother to make sure she didn't meet people, and the last time she had, she said there'd been an accident. What kind of accident? Obviously not an ordinary one, otherwise why isolate her? Could it have something to do with her gift? She could obviously change the structure of things she touched, but if she could do it at will, why try to commit suicide and then change the rope, make it stretch? That didn't make sense. Perhaps Cassandra had no control, and everything she touched changed.

Anne had reached the clearing where the studio stood. Crossing over to one of the windows, she perched on the ledge. Despite the fine drizzle, she didn't want to go inside. The smell of damp earth filled the clearing and she found it refreshing, touching something deep in her soul that brought her a measure of peace.

If Cassandra had no control over her gift, could circumstances around her be triggering it? When Cassandra had altered the rocks, she'd been happy and the "paintings" had reflected this. The second time, she'd been upset and angry and when she'd lashed out at the paint box, it had gone flying as one would expect, but the structural change had been one of decay—it had crumbled to dust on being touched. Perhaps her mood dictated the type of change.

That sounded good so far, but how did the change in the rope fit in? Maybe her ability had a built-in survival factor and she couldn't stop the rope from changing. Anne sighed. As a survival factor, it hadn't been particularly successful.

The sound of footsteps, followed by the flash of black skirts and swirling ginger hair made her look up.

"Cassandra!" she yelled, leaping to her feet. "My God, you're alive! Come back. It's me, Anne!" Anne raced across the clearing. "It can't be her, she's dead. Oh, please, God, let her have survived," she prayed, pushing the bushes aside as she tried to follow.

Beyond lay a narrow rabbit track. Dark footprints on the damp grass showed she was on the right path. Not stopping to think, she ran along it, following the footsteps till she burst out of the trees onto the headland not far from the croft where Cassandra's family lived. Sides heaving, she looked around frantically, but apart from the croft, the grassy slopes were absolutely empty of human life. Maybe she'd overtaken her in the dash through the woods.

Logic told her that she couldn't possibly have seen Cassandra. Briefly, she considered going up to the croft, but she knew she'd no right to disturb the family in their mourning. Turning to leave she let out a muffled shriek as she came face-to-face with Cassandra's brother.

"God, you frightened me! I didn't expect to see you here," she said, backing off hurriedly.

"Who'd you expect to see? Cassandra?"

"No," admitted Anne, suddenly aware he was carrying a dead rabbit and a shotgun. "But I thought I saw her back by the studio. It must have been my imagination playing tricks on me."

"Must have," he agreed laconically, his dark eyes never leaving her face.

"She had a great talent. It's a pity that she didn't have the chance to develop it," she said, stumbling for something to say.

"Cassie didn't have a talent," he said, frowning.

"But she did. She was able to alter the rocks and paint into them. You must know she could change things."

"She never painted into any rocks that I knew of. Where d'you see these paintings?"

"On the path down to the beach."

Paris shook his head, a lock of black hair falling over his face, shielding his eyes from her. "I was down that way on Thursday and there weren't any paintings then. Reckon it's your imagination again."

"The paintings were there on Wednesday," began Anne, then stopped, her hand flying to her mouth in shock. "Cassandra," she whispered, pointing a shaking finger past him toward the croft.

"You should have listened to Cassandra and stayed away from us," he said sadly, shifting the rabbit off his shoulder and letting it dangle at his side. "Pity you had to find out. Cassie has our gift, all right, but it's wild in her. She can't control it. What she touches turns depending on her mood at the time."

Anne pulled her gaze away from Cassandra and looked back at the brother, sensing the menace in his tone.

"It was you who erased the pictures," she whispered, color draining from her face.

"To save you, missy, if you'd had the sense to let be," he said harshly. "You pushed her, reminded her what it's like to be one of your kind. It was just your bad luck that you were the one to find her body." His eyes narrowed and he lifted up the rabbit. "Our gift can create and heal, which is how we saved Cassie, but it can destroy, too." He tightened his grip on the rabbit's body and as he squeezed, before Anne's horrified eyes, it began to decay. The skin swelled, oozing a yellowish-gray liquid. The stench of putrefaction hung heavily in the air.

Anne glanced back at Cassandra, a small figure in front of the croft, but near enough for her to tell that the girl was no less terrified than she was.

"We can't let you leave now, you know that, don't you?" he said almost conversationally, tossing the decayed body to one side. "Every time this happens, we have to move on, keep hiding from the normals like you. After thousands of years, we finally thought we'd found a place where we'd be safe."

His stare became hypnotic, and Anne found she was unable to look away. Her willpower gradually began seeping from her and though she stood passively waiting, her mind screamed in raw terror.

He stepped forward, and his hand reached out for her.

"You should have listened to Cassandra, she knows the truth, but then, you're not the first to ignore her warnings of danger. It's her curse, you see."

THE KILLING OF BAD BULL

by Alan Dean Foster

Alan Dean Foster was born in New York City and raised in Los Angeles. He has a bachelor's degree in Political Science and a Master of Fine Arts in Cinema from UCLA. He has traveled extensively around the world, from Australia to Papua, New Guinea. He has also written fiction in just about every genre, and is known for his excellent movie novelizations. Currently, he lives in Prescott, Arizona, with his wife, assorted dogs, cats, fish, javelina, and other animals. He is currently working on several new novels and media projects. His recent books include the third volume in the *Journeys of the Catechist* series, *A Triumph of Souls,* and *Reunion.*

The saddest thing about it was that it was his own people who were trying to kill him. The rest of humanity didn't give a damn. Of course, the rest of humanity didn't know about him. Which was why his own people were trying to kill him.

A quick stroll around the casino revealed nothing out of the ordinary. Here in Salvador, on the north coast of Brazil, the men and women sitting like sphinxes in front of the slot machines and laughing as dice ricocheted around the craps table were nearly all locals, with only a smattering of foreigners. Being Pima-Cheyenne, it made it easier for him to pick out strangers, since the local Indians were considerably smaller of stature than their more robust North American cousins. This was important, since strangers might be looking for more than just entertainment, or a chance to make a quick dollar.

They might be looking for him.

They'd chased him clear across the U.S.; from Vegas, to the riverboat casinos of the Mississippi, to the enclosed gambling palaces that ringed the Great Lakes, and finally to Atlantic City. Then through Europe, where he had finally succeeded in giving them the proverbial slip. Upon reaching South America, he'd begun his run in Rio before moving on to São Paulo, and now found himself here. For the well-traveled Bull Threerivers, Salvador was a comparative backwater, big city or no.

He took only one carry-on bag with him. It contained a few items of personal interest, one change of plain clothing, one of exceedingly expensive custom-tailored attire, and little else besides his passport and a dozen bankbooks held together with rubber bands. The bankbooks listed accounts under half a dozen aliases in Switzerland, the Caymans, and the Cook Islands. Cumulative numbers in those books reached seven figures. When they reached eight, Threerivers would stop. That was the goal he had set for himself. That was when he felt he could safely stop working.

The people who were after him wanted him to stop *now*. He'd been warned. Ignoring the warnings, he had fled eastward from his home in Los Angeles. Twice, they had almost caught up with him. Once in Connecticut, and later in Monaco. Both times he had slipped away, though not before taking a bullet in the shoulder before leaving France. He'd had it removed, and had waited for the wound to heal, in a rented private residence on the borders of the souk in Casablanca. Money bought speed and silence.

He did not know if they had been able to track him to Brazil. Logic dictated a move on his part from Europe to South Africa, where the casinos, and the pickings, were bigger. By recrossing the Atlantic, he hoped he had finally thrown them off his trail. His confidence had been buoyed by his successes in Rio and São Paulo. From Salvador, he intended to move on to other major South American cities, then to Australia, concluding his odyssey of personal financial enhancement with a visit to the fleshpots of Asia. As to where he would retire, he found his present surroundings more than congenial. Though he hailed from another continent, his Indian features allowed him to move easily among the locals, and both the food and climate suited him.

No one paid any attention to him as he wandered through the casino. There was no reason why they should. Though tall for a local Indian, he was not of eye-catching height or appearance. He flourished no jewelry and flaunted no evidence of the considerable wealth he had steadily accumulated in the course of his travels.

From time to time he would pause, seemingly at random, before a slot machine and drop a few coins. That was his modus. After half a day or so of aimless drifting he would zero in on a chosen machine. On the right machine. On the one with just the right scent of ripeness.

Bull Threerivers could smell electricity.

Not the way ordinary folk smell a wire that's hot and burning. Most people can do that. With a sniff and a pause, Threerivers could scent the actual flow of electrons; could detect their moods and motions, their flux and flavor. It was a talent he had not realized was unusual until he turned nine and observed that none of his playmates in the run-down L.A. neighborhood where he grew up could do it. Even then, he thought little of the odd aptitude, and kept the knowledge to himself. No kid likes to be thought of by his peers as "weird."

It was only when he reached his teens, an age traditionally devoid of rewarding prospects for members of his ethnic faction, that he realized it might be useful in finding a job. He actually found two. Alternating between the auto electronics repair shop and a small local store that fixed TVs and other appliances, he demonstrated what seemed to his bosses an uncanny ability to find the source of any electrical problem in any device within minutes. Often, he killed time taking them apart to make it look like he was working.

What he was actually doing was sniffing out the location of the defect. Short circuits, for example, had a sickly, unhealthy aroma. Dead contacts smelled— not dead, but rather like burnt cinnamon. Weak connections stank of wet sesame seed. Misbehaving chipsets reeked of rotten eggs. And so on, with each flaw possessing a distinctive aroma of its own: a unique identifying fragrance only he could detect. Struggling to find an explanation for his condition in the local library and on the net, he could uncover nothing like it in the medical literature. It was then he decided that his situation was unique. Something was cross-wired in his olfactory nerves, something that enabled him to sense the ebb and flow of electrons in a current the way a master chef could taste the difference in the same kind of spice that had been grown in differing locales.

From helping to fix car stereos and auto diagnostic systems on the one hand, and toasters and microwave ovens and vacuum cleaners on the other, he moved on to computers, pinpointing the location of hardware problems so intractable that the owner of the business where he had been working literally cried when Bull announced that he was leaving. Even the offer of a doubling, a tripling of his salary was not enough to induce him to remain. Because Threerivers had found a far more lucrative application for his peculiar ability.

He'd started in Las Vegas. If he had confined his activities to Nevada, and perhaps New Jersey, his singular activities might have gone unremarked upon. But he made the mistake of spreading himself around, in a sensible effort not to draw attention to himself by winning too much in any one place. His travels soon led him to the many casinos that were located on individual Indian reservations throughout North America. He was observed, and then followed. For some time, Security personnel sharing information were at a loss to figure out how he was managing his remarkable success.

Then, running through tape after security tape of the extraordinarily lucky native American gambler, one particularly attentive agent with an open mind and no preconceptions happened to notice the subject of all the attention leaning forward to sniff a machine he was playing just before it paid off. Subsequent reviews of other tapes inevitably captured similar moments on video. Incredible as it seemed, and without understanding how or why it was happening, casino security personnel could agree only on the incredible obvious.

The subject, a certain Bull John Threerivers of Los Angeles, California, could somehow smell a slot machine that was about to pay off.

Tribal owners and administrators engaged in soft-voiced but quietly frantic caucus via telephone and fax and e-mail. It was not the money they were losing that set them on the knife edge of panic. It was something much worse and of potentially far greater import.

And so the pact was made, and the decision taken, that as quietly as possible, this one seemingly innocuous if fortunate gambler had to be stopped. A delegation from several tribes had been appointed to confront him at his modestly lavish condominium in Los Angeles. Inviting them in, he had listened politely, even intently, to their expressions of concern. When they left, it was with his assurances that he understood the gravity of the conundrum, and that he would take appropriate steps to see that their concerns were fully addressed.

When they came back to check on him in person, after discovering that his phone had been disconnected, it was to learn that he had moved out the day after their visit. That was when it was decided that, given what was at stake, stronger measures would have to be implemented.

Threerivers had barely escaped the first attempt on his life, which took place in the parking lot of a riverboat casino docked outside Memphis. Only the timely arrival on the scene of a bunch of semidelirious college students on spring break had forced the three men who had pinned him against the side of a truck to let him go. Bull had never been so glad to see a bunch of drunken white men in his life. After that he moved fast, erratically, staying in no one place for more than a few days. He thought he had shaken his pursuit when he shifted his activities to Europe, but soon found them on his trail once more. Fortunately, the presence of several large Amerindian males in a casino in, for example, Copenhagen, was obligingly conspicuous. On such occasions he was always able to flee prior to any actual confrontation.

A distinctively sharp stench caught his attention as he patrolled the rows of gaudy, garish, insistent slots. The seat in front of the progressive poker machine was empty. His nostrils quivered. It reeked of readiness. No one else in the room, no one else in the city, and in all likelihood no one else on the planet could detect the distinctive fragrance that reminded him of sweet onions sizzling in a pan that was presently emanating from the machine. It was a scent he had come to recognize without trying; the scent of a slot machine about to pay off.

Taking the seat in front of it, he took his time arranging a handful of tokens by the side of the machine. Then it was feeding time. It ate two, four, six of the shiny base metal medallions. By the time he dropped in the eleventh coin, the perfume was so overpowering that his eyes began to water. Following the application of the twelfth, four aces lined up in the window before his eyes. Instantly, lights strobed, sirens wailed, bells rang, and excited fellow players in the immediate vicinity abandoned their machines to rush over and bathe in the audio-visual display. He sat contentedly before the fireworks, trying not to look too bored, his nose wrinkling at the stench of it. He'd sat through hundreds of similarly celebratory scenarios during the past year. One more year would see him finished with it.

For now, though, he smiled as he accepted the congratulations of the excited gamblers who crowded around him, hoping that some of the "luck" that had adhered to this undemonstrative foreigner would rub off on them. Well-wishes in German and English in addition to the ubiquitous Portuguese filled the air around him. One well-dressed businessman had in a pocket of his suit a palm computer that was about to succumb to a particularly nasty virus. Threerivers felt bad that he could not warn the man about it.

Two smiling men in neat suits arrived very soon and led him away. At the office, he received more formal congratulations from one of the casino directors. They would want to take a picture of him holding an oversized check spelling out his winnings, he knew. That was standard casino procedure in the case of big winners. He could hardly refuse without raising unwanted suspicions. It was not a big problem. He had long since developed a procedure for dealing with the situation. He would be a thousand miles or more away from Salvador before the picture appeared in any Brazilian paper.

Those who pursued him could have put a stop to his activities by passing his curriculum vitae on to every large gambling establishment on the planet. But they couldn't do that, he knew. Such an incredible revelation was bound to lead to inquiries: public, scientific, and commercial. Those who had especially sensitive reasons for wanting to stop him did not want inquiries—they wanted him dead. Their conundrum bought him time.

He had to convert his Brazilian heais into dollars, then find a bank that would handle the wire transfer to Zurich. That took the rest of the day. By the time evening approached, his latest winnings were on their way out of the country and his fanny pack contained a newly purchased first-class ticket to Lima. There was a nice casino in the district of Miraflores, he had read. He was anxious to pay it a visit.

He had chosen a hotel on Itapua Beach north of

the city, having reserved a room for the week. It had taken only two days to find the right machine in the casino. As he exited the taxi and entered the lobby of the hotel, he located a desk clerk with some command of English and informed him that management might want to send someone to check the main transformer on the street outside. Threerivers thought he might have seen a spark, or something, he explained. Actually, he had seen nothing at all, but stepping out of the cab he had smelled sage and thyme—essence of capacitor overload, as he had come to know it. He could have cared less about the transformer, or the neighborhood in which it was situated, or the hotel, but he did not want his bed to burn up before he checked out the next morning.

He had the key in the lock to his room when he hesitated. Something on the other side of the door was tickling his nose. He always made it a point to memorize the smell of a new room whenever he checked in. The TV, the electrical outlets, the lamps, all had their distinctive aromas. Here, something smelled different. The discrepancy was slight, but unmistakable. Slowly he removed the key from the lock, trying not to make any noise as he did so.

Someone pushed a hard, unyielding something into his back. "Don't turn around. Walk down the hall, toward the beach." Reaching out, the man behind Threerivers rapped on the door twice, then twice again. It opened to reveal a tall Amerind who slipped a small gun into his pocket as he emerged.

"He knew you were in there," explained the man behind Threerivers. "He was starting to back out. I was afraid he might bolt."

"How?" The other man's face was a mix of concern and confusion as he stared not at his partner, but at their stoic captive. "I didn't make a sound."

The other man gestured. "You wearing anything electronic?"

Shutting the door to Threerivers' room behind him,

the intruder considered the question. "Only a watch. And my cell phone is off."

"But charged," replied his partner. "He probably sniffed it. Same way he does the machines." The small, hard pressure in the middle of Threerivers' back pressed sharply inward. "Didn't you?"

Threerivers shrugged indifferently as he started down the hall. It was late, and none of the other guests were out. Hopefully, they would encounter a maid, or someone checking hotel security. The main building had only two floors, and was situated right on the sand. Right now, the beach would likely be completely deserted. That was not good.

"Cell phones stink of spoiled fruit juice," he murmured absently. "A watch hardly smells at all."

"Freak," snapped the man who had been concealing himself in Threerivers' room.

Bull replied in Cheyenne, which neither of his captors understood. "There's no need for this," he insisted as they walked him down the hall in the direction of the dark, empty beach and the wide Atlantic beyond. "Whatever they're paying you, I can add zeros to it."

"Sorry, brother," responded the one holding the pistol. "It's all been explained to us. There's too much at stake here."

"What? A few winnings?"

"Millions, is how I hear it," declared the other man. "It's not the money, though. You know that. You know what it is. The Elders told you."

"Maybe I don't." Threerivers was defensive. "Why don't you explain it to me again?"

"All those hundreds of millions pouring into reservation casinos every year," the man with the gun told him. "The salvation of dozens of tribes. The basis for the preservation and the resurrection of the Indian nations. Everybody's happy with the arrangement: the white folks who happily gamble their money away and the tribes that gladly collect it. Then you come along. An Indian who can smell out a winning jackpot. What happens if the white media get hold of a story like that?"

"I'm the only one who can do it," Threerivers explained.

"Maybe," admitted the hired assassin. "A lot of elders and council members sure hope so. But try and tell the white man that. If they think there's one of us who can put the fix on slot machines, they'll start wondering if there are others. And if they start wondering if there are others, they're liable to stop using the casinos on the reservations."

"I haven't been on a rez since I left New York for London," Threerivers protested. "I haven't cost one tribe an Indian nickel in the last year and a half."

"You're too dangerous to have around," the other man pointed out. "If anyone, anywhere, finds out about what you can do, the news will get back to the States. And then we have the same problem. Once the wendigo is out, you can't put him back in his hole." He gestured. "Mind the stairs."

Threerivers turned left instead of right. Before they could question his decision, they found themselves confronted by a waiter wheeling a hot dinner for two toward a second-floor room. Threerivers had turned that way because he had smelled the electric food warmer approaching. He was counting on the fact that the assassin wouldn't risk shooting the waiter, and that the pistol he was holding was not equipped with a silencer. When he made his break, darting forward and around the startled server, he gave the food cart a hard shove sideways. Fine Brazilian food went flying, the waiter yelled in surprise, someone stuck his head out a door to see what was happening, and Bull was sprinting for the service exit. Whenever he checked into a new hotel, one of the first things he did was mark the location of alternate exits.

They didn't catch him. By the time they found the service exit, he had managed to flag down a passing car. Waving a fistful of bills to persuade the startled driver, he was soon speeding away from the threatening ocean. His pursuers went straight to the airport, but they were not sanguine about encountering their quarry there. In this, they were right: Threerivers was too smart, too experienced to chance taking the first plane out of town now that his presence had been detected.

When the old bus finally rattled into Recife days later, he booked a cabin on a freighter and vanished into the Atlantic. They never caught up with him again. In the course of his travels, Threerivers had learned a lot about gambling. Despite his peculiar talent, he knew when to quit. If only his pursuers could have accepted his word that he would, his last flight would have been unnecessary. Seven figures, he decided, were of more comfort to a man alive than eight to a man sleeping in the earth. He never set foot in a casino again—or for that matter, in a city that boasted a casino.

They kept searching for him, of course, not willing to take the chance that he would keep his ability permanently under wraps. They didn't find him. No one thought to look on the coast of the island-nation of Sri Lanka, a hundred miles south of its sultry capital city of Colombo. There it was that a certain expatriate Amerind lived in quiet luxury amid beautiful people who were darker than himself. He married, and had four children, two of whom demonstrated the most curious propensity for fixing obstreperous computers and stereos, and a perfectly beautiful little girl who spoke repeatedly of her intention to one day start her own software company. Her friends chattered instead about boys and music and movies and school, and sometimes they laughed at her behind her back.

But then, none of them could feel the Net.

IN THE DARK VALLEY
By Brendan DuBois

Brendan DuBois is the award-winning author of short stories and novels. His short fiction has appeared in *Playboy, Ellery Queen's Mystery Magazine, Alfred Hitchcock's Mystery Magazine, Mary Higgins Clark's Mystery Magazine,* and numerous anthologies. He has received the Shamus Award from the Private Eye Writers of America for one of his short stories, and has been nominated three times for an Edgar Allan Poe Award by the Mystery Writers of America. His most recent novel, *Resurrection Day,* is a suspense thriller that looks at what might have happened had the Cuban Missile Crisis of 1962 erupted into a nuclear war between the United States and the Soviet Union. This book also recently received the Sidewise Award for best alternative history novel of 1999. He lives in New Hampshire with his wife Mona.

It was three PM and the snow was heavier than Claire Pembrose had expected. She swore under her breath as she drove the old Saab home, after spending a dreary final hour at the library. The solitary plow for the small town of Machias, NH was probably out there somewhere on the town's many narrow streets, but it sure as hell hadn't been on this road. She set the wipers on slow and looked through the windshield, feeling her hands tighten on the steering wheel. The day of escape was right now, and she wasn't going to let snow, wind, rain, or a tidal wave hold her back.

She could sense the rear wheels of the Saab slip as she drove. Snow was coming down in whipping sheets of white, obscuring the high hills and mountains that

surrounded the town. The homes in this part of Machias were single family or double-wide trailers, and
even at this early hour, lights were on inside all of
them. It was a cheery sight, and since she now knew
most of the people in this town, it would be easy
enough to ask for help if she got stuck, but on this
late afternoon January day, she didn't want to talk to
a damn soul in Machias.

She slowed as she got to the old Victorian that she
and Tom Watkins called home, and she swore again,
louder. The downstairs lights were on, and Tom's
Lexus was parked in the driveway. Damn it, he wasn't
supposed to be home now. He had said to expect a
late night, that it would be doubtful he'd be home by
six PM, and here he was, three hours early, and on this
day, this special day of escape.

Damn it again. She stopped the Saab at the intersec-
tion, not daring to go any farther. Knowing Tom, he was
probably downstairs, reading the day's *Union Leader* or
the week's *Machias Times*. She hoped he hadn't gone
to the upstairs bedroom closet, where her bags had been
packed. She rubbed her hands against the steering wheel,
knowing with a sick feeling that she had no choice. She
had to get out of here, get out right now. If she gave up
now, she knew she would never get he courage to go
through with it again to leave him and Machias.

The windshield wipers moved back and forth, the
snowflakes building upon the sides of the glass. She
felt her throat thicken as she looked at the gas gauge.
Only a quarter tank left. How far could she go on just
a quarter tank of gas?

Far enough. She backed up the Saab in a neighbor's
unplowed driveway, got caught for a moment, and
then headed away from her home and her husband.

No matter the weather, no matter the abandoned
belongings, no matter what, she had to get out of this
town tonight.

But nine months earlier, oh my, how things had
been different. Tom had been driving, laughing and

often squeezing her leg with a free hand as he maneuvered the Saab through the Machias Range, heading to the small town that Tom had grown up in, and that they were now both going to call home. They had met while at the University of Maine, where she had studied journalism and he had studied business administration. They had dated off and on until graduation, and nearly two years later, they had met again. She had been working for a daily newspaper on the coast of Maine in York, and Tom had worked for one of the large credit card companies that had set up shop in the area, looking for cheap and relatively well educated labor.

Whirlwind . . . she wasn't sure what described a whirlwind romance, but this must have come pretty close. Meeting again after college, something had clicked, something had just seemed so right. They had moved in together after six months, and six months later, a quick marriage ceremony before a justice of the peace with just a few friends from the newspaper and his place of work. All through those busy weeks, not a moment of doubt, not a moment of reconsideration.

Family members? She shuddered at the thought of having wizened old Aunt Meg and Uncle Hubert show up at something so wonderful. They had raised her since she had been an infant, after her parents had died in a car accident, and while the upbringing had been proper and correct and relatively comfortable, it hadn't been loving, not for a moment.

And for Tom, well, his large family never got out of Machias much, and they hadn't gone to the wedding either. "Not to worry, m'love," he had said. "There'll be plenty of time to catch up later. I'm sure they'll love you, and I'm positive you'll love them and Machias."

Okay, she hadn't been too thrilled with the idea of bailing out of the coast of Maine and going into the deep woods of New Hampshire, but then Tom had come to her with a bombshell: a well-off uncle was

going to stake him in an investment company that
could work out of anywhere, so why not Machias?
And the money Tom would make could easily mean
that her first dream, the primo dream of all, of sitting
home every day and working on a novel, was about
to come true, twenty years ahead of schedule.

Tom squeezed her leg again, as they started descending down the road to Machias. "Here we go,"
he said. "Look up here and we'll stop for a sec, show
you what we're getting into."

He pulled the Saab over to a paved overlook, and
they both got out. Below them was a small town, nestled in a bowl of green with a river running through
it. Craggy peaks of granite and tall pines surrounded
the town. Tom put his arm around her and said,
"There it be, Claire. Machias. Population about a
thousand. Only two ways in and out of the town. To
the east, over the Piscassic River, and on this little
paved highway, the Machias Mountain Road, also
known as Old Route Five."

"It looks so remote," she said, looking down at the
small collection of buildings.

He squeezed her shoulder. "Part of the charm. I
was a teenager before I learned people in other towns
locked their doors at night and didn't leave their keys
in the cars. Imagine that."

She looked over at her newly-minted husband, at
his dark brown eyes, light brown skin, and laughing
smile. He was six feet tall and well-muscled, and except for a furrowed scar on his left forearm—"hunting
accident when I was much younger"—he looked damn
near perfect. She had been curious about his family
background, and he had just shrugged and said, "New
England mongrel. Irish, Norwegian, French-Canadian
stock, and some old Indian blood, I'm sure."

Sure. She hadn't cared, not one bit. She wrapped
her arm around his strong waist and said, "Yes, imagine that."

They got back into the Saab and started descending
the narrow road, full of switchbacks and hairpin

curves, and then, curious about something, she popped open the glove compartment and pulled out a state road map. She looked and looked again, and then glanced over at her husband.

"Tom?"

"Yes?" he said.

"Uh, funny thing here," she said. "This road map. It doesn't even show Machias."

He smiled and looked back. "Another advantage of being in a small town. Sometimes you fall off the radar screen or the map. Makes it nice and quiet."

"Oh," she said, folding up the map. "I guess you're right."

She drove east, heading to the town bridge and her way out. Guessing right, she had recalled. I guess we screwed that one good. She hadn't guessed right at all once she and Tom had set up housekeeping in Machias. She kept the speed of the Saab slow, feeling the wheels fight as the snow accumulated. Up ahead was Conyer's Grocery, the only place in town that sold gas—from four pumps out in front of the wide farmer's porch of the store—and she pulled up in front of the store, mentally calculating how much cash she had in her purse, and she saw a cardboard sign flapping in the snow and the breeze. Three little words, written in black crayon. OUT OF ORDER.

She gunned the Saab and got back onto the road, looked again at the fuel gauge. One quarter of a tank. How far could she go? Taking the road that spanned the Piscassic River meant going into the White Mountain National Forest for a while, before ending up in the equally small town of Gilead. If she ran out of gas in the middle of the national forest, well, it certainly would get dark real soon, and who would be traveling at this hour, in such a storm? But if she got within walking distance of Gilead, she was sure she could make it. At least that town was real, she thought. Gilead existed on road maps and atlases and every place else. Machias, on the other hand . . .

Sure, it was real, but it was also something horrifyingly else, something dark in this hidden valley.

She pulled her eyes from the gas gauge, kept on driving.

The first few weeks of her life in Machias had been a dizzying set of parties, lunches and get-togethers, as she met Tom's extended family. Tom had three brothers and two sisters, and an endless series of cousins, aunts and uncles, nieces and nephews. His parents had died some time ago, but amazingly so, one of his grandmothers was still alive, an old woman who had sat in the corner of one of the uncle's homes, dressed in black, her skin wrinkled, most of her teeth gone, and her light blue eyes looking large behind thick glasses. She had nodded at her when she was introduced, and when she had grasped her hand, it was like coarse sandpaper upon her skin. She muttered something and later Claire said, "What did your grandmother say back there? I couldn't quite make it out."

Tom laughed. "Oh, Grandmama Watkins said welcome home. That's all. Welcome home."

"Welcome home?" she said. "I just got here."

"Sure, but she wants to make you feel welcome."

"Oh," she said. "Well, I certainly feel that." Which was true. She had been nervous at meeting Tom's family, knowing how small towns often have equally small minds, but they had been so warm and open and welcoming, it was almost intoxicating after the years of the dry and proper relationship with Aunt Meg and Uncle Hubert.

Later one night, as they were having dinner in their Victorian home—lovingly restored and filled with new furniture—Tom had brought a bottle of water to the dinner table. A small label on the side said Machias Crystal Springs. She had raised an eyebrow at that. "What's the matter, the town water not good enough for us?"

He unscrewed the cap, poured a glass. "Small towns

like this, hon, the water system doesn't get much of a budget priority. But there're a couple of wells in town that have the freshest, cleanest water imaginable. Here, have a sip."

She did, wondering what she was getting into, but Tom was right. The water was light and refreshing, and almost had a taste of lemons in it. Drinking it made her think of hot hayfields and cool picnics under old oak trees and the comforting buzz of crickets.

"Mmm, that is good," she said. "Oh, Tom?"

"Yes?" he said, spooning out a plate of pasta for her. He made two thirds of the meals for dinner, and Claire was sure that if some of her former female coworkers back at the newspaper had known that, they would have tried to snatch him away from her.

"Your Grandmama Watkins. She looks incredible. How old do you think she is?"

He shrugged. "No one's quite sure."

"What do you mean? Doesn't she know?"

He spooned some pasta for himself. "I'm sure she has a vague idea, but she's getting along in years, and is beginning to forget things. Plus, back in 1921 or thereabouts, there was a fire that destroyed the town hall and a lot of the old records, including birth certificates. So there you go."

She poured a glass of Merlot for each of them. "Well, I'll bet she's close to being a hundred. At least."

Tom smiled at her, a look that still made her feel so warm and loved. "At least."

And as she ate in the candlelight and her new house with her new husband, she thought this was about as perfect as a day as one could ever have.

Perfect. How true. And that had been one of the last perfect days, for that night, the dreams had begun.

She slowed the Saab as she saw the flashing lights up ahead. There were two fire trucks, a tow truck and the sole police cruiser for the town of Machias, blocking the bridge over the Piscassic River. A figure in a black wool hat and bright orange slicker and carrying a flashlight ambled over to her, and she lowered the window, flinching as the snow flew against her face and came inside the car.

Sam Conyer came up to her, the sole police officer—and therefore the chief—for Machias. "H'llo, Claire, a nasty night to be out, isn't it?"

"Sure is," she said, speaking loudly over the wind. "What's going on?"

"Got a fender-bender on the bridge," he said. "Young Jimmy Magruder slid into Miriam Norton's brand new pickup truck. Nobody hurt, but a hell of a mess."

"I can see that," she said. "Any idea when the bridge will be opened up? I've got to get to Gilead tonight."

His face was impassive and his eyes didn't let on a thing as he slowly said, "Now, Claire, why would anyone want to get to Gilead tonight? That national forest road ain't going to be plowed worth shit, and I'd hate to see you go over into a ravine. Thing is, you should go home, that's what you should do."

She looked around, saw how the volunteer firefighters and even the tow truck driver was looking in her direction. "Please, Sam, I've got to get to Gilead tonight. Can't you just make enough room for me to pass by. Please?"

A slow shake of the head. "I'm afraid I can't do that, Claire. Not at all. I'm still working the accident scene here. Could be another couple of hours before the road is opened up. You should just back up and head home, if you want my advice."

She clenched the steering wheel hard, remembered a time before she came to Machias when she'd have chewed up one side of him and down another. That seemed like a lifetime ago.

She meekly nodded and said, "Chief, you're right. I think I'll go home right now."

Now he smiled. "That's good to hear. You say hi to Tom for me. All right?"

"Sure," she said, and a couple of minutes later, she had turned the Saab around, and was headed back into town. She shivered as she spared a quick glance in the rearview mirror, and saw the little clump of men back there, all looking at her as she headed away.

The dreams. Yes, the dreams had started right after that night when she had drunk the water from Machias Crystal Springs during that dinner. An odd night. She had seemed quite tired and dropped off after only reading a few pages of a thick mystery novel. And it was like she slid right into this dream. Or dreams. Nothing involving flying cats or castles made of crystal or missing an exam while in college. No, this one had seemed quite real, like she had been picked up and dropped into another woman's life. It had been cold and she was wearing lots of heavy, smelly clothes, trying to keep a fire going in a large, stone fireplace. Her hands were rough and chapped and a couple of her teeth ached, and her name was Elizabeth and she was from Newkirk and now she was in this muddy village, trying to wrestle a life in the New World, and she still had terrifying memories of the months-long voyage over the Atlantic in the leaking boat where one of her young nephews had died and his body had been commended to the deep, and now it was winter and the root cellar was almost empty and her three children were crying with hunger, and her Abraham was out with the other men in the village, trying to hunt, trying to survive . . .

And then the dream flicked, like a television channel being changed. Flick. Just like that. And she was Mist On Waters and she was in her lodge, beaver pelts about her legs, stirring a small bowl of broth for her son, cuddled up against her breast, the cold wind seeping through the cracks in the lodge, her eyes watering from the smoke rising from the small fire, feeling warm and comfortable but also scared, frightened of the strangers who had moved into their lands, burning the fields, cutting down the trees, moving and arguing and pushing, and there was talk in the tribe, of blood being spilled and she felt frightened for her man and her brothers and her father, the sachem of this tribe, trying to survive . . .

She had woken up with a start, breathing hard, the blankets and sheets wrapped around her legs, her heart thumping and racing along, and she felt guilty for a moment, that maybe all this thrashing around had woken up Tom. But her husband was there, breathing soundly, resting, and she leaned over and kissed the top of his head, and then lay down again.

Dreams. That's all. Just dreams.

But after the dreams had begun, she found she couldn't write anymore.

Claire found the roads empty, frighteningly so, and she kept the Saab in the middle of Main Street, cursing herself for having tried to have gone out to Gilead. The gas she had wasted out there, she'd probably need when heading up the mountain road, heading out of the valley. She should have gone out through the mountain road first. So what. If she had to walk, she would do it, even if it meant crawling on her hands and knees to get out of this town.

She shivered again, noticing something else. She was being watched, she could tell it. From the doors of Conyer's Hardware to Magruder's Cafe to Watkins Garage, people were watching her. The good people of Machias. All watching her, all gauging where she was going. And she remembered the first time she had really been frightened, those first days when she couldn't stand to sit in front of the computer.

Right after the dreams had begun—and most of the dreams were the same, of being a colonial settler or Native American, scratching out a living in this valley—she would spend hours, staring at her computer screen, in an office she had made up in a spare bedroom. And nothing would come out. Not a thing! And it disgusted her! For when she had been a college student and an intern and then a reporter in Maine, she had prided herself on being able to write anything, at any time, no matter the pressure. Once she had been covering an apartment building fire and when she got back to the office, she had sixteen minutes to turn out a page one story. And she had done it almost automatically.

What made it doubly frustrating is that she always told herself that if she had just had the time, she would turn away from journalism and start writing a novel. Not the Great American Novel, but maybe the Somewhat Adequate Regional Novel. But nothing would come. Not A Thing. She would spend the hours watching television, making the beds, washing the floors, gardening outside, and every time she sat in front of the computer, staring at the blank screen, it would seem to mirror her own mind. Blank. It even got to the point one day when she was flipping through the thin phone book for Machias, something seemed to jump from the pages and sit in her lap, demanding attention.

It was the names.

Magruder. Conyer. Watkins. Norton. Moore. Almost every name in the phonebook had the same last name. Almost every single one.

Later that night, she had mentioned casually to Tom, that it seemed odd that almost every name in the book belonged to one of five families, and Tom had just shrugged.

"Those were the founding families, that came to this valley back in 1710. The valley's been so remote and isolated, not many other people manage to find their way here."

"But Tom," she protested. "There's roads, television, telephone. Surely more people could have moved in by now."

He gave her a smile that wasn't very comforting. "Oh, some do move in, but they don't stay long."

"Why?"

"I guess they get tired of the rural way of life."

I guess, she thought. I guess.

*   *   *

The windshield wipers began to cake up, as freezing rain started to mix in with the snow. After almost sliding into a snowbank on one sharp curve, she backed down her speed.

She had this horrible task, of trying to balance getting out of Machias as quickly as possible, with the certainty that if she drove too fast, she would crash the car. And the added fun that the freezing rain was going to make that long drive up the Machias Mountain Road. She remembered the times she had driven with Tom, even in the middle of summer on a dry and clear day, how the sharp hairpin curves and switchbacks would make her grasp the side of the door.

Now, she was going to try it in the middle of a raging snow and ice storm, and she knew she had no choice, no choice at all.

She turned up the defroster, to warm up the windshield, and kept on driving.

After a while of staring at the computer screen, of trying to find an idea of what to write, she broached the idea of a new book while eating dinner one night with Tom.

He looked so darling, in his gray slacks, pressed light blue shirt, and red necktie. His investment business was doing well, and he told her that he loved the idea of going head-to-head with other firms in Boston and New York City, all the while staying in the comfort of a small town.

As he chopped up some greens for a salad in their large kitchen, shirt sleeves rolled up to reveal that old scar on his arm, she sipped a glass of Machias Crystal Springs water that had floating slices of lemon in it.

"Tom," she asked.

"Yes, hon," he said, his back to her as he worked by the sink.

"I've finally come up with an idea for my book," she said.

"Hey, that's great. What's it going to be about?"

"Well, I've been stuck on doing a work of fiction. Nothing was coming up, so I decided to try to do something else. Nonfiction. A work of history, in fact. A history of Machias."

Tom's knife halted in mid-slice, and the back of his neck turned a bright crimson. He paused for what seemed a long time, and said, "A history of Machias. How interesting. Why would you pick something like that?"

She felt like she had been walking far out onto a frozen lake, and had suddenly heard the first cracks of thin ice. She took another sip of the water. "Well, I had to pick something. And here we are. This is a fascinating little place, and I thought I'd dig around and find out what I can."

He managed to turn and smile thinly at her. "Good luck. I doubt you'll find much. This is quite the boring town."

She eyed him in return. "Then I guess it'll be a thin book, won't it?"

The ice started clumping up on the windshield wipers, slowing them down and reducing their effectiveness. She slowed and pulled to the side, and got out, wincing as the wind cut through her. She thought about the bag she had left behind, back home. Spare hat and gloves, and warm clothes, and lots of memories and scrapbooks and computer diskettes. All left behind.

She pulled chunks of snow and ice away from the wipers, looked back behind her. The wind was whipping the snow across the road, causing little drifts to form. After only a few minutes parked here, she could hardly make out the tracks of the Saab. There were no homes on this stretch of the road. Back there was Machias. Back there was Tom. She wondered what Tom was doing. She wondered at what point he would worry about her, at what point he would go out and look for her. She was under no illusions. She knew that the police chief, Sam Conyer, probably got on the phone not so long ago and told Tom the odd tale, of his wife trying to drive into Gilead during one of the worst storms of the year. After all, it was what someone did in a small town like this, to look out for each other, and besides, in Machias, everybody was related to everybody else. Except for the few interlopers—like herself!—it was like one big circle: Magruder to Conyer to Watkins to Norton to Moore.

And even after almost a year here, she knew she still didn't belong.

The dreams had become even more frantic—this time with the colonial woman and the Native American woman both feeling faint from starvation—but she still managed to get to the tiny Machias Free Library, to do the research for her book. The library was brick and granite and about the size of a two-car garage. It was open Mondays, Tuesdays, and Saturdays, and the librarian was an older woman named Mrs. Moore. She was heavyset and wore black stretch pants and red sweaters—even in summertime—and she frowned as Claire told her what she wanted.

"I'm not sure what we have, but in the third shelf back there, we have some histories of the state and New England. I don't think anyone's ever done a history of Machias."

It was comforting, almost, to be in a library with a reporter's notebook in her hand. It was like she was finally doing something that she had been trained to do.

She spoke up. "I thought most small towns always had a history written, for a bicentennial or tricentennial."

The librarian gave a good-natured shrug. "This has always been a poor little town. We don't have the money to have someone write a book up and then print it up."

"All right, then," she said. "Old newspapers, like the *Machias Times*. How far back do your bound issues go?"

"Oh, until 1921. There was a terrible fire back then, you see. Destroyed a lot of buildings, town records, and such. The bound books are in the periodical room. Anything else?"

"No, I'll be fine, I'm sure," Claire said, and she went back to the shelved area. She ran her fingers across the spines of the books, enjoying their touch. She had always loved libraries. She had found earlier on that she could escape from her Uncle Hubert and Aunt Meg for hours if she claimed she was going to the library for some school project, and she loved those long minutes of escape, going through the books.

Then she remembered she wasn't sure which shelf Mrs. Moore said the histories were on, and when she went back, she saw the older woman talking quietly into a phone. She strained her ears, and was positive that she heard the name Claire mentioned more than once.

After cleaning off the windshield wipers, she stood in the falling snow and ice, holding onto the door handle, just waiting for a moment. She thought again about Tom. His easy way of looking at things, his ready smile, the way he did things about the house. Not like a lump sitting on the couch, grunting for another beer or for when dinner was ready. He was loving in his own special way, not like anyone she had ever met before. For the most part, it seemed like he had a sense of anticipating what she wanted, what she desired, whether it'd be a weekend trip to Boston or a romantic evening in front of the fire, complete with wine, strawberries, and footrubs.

The ice was cold in her hands. She imagined how warm and comfortable the house would be. In weather like this, she was sure he had built a fire. Having gotten home earlier, he was probably getting dinner ready. She thought about what it might be like, to turn around and head back. She could come up with some story about why she wanted to get to Gilead on this horrid night, and maybe, just maybe, she could try again.

Why not. Turn this rig around and in ten, fifteen minutes, she'd be safe and snug at home, with Tom and his friends and the family, all of whom had done their very best to make her feel warm and welcome here, from family picnics on the town common to canoe trips on the river, to the various birthday parties for the different nieces and nephews. Nothing like those long days growing up with Uncle Hubert and Aunt Meg, sitting as a youngster on the polished wood flooring of the living room, playing silently with her dolls, the only sound being the ticking noise of the grandfather clock and the rustle as her aunt and uncle turned the pages of their newspapers.

Why not? She felt something tugging at her, a sense of loss and regret. Go back, the voice said. Go back and be safe. Be safe and warm and belong . . .

She took the chunk of ice and rubbed it on her face, blinking hard at the icy cold. She shook her head and whispered, "Damn it, that was close."

Claire put the car in drive and kept on going, remembering what had happened back at the library earlier today.

The first two visits had gone all right, leafing through back issues of the *Machias Times,* finding very little of interest. The usual small stories about a small town. She sat in one corner of the periodicals room, going through page after page of brittle newsprint. Her notebook was at her elbow, and other residents of Machias wandered in and out, but she remained focused on what was before her, as she flipped back the pages on the history of her new hometown.

And after two full afternoons of visits, exactly one half page of a notebook had been filled with scribbled notes.

Half a page.

Having been a newspaper reporter, she could not believe how deadly dull the pages of the *Machias*

Times were. Oh, she was under no illusions, none whatsoever as to what kind of news would appear in the paper. But a front page story—complete with photos—of John and Terry Conyer, returning from their honeymoon in France? On the front page? The rest of the newspaper wasn't much better. Grange meetings, square dances, church suppers. Flea markets, building permits, weather reports. Photos of prize-winning pumpkins, squash and corn. Births, marriages, arrivals. First snow, first ice break in the Piscassic River. A photo of a moose wandering down Main Street.

Occasionally, though, a piece of real news managed to struggle its way in. An Army Air Corps pilot in 1944 had to bail out of his fighter aircraft, and was rescued up on Nora's Hill. A brush fire made its way to the edge of Wally Tompkins' farm in 1957. And in 1973 and in 1959, avalanches closed off old Route 5, isolating the town even more, if that was possible.

That was it. And as she wearily replaced the last bound issue of the *Machias Times* back up on the shelves and made he way home, her head throbbed and her throat was scratchy from having breathed in all that dust. *If you don't do better,* she had thought, *then it will be one thin book indeed.*

That night, after a fine dinner from Tom—his own lobster stew, which was marvelous—she had gone to sleep and the dreams had returned. Again, fading in and out, she was a colonial settler woman, or a Native American woman, both trying to survive, both fearful for their children, both fearing death for their loved ones, both—

She woke up, breathing hard, sheets clenched in her fist. Something was there, something on the tip of her tongue, something from the dream that was important, something tat was fading away. Tom murmured something and rolled over to face her and she had an urge to stroke his face, kiss his forehead, but instead she clenched her teeth and tugged at the sheets, knowing it was close, so damn close . . .

Fear. The women in her dreams. Fear of death, of dying.

Death.

She sat up, her hands now trembling as she held them together.

Where in God's name were the obituaries?

She wiped her face, felt the slickness of her forehead.

Obituaries. There hadn't been a single one in a single issue of the *Machias Times,* going back nearly eighty years.

Not a single one.

The road began rising up to the hills, and she said to herself, "Girl, if you think the driving's been awful so far, you ain't seen nothing yet."

She turned the windshield wipers on high, as more clumps of ice began to form along the edges of the windshield. They seemed to grow with each passing minute, and she knew she should get out to clean off the wipers, but she was afraid of slowing down and not being able to start up again, as the road inclined higher with each sweep of the wiper blades.

She was too far to walk to the other side of the notch, and she lowered the driver's side window, thrusting out her arm. Each time an ice-encrusted blade got close enough, she grabbed it and yanked it up. The blade would come out a few inches and snap back on the windshield, causing chunks of ice to break free. It was the best she could do.

At breakfast the next morning, after making both of them a pot of tea, Tom looked at her with concern in his eyes. "Hon, you okay?"

"Sure I am," she said, buttering a piece of toast. "Why do you ask?"

He took a bite out of an English muffin, opened up a page of the *Wall Street Journal*—delivered a day late to Machias, of course. "I don't know. You look like you didn't get enough sleep last night. Are you having any bad dreams at all, dreams that you don't like?"

She quickly took a bite out of her own toast, so she wouldn't have to answer right away. Dreams. Sure, Tom. Let's talk about dreams. Ever since I've been here, I've been having dreams. About women who've been dead for centuries. But these dreams aren't like the usual ones, about arriving to a college exam in your underwear or being chased by monsters or floating over a dreamscape. Nope, these dreams are so real that I'm sure I can smell wood smoke in an Indian lodge, feel the rustle of a corn husk mattress in a colonial garrison house, feel and taste and smell everything so much that when I wake up, it takes a minute or two to remember that I'm Claire Pembrose, of Berwick, Maine, a college graduate and writer.

Those are the kinds of dreams I'm having. And how about you, my husband? What's traipsing through your mind at night? Or are you awake beside me, watching me murmur and twitch and whisper? Is that what you're doing?

She swallowed the piece of toast. "No, no dreams. But thanks for asking."

But when Tom left that morning for work, she went upstairs and started packing some of her most precious things.

Just in case.

Just in case.

And then she left for the library one last time.

She looked down for a moment at the gas gauge, saw the needle fluttering toward the E, and when she looked up, the road had disappeared. Just like that. All about her was snow, flying and battering and blowing, and she couldn't make out a tree, the road or anything.

Then the steering wheel shuddered in her hands, and the Saab growled and started tilting over to the left.

She screamed.

*   *   *

At the library she went back to the *Machias Times* for another quick look, to make sure she hadn't been making things up. And she hadn't. Not a single obituary.

In the dusty confines of the periodical room, past the plastic-covered protected copies of magazines like *National Geographic, People, Time, Newsweek,* and *Sports Illustrated,* she almost felt like laughing. What's going on, girl? Losing your mind? Thinking you've stumbled into a New England Brigadoon? Sure, complete with phone service, the mail, and television. Makes a lot of sense.

Who knows? Maybe it's such a small town, you don't have to print an obituary. Everybody knows everybody else so well. Maybe the church bulletins take care of printing information like that. Makes sense, doesn't it? I mean, come on! Brigadoon in New Hampshire!

She went back to the rear shelves, looking for history books of the region, and she found three that mentioned this region of the White Mountains, and even more briefly, mentioned Machias.

One mentioned was just a throwaway line, how toward the end of the nineteenth century—the 1800s, lumbermen in Machias would ship their wood downriver to Gilead, on the Piscassic River, until most of the salable lumber had been harvested. The second mention was a more detailed story about that 1944 Army Air Corps pilot who had parachuted into town. And the third mention . . . well, that was interesting. It was a reprint of a history written in 1785 by Dr. Jeremy Belknap, the real first historian the state of New Hampshire ever produced. And in one line, the library seemed to darken and get cooler: "In the reaches above Gilead, in the dark valley, there is the town of Machias, a place not frequented by its neighbors in the county, due to legends and sorceries which I feel not proper to put down on paper."

She read and reread that sentence, over and over

again, and then she copied it, word for word, in her notebook.

Then, putting the book back on the bottom of the wooden shelf, her fingers touched a folded piece of paper, stuck far behind.

The car seemed to fall forever, and then hit something with a horrible crunch. Even with her seatbelt on, she lurched about, striking her head on the roof, and then the windshield smashed in and the damn car kept rolling, and rolling, and her handbag flew past her face, hitting her in the nose, and she screamed again, as the damn car rolled and rolled.

Sitting awkwardly on the floor of the library, she opened up the piece of paper, which had been folded into a tight square. It was a page from another history book, *Legends and Whispers of the White Mountains*— and she checked the other books on the shelves and didn't find it at all. It was like someone had removed this page, hidden it, and then taken the book away. The page seemed old, at least a hundred years, and what she read caused her legs to begin quivering with fear.

One more roll, one more bang. The car came to a stop. She spit out blood and saliva, saw it fall away. She was upside down. Her legs couldn't move. Her arms couldn't move. She struggled and coughed again.

One side had a woodcut illustration of a railroad. On the other side, the bottom part of the torn-off page said:

"In the dark valley above Gilead there is a town steeped in mystery and superstition, called Machias. Not many trade or shop in this small village, due to the hostility of the locals, made up of five or six families who first settled this valley nearly two hundred years ago. Many in these families have lived

their entire lives within the confines of the small
town and have never left.

Rumors have it that the first families intermarried
with the Passaconaway tribe residing in the valley,
and that the descendants years later have a mix of
the old settler and Indian blood. One other rumor,
almost too fanciful to bear repeating, is that often
young men will leave the town to seek a bride "from
away," and bring her back for unspeakable ceremonies and acts such as

The page ended before the sentence did. There was
nothing else. Nothing else save what had happened to
her. How Tom had met her in college, and how he
had accidentally met her again in York, and how he
had brought her back to Machias. For what? Love? Or
as the old book said, *unspeakable ceremonies and acts*?

She folded up the paper, shoved it back where she
had found it, and then left the library, determined to
grab her things and leave, never to return.

It was now dark. Her teeth had started chattering
and she was sure she was hallucinating, for she could
hear voices out there in the darkness, the low murmur
of a group of people, seemingly talking about her.

Then she shrieked, as a light came on, playing about
her cold face and weepy eyes. "Claire?" came the
voice of her husband. "Claire, are you all right?"

"Tom!" she yelled. "Tom, please get me out, please
get me out! Please!"

In a confusing handful of minutes, Tom had wiggled
his way into the wrecked Saab and managed to free
her and lower her down. He had brought a heavy
down blanket and had wrapped her up, and though
she was thirsty and achy, she instantly began to feel
warmer.

"Are there . . . are there other people out there?"
she murmured.

"Yes. The volunteer firefighters, the chief of police,
others. We're all looking for you."

"But . . ."

He squeezed her. "We needed to bring you home. Needed to bring you back. No matter what you were trying to do by leaving tonight. Tell me, what do you know about your parents?"

The question stunned her, being asked in the wreck of their car. "My parents? Not very much, my aunt and uncle—"

He squeezed her gently again. "They were not your aunt and uncle. They were foster parents, from the state. Your true parents came from here, Machias, and it's true they died in a traffic accident, but it's not true those two were related to you. It took many years to find you, but we did, so we could bring you back where you belong."

She felt a flash of anger, despite the giddiness of being rescued. "Was that your job? To pretend to be my husband? To drag me back here?"

Tom stroked her forehead. "Yes, that was what I was going to do. And instead I fell in love with you. The moment I saw you, Claire. The very moment I saw you."

"You're lying."

"No, the truth."

She coughed up some more blood, could sense even more the people out there in the snowy woods, waiting for them. "Then tell me everything. Tell me the truth."

"All right. The truth."

Another gentle stroke of her forehead. "In this small town reside a special group of people. A mix of the old settlers and the Indians who lived here first. They came together out of necessity during a very harsh winter that very first year of colonial settlement, when food was scarce. The colonials had gunpowder and firearms, and could hunt deer. And the Indians, well, they had a special spring, something spiritual and magical. It was a fair trade."

"The spring water," she said. "What does it do?"

Tom said simply, "It gives us long life."

She choked for a moment. "Long life? Immortal?"

"No, not immortal. We can be killed, like your parents. But if we are careful, if we stay here and drink the spring water, we can live for a very long time. But one should start drinking at an early age. If you first drink it after puberty, there are side effects."

"Dreams," she said.

"Yes, dreams. About the early times. All of us here are connected in ways we don't understand, and we don't want to understand. If the scientists and the reporters and the government found out what we had here, what would happen? We would all die. There would be panic. Wars. Conflict. Over the fact that a fountain of youth had been found. Something we would not allow to happen."

Claire thought for a moment. "Grandmama Watkins . . . how old . . ."

"One of the last of the first settlers, Claire. The oldest one here in the valley."

She wiggled against his grip, felt a flash of pain, knew she had to get out of the car, no matter what nonsense he was spouting. "Tom, please . . . I have to get out of here . . ."

He bent down to kiss her forehead. "Of course, m'dear. But we need to know something. We need to know if you intend to stay and live here where you belong."

Another flash of anger. "Or what? You'll leave me here?"

He looked at her, smiled again. "We need to know. That's all."

She was cold and she was tired and she ached and she was angry, but something inside of her deflated, something about the old Claire Pembrose from Berwick, Maine, just packed up and went away. She was feeling warmer, and she knew why. She had truly come home. She truly had. And if Tom and his relatives wanted to believe they were immortal, so what. As long as it got her out of this wrecked car. And if they wanted to tell her what her real name was—

Conyer or Moore or whatever—so be it, as long as she got someplace warm.

"Yes," she said, her voice hoarse. "I'll stay here and build a life with you, Tom. Whatever you say."

"Wonderful," he said, and as he maneuvered the heavy flashlight around, the sleeve of his jacket exposed his forearm and the old puckered scar there, and she touched it and said, "The truth, Tom? Where was this from? Not a hunting accident, was it?"

He pulled the sleeve back. "In a manner of speaking, it was a hunting accident. Men hunting other men. In wartime."

"Oh," she said, her mind now confused again. "Where? The Gulf War? Vietnam?"

He bent down to kiss her gently. "At a place called Gettysburg."

BEHIND HIS GATES OF GOLD

by Karen Haber

Karen Haber's short fiction appears in *Warriors of Blood and Dream, Animal Brigade 3000, Elf Fantastic,* and *Wheel of Fortune.* Her novels include the science fiction trilogy *Woman Without a Shadow, Sister Blood,* and *The War Minstrels.* She lives with her husband, author Robert Silverberg, in California.

The gates of Prosper Mephisto's estate were golden arabesques that seemed to melt and writhe in endless curling patterns under Brazil's relentless December sunshine.

Hugh Carter, former roving reporter for EuroNews Web, whose rugged good looks and sea-blue eyes had helped win him high ratings from viewers—especially female viewers—counted out *cruzeiros* for the cabbie, grabbed the handles of his calf-leather bag, and stepped through the glittering portal. This, then, was to be his home for the weekend. Of late he had enjoyed far less luxurious accommodations, a fact concealed, along with his journalist past, by his current masquerade as a fledgling tycoon.

The taxi driver's irises were an odd yellow-green, one of the sure signs of mutancy. Carter had been surprised to see a mutant at the wheel until he remembered that Brazil, unlike the United States and most of Europe, had no protectionist laws and anti-mutant lobbies. Here it was perfectly legal to employ mutants in the service industries.

The driver's chartreuse eyes had gone wide when

Carter gave him the address. "There? You want to go there?"

Carter's chuckle rasped in his throat. "Why not? What's wrong with that place?"

The man's face closed like a slammed door. "Nothing."

"Then let's get started." Carter tossed a carefully groomed golden forelock. He prided himself on his nerve. And, indeed, it had taken him through Chinese-controlled Tibet on horseback tracking rumored mutant monks, over the jagged Himalayas, aboard a rusting merchant freighter bound for Indonesia to probe the drug trade, and into the back alleys of Moscow at midnight. Unfortunately, it had also taken him into the wrong bedroom with the wrong woman at the right time: his producer's wife.

In free fall after his *resignation,* he had finally snagged a toehold with EyeNet, a freelance investigative service that paid a fifth of his former salary. On behalf of EyeNet, he was disguised as a sleek and pampered playboy, heir to a real estate fortune. His supposed net worth had gained him access to the Diamond Club's Hundred Carat weekend, an annual bacchanal held by a coterie of the super rich, hosted in turn by the wealthiest members of the elite club.

Carter's faked ID and bank statements had cost him a month's income but had passed the scrutiny of the notoriously picky Diamond Club membership committee. And this year the party was being held by flamboyant tycoon Prosper Mephisto.

He gazed at the graceful grounds and buildings of Mephisto's elaborate compound. *Mephisto,* he thought, *you certainly know how to live well. And before the weekend is over, I'm going to uncover the man behind the myth and use that information to buy my ticket back into the big leagues of Web reporting.*

Mephisto was the tenth richest man in the world, and certainly the richest by far in his adopted homeland, Brazil, where he lived like a pasha, just an hour south of Rio. He had burst upon the world like some

Houdini of high finance fifteen years ago, his appearance heralded by several adroit maneuvers in cutting-edge technology and pharmaceutical stock that quickly made him a familiar name in the business vids.

In public, he always appeared in formal attire and mask. Adding to his mystique was the fact that no one knew what he really looked like. The paparazzi swarmed around him, and he amused them with flower bouquets which sprang from the silver cap of his ebony cane or a white rabbit clambering out of his silken top hat. Mephisto, the flamboyant trickster, managed to keep his face hidden despite the closeup scrutiny of the vid camera.

Despite his stunts, he was an acknowledged force in world finance, his name invoked with awe in boardrooms and news reports. His origins and early life were as mysterious as his true appearance. It was rumored that he was either the bastard son of a Tajikistani warlord or a desposed South American dictator.

There were other rumors as well, tales that Mephisto dealt in black market goods, bits and pieces of Russia's nuclear armory, gemstones that had not been seen since World War II. He was, it was said, a ruthless negotiator, an amoral dealer in all sorts of forbidden merchandise.

Whispers had it that he possessed strange powers of perception that had enabled him to employ his investments in such a way as to quadruple his riches. Prosper Mephisto did nothing to defuse these tales. He lived well and yet in secret, appearing and disappearing from the center of the action, a global will-o-the-wisp.

Carter wasn't buying it for a minute. He knew—he felt it in his very bones—that this Mephisto was some sort of charlatan, a phony preying upon Carter's more easily impressed colleagues. Well, this assignment would put an end to that b.s. once and for all. Carter might have been sent here to attend the Hundred Carat party, but before he was done, he would expose Prosper Mephisto for the empty joke that he was.

With a story like that in his pocket, Carter would quickly recapture his own credibility as a hard-hitting reporter. He only hoped that his assistant, Janny, was doing all the research he had asked for, tracing Mephisto's financial maneuvers and not goofing off with her boyfriend while the boss was away.

A terrible scream pierced the air.

Carter jumped. "What the hell?"

Above his head ivory-winged gulls cut across the blue bowl of the sky.

The scream sounded again. It was the birds. Their almost-human cries split the air.

As Carter's pulse settled down, he turned his attention to Prosper Mephisto's estate. The main dwelling, he saw, was a huge affair, all glass and soaring arches. He had spent nights in palaces that were mere flophouses by comparison. Subsidiary buildings, mostly domes, popped up like mushrooms across the lawn, as though the main house had sent underground runners to expand its domain. This part of the compound was punctuated by spiky agaves and clusters of palm trees.

Graceful rows of purple-flowered jacaranda trees lined the driveway. The velvety lawns flowed in unbroken undulations down to the dunes that ran like a tawny lion's back along the edge of the compound. Beyond was the blue-white Atlantic, its waves growling as they battered the beach.

A golden spider, fat and complacent, clung to the doorframe of Mephisto's mansion. The doorbell, Carter realized, and reached for it. A sudden stabbing pain shot through his thumb, making him gasp. The voluptuous orange flowers that framed the door hid wicked dagger-sharp thorns. Cursing, sucking his wounded thumb, Carter pressed the golden spider's back several times, hard.

A tall, shapely red-haired woman opened the door. She wore a silk sheath the color of the sky on a stormy day. "Mr. Carter? Please come in. Mind the vine. It has lovely flowers, but the thorns are wicked."

"So I've noticed."

Her smile was sharp. "Yes. Mr. Mephisto can't bear to cut it until after it's bloomed."

"Then he ought to put out warning signs." Carter edged past the flaming petals into a vast vaulted space of bronzed walls and tinted glass. A strange sweet smell pervaded the hall. Honeysuckle, he wondered? Myrrh?

"I'm Ariel," said the redhead. "Mr. Mephisto's official greeter, among other things. You're a new member of the Diamond Club, aren't you?"

"Yes. This is my first Hundred Carat Party. Do you have any advice?"

"Keep a supply of aspirin handy, and don't eat the smoked oysters after three in the morning. Oh, and watch out for flying crystal. But they usually don't begin smashing the glasses before five AM."

"Thanks for the tip."

She shepherded Carter along a hushed corridor whose floors of stained and inlaid wood gleamed like precious jewels. Massive crystalline lilies quivered in glass niches, shattering light into a dozen colors. Overhead, lamps winked on at their approach and off behind them. In and out of the shadows they wove.

Ariel was barefoot—an odd touch—and walked so lightly that she appeared to almost float. Surely, Carter thought, that was a trick of the shadows, the odd bright and dark illumination. He clomped along behind her feeling large, loud, and graceless.

Music, odd and compelling but hardly rising above a whisper, wafted through the air. Did rain fall, Carter wondered, a gentle mist, from pillar tops, sinking down to cool the sunlit room, evaporating before it touched the ground? The floor seemed to glitter with cool streams. Yet his feet, and those of his guide, were dry.

They passed a room where a string quartet, three women and one man, sat enraptured, playing for all they were worth. At first Carter thought that they were the sources of the ghostly music. Then he looked closer and saw that the cello—in fact, all of the instruments—had no strings, none whatsoever.

Very cute, he thought. *It's the odd "synthesizer hidden in the instrument" trick.* Mephisto was going to have to do better than that to impress him.

In another alcove a solitary woman in red lace sat before a loom, weaving a dazzling golden tapestry. As she worked at warp and weft, rich, honeyed tones came forth from the heart of the machine.

Carter suppressed a chuckle. *What next?* he wondered. *Singing shoes? Tiny elves to bid me welcome?*

In the wood-paneled library, a dozen books sat open on a massive oak table, murmuring among themselves. Carter was tempted to applaud. This Prosper Mephisto was an artful fellow, no mistake. Carter couldn't wait to ask him where he had hidden the wires and speakers.

"Here we are," Ariel said. "Watch your step."

Carter stepped up and into a vast suite that appeared to have no far wall. Then he realized that he was staring through the wall—a wide and perfect window—into the verdant rear garden.

Ariel pressed a spider button and the roof retracted partially, leaving Carter standing in an open patio. The cries of the gulls echoed eerily in the courtyard.

"Will you be needing anything at the moment?"

Almost reflexively Carter turned on his "you are the most fascinating woman I've ever seen" smile and said, "What time do you finish work?"

"My work is never finished," Ariel said. She flashed him a saucy grin and vanished down the corridor.

Carter blinked. She was quick on those bare feet of hers. Well, he would find her again, and invite her to have a drink with him anyway.

A brief inventory of the room revealed that it was equipped with everything he might want. The chairs and sofa were upholstered in golden silk. A silver tray was balanced upon a hassock, holding a tall pitcher filled with a tempting icy green liquid. Fresh fruit was set in swirling slices around a delicate white cheese.

The artwork in the room would have filled an exclusive gallery. Carter recognized a Matisse watercolor, a Picasso sketch, and what he took to be a small Teniers oil-on-copper-plate.

Soothing jazz—piano noodlings—emanated from a hidden speaker. The scent of lavender that had been on the stem moments before perfumed the air.

Mephisto might be a phony, but he certainly knew how to treat his guests, Carter thought. He munched on a piece of mango as he sank into the deeply padded armchair and contemplated the array of single malt Scotch bottles lining the bar.

A high, thin cry cut into his concentration. It could have been a bird—no, a woman, it was definitely a woman—wailing in distress in the corridor. Screaming.

Carter was on his feet and through the door. He nearly collided with a man clad in glossy black pants and sweater.

"Did you hear that?" Carter said. "A woman screaming?"

The thin and elegant stranger arched his slender eyebrows in a disdainful manner. "Mr. Carter?" A faint sibilance in his speech betrayed foreign origins, difficult to place. "I am Stephanos, Mr. Mephisto's personal assistant. I see to all guest's needs. This is your first time here, yes?"

"But the screams, man. Didn't you hear them?"

Golden-brown eyes, nearly amber, stared at him, impassive. "I heard nothing."

"But—"

"Perhaps you heard a bird, Mr. Carter. Please don't distress yourself further. Would you care for a tour of the grounds? Come." Without waiting for a reply, Stephanos turned. He walked lightly on the balls of his feet—bare feet again!—with liquid grace.

He's right, Carter decided. *Must have been a bird. Another one of those noisy damned seagulls.*

They turned down a corridor, and the walls were lined with elaborately framed paintings. Carter saw what appeared to be a bald man wearing a starched

white Puritan collar. His hands were clasped primly in
front of him. There was something wrong with the
fingers, but Carter was around a corner and the painting out of sight before he had time to turn and look
back.

And here, in another portrait, the bones of a face
seemed to be pressing up and out, attempting to sub-
sume the flesh in much the same way as ancient tree
roots grew over and into and around restrictions.

"As you have no doubt noticed," said Stephanos,
"the master is a collector of the first order. He has a
most discerning eye and quite eclectic tastes. Luckily,
he possesses many mansions and in them are many
rooms."

"So I've heard." Carter was getting impatient with
this Stephanos and his guided tour. Of course he had
heard about Mephisto's art collection. Who hadn't?

Stephanos turned. His eyes caught the light in unset-
tling amber flashes. "These, as you can see, are the
gardens. Mr. Mephisto is quite proud of them. Magnificent, yes?"

"Yes." Carter listened to the catalog of agaves,
aloes, and rare trees until his own eyes began to
glaze over.

"Designed by internationally acclaimed landscape
artists."

Beyond the acclaimed aloes, Carter saw a golden-
domed building with opaque windows. "And that?"

He might have told Stephanos that his fly was open
for the stern reaction he got. "That area is off-limits
to visitors. Of no possible interest. This way, please."

"But—"

"Over there is the swimming pool. Suits are provided in the poolside cabanas if you wish. The pool
and hot tubs are swimsuit optional. Massage and skin
treatments are also available."

Carter gazed at the expanse of blue water glinting
like a jewel. Several of Mephisto's guests were already
gathered by the poolside and both male and female
were taking advantage of the nonswimsuit option.

"If you prefer the beach," Stephanos continued, "we can provide you with a portable cabana, attendant, snorkeling equipment, and whatever else you desire."

"And this evening?"

"There should be a schedule of events in your room. We'll have cocktails in the atrium at six-thirty, and diner in the ballroom at eight. Dress is, of course, formal."

"Of course." The pool did look tempting to Carter, but duty called. "And may I stroll in the gardens?"

"By all means." Stephanos gave him a brief nod, before slinking away into the shadows.

Carter wandered through a phantasmagoria of plant life that dripped and oozed seductive perfumes. Blood-red lilies stretched lascivious petals toward him, yellow pistils flaming at their centers. Passion-flower vines entwined the limbs of saplings, covering portions of the garden with a blue-and-green canopy. Strange gray-leaved trees spread their enormous roots across the ground like writhing snakes. And over here, row upon row of Venus flytraps raised speckled maws, waiting for their next meal. Huge black-winged butterflies skittered through the air. When the sun caught them, their wings glittered like polished opals.

It was lush and exotic and strange and all disappointingly innocent. To his chagrin, what Carter saw about him were the well-tended gardens of an extremely rich man who had unusual taste in plants, nothing more. No clue to the man behind the gardens, and the mask.

The other buildings on the property seemed to function as greenhouses, cabanas, and gamerooms. Every door he touched opened, every building welcomed him. He found no dark shadows, no sinister hidden rooms.

Suddenly the underbrush heaved and shuddered, scattering sharp-edged silvery leaves. Hysterical squawking erupted and grew in volume as the thrashing beneath the leaves became truly frantic. Then,

slowly, it diminished. Carter peered between fleshy
pandanus leaves and spied a yellow snake enfolding a
gull in its fatal embrace. He had seen plenty of death,
but nevertheless, he shuddered and looked away.

* * *

The dining hall glittered with fine crystal and golden
plates set upon ivory damask cloths. Long tables were
laden with delicacies and bottle upon bottle of rare
wine.

The Diamond Club, an international flock, stood in
small groups, chattering with easy familiarity. They
were tanned and bejeweled, the men broad-chested
and glossy in their black dinner jackets, the women
sparkling in gossamer gowns that set off the lush oiled
darkness of their skin. Gems glinted from chignons, at
ears and necks, hands and ankles.

Carter heard fragments of conversation—most of it
money talk—as he took a quick survey, putting names
to faces. Over there, the blonde with a fortune in yellow diamonds cascading into her cleavage, wasn't she
the British wife of the Iranian soccer star who had
retired with millions? And near the door, a short bald-
ing man with a thick cigar held forth to a spellbound
group. It had to be Balto Schmidt, the bold entrepre-
neur whose mobile radar vans and microwave trans-
mitters had nearly single-handedly revived the sagging
telecommunications industry in the former East Ger-
many. A Taiwanese tycoon offered a martini to an
Israeli computer billionaire. A Mexican silver magnate
gossiped with the former minister of French culture.

Noise levels rose as the chic crowd twittered and
crowed.

—"Cashed in all my closed-end funds for the Tahiti
house—"

—"The night-diving scheme worked perfectly. In
three months we ruled the Tahitian pearl market."

—"Bought Tevcom on margin and sold it for three
times what I paid before the call."

A deeply tanned man approached Carter and offered his hand. "I'm Ralph Anderson." His accent was American, but his refined manner was not, and his grip was surprisingly strong. "I've seen you somewhere before, haven't I? Movies?"

"Uh, no." Carter pretended to be flattered. "Hugh Carter. This is my first Hundred Carat party."

"That so? A dot-com millionaire?"

"I wish. Nope. Just chose my ancestors wisely."

Anderson's grin flashed bone-white in his deeply tanned face. "Old money is the best kind, isn't it? You're lucky to be making your maiden voyage at Mephisto's."

"You've been here before?"

Something flickered in the depths of Anderson's eyes, smoldered, went out. "Many times. I recommend that you reserve your pool chair early or you'll have to plow through bodies to find someplace to sit. And ask for Denice for the massage. She's the best."

"I appreciate the advice." Carter nodded his thanks as Anderson handed him another drink.

Anderson leaned closer until Carter could smell the liquor on his breath. Anderson was, he realized, completely smashed. "And whatever you do, don't go near the golden pavilion with the dark windows. Don't even think about asking about it. It's off limits, absolutely untouchable."

The dark windows. The look on Stephanos' face. Carter remembered the forbidden pavilion, and a thrill went through him.

"One more piece of advice. Watch your step around that assistant of his."

Carter allowed himself a smile. "Stephanos. Yes."

Suddenly, something exploded in the center of the room. The women shrieked and backed toward the entrance with the men close behind.

From out of the cloud of dust walked a particular figure.

He was tall and thick-framed, with the slow deliberate movements of one whose flesh lay heavily upon his bones. His features were covered by a close-fitting mask that had been bisected into jagged areas of white and silver.

The mystery man wore a dark top hat and tails, but Carter saw that there was nothing delicate or elegant about Prosper Mephisto. He was not at all the effete boulevardier whom Carter had expected. Mephisto could indeed buy and sell small countries, but he looked as though he could also wrap them up for shipping with his bare hands.

"Good evening, friends. I'm delighted to see you all, and to be hosting the Hundred Carat party this year."

Mephisto's voice was mellifluous, a marvelous mid-Atlantic baritone, impossible to place. Rich and full, Mephisto's voice had so much resonance that Carter wondered if he had trained professionally for the stage. Despite Mephisto's dramatic appearance, his charisma resided primarily in his voice.

Carter watched his move through the room, greeting guests in their native tongues, conversing easily in a dozen languages. With elaborate flourishes of his cane he produced boutonnieres for the gentlemen and nosegays for the ladies.

And yet, despite his magic tricks and easy patter, Carter detected a certain aloofness in his host. He seemed completely unengaged by the social rituals in which he was participating, almost mechanical, in fact.

"And this is Mr. Carter," Stephanos said. "Our debutant."

Carter turned on his strictly-for-closeups smile. "You have a beautiful home, Mr. Mephisto. I'm delighted to be here, and to be a member of the Diamond Club."

Mephisto's eyes were shadowed behind the mask. With a flourish of his hand he made an elaborate bow. "Very kind. Glad to have you. If you have need of anything, any little thing, please don't hesitate to ask. I'm sure we'll talk more tomorrow." He squeezed Carter's hand and moved past, leaving in his wake an impression of manufactured and professional hospitality. Carter shivered.

He found his seat, wedged between a wide Hungarian countess with diamonds in her hennaed hair and a narrow sharp-jawed woman who wore a severe black pantsuit and no jewelry, not even a simple gold ring. Hugh Anderson was seated on her left. As a neophyte, Carter had expected to be exiled to the far edges of the room, but, to his surprise, he saw that his table was close to Mephisto's own.

Carter quickly learned that the countess had a great many opinions on a great many things. Only the actual appearance of the waiters bearing the first course of seafood mousse rescued him.

Anderson, he saw, was drinking steadily during the meal. Midway through the foie-gras-stuffed duck, the man lurched to his feet and, walking unsteadily, left the room.

The waiters whisked away their dishes, setting down small iced silver cups.

"Oh, wonderful," said the countess. "I so adore a citrus granite before desert, don't you?"

As the waiters laid in the utensils for dessert and offered coffee and tea, Carter realized that Anderson had not yet returned. His host, he saw, had noticed as well. As he watched, Mephisto summoned Stephanos and gestured covertly toward the empty seat. The major domo's lips tightened, and he left the room at a near run.

Carter commiserated with the Hungarian countess over the high price of emeralds while keeping an eye on his host. Mephisto drummed his fingers upon the table. The minutes ticked by, and then Stephanos materialized, practically towing Ralph Anderson behind him.

Carter strained to hear Stephanos' exchange with Mephisto. "He was near the front door. Says he got lost looking for the men's room."

"No doubt," Mephisto replied. "We must be certain to give him better assistance for the remainder of his stay." A look, severe and unreadable, passed between the two men.

Mephisto's powerful voice took on a sandpaper edge as he said, "Welcome back, Mr. Anderson. We would have hated for you to miss dessert."

"Sorry. So sorry." Anderson toppled into his chair beside the woman in black.

The door. Carter could only wonder what that meant. "Anderson, are you all right?"

His tablemate flashed him a desperate look. Carter could have sworn he was stone cold sober. But a moment later, the inebriated mask was back in place, and it stayed there for the rest of the evening.

* * *

It was half past midnight when Carter opened the door to his room. The whisper of movement, there in the darkness, made him pause in the doorway. He sensed a presence. Ready to fight or flee, he flicked on the light.

"Hello." Ariel was curled on the couch like a cat. The lamplight caught her dark red hair and turned it to molten gold. Her smile contained every enticement that Carter could imagine.

Carter took a step toward her. "I was hoping to see you at dinner."

"And here I am."

Before he could respond, she had uncoiled from her cushions and swept him into a kiss that took his breath away.

He didn't know how they made it to the bed, and he didn't care. She seemed to understand and anticipate everything he wanted, everything he liked.

As her face contorted over him in passion, it seemed to flow and change, to become something frightening and inhuman.

Her lips—the fangs—her eyes—the claws.

His own climax carried him up and above that vision, far away, and down into the splendid darkness of sleep.

He awoke, his head throbbing in three different places.

"Ariel?" He reached toward her, touched empty air. Her place on the bed was smooth and cool.

The pain in his head increased.

"God, what was in those drinks?" he muttered. "Got to be some aspirin in this fancy bathroom." He heaved himself to his feet and rummaged through the medicine cabinet.

High-pitched cries cut through Carter's search. He froze at the sound.

The cry, when it came again, sounded like a hawk or eagle on the hunt. But the longer Carter listened, the more convinced he became that the cry was that of a human being. A high-pitched man's cry or, more likely, that of a woman.

He opened the shutters and peered outside. The yard was ghostly lavender in the early morning light. Something pale and thin was moving about slowly down near the sand dunes. Carter squinted. His eyes widened.

A vision out of a nightmare stalked through the garden: half serpent, half woman, with scales and claws and awful glowing eyes.

Carter blinked incredulously, looked again, and saw a woman in a silken gown. Long-limbed, with a mane of red hair. Even in the dim light her beauty was unmistakable.

Ariel.

Across the garden a man emerged from the bushes. He wore evening garb and appeared to be reeling on his feet. Ralph Anderson.

Ariel held her arms wide, entreating.

Anderson hesitated.

She was so beautiful, golden and willowy.

Again Ariel reached toward Anderson.

Carter felt a stab of envy—and rage—as he watched

them embrace. Slowly, very slowly, they sank to the ground into the shadows.

Carter slammed the blinds closed. His emotions were roiling in his gut. How could Ariel have spent that marvelous time in bed with him and yet, only an hour or two later, be roaming the garden in search of further amorous adventures?

Through the closed blinds Carter heard a high, triumphant sound, like a bird of prey trumpeting its kill. He shook the notion from his head. All was silent. Now, at least, he might get back to sleep.

But he tossed and turned, haunted by the imagined scenes of passion outside his window. Finally, he fell asleep and dreamed of gulls weeping above the sea.

* * *

Carter awoke with a heavy head and laden body. He remembered blurred scenes from the previous evening, the feel of silken skin against his, and some strange predawn vision on the lawn.

He opened the blinds.

Ralph Anderson, clad in his black satin tuxedo, lay on his back in a bed of orange flowers.

That's a hell of a place to sleep it off, Carter thought. He tapped on the window. "C'mon, buddy. Get up and go to bed."

It took him a moment to realize that Anderson's eyes, like his mouth, were wide open, vacant and unmoving. He didn't appear to be breathing. There was a strange waxen texture to his skin. He resembled a corpse or, worse, a humanoid dummy.

"Jesus!" Carter fumbled with his pants and, bare-chested, raced out in the hall.

Before he had taken more than a few steps, Stephanos materialized, barring his way.

"There's a guest," Carter said. "Ralph Anderson, in the garden. I think he's unconscious or dead."

Stephanos gave him a cool, disdainful look. "I beg your pardon?"

"Didn't you hear me? One of your guests is lying dead in the garden."

The major domo's expression warmed toward something that might have been amusement. "I assure you that there's nothing of the kind in the garden."

"Dammit, man, I just saw it."

"Saw what?" Stephanos gestured toward the window.

The lawn was empty.

Carter felt his mouth fall open. Had he imagined? No. No, he knew he had seen it, seen Anderson with his dead eyes and waxy skin. Someone had removed him, just now, while Carter's back had been turned.

Was that amused malice dancing in the amber depths of Stephano's eyes? "I'm to tell you that there's been a seminar added to the schedule. The title is 'Why Swiss Bank Accounts Make Sense Now More than Ever,' and it will be held in the library at two."

"Thanks."

"And may I suggest that you wear a shirt? The master is quite meticulous about such things."

* * *

I'm not crazy, Carter told himself. *I know what I saw.* He buttoned his shirt. Who had taken Anderson's body, and why?

He shivered as the image of Ariel floated out of his memory, half-woman, half-monster, poised above him in wild passion. That was one for Dr. Freud, all right.

Shifting his gaze, he looked out the window and saw a man dressed in black. His face was in shadow and his body moved with unusual grace.

As Carter watched, the man gestured toward the underbrush.

The yellow snake emerged and slowly twined itself around his outstretched arm.

The man appeared delighted to have the massive

thing attached to him, and petted a sinewy coil as he sauntered off into the bushes and out of sight.

Carter shook his head. Was this another side-show attraction arranged by Mephisto for his guests? Or had that been Mephisto himself, exercising his so-called magical powers? He was getting a little tired of his host's stunts.

He needed some fresh air. Perhaps a stroll down to the swimming pool would help him sort out things. Just a little walk in the morning sunshine. What could be nicer, provided he didn't run into Stephanos, or the man with the snake.

The hallway outside his room was deserted and silent. Where was the music? The wonderful perfume? Carter prowled uneasily, retracing his path from yesterday. The halls echoed with his footsteps.

He came to the library and the music room. Both were empty, as was the alcove where the woman in red had played the loom, and the corridor where the columns had exuded blue mist. The sunroom, the conservatory, even the ballroom were completely depopulated. Where was everybody?

Carter decided that the other guests were either sleeping in, at the pool, or engaged in other pleasurable diversions.

He pondered his options. He couldn't just wander the house, hoping to sniff out some information about his host. Nor could he spend every waking hour at the pool. He was getting nowhere.

Whatever you do, don't go near that locked pavilion.

Carter felt the hair prickle on the back of his neck. *Don't ask about it. Don't even think about it.*

Of course not. Except that he had to. This was the reason why he was here, wasn't it?

The forbidden pavilion. Yes. Yes, yes, yes. He had to find out what was in there, and right now.

Outside, he passed the cabanas, the gardens with their carnivorous plants, and the tennis courts. Passed the pool and waved at a shapely brunette who was

standing on the diving board. Then he was safely past
all possible witnesses.

There.

The golden pavilion sat, locked and ignored, in its
corner of the compound.

Carter scanned for servants or groundskeepers, but
the area was deserted.

The door to the pavilion had a simple single-bolt
lock. Carter remembered an old-fashioned trick he
had observed years before, in Paris, and pulled a
credit card from his wallet. He ran it lightly along the
door's edge. With a click and a whisper the door slid
back into the curved wall.

A gust of warm air brought the scent of hay and
animals.

Carter stepped inside. The door slid shut behind
him. When his eyes adjusted to the dimly lit room,
he chuckled.

A zoo, he thought. *It's a goddamned zoo. But why
is it off-limits?*

This particular zoo seemed to have been drawn
from an elaborate Victorian daydream. The cages
were gold, although Carter couldn't quite believe that
they were solid gold, and the bars scrolled and wound
about with bas-relief leaves. The impression was one
of gaudy anachronistic radiance, of elaborate decora-
tion worthy of a king's hothouse.

The denizens of the zoo were as unlikely and remarkable as the place that housed them.

A four-footed duck was the first wonder that Carter
saw. The rest of the duck had a normal appearance:
teal head, brown feathers, but there were, undeniably,
four blue-webbed feet attached to the plump body.
With odd and stately grace, the thing waddled past
Carter and settled happily into its private pond.

An engraved nameplate in elaborate script read:
"Quadruped Booby."

In the next cage, according to its nameplate, was a
"West African Leucrocotta."

Carter stared at the creature and shuddered. It was

nearly as tall as he, with a vast saurian head topped by two rolling yellow eyes. Its broad mouth gaped open to reveal double rows of bright blue incisors.

The Leucrocotta stood on its hind feet and took several steps toward him on its curiously dainty hooved feet. It had fine blue-green hair from hoof to knee, where the hair changed to iridescent scales that coated the rest of its formidable bulk. The Leucrocotta grinned hungrily at Carter and he was very grateful for the thick bars that separated them.

The next cage held a "Getulian Mimicke Dog." A small foxlike animal waved its wispy tail as its hide flashed from green to red to brown reticulations. Its head was oddly rounded and resembled that of a giant squirrel, with a flat nose and huge front teeth. It whinnied like a horse, shifted in hue from brown to green, and began to shriek like a mynah bird.

Carter's pulse began to race. He'd never seen anything like these animals. Where the hell had Mephisto found them?

Carter wandered dazedly past a "Purple Seapig." It was curled in its nest, eyes closed. Its head was cradled on its front flippers and it appeared to be asleep. But on its purple, scaly hide were other eyes—golden ones—scattered like a leopard's spots. They blinked and swiveled, following Hugh's movements even as the Seapig muttered in is dreams.

He walked past a stout Libyan Giraldus with the saucerlike eyes of a night hunter, a snow-white Scandinavian Golun ramming its single black horn into a stack of grass cubes, and a tricolored Eale with winding crystal tusks.

A tiny bell rang with tinny sweetness. Carter turned toward the sound and saw another door, even more magnificent than the last. What marvels would he find behind it? What rarities? A dodo bird? A sphinx?

He turned the knob and found himself in yet another section of the zoo. This was a smaller room, dimly lit, with only a few occupied cages.

What'll it be this time? Carter wondered. He half

expected to see a dog-faced boy or bearded lady. He walked up to the first cage. The lights came up as he approached.

"Jesus!"

Ralph Anderson sat limply upon a bunk.

"Ralph! Ralph, can you hear me?" Carter waved his hands in front of the man's face.

If Anderson heard or saw him, he gave no response. His eyes were open, but there was no comprehension within. He sat like a spent puppet, awaiting the puppeteer's whims.

Carter tried to find the door to Anderson's prison, but there was no access, no opening. He pounded upon the smooth glass fronting the cage. Anderson didn't move.

This was bigger, much bigger than Carter had dreamed. Mephisto, a human slaver? He cast his gaze around the room. There were other human shapes in the darkened cages. The Hungarian countess was to his left. She still wore her tiara and evening dress, and was seated in a chair, eyes closed. Carter recognized several of the other party guests as they sat, drooping, in their golden cages.

And then Carter saw it. A narrow line of light split the wall on his right. A doorway, with a staircase within leading down.

Carter was light-footed on the metal steps. He went down one floor, and then another before he came to a portal.

Through it he found a vast subterranean room. In it were dormitory bunks, a computer area, and what was obviously an armory. At the moment it was empty, but there were signs of recent occupancy: clothing strewn over the cots, cups of coffee sitting on a small round table.

So, Carter thought, Mephisto was housing his own little army down here. Or was this the place where he kept his guests before he penned them? No, Carter decided. The armory looked too accessible. An army, then.

"Mr. Carter, what are you doing here?" It was Stephanos, poised above him on the stairs. With a graceful leap, the major domo was over the banister and on the ground, reaching for him.

Carter plunged into the dorm room. Stephanos was close behind him. Desperately, he knocked over cots to trip his pursuer. If he could just make it to the far stairs . . .

But Prosper Mephisto was there, blocking his path, standing like an avenging demon with arms outstretched. And Stephanos was gaining.

Carter turned on his heel and bore down on the computer room. He had to get help, raise the alarm. He had to get away. There, that row of shelving as tall as a man. He put all his strength into the shove. The entire metal skeleton wobbled and began to topple onto Mephisto's servant.

Mephisto made an odd sound.

The shelving paused in midair and slowly, very slowly, began to right itself against the wall.

Carter stared. "What the hell?"

Mephisto and Stephanos exchanged a look.

Suddenly it all fit into place. The shock of it made Carter fall back against the wall, suddenly weak. "You're mutants, aren't you? That's what's behind your magic act and all this mystery."

"Mr. Carter, really, what am I to do with you?" Mephisto sounded regretful, almost sad. "You abuse my hospitality. You disregard my wishes. I'm not accustomed to having my guests behave in such a manner."

"Your guests—your household staff—the creatures in your zoo . . . are they all mutants?"

"Well, not all. The animals are, obviously, projections."

"But you and your staff, you're all mutants."

His answer was a curt nod.

Carter thought of Ariel, the startling image of her as half human, half something else. Now it made sense. Awful sense. "And those things I saw in the garden—"

"Were intended only to keep you off balance. Practical jokes, if you like. Except for Ariel disciplining Mr. Anderson. You were not intended to see that. She should have known better and taken care of it elsewhere."

"He was slipping out of your control, wasn't he?"

"Let us say that his connection to us had frayed a bit."

"And the staff, are they under your control, are they your prisoners, too?"

Mephisto's laugh was sharp and bitter. "Hardly. They came to me for shelter."

"From what?"

"A society—a world—that would abuse and enslave them. My money provides safety."

"And what about your so-called party guests in those cages? What about them?"

"They all came here of their free will, too, in the beginning. But not with pure intentions. Some wanted to use me. Others planned to spy no me."

"What about Ralph Anderson?"

"Oh, he came here, like you, prying, spying. Then he worked for the CIA. Now I suppose you could say that he works for me. It's useful to have regular guests available for my parties, and to reassure visitors, at least until I've had time to scan them thoroughly. Especially at these Diamond Party events. Somebody often tries to slip in, as you did."

'This looks like a military barracks."

Stephano's eyes glittered, but Mephisto held out a warning hand. "I've told you. This is a place of security for mutants who are not safe among the so-called normal humans who control this sordid world."

"What are you going to do? Stage a revolution? Take over this country?"

Mephisto laughed again. "Brazil? Hardly. I have enough responsibilities as it is. Besides, I'm not in a position to take over anything. Believe me, those weapons you saw are intended for defensive use only. Someday I hope that we'll be able to claim our rightful place in society. But that day is far away."

"I don't believe you."

"Imagine, Mr. Carter, that you have a very strange, very valuable talent, one that many unsavory people—and powers—would like to use. You are small and alone, and it is only a matter of time before you are forced to choose which master to serve. I provide an alternative. A sanctuary, if you will."

"Seems to me that you're the master here."

"I am first among equals. And what is important is that we are growing in strength. We protect one another. And I protect us all—from outsiders."

"Then why hold such elaborate parties?"

"Often it's best to hide in plain sight. You can spot your enemies that way. And maintaining our frivolous facade distracts others from the truth. However, when we had Ariel probe your—"

Carter was edging toward the door. If he could just get up the stairs . . .

"Stop!" Mephisto's voice was utterly compelling. Carter felt his muscles freeze.

Heart pounding, he watched as Mephisto peeled away his mask. His true face was barely human, frightening, all sharp planes and angles, with terrible livid eyes. It was the face of a monster. Carter wanted to look away, but those terrible eyes held him helpless.

Mephisto continued as though nothing remarkable had happened. "As I said, we had Ariel probe you last night, and she discovered that you were an impostor. We knew that we would have to watch you closely. But we never expected anything like this. However, the damage is done." He gestured and in a moment, soundlessly, Ariel was there.

She stared at Carter with an almost feral hunger.

"No!"

She came closer. Closer. Her eyes, he saw, were a peculiar yellow-green and they held his gaze with implacable strength.

"No, you're making a mistake—"

Without a word she wound her arms around Carter and pulled him close.

He had a brief scrambled sense of searing light invading his mind, his body. Those eyes. He was falling into them. He wanted to say something, to plead, protest, but his mouth wasn't working. And then he knew nothing, nothing at all.

* * *

RIO: AP NEWS

An American tourist is feared lost off the coast of Brazil. Hugh Carter, 32, a former employee of EuroNewsWeb, is presumed to have drowned in the Atlantic Ocean. Although his body has not yet been recovered, his clothing and possessions were found on a beach along the southern Brazilian shore. Witnesses told police that they had seen him enter the surf, but he never came back to the beach.

* * *

In the main house of Prosper Mephisto, subtle perfumes fill the air. Music, hardly rising above a whisper, wafts along the golden corridors. The crystalline lilies quiver in their niches while gentle mists tint the air with blue coolness.

The loom sings under the woman in red's hands. The books in the library murmur to one another. The Leucocrotta grins its ugly unreal grin.

In his quiet golden age, Hugh Carter sits, head down, gazing upon nothing. To his left Ralph Anderson, to the right, the Hungarian countess.

Prosper Mephisto gazes upon the newest addition to his collection and nods with satisfaction. Then he turns off the light and leaves the room, locking the door behind him. He is expected at dinner. There are new guests waiting for him, new acquisitions to be made.

INTERVIEW WITH A MUTANT

by Janet Berliner

In her twenty-five years as a writer, editor, and publishing consultant, Janet Berliner has worked with such authors as Peter S. Beagle, David Copperfield, Michael Crichton, and Joyce Carol Oates. Among her most recent books are the anthology *David Copperfield's Beyond Imagination,* which she created and edited, and *Children of the Dusk,* the final book of *The Madagascar Manifesto*, a three book series coauthored with George Guthridge. Currently Janet divides her time between Las Vegas, where she lives and works, and Grenada, West Indies, where her heart is.

This morning, at a Kinko's in Las Vegas, I made a copy of the transcript of several micro-cassettes, put the pages into a preaddressed FedEx envelope, and wrote a note to my online editor:

Dear Ellen,
    Yesterday, I came across a Reuters follow-up to what was ostensibly the world's first hand and forearm transplant.
    It wasn't—the first, I mean.
    In the case I read about, a New Zealander named Clint Hallam, received the transplant from a brain-dead 41-year-old motorcyclist. He was fine until 1998, two years post-surgery, when he began to complain about pains which included a burning sensation. He has appealed, without success, to the British surgeon involved in the original operation at the Edouard Herriot hospital in Lyon, France, to amputate the transplant.

Were I to find Mr. Hallam, who is apparently here in Las Vegas in search of a surgeon willing to perform the amputation, I'd send him to Dr. Piet Runolo. But first I'd ask him to talk about how the transplant affected his persona and his life in ways other than the expected. I'm willing to bet it did. If he's alive and still has that cyclist's hand, he's probably using it to drive a motorcycle into the desert.

The question is, what would that make Mr. Hallam? Is he still Clint Hallam, or has he mutated into an extension of the brain-dead cyclist?

Should his pain be treated by psychiatry, drugs, prayer, witchcraft? A combination of all four?

Would his insurance pay?

Probably not, though it is the twenty-first century and times they are a-changing—perhaps even for the better.

You and I have often bemoaned the primitive attitude of the AMA and medical insurance companies regarding alternative medicine. That's why I'm sending you this transcript, which is based on a series of things I saw and experienced earlier this year, more of which would have impacted me had I not, in '86, completed an assignment for Monterey Life *interviewing a group of doctors' wives who piloted discarded medical equipment to needy Third World countries.*

Here's what happened.

I interviewed Dr. Piet Runolo for Monterey Life *because they'd suggested a follow-up piece about Interplast. I did the article they wanted, but did not touch upon what followed the interview because I thought it would someday make a fine backstory for an Orwellian sequel. However, in light of Mr. Hallam's experience, the truth is probably much too strange to couch as fiction, in which guise readers might not have been able to suspend disbelief.*

Make of these pages what you will; use them, or don't use them, as you see fit. Whatever you do, it might be wise to change the names. I wouldn't want Piet after my butt, or yours. The intense heat of immersion in an HBO unit cannot be overstated. That being his favored

mode of God-playing—albeit mostly for good—I'd pre-
fer to keep his real identity hidden.
    Love, J.

Life-altering experiences never approach me politely, from a place where I can look them in the eye.
This time was no different.

It started innocently enough when I interviewed Dr.
Piet for *Monterey Life.*

Why Piet?

Mostly because he was accessible. He was a recon-
structive surgeon, director of a large burn unit, and a
frequent flyer with Interplast. He was willing to talk
to me; he was a South African who had completed his
degree at Groote Schuur under the sponsorship of Dr.
Christian Barnard—father of the heart transplant—
and I'd been told he was cute.

At his request, I met him at a small tea-and-
groceries shop in East LA called *Africa Hut.* Apparently he had laid some heavy bets on a soccer game;
that was the only place he could drink hibiscus tea,
watch the game on TV, and do a little delicacy shopping on the side.

Ultimately, I would learn that Runolo had a rough
time doing fewer than three things at once. For now,
my lessons included little except his admission that
only two things in life made him high: gambling, and
doing surgery. He told me that the reason he got involved with Interplast was that he gets crazed if he
goes too long without practicing what he called "real
medicine," using the tools at hand and elbow-deep in
blood. He said he flies mostly to South America where
they desperately need medical help, chews coca-
leaves, stays up three, four days and nights in a row
working on deformed children. Cleft palates, mostly,
he said, which needed multiple surgeries and grafts.
He said the most successfully absorbed grafts are done
with human fetal tissue. Of course, America disap-
proves, but he often flies to foreign parts and brings
back ice-packed embryo tissue. Carries it himself. On

his lap. The second best is from pig embryos, he said, but the animal activists object.

"My Interplast trips are my vacations," he said. "It's not only because of the satisfaction I derive from the work I do on those trips. I also get to dance and drink and live for a while with the natives—like the natives. How many people get the chance to do that? I've been to India and to Japan more than once. I've flown to Europe and Equador, to Peru, Honduras, Brazil, all over Africa.

"There's something else," Runolo went on. "Interplast provides the best teaching in medicine. We take interns, young doctors. We go out and see four or five hundred cases, and we have to deal with them."

I asked him what kind of equipment they took along.

"I tell Interplast I don't want to bring anything—I just want to use what they have right there, on the spot. I take my Humbly knife and that's about it. Every once in a while some of the younger doctors talk about resuscitation or grafting and the lack of equipment. I ask what they have and I tell them we'll use that. They want me to bring down supplies, dressings. The younger doctors tell me they need antibiotics. My purpose with the Interplast trip is not to bring supplies, but to show the local healers how to use their own supplies. And their own knowledge."

"Have you taught their shamans how to use what they have to deal with problems when you get out of there?"

"Since time immemorial they have performed miracles undreamed of by the AMA. I have taught them no more than they have taught me," he said quietly, and I knew the interview was over.

When I transcribed the tape, I tried to add a description of Dr. Runolo. Cute, I thought, was distinctly the wrong adjective. Tall, intense. His father's East Indian cheekbones, a complexion like mocha moleskin, and a small scar on his left hand which I'd noticed because I'd looked to see if he was wearing a wedding ring. The man was interesting, fascinating, but definitely not *cute*.

I wrote the article, sent him a copy, and, for a while, hoped in vain that I would see him again. I did, but not for ten years.

Again, we met at a shop that sold African delicacies, this time here in Vegas. It was Mother's Day. I had walked there to pick up rusks, a treat my daughter would not have thought of sending me. He was once again drinking tea and watching a soccer game. He didn't seem to have aged at all in the ten years that had passed.

"We have to stop meeting like this," I said lamely, hoping he'd remember me.

"What's it been? Ten years?" He waved his hand in a friendly gesture and it occurred to me to wonder why he was wearing surgical gloves. "Sit down. Drink tea with me."

"Visiting Vegas?" I asked.

"Visiting my money," he said.

Turned out he was living here now, running a burn unit and occasionally moonlighting at the morgue. As it happened, I had been trying to find a way to watch an autopsy, so that I could complete a pivotal chapter in my novel. When the game was over, he said, he had to autopsy a prisoner, killed in a local prison. The prisoner's family requested and had been granted an autopsy.

We went there in his car. He drove with a sure touch, with a sense of calm and ease that I didn't recall from our first meeting.

I had seen a corpse twice before. One was my grandfather, the other on a date with a medical student who insisted on showing me what . . . who . . . he was working on. Neither prepared me in any way for this.

After having been buried for weeks, the corpse smelled putrid. Only my communion with my notebook kept me from passing out or running out. That, and my fascination with Dr. Runolo.

When it was over, he washed up and, keeping his back turned, donned clean latex gloves which he took from the pocket of his gown. I asked if he always wore them.

He nodded but didn't explain. "Was it what you expected? The autopsy."

"I . . . don't know." I pictured the deceased's skull being cracked open and laid back like a coconut husk; the moment his body was slit stem to stern; the scream of protest I imagined I'd heard from deep inside the long-dead body as a gray phantom emerged and dissipated.

"I hear it, too. Every time," Runolo said. "It's the soul exiting the body."

"How did you know I'd heard it?"

"I just knew." He looked at his watch. "Lunchtime. bet you couldn't eat a rare hamburger after all that."

"Bet I could," I said. And did.

He hardly spoke during the meal, nor did he remove the gloves. "I told you I always wear them," he said, seeing me stare at his hands.

"By choice?"

"No."

His beeper cut short any explanation he might otherwise have been willing to give me.

"Mother's Day," he said, checking the incoming number. "Worst day of the year for male suicide attempts." He signaled for the check. "Self-immolation of one kind or another is the number one MO. Last year a young man climbed a pole and fried himself on the power line. Did in the year before, too. He'll keep doing it until he gets it right."

"That was his *second* time?"

"Severe burn victims are often involved in more than one burning. As much as eighty percent of the time." He looked at me intently. "They wouldn't have paged me today if there weren't surgery involved. Want to observe?"

His smile was there and gone almost before it registered. "I'll catch you if you faint," he said. "I won't be doing the cutting. Not allowed to anymore. Not in America. Insurance won't cover me. I'll be talking someone through it and doing the healing."

"Why is that?" I was buying time.

"New hand," he said. "It belonged to a shaman. I'm not cleared to cut with it, but I am allowed to heal."

New hand? I figured I'd heard wrong.

Not wanting to sound uninformed, if not stupid, I veered sideways. "Do you miss it? The surgery?"

He stood up. "Would you miss breathing?" he asked. Then he turned toward the exit, knowing that I would follow.

After having observed (and smelled) an autopsy, the last thing I truly wanted was to observe surgery. But I did it anyway. When it was over, I left Runolo at the bedside of the patient who, though he appeared to be unconscious, screamed when the doctor made any movement which could have been taken to signal his departure.

I took a taxi home and, without showering or glancing at myself in the mirror, crawled into my bed. I knew what I smelled like, but I can only imagine what I looked like as, remnants of makeup on my face, half undressed, I fell into a dream-filled sleep. Bits of the last Clancy novel I had read cross-hatched with the events of the day to create fragments that contained every element of a thriller . . . CIA, plastic surgery done on the front lines to the powerful, the famous and infamous, guns and bullets and micro cameras, threats, high rolling, psychics, psychos, travel, disillusion, delusion. When I woke up the next morning, all I could think of was how fresh Piet had looked as we parted.

I showered, ate breakfast, and within the hour was looking for an excuse to call him. I told myself that the combination of biotechnics and pyrotechnics was fertile terrain for short and long fiction and that the world loved medical thrillers, but I did not make the call.

Instead, I watched the news at the top of the hour. The reporter was a fresh-faced unknown who was taking every advantage of her fifteen minutes in the spotlight.

"For those of you just tuning in, I am coming to you from Barstow, California, where early this morning all of the students at Kennedy Elementary School were taken hostage and held for ransom.

"Barstow is a sleepy, quiet town where nothing much happens, one of those hamlets where everyone is 'family' and no one's business is sacrosanct. The town has nothing special to offer the outside world. It is a place of boots and rifles, beer and barbecue. Most everyone has a dog, a cat, and a few chickens. The town does not ask much of the world outside of the safety and well-being of its children, for that is its most precious commodity.

"Dennis Bates knew this. So did his wife, Edna. He was a former Barstow policeman who was fired. She was his lover, a married woman who left behind two teenagers.

"The Bates' knew about Barstow's children—everything about them—which was precisely why they returned here. To walk into the elementary school and take the school hostage. The entire school. For its release, they demanded three hundred million dollars in ransom—two million per hostage—"

What distinguishes this catastrophe from others is the fact that the Bates' seem to have deliberately reenacted a tragedy which occurred on May 16th, 1986, in Soda, Wyoming. The perpetrators in the '86 ransom were identified as David and Doris Young. It is known that Doris was blown up during the course of events in Wyoming. According to reports, David shot himself through the head. His body was not recovered.

"The following clips from a movie based on the Wyoming tragedy show what the children there saw and heard ten years ago."

After a commercial interruption about swimming pool hazards by a company that manufactured pool

covers—summer was, after all, around the corner—
the camera focused on a room filled with children of
assorted ages. Some of them huddled in corners. Others stood with their backs against the walls. The youngest were being comforted by adults identified as
teachers.

"Don't worry," the woman playing the part of Doris
Young told the children. "David hates grownups, but
he doesn't want to hurt *you*."

"See this gun?" David lifted the weapon in his
hands, then pointed at a stack of three or four rifles
and a mound of shells and ammunition. "This is all
for the grownups. I have BB guns for you kids."

A voice, presumably that of the actress playing the
reporter's 1986 counterpart, said, *"Those weapons
were nothing more than distractions to the reverse Pied
Piper of Moose Lake County whose music was locked
into a homemade explosive device that lay in a shopping cart, in the place where a child usually sits, grab-
bing at candy and cookies and Spaghetti-Os."*

The screen filled with a close-up on a series-bomb.

"She said to call her Dorrie," one of the children
said. "She's a nice lady. She wants to help us."

Another close-up showed a clothespin with two
sheet-metal screws through it. A piece of wood between thin screws was keeping the contacts apart. The
trigger was attached with a shoestring to the wrist of
"Doris Young."

"Gotta pee. Don't move, Doris."

As "David" left the room through a door behind his
wife, the camera closed in again on the woman's wrist.

"I'm back."

In a celluloid slo-mo, "Doris" turned her head. Her
body followed. There was an explosion, a blinding
flash, like thunder and lighting all jumbled together.
The children's bodies flew through the air. They
screamed, bled, collapsed.

The movie reporter said, *"I can't understand why
they weren't all killed,"* and the screen returned to the
reporter in Barstow. "The smell of gasoline. That's

what I'll keep remembering," she said. "Standing here, one can only imagine the smell of burning flesh that I'm told hovers around fresh burns and the stale, acrid stench that lived permanently around old burns in the days before antisepsis.

"A few minutes ago, I asked one of the mothers why she thought most of the children had survived. She said, 'Because they were meant to live.' I suppose that's as good an answer as any.

"Wait a moment, folks." Her voice rose with excitement. "Here's one of the teachers who was there and came out of this alive. Let's see if she'll talk to us."

She placed the mike near the face of a woman who looked as if she'd come from a battle zone.

"He attached the . . . the . . . thing . . . to his wife, you know. He had to go to the bathroom. You believe that?" the woman said, pushing away the mike.

"We're told that the bomb that exploded was made up of ten to twelve milk cartons," the reporter said. "He gave the trigger to his partner when he went into the bathroom. She turned when he reentered the room and part of his bomb exploded. Part of the device didn't go off despite the connection . . . four back-up pipe bombs in a series. Resorting to his gun, he shot and wounded the music teacher, then shot himself in the head.

"Dennis Bates hated the system so much that he damned himself. His dirge, the song of the reverse Pied Piper, sent him to his own death. His song has ended, but the melody's discords are lingering all around me.

"Fortunately for the survivors of this tragedy, Dr. Piet Runolo, renowned burn specialist, has volunteered to medivac his burn team from their base in Las Vegas to help with the forty worst cases who will be taken to his hospital's burn unit for treatment. The team will be working on their own time, without remuneration. They include an occupational therapist with a specialty in treatment of burn victims—"

The telephone jangled. I picked it up, knowing I'd

hear his voice. Knowing what he'd ask me to do. Knowing that I would cancel a long-anticipated hot date for that night and do it.

I had enough time to throw a few necessities into a bag, grab my portable and cell phone, and get to the helipad in front of the hospital's main entrance.

"This will fill my beds." Runolo had to yell above the noise of the helicopter's engines. Still in his OR greens, he looked relaxed and comfortable, even ebullient, and I knew why. His burn unit's empty beds were about to be filled. His funding would no longer be endangered. He had told me about the funding the night before, during post-surgery down time. "The hospital board said, 'Fill them or take a long vacation. Go to Rio and do some tits and ass while we try to reestablish credentials for you and the hospital.' "

For a split second, following him into the helicopter, I wondered if, like some firemen, there were burn surgeons who were pyrotechnicians, setting fires in order to fill wards and win the Burn Unit War for grant money.

"Do you do them? Tits and ass, I mean?" I asked when we were airborne.

"I won't abuse that talent God gave me." He hesitated. "Well, maybe once a while, in extenuating circumstances."

It was not until much later that I understood that he was referring to the quick surgeries he did to support his nasty gambling habit which was threatening to cost him his cutting hand.

"You know what I want to do eventually," he said to the medivac pilot who was defying statistics on this flight. The most dangerous job in the world; too little sleep, too much tension, too few pilots. "I want to go back to the elements. I came in with nothing—I want to leave with nothing. I dream of giving away everything . . . not selling it—giving it away—and going back to being a patient's doctor . . ."

"There's a book in that if you do it," I said, thinking, I don't even have a toothbrush with me.

"You can buy what you need in Barstow," Runolo said, as if he had again read my thoughts. "First rule—never carry baggage that isn't directly related to your job."

I glanced down at my portable computer, imagined the book I might write about this healer-hero, and asked myself if emotional baggage was included in Runolo's rule.

It took around forty minutes for us to get to Barstow and another ten to reach the town's emergency clinic. I at once separated myself from the burn team and, not wanting to be in anybody's way, positioned myself on a hard bench in a courtyard near the entrance. The bench made a more than adequate work table; I was within hailing distance if I was needed inside, and I could be available to the less seriously injured children and various family members who milled around outside.

From what I'd seen en route from the field where the helicopter had landed, this part of town sported little more than one decent hotel across the road from a gas station, and a small Mom-and-Pop store that sold fishing licenses and beer and odds and ends. I'd been told there was one bar, hidden in a side street.

"There were more caps. If those had gone, off, too, they would all have been dead." A man, a father, mouth smiling at me over a warm, red beard that failed to distract me from the ice in his eyes. His arms were around a good-looking blond boy, a Siamese twin whose living but undeveloped brother remained attached to his burned hip in a kind of pouch, kangaroo-style.

"Do they call you Zach?" I asked, knowing his name was Zacharias.

"Nah. They call me 'Roo'—Bye!" Zach-the-Roo was off, charging head-on at Runolo who had stepped outside for a breath of fresh air. "I know who you are." He poked Runolo in the arm. "You're a doctor. You hurt people."

"I try not to hurt them, Zacharias," Runolo said solemnly. "Really I do."

The boy's father looked embarrassed. "Don't mind Zacharias," he said. "You know what it is with twins. He's just jealous 'cause he didn't get burned like Jeremiah."

A woman sat down beside me and tugged at my arm. Inside the building, her nine-year-old sat in a Hubbard tank. His neck was being debrided, peeled like a scalded tomato by a member of Runolo's burn team, a big man with experienced and emphatic hands. The act of debriding would minimize the child's risk of infection and cut down on scarring. His mother had told her story to journalists and in front of TV cameras, but she needed to tell it again. She would probably need to keep telling it until her son's scars had healed and they could both reenter a world which would never again be the same one they remembered.

I listened helplessly, because I could not alter the events of the past, and thought about Dr. Piet Runolo—an old-young, cafe-au-lait man, moving surely and quietly around the children. I had felt them respond to his presence as he talked, smiled, instructed. Not one of his team had eaten since the night before; not one of us asked for food.

We didn't need to.

We, like the children, were being nourished by the atmosphere of healing and hope and optimism.

With all of its attendant agonies, Runolo's story was the story of hope for the good that is in mankind. Like David Young in Wyoming, Dennis Bates was beyond pain, but the mother sitting on the bench at my side was alive. She and her son. Miserably alive.

A boy flew by on a scooter, hollering that he had come to see the famous doctor who had flown in to see the children. Parking his scooter in a corner, he licked the corner of his mouth, then screwed up his face as if to let me know that he was in plenty of pain.

"Been on TV lotsa times," he bragged. "Wanna know anything, you ask me."

"Okay," I agreed. "What was the craziest thing that happened?"

"The bomb, dummy!"

We were friends now. "What else?" I asked him.

While he was thinking about his answer, a little girl sidled up to my chair. She was golden and beautiful, even with the flaming red burn which marred the side of her smooth face. She clutched a soft doll in her arms.

"I've decided . . ." The scooter-boy came closer. "It was my friend's birthday, you know. We sang 'Happy Birthday' at school. The man—he sang, too. He couldn't even sing in tune." He shook his head in amazement and added, "A grownup and he couldn't even sing 'Happy Birthday!' "

The Byzantine quality of all of it came home to me. Two tragedies, one in Wyoming, the other on the outskirts of Death Valley, yet so similar that I could almost believe that David Young and Dennis Bates were the same person. Children's lives being threatened by a bomb made up of milk cartons—ten or twelve of them. A device that didn't fully detonate, despite there having been four back-up pipe bombs in series.

I wondered if David Young could sing 'Happy Birthday' in tune.

"We've had our psychiatrist see the kids," Runolo said, having disengaged himself from Zacharias. "I'll repeat a conversations I overheard between one of the children and the therapist. I'm sure it'll make you feel better.

"The psychiatrist asked the littlest guy if he would go back to school. The kid said 'Yup.' The psychiatrist asked him if he thought he would learn anything when he went back. The kid said, 'Don't think so. I think we're just going to play. Already know all about bombs!' "

The children were in this together. It was rather like the bond I'd observed between New Yorkers. A "bitching bond." A glue made up of anger at cab driv-

ers and at Con Edison's eternal "dig-we-must." Their
wounds were being tended by nature and medicine.
They were adjusting. I was less confident about the
adults. I compared them with some of the children to
whom I had spoken. . . .

Jamie, who said his greatest joy in life was
". . . bugging my sisters." There are six children in his
family. "I want to be a movie star. *No,* I guess I want
to be like he is." He pointed to the visiting doctor.

Greg, who came into emergency with his fingers
loosely bound after a motor-bike accident and confessed
reluctantly that he had not been burned. If someone had
handed him a pressure garment to wear, he would have
put it on and worn it like a badge of courage—even
though he had no burn scar to minimize.

"I feel . . . humble," I said.

Runolo laughed. "Don't get too humble," he said.
"It won't do you any good around doctors, you know.
It won't do you any good around the fish either."

"What fish?"

"We're all being picked up at four-thirty in the
morning to go fishing. The whole team."

I threw up my hands in a gesture of resignation.
"It's hardly an occupation for a nice Jewish girl," I
joked, "but why not! Actually, it sounds like fun."

Runolo laughed again. "Promise *I* won't tell the
fish, if *you* don't," he said.

Little did I know that I was about to been given an
essential transfusion of simplicity. The van picked us
up right on time and drove us to the Colorado River
outside Needles. Having breakfast on the sunrise en
route, I feasted on a surfeit of quiet and wandered off
alone to the top of a ridge. I could see Runolo below
me, slightly apart from the others, casting his line with
the grace of a dancer, his body one with the rod and
reel. Were it not for his omnipresent gloves, it might
have been hard to reconcile his T-shirt and blue jeans
with the white-coated man I had seen the day before.

"You must have fished a lot when you were a boy,"
I said later, when he joined me on the ridge.

He nodded. I felt momentarily close to him. "Have you ever been burned?" I asked.

"Guy Fawkes Day, 1950," he said. "I was six years old, by myself at the front of the house where the firecrackers had been lit at midnight the night before. How I loved those firecrackers." He turned to look at me. "The noisy ones especially enchanted me—the ones strung together in packages of anything from ten to a hundred child-finger-sized miniature bombs.

"The number of firecrackers lit by a family was relevant in our neighborhood," he explained. "A status symbol."

The night before had been clear; the family had lit between five and ten thousand firecrackers. That left plenty of half-burned ones lying around. Quietly—with the same intensity that would dog him for the rest of his life, he collected firecrackers. Leftovers, he called them.

"I was delighted that the night had not brought rain to limit my selection. I found fifty, maybe even a hundred of them, broke each one in half, and rolled the halves one at a time between my thumb and index finger until the powder spilled free." He rolled his fingers together, as though replaying the scene. "I'd disemboweled at least a hundred of them before I was satisfied."

I imagined the growing gray mound.

"I was sitting three or four feet away from a patch of aloe that was snuggled into the flora. My grandfather planted it. He swore aloe cured everything from warts and athlete's foot to sunburn and acne." He closed his eyes. "I can see my surroundings," he continued. "A tea plant, white plumerias with yellow centers and red-pink ones with white centers, crotons growing in a profusions of primary colors next to poinsettias and hibiscus. But it was the gray dust that fascinated me.

"I knew I shouldn't do it, I knew it was extremely flammable, but I went on building that small volcano. Then I struck the match!"

He rubbed his palm on his thigh.

"There was an explosion, a flash. I didn't have time to back away . . ." He inhaled deeply and continued, "I remember bending over the powder, holding the matches in my right hand. I remember that flash of light and instinctively lifting my left hand to protect my face, which is why it was the one that got burned.

"I suppose I felt pain, though I don't remember it. Nature is kind that way. It allows us to forget. Anyway, instinct took over again. I ran across the three or four feet that lay between me and the aloes, picked one, broke it, and rubbed it on my wound. Because the aloe was applied immediately, it reversed damage that otherwise would have been irreversible."

Frowning slightly, he looked at me and said, "I remember some comment later from my grandfather about my having been destined to become a doctor—a good one—because the first thing a good doctor has to learn to do is to heal himself."

The crisis Runolo had created was over within about six hours. ". . . I must have been in shock," he said. "I know they took me to the emergency room where they washed my hand and bandaged it up."

"How bad was the burn?" I asked.

"Pretty bad, they tell me. Swollen, blackened, singed. My fingers looked like small sausages. All I remember is how they peeled off the blisters.

"I was lucky." He removed his glove and showed me the white pinhead-sized scar I'd noticed the first time we met. "There was no way I could have known about the zone of stasis, the area in which burn damage is reversible for the first fifteen or twenty minutes if a compress, or better yet aloe, is applied."

"Why aloe?"

"The plant's effect is to increase antiprostoglandin activity. It acts a an anti-inflammatory agent, which in turn increases the blood flow and causes vasoconstriction. The result is that reversing process I mentioned. If you really want to know about it, read *Aloe: Myth or Magic.*"

"Magic," I mused. "Why not."

He put the glove back on. I wanted to ask him to take off the other one, but I didn't, at least not directly. "The other day I asked you why you weren't doing surgery. You said, 'New hand. It belonged to a shaman, so I'm not cleared to cut with it.' Could you explain what you meant?"

He waited so long to answer that I was sure he was offended. "Are you sure you want to know this?" he asked finally.

"Very sure."

"All right. I'll tell you. But I won't be insulted if you don't believe me." He paused. I said nothing. "Not long after we met," he went on, "I did another Interplast trip. We went back to a village near the Amazon, where I completed reconstruction of the cleft palate of a young woman who happened to be the favorite daughter of the village healer. After the surgery was done, I celebrated by cleansing myself in the river. Unfortunately, I encountered a hungry crocodile, and emerged from the water without my right hand.

"When I realized what had happened, I passed out. Apparently, the villagers found me and carried me to the healer.

"Here's the part you need not believe, though it is true. It seems the healer was so grateful for what I had done to make his daughter normal, that he at once chopped off his own right hand and transplanted it onto my forearm."

At this juncture, I must certainly have looked at Runolo as if he were insane.

"Would you like to see it? The hand?"

I must have nodded, because he removed the glove from his right hand. It was gnarled and wrinkled, and so dark as to be almost black. About an inch above the wrist, the skin shifted in a jagged line from wrinkled black to smooth latte.

"Now you've seen it and you know," he said.

He was right that I'd seen the hand, but what was

it he thought I knew? That being part Shaman had given him that uncanny ability to intuit what I was thinking? Probably. But it was more than that. Much more. I could not help but wonder, for example, how much of the sense of safety and healing he projected was the confidence of a highly-trained doctor, how much the natural healer, and how much the ancestral wisdom of the shaman whose hand he now bore.

Beyond all of that, would our AMA-driven system ever be advanced enough to fully accept the hybrid he had become and allow society to derive the benefit of the gifts he had to offer?

He started to put the glove back on, but I stopped him by placing my own hand over his. For all of his gifts, I thought, he was still a human being, with human frailties.

Until his pager called. Then he wanted only one thing, *was* only one thing: a healer; a human aloe in a world of deadly nightshades.

I started to close the FedEx envelope, but thought better of it and added a postscript to my note to Ellen:

> P.S. There are the unique among us who, having found their own design, glory in it: the writer who must give us Madame Bovary; the sculptor who must give us David; the man of science who must give us the Theory of Relativity. Give—because they do know their purpose and have no choice but to do what is demanded of them.
>
> We have heard their melodies, their lyrics, and we bow to their uniqueness. There is a light within them, a flame that surrounds them, made up of equal parts of art and skill, of passion and compassion, of obsession and love and human frailty.
>
> Piet Runolo is one such man. As life is flawed, so is he, but his flaws are the true measure of his humanness. The measure of his greatness lies in the fact that while he dreams of combing hidden beaches with a metal detector, while he wants a tailor-made tuxedo, a house

overlooking the Mediterranean, a Nobel Prize, he knows that his destiny lies with the three major traumas in life: birth, death, and burning.

I do not envy him his particular destiny, but I so deeply lust after his brand of knowing that I have been in search of my own. I am not there yet, but I have learned that, for me, there are two universal truths: thought and doubt.

Regarding the first, I have been unable to improve upon what Descartes wrote: Cogito Ergo Sum. I think, therefore, I am. Regarding the second, for those of us who think at all and wonder that life is all about, I would add, Dubito Ergo Sum. We doubt ourselves, we doubt others, we doubt the grand design. Above all, we doubt that there is a reason for each grain of sand, each raindrop, each two-legged sentient creature, the least purposeful of which appears to be man.

LUCKY GUESSES

by Marc Bilgrey

Marc Bilgrey has written for television and magazines. His short stories have appeared in numerous anthologies, including *Cat Crimes Through Time, Merlin,* and *Far Frontiers.*

I remember the day everything changed. I had just walked into the reception area of the company where I worked when Jan, the receptionist, told me that my boss wanted to see me. Since I hadn't been expecting a meeting with him, I had no idea what he wanted.

I was still trying to figure it out as I stepped into his office. He was talking on the phone, but motioned for me to sit down. Suddenly I knew I was about to get a raise. It was as plain as if he'd actually said the words out loud, only he hadn't. In fact, he was still talking on the phone at the time.

I was not reading his mind, I was reading his feelings. His enthusiasm, the thrill of telling me the good news. I didn't need to hear his thoughts, his emotions made his thoughts very apparent, at least to me.

When he finally completed his call, placed the phone receiver on its hook, and turned to me, it was all very anticlimactic.

"Doug," he said, smiling and adjusting his necktie, "you probably have no idea why I asked you here today."

"Uh, no," I said, because at age twenty-five I'd already had a lifetime of experience that had taught me it's best to pretend you don't know what people will say. It's very disturbing to them to be told that you know what they're feeling before they've expressed it in words.

"Doug, you've been selling more lithographs than anyone else in your department, hell, in the whole company. You're our best damn salesman and I thought you ought to know it."

"Thanks, Mr. Walters," I said. It was like watching a play you knew because you'd read the script in advance.

After a long pause, he said, "I'm giving you a raise."

"That's wonderful," I replied, hoping I sounded suitably surprised. But then I read his continued feelings of good cheer, and I knew he believed my reaction.

"You've earned this," said my boss, "and I want you to know that we're expecting big things from you." With that he stood up, shook my hand, and instructed me to "get back to the grindstone."

I left his office feeling oddly disturbed, but not because of the raise. No, that had seemed logical considering my sales record. What had shaken me up was how powerful I was getting. It used to be that I could "read" people's feelings intermittently, whenever the right mood struck. It was something that happened every so often, a few times a month, but now it was going on all the time. And before I hadn't always been accurate. Now I never missed.

I stopped by my cubicle, dropped some sales brochures into my briefcase, and headed to the elevator. As I walked into the crowded elevator, I picked up the feelings of a man who had just had a serious loss in his life. I focused in as if I were fine-tuning a station on a radio, cutting out the static. I saw that it was a close male relative of his, an uncle who had just died. I glanced at the man in the back of the elevator. He wore a suit and tie, was overweight, and his face was expressionless. There was no hint that he was experiencing such deep sorrow.

A minute later I was on the street, walking in the

direction of my first sales call. Instead of thinking about selling framed still-lifes and landscapes to the next office manager I would be meeting with, my thoughts drifted back to my childhood. I found myself thinking about what, as a child, I used to call lucky guesses, but now referred to as "the gift" or "the power." I remembered once, in first grade, asking the teacher why she was so sad. She denied it at first, then I asked her if her husband would be coming back. She had not given any indication that she had been having any marital problems. Why would she? We were a roomful of six-year-olds. She had me wait after class and then asked me how I knew. I said, "I heard you in my mind." I saw her eyes fill up with tears. She said, "Don't ever mention this to anyone." She never brought up the subject again and neither did I. I was too scared. I thought she would contact my parents, but she didn't. In retrospect, I guess she probably wouldn't have known what to say to them even if she had.

A couple of years after that incident, I was in my father's office one day (he worked for a real estate company) when I passed by a desk and saw a man sitting quietly looking at some papers. Instantly I knew he'd been stealing. The feeling was overwhelming. He was so happy with himself, pleased with his skill, satisfied with the results of his crime.

I asked my father why the man had been taking money that wasn't his. My father got very angry, slapped me across the face, and told me never to make up lies about people again. A month later his co-worker was arrested for embezzling and put in jail. My father, if he'd remembered what I'd said, never mentioned it. Not everybody, I realized, could do what I could, and talking about it would only get me into trouble.

Years went by, and there were other times that I read people's emotions. There were kids in school, people on the bus, but I kept quiet about it. And, since it didn't happen that often, it was best to pretend it wasn't happening at all, like an illness that only erupted occasionally, ignore it till the outbreak passes.

I went to my sales call. I sold the office manager three dozen prints. Mostly abstracts that matched the color of the company's carpet. I felt a pang of guilt as I wrote up the paperwork. She'd been so easy to read. Her surface bluster was just a hard phony edge that covered her insecurities. I knew exactly what to hone in on. In a way, I felt like I'd been cheating.

As I left her building and walked onto Lexington Avenue, I realized just how uncomfortable I'd been feeling lately. Of course I was the best salesman in the company, where was the surprise there? It was like hiring an Olympic swimmer and then throwing him in a pool with small children. But what was I supposed to do, disregard what I felt? Dismiss my conclusions? I had thought to try to stop the process, but I didn't seem to be able to shut it off.

As I walked, I passed people, strangers, and felt stinging surges of their emotions. I didn't want to know everyone's life story. Not that I had anything against being a voyeur in theory, it just got very tiring and draining after a while. In the previous few months, I had noticed my power growing. Why it was growing I didn't know. I wasn't even sure why I had it to begin with, though I had a theory.

Years before I was born my mother had worked at a secluded laboratory upstate doing clerical work. Apparently there had been experiments there with different kinds of radiation. It was all top secret, and she was only a low level employee with minimum security clearance. I have since tried to find out more information about this lab, but thus far have only managed to verify that it once existed. Whatever experiments were being done there are, to my knowledge, still classified.

I only began looking for explanations after college when the power had started to get stronger. By then I was going through everything I could find on ESP and psychic phenomena. After much research I came to the conclusion that I was an empath, someone who could read and feel other people's emotions. Maybe "feel" isn't even the right word, maybe "receive" is better. Language is very imprecise when it comes to describing anything beyond the five senses. In any case, it was good to finally be able to give a name to what I have. In my studies, though, I never came across anyone who was as consistently accurate as I was.

When I was done with my sales calls, I found myself, once again, on the street walking. I thought back on the day. Months earlier I had promised myself that when I got a raise I would get married. I had been going out with Deborah, my girlfriend for two years, and was not about to rush into anything without being financially prepared. And here it was, the day I had longed for. She, of course, had not yet been informed of my raise. I was due to meet her at her apartment after work.

Then I thought, why delay the inevitable? Now was the time to make the most of my good fortune. I walked to Fifth Avenue and into a jewelry store. After looking around for half an hour I found an engagement ring that I knew Deborah would love, paid for it, and left the store. As I walked north on Fifth, I pictured what the look on Deborah's face would be as she opened up the little white, velvet-lined box and saw the glittering stone inside. Of course she would say yes to the question, that was a given. I knew she loved me, and I her. If I was privied to strangers' emotions I certainly knew my girlfriend's in even greater depth.

My thoughts were interrupted by a sharp stab of pain in my right temple. I stopped walking and touched my head. Is it a headache, I asked myself? No, it wasn't. I was feeling, receiving someone's emotions. I felt the pain again; this time it was even more intense. I had never experienced anything like it before.

I shook my head. I was feeling someone's suffering,

strong despair and hopelessness. But whose? I turned to look at the passing crowd of people around me. The person I was searching for was not among them. I took a few steps backward. The pain lessened very slightly. I stepped forward again. The force increased. Whoever I was picking up was someplace in front of me, in the direction I was walking. For some reason I found myself drawn to the source of the pain. At first I thought it was just curiosity, but then I realized that whoever's emotions I was experiencing was in great distress and in need of help. And no one could hear her but me. Yes, it was a female, that much I did know.

I began walking faster. As I crossed the street to the west side of Fifth, the pain got even stronger. At Fifty-fifth I turned and started walking toward Sixth Avenue, then Seventh. When I got to Eighth I stopped in front of a ten-story apartment building. Whoever was sending the signal was someplace inside. I hesitated. I would be trespassing, it could be dangerous, anything could happen. I dismissed my concerns.

I opened the building's front door and went into a small vestibule. A locked glass door prevented me from going any further. On the wall to the right was an intercom system. I scanned the names next to the buttons. The pain in my head was coming in spasms now like a broken car alarm. I ran my fingers along the names of the tenants. At apartment 5-B (the name was Ross) I felt as if I'd placed my hand near a lit match. I pressed the button. There was no response. I tried a second, third and fourth time. I had to do something. I pressed a button marked "Super," 1-A. The glass door opened with a chirp. I went inside to a dimly lit lobby. There I heard locks turning, another door opened, and a man with a mustache and a five o'clock shadow looked out at me.

"Yeah?" he said.

"Are you the Super?" I asked.

He nodded.

"There's a woman in apartment 5-B, she's in trouble, in danger," I said. Even as I spoke, the words sounded strange to me, almost as if someone else were saying them.

"What do you mean?" asked the Super, who had the name Joe sewn in script on his gray shirt.

"She's not answering her door," I said, breathing heavily now. "Do you have her key?"

"Yeah," he said, looking me up and down and squinting, "you a friend of hers or something?"

"Yes, I'm a friend. But we've got to get up there now, she's in real bad shape. Please, you have to open her door."

He took another look at me, I suppose trying to access my credibility, then disappeared into his apartment for a few seconds and returned with a ring of keys. He closed his door and led me to an elevator.

As we rode up in the elevator he said, "You tried calling her?"

"Yes," I lied, "there was no answer."

He glanced at me again and said, "I don't remember seeing you around before."

"I've been around," was all I could come up with.

At the fifth floor we got out and walked to an apartment near the elevator. The Super rang the doorbell, received no response, found a key on his ring, and placed it in the lock. He then turned the doorknob and walked into the apartment.

"Ms. Ross," he said, calling out in the dark living room. No one answered. There were a few theatrical posters on the walls. We went into the bedroom and saw a blonde-haired woman in her thirties, wearing a green dress, lying on a bed. Her eyes were closed. On the night table was an empty prescription bottle. A label had the name Rebecca Ross typed on it, under that was the word Valium.

I shook the woman as the Super stood watching. She didn't wake up, though I heard her moan. I picked up a phone and called 911. I gave the operator the address and the apartment number and told her to send an ambulance and prepare for a possible drug overdose. After I hung up I noticed a handwritten note that must have fallen to the floor. It read: I am so sorry. God, please forgive me.

The Super stood staring at the woman on the bed and shook his head. "Beautiful girl," he said. "She was trying to be an actress. She gave me an autographed picture."

"How was the acting going along?" I said.

"I don't know, but she was a month late on the rent."

I waited till the emergency medical people got there, followed them to the street, and watched as they put her into the back of the ambulance.

"Where are you taking her?" I asked.

"Roosevelt Hospital," one of them said, as they got in. Then the ambulance zoomed off, flashing red lights and siren blaring.

When the ambulance disappeared into the evening traffic, I noticed the Super standing next to me.

"Good thing you came along when you did," he said. Then he started walking back into the building. "Such a pretty girl."

I called Deborah from a pay phone and canceled our meeting. I told her nothing except that I wasn't feeling well, which was true. Aside from what must have been some kind of shock, I was also experiencing a great fatigue. The pain that I'd had in my head vanished within minutes.

I went back to my apartment on West Seventy-eighth Street and tried to make some sense of the day, only it didn't really lend itself to much sense. I took the box with the engagement ring I'd bought and tossed it on my table. Then I ate a few pieces of soggy, leftover Chinese food I found in my refrigerator. A couple of hours later I called Roosevelt Hospital and asked about Rebecca Ross.

"Condition stable, resting comfortably," said a woman in a monotone.

*   *   *

That night I didn't get much sleep. In the morning I called in sick. My boss was amused. "Here I go and give you a rise and then you wimp out on me? What'd you do last night, booze it up celebrating? Don't worry about it; with your sales record, take a day off. If the rest of your department could sell as well as you do, I'd let them have extra sick days, too."

I got dressed left the building, and started walking downtown on Amsterdam, wondering what I should do. It occurred to me that I'd never missed a single day of work in the over three and a half years I'd been with the company.

Then I thought back to my girlfriend. I had not canceled a date with Deborah that I could remember either. And what a date it would have been, too. The night I was going to propose. I'd gotten a reprieve, I thought, then smiled. I looked at my hands; they were shaking.

As I walked, I saw a homeless man sitting near a parking meter selling some old magazines. I felt joy emanating from him, but it had a confusing, bizarre quality to it that I had not encountered before. Then I realized that he was high on something.

A skinny man passed me. He radiated intense anger toward someone. A relative? No, it was his wife. On the next block a woman holding a shopping bag was frustrated with a friend who, she felt, had betrayed her. A man walking a poodle loved his dog more than he cared for any human being.

What was going on? Was I short-circuiting? The worst part was there was no one I could talk to about it. Deborah didn't even know what I could do. Sure, there had been a few times that I had seemed to "read her mind," as she put it, but she'd dismissed them as coincidences. Was there a doctor I could see? Yeah, a shrink, and by the time he or she was done with me, I'd either be heavily sedated or locked in a padded cell or both.

On Fifty-ninth Street I turned west and was soon in front of Roosevelt Hospital. After evading a security guard I found the floor that Rebecca Ross was on. I went to her door and walked inside the room without knocking. She sat up in bed and looked at me.

"I must have the wrong room," I said, "I'm sorry."

"That's all right," she replied, smiling. "Today, I'm glad to see anyone and everyone."

I left the hospital.

In the late afternoon I went to Deborah's apartment. She'd come straight from the bank where she worked as an assistant manager and was still dressed in her conservative black suit and white blouse. I told her everything, except for the part about buying a ring. I filled her in on my childhood experiences, my mother's job at the secret lab, my growing powers, my boss giving me a raise, and then about finding Rebecca and getting her to the hospital.

I also told her about how different I now felt and that I was having serious doubts about continuing in my job; that I was considering quitting and seeing if I could put my abilities to a better use than selling.

"Quit your job?" she said softly.

I looked into her eyes and felt her profound disappointment.

"What are you going to do," she asked, "walk around the city every day looking for people to save?"

"Well, no, not exactly," I said. "I just thought that maybe I could explore the possibilities of my power and somehow find a way to—"

"You can't quit your job. You've worked very hard to get where you are."

For the first time since I'd known her, I perceived that it wasn't just me she cared about, it was my status and how much money I made. I hadn't thought it mattered to her, but now I realized she wanted to be an executive's wife with all that went with it. We'd occasionally talked about buying a house in Connecticut, but only casually. Apparently, there was nothing casual about it. If I left my job to go on some kind of, for lack of a better term, spiritual quest, I would lose her.

She smiled. I still loved her. I wanted to have a life together, and on some level I couldn't blame her for being surprised and angry. We'd often discussed our plans. There was nothing wrong with wanting a financially secure future. She was decent and kind, and we cared deeply for each other.

I left her apartment more confused than when I'd entered it.

The next day I went to my office and checked in, with every intention of doing an honest day's work. But as soon as I headed out toward my first sales call of the morning, I decided that I couldn't go through with it. I called and canceled, then did the same with all the other appointments I had.

I was too upset to concentrate; my mind was a jumble of disconnected thoughts. I began walking aimlessly. Sometime later I found myself on Fifty-ninth and Fifth entering Central Park. I passed a couple of people jogging and a hot dog vendor who looked bored. I found a bench, sat down, and thought about getting a raise. Eventually I'd get a promotion which would make me head of the sales department. I thought about Deborah and our dream house in Connecticut. Maybe she'd been right. Maybe I was crazy to consider throwing it all away. And for what? Some vague ideal? She did have a valid point; I certainly couldn't patrol the city every day like a demented comic book vigilante righting wrongs. Still I knew that I'd been profoundly moved by my experiences.

Yet people do have transformational moments—births, deaths, spiritual awakenings—and they manage to integrate them into the fabric of their lives without giving up everything that went before. And wasn't marriage itself one of those sacred rites of passage?

An old woman with a wrinkled face, dressed in a black coat, sat down at the end of the bench. She was dying; I could feel it. She was very sad about dying. She had no friends or relatives.

After a minute, I turned to her and said, "Beautiful day, isn't it?"

She eyed me suspiciously at first, then replied, "Yes, it's beautiful."

Without even thinking, I said, "I have a friend who's very sick, and very scared."

The old woman stared at me.

"My friend sometimes comes to the park to try to forget about her illness."

"Does it work?"

"No, but really she just wants to be talked to, hear something positive, feel like she's part of the world for a few minutes." I saw the woman's eyes fill up with tears.

"I know just how your friend feels."

"I thought you might. My friend is a lot like you, she's emotionally strong and brave. She knows that in some way we're all connected."

"Thank you," she said, and extended her hand.

I went over to her and held her hand for a few seconds. I felt the woman's fear and loneliness lessen. Then I let go of her hand and started walking out of the park. My powers did not extend to precognizance but that day I knew the future, if only my own. I would return the ring I had bought and quit my job. I had no idea what I would do or where I would go just that I could not return to my old life.

I thought about my first grade teacher again, the same one I had told about her bad marriage. One day one of the kids took out a candy bar and began eating it. She said, "Either share that with everyone, or put it away."

Well, I thought, it was time to share.

EXCITING RADIATION TALES QUARTERLY
June 1952
MUTANT MOTHER FROM HELL
A 'FIZZ SMITH' STORY
by David Bischoff

(author: Puce-Galaxy Warriors, Cosmic Beam from Uranus)

David Bischoff was born in Washington D.C. in 1951 very close to where Michael Rennie and Gort landed in *The Day The Earth Stood Still*. One of his favorite books as a child was Edith Hamilton's *Mythology*. He attended the University of Maryland and graduated in 1973. Thereafter he worked for NBC in Washington where he started writing stories and novels. He now writes full time, including nonfiction books and articles in his repotoire. His latest books are *Philip K. Dick High* and *Tripping the Dark Fantastic*.

He just wanted to cut the apron strings. Mom wanted to cut something else—off!

Note from the Editor:
   We're very thrilled to have this new series of stories by that old vet Scientification author David Bischoff, who won the Bugga-Boo award last year for his masterly novelette "Spankers from the Dead Asteroid." When we showed this to another fine writer and our good friend, Henry Kuttner, he said. "Damn! Did I write this?"

I

MOMMY'S BOY-THING

His name was Fizzington Smith. Although he would have preferred to have been called "Zing," he was called "'Fizz" by his few friends, "Fizzle" by his enemies, and 2345-432-4324-4323434-43975-A43 by the government (no nicknames from them.) Upon graduation from Idaho Middle College in the year of 2345 AD, he attended a government-sponsored interview session in a search for a job. The transcripts of the interview read thus:

"Mr. Fizzington Smith?"

"Yes. So nice to meet you. I hope you had a nice trip to the campus—"

"You're hired. Please report for duty at seven hundred hours, July 19th. Next, please."

Thus, did Fizz Smith become a bureaucrat, an unlikely first step on his road to sex, intrigue, conspiracy, violence, and the wildest journey through interstellar space on record, to say nothing of winning the Pan Stellar Chili Cook-off.

This story, though, has none of these, because it's about how Fizzington Smith managed to get away from a clinging mother.

Oh, yeah.

Fizzington Smith was a mutant.

Nor was Fizz Smith a mutant in a subtle way. Nor did he have any special powers. Nope. There was a big point on top of Fizz's head, he had an eyeball where his ear should be and his tongue came out of the middle of his face and that monstrous thing had an eyeball, too. Yep. An eyeball, and a damned efficient one, too, if he ever had to fight in trench warfare.

Other than the rearranged face, Fizz was a handsome young man, with nice eyebrows, nice nostrils, perfect teeth, and a strong country lad's chin. True, they weren't exactly where they were supposed to be, but if you were a cubist, you got the idea.

When Fizzington Smith went home to his mother and pseudo-father to tell them about his exciting new career that fateful day just before his graduation, he had to wait for a time in the kitchen of the pomato farmhouse while they finished what they were doing in the bedroom.

After a little thought he went into his bedroom in the storm cellar, packed a bag, and set it out by the door, just in case.

With Mother Smith, you could never be sure.

Fizz sat down at the kitchen table, eating a pomato salad and washing it down with a glass of milk, listening to the bedsprings ricochet above. Mother Smith was a sex fanatic of long standing, and she went through a pseudo-dad a year if the pomato harvest was good. If not, she just hauled out the Acme Vibration Equipment and drained electricity for a while.

By the time the pomato salad was finished, so was Mom. She came out into the kitchen for a snack wearing only a tatty bathrobe, muttering under her breath about something significant breaking off the pseudo-dad and needing to go to the bio-store sometime this weekend. She opened the fridge and stood, dripping ashes from her cigarette, squinting through a squiggle of smoke.

"Damn! Who ate all the pomato salad?"

"Mom, I'll make some more! We've got enough!" murmured Fizz solicitously.

Mom swung around, windmilling her shedding tassels, the dust-eaters on her slippers coughing and hacking from overwork. "That's not the point. I made that pomato salad fresh this morning for me and spent a goodly time herbing it up good. Wasn't for you, Fizz Smith. For *me!*"

Mother Smith was nothing if not rather fearsome when she got riled, the varicose veins on her legs popping out like relief maps, the wide-spaced eyes red, the single caterpillar eyebrow wiggling lowly and darkly.

Even old radiation burns on her neck glowed a livid purple of fury.

This was not a good time to let her know that he'd accepted a job in Washingtron as a Class G bureaucrat and, no, Mother Smith's oldest boychild would not be in training anytime soon to take over management of Smith, Smith, Smith, and Smith Pomato Producers, allowing Esmeralda Smith a life of ease to wear out pseudo-fathers.

"Sorry, Mom. I'll make you some more. Right away."

Mom produced a sound somewhere between a grunt and a harrumph, and she waddled her hefty rear over to the table, poured herself a cup of coffee, and sat down across from her college boy. "Yah. You do that, you little snot."

"Mom. I think we really should have a discussion about the future," Fizz blurted. The eye on top of his head looked down at the floor and his tongue scratched at an eyebrow, which itched. He was feeling worse tics coming on, but suppressed them. Poor Fizz got all tied up in knots when he talked to Mom Smith sometimes. Sometimes it took days to untie himself.

Mom coughed. She dropped the cigarette into the cup of coffee, stirred it, and then drank a mouthful. "Yah. The future. Dat's what we're in, ain't it? Da great Future. Da Land of Possibility and Imagination." She drank another grainy swallow, a remarkably large Adam's apple for a woman upping-and-downing like a yo-yo. "I tell you, though Fizzington. I freaking bought that genetic kit *guaranteed* to mix up with one of my eggs in the right way to produce a strapping farm boy and what do I get? You!" She took a swallow of coffee, picked out a piece of cigarette paper from between her teeth and flicked it into the edge of a garbage machine. Sensors detected it, and a plastic tendril whipped out and snatched it into a grinder.

Fizz Smith sighed. That particular speech was something he'd hard thousands of times, a refrain to the song of his life, according to his mother.

Somehow, he had not turned out muscle-bound, or even particularly coordinated or even especially able to repair farm equipment. What he was was Fizzington Smith, which he accepted but that Mom never really could.

Fizzington Smith, at five foot six, was quite short in twenty-fifth-century terms. Not precisely midget sized, but in an era where nutrition had upped the average size to about six-five in men, he was a bit of a runt. Fizzington Smith was a bland-looking fellow with corn-silk-colored hair, parted in the middle to accentuate the perfect bump on his head. It was the favorite hairstyle of his Geek Fraternity, Psi Phi Gamete. His chest was peculiarly concave, and his limbs were twiggish rather than the logs that Mom Smith had hoped for her *in vitro* baby of twenty-one years ago. His most peculiar feature other than the aforementioned, however, was his lips. His lips were rather large and bulbous fishy things, protuberant past small narrow teeth, the color of—well, rather the color of pomatoes. Whether this was because of the steady Smith diet of pomatoes or sheer coincidence is not readily ascertainable.

Pomatoes, of course, were a hybrid of potatoes and tomatoes that were one of the staples of the galaxy, and one of the few things the depleted and half-scorched agricultural lands of Terra were capable of growing. Botanically an unlikely pair, nonetheless, the great biofusionist George Washington Burbank (melder of the culinarily audacious artipeach, the outrageous pinecarrot, and the truly masterful blending of animal, vegetable, and mineral, the Stewcreature) had always been a fan of potato and tomato sandwiches, and had been fooling around with gene-slicing one day while consuming one. The idea of the hybrid had naturally popped into his head, and since much of the livable part of Terra at that time was underground, and the hybrid was the perfect stuff for hydroponic growth, it was inevitable that, after much trial and error, the great scientist would finally stumble upon the right

DNA combination. The resultant pulpy, red-jacket combination was not only a deliciously sweet and nutritious tuber-vegetable, but absolutely first class for throwing purposes when slightly rotten.

The Smith Family had been one of the first to venture out of the Under-warrens over a century back (still a little glowy from nukes) and they'd settled this area of Idaho, not very close to Boise at all. After terrible failures with corn and wheat, Blizzlehead Smith had discovered that pomatoes grew like nobody's business in the funky farm dirt available. Very soon, the Smiths were making a decent if unspectacular agronomic living upon the stuff, and thus a modest empire arose. Alas, then came Great Matriarchal Shift, involving mass castration as a solution to Terran tendencies toward war. Men without testicles, with prosthetic tubes for penises, tend to be less than interested in weapons and aggression and stuff like that— alas, they were also uninterested in positions of authority. Only in the last thirty years had males been allowed to keep their gonads—and Mom Smith the Fourth had jumped on the opportunity of having someone else to run the farm and so had brewed up Fizzington and his three younger brothers: Burlington, Hemingway, and Joe. Alas, the other brothers: away at school now, were much younger than Fizz and wouldn't be able to take up the business for years; hence, Mom Smith's glee about son Fizzington's impending graduation from his agricultural and business curriculum at college.

"Mom. I'm legal age to make my own decisions now," said Fizz, squaring his shoulders in sadly roundish kind of way. "And I—I—I . . ."

Fizzington Smith tended to stutter at times of great stress, raining great rivulets of mucus down from the five nostrils in the middle of his face.

"Goddammit, Fizz!" said his mother, slapping him on his head. "Spit it out, boy! You sound like some kind of broken record!"

"Mother Smith, I've accepted a position with the

government. I'm going to be a Class G civil servant in Washingtron!"

Mom Smith blinked. The left corner of her mustached upper lip quivered—a facial tic that came on her at times of extreme stress. For a few stressful moments, she just sort of quivered, metaphorical steam flowing out of her large jutting ears.

"You *what*?"

"I'm moving away, Mom. I'm not going to work on the farm. If you need money, I'll send some back. But I need to pursue a more exciting future than growing pomatoes. Can't you understand? I've got *potential*!"

"Fritz!" she cried suddenly at the top of her lungs, her fleshly limbs trembling. "Would you come down here immediately and speak with your son!" She turned a baleful glance at Fizz, fully capable of withering a pomato vine in the bloom of youth. "Wait until your father hears this."

Fritz wasn't Fizz's real father, of course. Fizz' real father was genetically-futzed-with sperm from chopped up and frozen testicles from the Time of the Great Ouch. However, Fritz had the authority to beat the shit out of the fellow, so Fizz felt a thrill of fear run down his spine like a jolt of electricity. He made to start away toward his suitcase, but his mother's meaty fist reached out and grabbed him by the collar of his shirt. "Don't you go *anywhere*, boy, until your father's had a chance to discuss this matter with you!"

For some reason, Fizz did not try to break away. Perhaps it was the years he had spent under the iron rule of Mom Smith—and then again, perhaps it was because the sight of the gleaming, sharp pomato knife she'd taken off the table and was pointing toward his stomach had petrified his muscles and he simply could not move. Whatever the reason, he lingered long enough for the arrival of his pseudo-father.

Fritz Mark 29 strode down the stairs in the casual but authoritative stride characteristic of his manufacturing class. For all intents and purposes he seemed quite human. He wore a suit and a subdued tie, and shiny black Oxford shoes. He wore his hair short and swept back, very neatly groomed. A long pipe was clenched between his teeth. Mild brown eyes surveyed Fizz as he arrived.

"Now, then," he said in a rich baritone voice. "What seems to be the matter?"

Yes, he certainly *looked* human enough.

However, he wasn't.

He was a specially manufactured android . . .

"Fizzington here says he's accepted a job in Washingtron. He wants to be a bureaucrat," said Mom Smith.

. . . in a manner that would fulfill the psychological needs of children for a testosteroned role model, and also satisfy the physical needs of the matriarchal head of the family without threatening her position of authority.

Fritz's eyebrows creased with a frown. "Ah. I see. Well, then, young lad. Perhaps you and I should adjourn to the parlor for a little father-son chat!"

Fritz 29s were modeled specifically after Ward Cleaver of the *Leave it to Beaver* show, one of the video tapes discovered in the Sacred Cache which resulted in the Tertiary Haploid Renaissance of the twenty-third century. However, there was also a slight resemblance to one of the Gods of the current Terran pantheon—Bob of the Church of the SubGenius—but not enough to be sacrilegious.

Apparently confident in the ability of her pseudo-spouse to deal the situation, Mom Smith put the pomato knife down.

"I really don't think that's necessary!" said Fizz. "I'm not going to stay. You see, I've decided, Mom . . . Well," he said sheepishly, embarrassed to be talking about such things with his mother. "I'd very much like to keep my genitals, and being a bureaucrat, you get to be in a different class of society that lets you do that and— well, shucks, Ma, I'm just nuts about girls!"

Mom Smith took in a sharp breath. "May God in Heaven have mercy on your sinful soul! I should have gelded you years ago, Fizz—but I wanted some muscles on you! And come to think of it, I'm still waiting for those." She shook her head, aghast at this blasphemy being uttered by her own flesh and blood. *All* males of the Church of Hilda and the Saints of Tomorrow had to be castrated by the age of no later than twenty-two—and they had to have their virginity registered to make it that far, along with regular visits to the local sperm bank for donations to make their active glands useful in a clinical fashion. The idea of her son, her *baby*, sticking his thing into some heaving hussy made Mom Smith absolutely chartreuse with rage. "You'll be damned to eleventh level Perdition, son, along with the psyche-whores and the chiro-heli-practors!"

Fizz walked over to the door resolutely and picked up his bag. "I'm sorry, Mom. The decision has been made. I just wanted to tell you, and hope for your understanding."

The pomato knife was back in Mom Smith's hand. However, this time, she did not wield it threateningly. Instead, she handed it to the Fritz 29.

"Fritz," she said, her features gnarling into a carica-ture of motherly outrage. "Maybe we'd better take care of that gelding business now. I'll go and get the Servo-Med Kit and cauterizer, and you deal with this so-called son of mine."

"Yes, dear."

The pseudo-father placed his pipe on a table. He took the knife. As Mom Smith left the room, Fritz started out for Fizz, the gleam of the knife matching the sudden gleam in the pseudo-Daddy's eye.

II

THEY CAME FROM BEYOND TUESDAY

By the twenty-fifth century, there was a great deal of human history under the bridge.

Alas, it was during the World War Seven and a Half, The Sequel, in the twenty-second century that much of that history was effectively *erased*, to say nothing of the memories and personalities of human beings.

All this by way of explanation as to why things are the way they are in the twenty-fifth century, and maybe some insight into why a mother would be so intently trying to castrate her own son with a pomato knife.

By the twenty-second century, mankind had practically given up on colonizing the stars. Somewhere along the line, the promise of technology had simply dried up. Engineering dreams of building at the very least a generation ship to the stars had collapsed in ruin, after a faster-than-light drive had become a sad and sick joke. The human heart's urge for expansion had to be satisfied with modest colonies on Mars, the asteroid belt, and Titan—more outhouses of humanity than outposts.

In the meantime, the nations of the world did what nations do: war. After the Third and the Fourth World Wars, contained and limited nuclear weapons proved conclusively that even restricted radiation was good for nobody, so the few remaining nations discretely ditched their remaining warheads. However, mankind being mankind, even more weapons were developed. For even though technology was crapping out in the exploration of the wonders beyond the solar system, it enthusiastically forged ahead in its dutiful endeavor to destroy human life. Baroque fighting machines were created; monstrosities of the earth, the air and the sea, gnashed and scratched at one another in the fight for precious un-nuked land. Subtle poison choked soldiers; dire chemicals ate away skin. Strange rays turned bones to Jello. However, humanity managed to remain intact until the fateful year that the most awful weapon in history was developed.

The Tabula Rasa.

Dr. Naughtus Zero was, of course, the man who invented this terrible device. Dr. Zero was a German midget in the Traveling Freaky Scientists show—a research group who earned money by displaying their various curious deformities to the public. "Oh-oh" to his distinguished misshapen colleagues—such as the famous gynecologist Dr. Ernst Dildo, whose sexual organs had somehow grown out of his face instead of his groin, and Dr. Eva Zevanshanz, a hunchbacked xenobiologist bent on proving that Earth was the only planet in the universe containing life—Dr. Zero was scientific follower of the philosopher Rousseau. Like Rousseau, he believed that man at heart was good. It was civilization that was corrupt. If the evil part of civilization, of culture, could somehow be *erased* from a man's mind, then he would be good, pure, and remember to put the toilet seat down when he was finished peeing. To this end, the Doctor invented a device that emitted electro-magnetic particles that demagnetized selected memory nodes of the human mind, thus causing selective amnesia.

Now, even as Dr. Zero perfected his device (and enroute created the Cult of the Blissfully Forgetful Monks) the nation of South Africa was emerging as the dominant military and economic power on the globe. South Africa had brought back its policy of *apartheid,* however—with a significant difference. Whites and blacks should indeed be apart, the politicians held, apart the greatest distance possible: whites should be alive and blacks dead. Since they felt that by now most of the rest of the world's nations were infected with negroid blood, South Africa felt that all other nations should be exterminated. To this end, not only did they secretly redeploy nuclear warheads, but an intelligence agent stole the secret Tabula Rasa weapon. The South African general intended to direct these rays at the enemy's technology operators so that they would forget how to use their weapons. When World War Seven and a Half, the Sequel, broke out, however, the Tabula Rasa devises worked only too well. Not only was half the population of the Earth wiped out—those that survived had been so riddled with the powerful Rasa rays that they all had partial

amnesia. Enough memory and personality remained
in people that for the most part they were able to
survive. And because they forgot their glorious cul-
tural heritages as well as their prejudices and hatreds,
people actually stopped killing each other.

The Comeback Years were an exciting time—but
especially difficult, since all records of the past had
been demagnetized, all libraries had been burned, all
microfiche had been macro-destroyed. People had to
wing it from bits and pieces of memory that floated
to the surface, odd scraps discovered in charred, radio-
active buildings.

However, in the third year of the Comeback, an
exciting discovery was made in the Midwest of the
United States of Canada. The small prairie town of
Oshgosh, Kansas, had somehow survived the frazzle-
bombing. Stored in an old-fashioned fallout shelter
was a discovery as exciting as a suddenly restored Alex-
andria Library might have been to the ancient world—
an extensive collection of books! Here, thought the
leaders of the world, were the keys to the riches of
the past! Here, thought the baffled and muddled peoples of Earth, were the keys to prosperity and understanding for the future. After much work by great
scholars, reading was rediscovered and the long road
of deciphering this mass of literature was begun.

What the people of the twenty-second century did
not realize was that safely tucked away in the hermeti-
cally sealed fallout shelter had been Irving Furmeister's collection of science fiction and twentieth century
crackpot literature.

Science fiction, of course, was the curious brand of
writing popular only in the twentieth century when
progress was a given, and the stars seemed only a few
decades away. Once mankind accepted the fact that they
were stuck in this obscure corner of the Milky Way
Galaxy, the literature died and rotted away, replaced by
a resurgence of men's action-adventure kill-porn, and
women's nurse novels. Surely it would have been a dif-

ferent world if a cache of these had been discovered, and not Irving Furmeister's sci-fi collection.

Particularly curious, however, were the masses of magazines and nonfiction books in this underground library, which the scholars presumed to be the History of the World. There were the Eric von Daniken *Chariots of the Gods* books; a whole shelf of Rosicrusion literature; a wealth of Scientology books (including an autographed copy of the original Dianetics article in *Astounding Stories* by L. Ron Hubbard himself); four thousand UFO books, a complete run of *Fate Magazine,* and all the Shirley MacLaine books, three copies each. There were books on dowsing, crystals, reincarnation, conspiracies, the Illuminati, the Masons, the Mormons, and virtually every nut-cult in US history—but nary an actual Bible or more bland publication from the mainstream of religious faith. There were books and articles on EST, rebirthing, shamanism, feminism, McCarthyism, Rahjneeshism. There were decks of tarot cards, astrology charts, Tao Chi sticks, crystal balls and eight balls. All this and much much more than the modern amnesiac scholars had to shuffle through with the sole help of a bank of cross-referencing including such works as the *Star Trek Encyclopedia* and *New Age Terms.*

Needless to say, the scholars were somewhat perplexed.

Soon enough, however, the printing press was rediscovered. The more interesting items of the Irving Furmeister collection were reprinted and distributed among the peoples of Earth. Unfortunately, very few had taught themselves to read, so it was left to these one-eyed folks in the kingdom of the blind to read aloud the works of the past. These First Readers became somewhat like priests more than anything else, and naturally, opinion and narrow-mindedness being human qualities that could not be eradicated by mere amnesia, these priests latched onto various of the books and created their own cults, their own religions and their own Masonic Lodges for the Sacred Study of Science Fiction.

And from this font burst forth a spring of new civilization, a Renaissance of thought unseen in human history since the discovery of the flush toilet.

Technology forged forward again. Nations were formed, but a central government ruled the earth, so that no more devastating wars could be fought—skirmishes between provinces were the limit. After all, there were the Aliens to deal with—the Aliens out in the sky beyond whose sole purpose was to crush out the valiant flame of humanity. Somehow, the scholars had gotten the science fiction mixed up with the crackpot literature, it seemed, and construed the words of such worthies as A.E. Van Vogt, Robert Moore Williams, and Eando Binder (among numerous others) as profound cosmic visions into a very real future.

This attitude had its definite advantages. While it certainly bred a definite xenophobia, the fear of extraterrestrial, UFOs, and dwellers from other murkier dimensions banded together the normally fractious human race into a whole intent upon survival and perpetuation of the human species. Weapons were built, but solely for defense of the Earth—and for the fleet of spaceships fully developed a century after the Great Brain Drain. Not only that, but by the end of the twenty-third century, something previous unattainable was grasped. A barrier was broken.

Faster-than-light space travel was discovered.

Unaware of the impossibility of such an achievement, and assuming that it was inevitable because of the works of such SF greats as Robert Heinlein, Isaac Asimov, and the most popular of all, Stanton A. Coblentz, space scientists routinely hurdled such previously indestructible barriers as Einstein's Law of Relativity, slaughtered Schrodinger's Cat, slid down Occam's Razor to produce the marvelous and amazing Campbell Drive, named after that great SF editor and author and founder of Campbell's Soups, John W.

Campbell. The Campbell drive operated on the Collision Principle. It was discovered that if an Immovable Object met an Unstoppable Force they would both hurtle somewhere Faster than Light. By strapping spaceships onto this phenomenon (best achieved by mechanically hurling excrement at atomically fused Pet Rocks) mankind was able to visit the stars.

Thus was the Galactic Umpire was born. (The Great Scholars of the Irving Furmeister Cache got the occasional vowel and consonant wrong, a mess-up later titled "malapoopism.")

The far reaches of the Galactic Umpire, of course, were the destination of our hero, Fizzington Smith.

But whether he went there with his reproductive equipment or not is the subject of the next chapter.

III

THE FLAMING BLADES OF EXO-DEATH

It must be understood that Fizzington Smith was quite attached to his reproductive equipment.

Most boys of his class had their removed before they quite understood the significance of those curious dangling oddments of anatomy and go on quite well without them. However, since Mother Smith had signed for an Extended Biological Extension of Hormonal Producing Glands in order to create a properly equipped farmboy, Fizz had discovered the joys and hopes of glandular secretions and rather hoped to extend his enjoyment and achievements with them in partnership with beautiful blondes with very large breasts. He also discovered marvelous uses for long tongues—and hoped he could thus impress the ladies.

Therefore, his alarm at the sight of his pseudo-father heading his way with a carving knife is quite understandable.

"Don't move, you little shit!" the android roared,

his mouth twisting out of shape with blood-lust. "Stay still and let me cut them off!"

Fizzington Smith, of course, did not stay still.

Fizzington Smith grabbed his suitcase and proceeded to try and run away.

Unfortunately, Fritz the pseudo-father was quite fast, and caught him easily, manhandling him in the peculiar and brusque manner programmed into his class. There was the traditional Boxing-of-Ears. The Whacks across the Face. The Whipping with the Belt. All these things Fizz was quite used to and responded to in a passive fashion; pure knee-jerk survival on his part. However, when Fritz went for the pants and the knife flashed up like a piece of lighting another automatic response triggered in Fizzington Smith: The Urge for Survival.

A tremendous scream tore from the fellow's lips; a scream of proportions unheard in the Smith household (and there had been some whoppers there unstoppered in the near-century of mercurial matriarchy). Now, this scream so surprised, so unnerved the android, so knocked his cheap ball and hammer through his cheap Yugo-Ukrainski eardrum, that for a moment he was frozen, stunned, the knife halted in mid lunge for the Fizz privates.

Again, survival drove the young man. With all his might he struck his pseudo-father in the face with a fist. Half of the fellow's vat-o-flesh ripped from its mooring around the right cheek; the android windmilled backward, whirled along the floor in an imitation of a somersault, and landed (clang) by the garbage disposal unit.

The disposal unit was set on a Wide-Range garbage. And since the pseudo-father was essentially built only to last for not much over a year, and because the shoddy bio-merchandise was coming apart at the seams, and since the disposal unit sensed deterioration (and quite a large amount of it) it issued forth its full five tendrils and maximum strength, pulling Fritz the pseudo-father's head into the whirring micro-nuke interior and blasting it to ashes. The headless body spasmed for a few seconds and then was still.

Fizz Smith could only stand, petrified with horror at what he had done.

Mom Smith rolled her Medikwak device (a contraption that would surely have made Torquemada roll his eyes with envy) into the room. "Oh, I heard the scream, darling! You must hurt, darling. Come here and mommy will make it all bet—" She stopped, staring down for a full beat at the headless body, which the garbage disposal arms were attempting to pull into its maw.

"Fritz!" she cried. She swung a glower to her eldest son. "You nuked Fritz!"

"Mom! It's that goddamned machine. I'm—"

Mom Smith hit the start button on the Medikwak. Crustaceanlike arms reared up, the twisted apparatus clicking and glinting. Hypo-mandibles spurted, snapping toward the poor lad as the infernal device clunked and clawed its way toward him.

Fizzington Smith had always hated the Medikwak. From the very moment he had seen it as a small child when Mom Smith had gotten it for his bum-booster shots through the horrible hot oil enemas and the Boraxo dewormings to the regular forced cod-liver feedings, Fizz had always associated the Medikwak with the very worst his farmish life had to offer. So another Pavlovian response took hold of the fellow.

He grabbed his suitcase, opened the front door, and he scooted away, fleeing for his life.

Mom Smith's wails and threats followed him.

"I'll find you! I'll find you, you faithless, worthless piece of traitorous shit! I'll find you wherever you go! And then you'll be as sorry as I am I didn't strangle you with your own umbilical cord!"

All in all, a very manic-depressive kind of day in the life of Fizzington Smith. Who knew that soon, macrocosmic greatness would be thrust upon him by the universe?

And through what mutant orifice?

The End

Another Note From Editor: Be sure to pick up the next thrilling Fizzington Smith story in the next issue of *Exciting Radiation Tales*. It's called "Mr. Smith Goes to Washingtron," and good buddy Alfred Bester says about it: "Bischoff is rapidly becoming the new Stanley G. Weinbaum of scientification stories."

Ye Crusty Olde Ed.

FAMILY
by Fiona Patton

Fiona Patton was born in Calgary, Alberta in 1962 and grew up in the United States. In 1975 she returned to Canada, and after several jobs which had nothing to do with each other, including carnival ride operator and electrician, moved to seventy-five acres of scrubland in rural Ontario with her partner, five cats of various sizes, and one tiny little dog. Her first book, *The Stone Prince*, was published by DAW Books in 1997. This was followed by *The Painter Knight* in 1998, *The Granite Shield* in 1999, and *The Golden Sword*, 2001.

The arena's gravel lot was full, with cars parked all along both sides of the road and into the field beyond. Brandon Geoffries and his brother Fred sat on the hood of Brandon's '86 Plymouth station wagon watching the police cruiser that slowly wove its way through the rows of pickup trucks and four-by-fours. They glanced at each other, then both men's eyes went dark. The cruiser passed two cars with broken headlights and three with expired license stickers before it came to a halt in front of the two men. Fred grinned. Brandon merely lit a cigarette with an even expression.

The cop craned his head out the window.

"Hey, Brandon."

"Ken."

"Cheryl gonna baby-sit this summer?"

"I guess."

"Same price as last year?"

"She's over there talkin' to Lisa and her Mom. Why don't you go ask her?"

The cop nodded and carried on toward the three women standing by the arena's main doors.

Fred chuckled. "Lisa won't thank you for that," he noted. "She hasn't paid those speeding tickets she got last fall."

Brandon shrugged. "Ken won't bother her tonight. His wife's havin' another baby, and he's probably gonna need Cheryl and Lisa both to watch the four older kids."

After a moment the police cruiser carried on, and the three women made their careful way around the lot's myriad of pot holes to the car. As they came up, Brandon tossed his cigarette on the ground.

"Hey, Lisa, Ken gonna haul your ass in this time, or what?"

"Fuck you, Brandon." Lisa shot him the finger before fishing Fred's cigarettes from his pocket. He wrapped one arm about her ample waist.

"You ready to go?" he asked.

She nodded.

"You comin' with us, Janet?"

Lisa's mother shook her head. "I'll catch a ride with your Uncle Lloyd later. The W.I. wants to take this stuff over to the McFauls right away."

Brandon glanced over. "We bring in much?"

"About five hundred dollars, a couple of beds, a kitchen set, enough clothes to hold them over the summer, some toys for the kids. Thank your mother for all that bedding when you see her. It'll really come in handy."

"They find out what caused the fire yet?"

"Wiring."

"They gonna rebuild?"

"Come summer, once the ground dries out. When they do, they could really use a couple of Geoffries boys helpin' out."

"Well, tell 'em we'll be there."

She nodded. "I'll see yous all tomorrow, then. I'll

be bringing Debbie by, Lisa. Joe says she wants to see the family."

Fred grinned. "That kid's getting stronger everyday. Must take after our side of the family."

She snorted. "Not likely, Frederick Geoffries. He's a Mynaker through and through, and you know it." She turned to go. "Will you be heading straight home, Cheryl?" she asked over her shoulder.

"Probably."

"Then I'll bring that cat by after we're done."

She gave a brief wave and disappeared back into the arena as Brandon shot his girlfriend a suspicious glance. "Cat?"

She just shrugged. "One of Rick MacConnell's. It got hit by a car, and he can't afford to take it to the vet's. You know how it is."

"Just as long as we're not keepin' it. The drive shed's full of your little hairballs already."

She merely smiled at him.

"I mean it, Cheryl."

"Whatever."

He caught her up in his arms. "Frawst girls, they just can't help takin' in strays."

"That's how we end up with so many Geoffries boys. C'mon, take me home. I've go a cat to make ready for."

Brandon slid off the hood. "You wanna go first, Fred? I've got a headlight out."

"Sure."

"Son of a bitch!"

Teeth clenched, Brandon spat the curse out past the remains of his cigarette as he turned his head to glare into the headlights of the car behind him. "Fucker."

"What's wrong?"

"Bastard's tailgating me with his fuckin' high beams on," he answered, anger overcoming his usual laconic temperament.

Cheryl craned her neck to peer at the station wagon's speedometer. "You're going the speed limit?" she asked, her voice incredulous.

Brandon shrugged. "Fred's truck won't go any faster."

Ahead of them, his brother's half ton belched black smoke from the tail pipe as it rounded a corner. In Brandon's single headlight, Cheryl could just make out the mud-splattered license plate tied on with binder twine.

"Why'd Fred driving his huntin' truck?"

"Dad's got the other one. Shithead!"

The lights were so bright inside the car that Cheryl frowned as she, too, turned to glare at the vehicle behind them.

"It's a sport ute," she observed.

"Fuckin' tourist."

"Maybe we should just pull over, Bran."

"Screw that, it's not his road. Besides, even if we did, which we're not, he'd just pull the same shit on Fred, and *he's* liable to shoot the fucker."

As they slowed to round the corner, the other vehicle drew even closer. With an incoherent growl, Brandon shot the cigarette butt out the window. "Okay, that's fuckin' it. Can you drive?" Without waiting for an answer, he released the wheel and turned around to glare into the approaching head lights, his blue eyes already wide and dark. The static electricity inside the car rose suddenly, sending his dark blond hair dancing across his shoulders.

Cheryl caught the steering wheel with one hand. "What are you doing?" she demanded.

His eyes impossibly wide in his thin face, Brandon grimaced. "Imagining a big . . . brick . . . wall."

She frowned. "Don't kill him, Bran."

"Who said I was gonna kill him?"

"I mean it, Brandon."

"Fine, if you're so eager to save his ass, flip it outta there on impact, 'cause there's going to be one, big, fuckin' impact."

Glaring at him, Cheryl's own blue eyes went dark. "Fine."

"Fine."

"Fine!"

"Shh."

Brandon raised one hand, then smacked it against the side of the car. Within seconds there was a terrible crash behind them and the headlights snapped off. Brandon turned back to the road, accepting the wheel again with an even expression. Glancing into his rearview mirror at the comfortable darkness, he nodded grimly. "That's more like it."

Next morning, they pulled up in front of Fred and Lisa's trailer. It sat in the middle of a wide pasture field with two strands of electric fence keeping the nearby herd of cows at bay. As they parked, they spotted Lisa sitting outside with her mother and two sisters, while half a dozen children and as many dogs and cats played among the piles of rusty farm machinery and old auto parts that littered the front yard. Brandon paused to light a cigarette before reaching through the window to open the car door from the outside.

"Hey, Janet."

The older woman nodded back at him.

"Auntie Cheryl!"

Cheryl was immediately swarmed by children as Brandon made his way into the trailer, passing so that Lisa's sister Anne could give him a big hug.

"Hey, Anne."

She smiled mutely at him.

"You lookin' after everyone today?"

She nodded happily.

Brandon squeezed her shoulder and continued on through the patched screen door.

Fred was seated at the kitchen table working on a weed whacker. Brandon shook his head.

"Haven't you got that fixed yet? You've had it a week."

Ignoring him, Fred pulled the starter cord. Pieces of grass and yellow nylon began to spew from the engine which then began to smoke. He snapped it off with a curse. "I've had it fixed three fuckin' times this week," he growled, reaching for his cigarettes. "I swear Dad's goin' blind."

"So why don't you get Lisa to do a little mojo on it?"

"Because I don't need her to. It would work fine if Dad would stop catching up wire and fuckin' binder twine." He glanced up. "Get a beer, I'll be a while."

"Please Auntie Cheryl, please."

"Aw, c'mon, Auntie Cheryl."

"Pleeease."

By the time the two brothers left the trailer, Cheryl had made her way to the front steps, but was still surrounded by children. They kept up a constant barrage of begging and, as Brandon dropped down beside her, he clapped his hands over his ears. "What's goin' on?" he demanded.

A small, blonde girl of seven turned an aggrieved expression in his direction. "Auntie Cheryl won't let us go flying."

"What, you're still too little to do it yourself, Caitlin?"

The girl jerked her head in indignation. "I can do *me,* Uncle Bran," she answered in a voice dripping with condescension, "but I can't raise everyone by myself, and Cousin Debbie wants to come, too."

"Oh, she does, does she?"

Brandon glanced at the small, dark-haired woman seated in a wheelchair beside Janet. She stared off into space, oblivious to the chaos around her. "Says who?"

"Says Joe."

He turned to the older boy standing beside Cheryl, who nodded vigorously. "I felt it," he declared. "She's bored and she wants to fly. C'mon, Auntie Cheryl. Please." His voice changed to a more manipulative tone. "Daryl and I'll dig up that garden for you. You know Uncle Bran'll never get around to it."

Brandon gave Cheryl a sideways glance to see if she

was wavering. She sighed. "All right, but, Caitlin, you have to help me."

The girl jumped up and down excitedly as Cheryl stood. "Right then, everyone who wants to fly get in a big circle, but make sure yous hold onto Debbie nice and tight now, I don't want any accidents."

The children scrambled to do her bidding. Joe unlocked the lap belt around Debbie's waist and helped her to stand as a dozen little hands caught hold of her.

"Ready?"

"Ready!"

"You comin', too, Uncle Bran?" Daryl called over his shoulder.

"Naw, last time I let your Auntie Cheryl fly me, she tossed me down next to the lawn mower and I don't have time to mess with it right now. Fred and I have important business in town."

"Like what?" Lisa demanded.

"Like a job search?" Janet interjected hopefully.

"Like using my beer money to pay your daughter's speeding tickets before she gets busted," Fred answered smoothly. The two men headed down the driveway as the ring of children, Debbie in their midst, began to rise off the ground.

"Don't be cuttin' through Lewis Clapp's old field today," Janet called after them. "That fella who bought the place last year moved in yesterday, and he's already got a bunch of no huntin' signs up."

Brandon shrugged. "And?"

"And keep away from him," Lisa added. "I ran into Christine from the real estate office in town this morning and she say's he works for some Toronto tabloid as a writer or a reporter or something."

"So?"

"So, brain case, this," she gestured at the children already hovering four feet above the ground, "is probably why he's here."

"Big deal," Fred sneered. "We've had guys like him snooping around before. Nobody tells him anything, and after one summer of dodging mosquitoes and black flies he'll piss off back to the city."

"It's not that simple this time, Fred," Janet answered.

"Why not?"

"Because his grandmother was Dorothy Mynaker."

"Aw, shit."

Slowly the children sank back to the ground.

"Hey, isn't that Lisa's newspaper guy?"

Brandon glanced over to where Fred was pointing. Down the driveway of an old stone farmhouse, a heavy-set man in his early sixties was hosing bird droppings off the roof of his car.

"Could be."

"Shit, another damned sport ute. What is it with those things?"

Brandon made a tight u-turn through the shallow ditch on the right, and Fred glanced at him curiously.

"What're you doing?"

"Meetin' our new neighbor."

"You can't."

"Why not?"

"What do you mean why not. Because his grand-mother was Dorothy Mynaker and even two genera-tions past the Mynakers still have the Sight. You can't take the piss with him, Bran."

His brother grinned. "Who says I'm going to," he answered, the growing darkness in his eyes belying his words.

"He'll know. The Mynakers can See right through the best illusion you could make."

"Maybe the best I could make, but I bet he wouldn't be able to See through the best both of us could make."

Fred shook his head vehemently. "No way. Lisa'd kill me."

"Whose gonna tell her?"

"She'll *know*, Bran."

"She takes after her Dad. Just think about power tools for a couple of hours and she'll never catch on."

"You're a fucking idiot, you know that?"

"Just do it, eh?"

Fred growled an incoherent reply, but by the time they reached the driveway, smoke was pouring from the sport ute's engine. The man was standing by the open hood, a fire extinguisher in one hand and a panicked expression on his face. He looked up as the two brothers got out of the car, and Brandon immediately noticed the distinctive Mynaker nose. Pushing up his ball cap, he made his way over.

"Mornin'."

"Good morning."

"Havin' a bit of trouble?"

"I am." The man wiped his hand clear on a rag before sticking it out. "George Prescott."

Taking quick note of his good shoes, new jeans, and expensive watch, Brandon shook his hand with a faint smile. "Brandon Geoffries, this is my brother Fred. You'll wanna get that looked at."

"I will, yes. The problem is I just moved in last night, and the phone won't be hooked up until Monday morning." He frowned. "My cell phone doesn't seem to work out here either."

"No, it wouldn't," Fred answered, his head already buried in the sport ute's engine.

"We're in a dead zone," Brandon explained. "From Mill Valley all the way out past Rocky Point. You'll need a big antenna to get clear TV or radio reception, and cell phones don't work at all." He glanced over the farm house. "Irene Clapp never did get an antenna; she didn't care much for TV. You gonna be here long?"

"Just for the summer likely."

"Right." Brandon's gaze took in the dilapidated side porch. "You'll want to get that looked at anyway before it falls down on top of yous."

"And cleaned as well. It has a very funny smell."

"Yeah, well, it would. Lewis Clapp used to keep pigeons in it. When he died, Irene just closed it up and used the back door from then on."

"That would explain all the droppings."

"Likely." Brandon lit a cigarette. "So I hear you're Dorothy Mynaker's grandson."

George looked over in surprise. "Yes, yes that's right." He laughed a bit nervously. "Small towns, eh?"

"Yeah. We'd be related, then."

George suddenly smiled. "Really?"

"Yeah, more or less. Dorothy's Uncle Paul was my great great grandfather. So you're a Geoffries through your Great grandmother Sarah. That makes us third cousins, I figure."

A sudden hungry look flashed in the other man's eyes. "So you know the family history," he asked hesitantly, "the Mynaker history, I mean?"

"Sure. Don't you?"

"Not really. I only know what my grandfather told me. He met my grandmother during the war, you see, and the First World War at that. She was a nurse, and he was an army medic. They married after the war and moved to Toronto where his family was from. She died of rheumatic fever soon after my father was born, so all I really know is her name and that she was from a tiny place called Blind Duck Island. I thought about getting a place out there, to—well, you know—but the real estate agent said no one lives there anymore. A pity."

"Yeah, a pity."

The sound of Fred banging the hood down interrupted their conversation. Brandon turned. "Can't work it?"

Fred shook his head in disgust. "Looks like you've got multiple problems with your electrics there," he said, shooting a glare in his brother's direction. "These new sport utes are tricky."

George deflated, and Brandon cocked his head toward the station wagon.

"We can take you up to Mill Valley," he offered. "There's a pay phone at Barry's General Store. You can call a mechanic from there."

"Thank you. That would be wonderful. Just let me get my jacket."

The older man headed into the house and Brandon turned. "I thought you said we couldn't take the piss on him?" he asked in a smug tone.

Fred shot him the finger. "We didn't. His engine's a mess. I'm amazed the thing didn't break down on the way here. It was only a matter of time."

"Yeah, well, now you don't have to worry about Lisa killing you. We're doin' him a favor." Brandon glanced over as George came out the front door, carefully locking it behind him, and shook his head.

"Like a lamb to the fuckin' slaughter," he muttered. "Come on."

Barry Thomson was busy at the postal counter putting stamps on a stack of letters for an older woman. He grinned at the three men as they came in.

"Hey, Bran, Fred."

"Hey, Barry." Brandon pointed George in the direction of the pay phone before heading toward a wall of videos.

"Did ya hear about the big accident out on County Road One last night?" Barry asked, leaned eagerly against the counter.

Squinting at the back of a dusty video box, Brandon shook his head.

"Big sport ute. One of the new ones. Hit a tree out past the old Dulmage place. The driver walked away, but the car's totaled."

Fred glanced from Barry to Brandon and back again.

"Deer?" he asked in a neutral tone.

"Maybe. Ken said the guy kept babbling about this big wall suddenly appearing out of nowhere right in front of him."

"No kidding."

Brandon returned the video to its slot on the wall and pulled out another one. "Must have been drunk," he observed mildly.

"Yeah. Must have been."

"Excuse me?"

Barry glanced over, took in George's clothes and demeanor as Brandon had done, and his mouth quirked up slightly.

"Help you with somethin'?"

"Yes, you could actually. I need a tow truck and a good local mechanic. I was wondering if you could recommend anyone for me?"

"I guess I could. You're from Toronto, eh? Bought Irene Clapp's old place last fall?"

"Yes. That's right. I supposed everyone knows by now."

"Probably. Well, there's Gary Wallace. He's got a garage in Greenville."

Brandon glanced over. "Turns out George is Dorothy Mynaker's grandson, Barry."

A slight widening of the eyes was the store owner's only reaction. "Call Art Akorman. Likely he can fix it up right no the spot." He glanced over at the two brothers. "I'm surprised Fred here couldn't get it running for you," he noted. "He's a real wiz with mechanical things. Not as good as his wife, mind." He winked at Brandon. "But, hell, she's Art's daughter, so he's laboring under a handicap, I guess."

Fred bared his teeth at him. "It's got nothing to do with being a wiz at anything," he growled. "I'm not good with complicated electrical shit, you know that."

Barry just laughed. "If you take him up to Art's place now, you could deliver his paper for me." He turned toward the backroom. "Hey, Shirl, you got Art's *Gazette*?"

The newspaper came flying toward his head, and only Brandon noticed that Cheryl's cousin Shirley hadn't bothered to actually touch it. Barry caught it before it put his eye out and tossed it to Fred in a more conventional manner. "That way he could run George back to his place and have a look without coming into town," he finished.

"I don't want to be any trouble," George said diffidently. "I could just catch a cab back and wait for him at home."

The three men turned to stare at him.

"Don't be a fool, George," Brandon said wearily. "You don't take cabs when you have family."

"Shit, even if you don't have family, you don't take cabs," Fred scoffed. "It'd cost you twenty bucks to get out there."

"Well, that's not so much, is it?"

Brandon sighed. "Just get in the car, George."

On the way to Fred's father-in-law's, George turned a curious look on Brandon. "Gary Wallace is not the best mechanic in the world?" he asked with mock innocence.

Brandon glanced over with a smile. "Oh, he's all right," he allowed.

"When he's sober," Fred added.

"He just has a little trouble adding up the bill right. But he's okay for some folk."

"For city folk, you mean?"

"For city folk who don't know any better," Fred expanded.

"Good thing I'm Dorothy Mynaker's grandson, then, isn't it?"

Brandon kept his eyes fixed on the road as a line of gravel trucks drove past them. "Yeah," he answered quietly. "It is."

Art Akorman was only too happy to accompany the three men back to the sport ute. Once there, he and Fred huddled over the engine while Brandon and George took a seat on the weathered planking around a old willow stump.

Brandon lit a cigarette, staring out over the distant fields before speaking.

"So you're here to look up Blind Duck Island, then, eh?" he asked casually.

"That's right."

"Awful big purchase, this. For a summer visit, I mean."

"Well, the price was right. I thought if I liked it I might retire out here, if not, I could always fix it up and sell it again."

"You're not retired yet?"

"Why, do I look that old?" the other man asked with a chuckle.

Brandon looked over at the lines about his mouth and eyes and shrugged. "You look like you might be," he said truthfully.

"Yes, well. I'm on a medical leave of absence, actually. My paper insisted after my third heart attack. You did know I was a journalist."

It wasn't a question and Brandon just nodded. "Sure. Your cousin Lisa's already got the scoop on yous from your real estate agent this morning."

"My *cousin* Lisa?"

"Yeah, Fred's wife. The girl who's better at mechanical things than he is," he added loudly.

A muffled, "Fuck you, Bran," could be heard from the depths of the engine.

"I thought Fred was my cousin, too," George asked with an amused smile.

"Sure he is, third cousin. Lisa'd be you second cousin through Dorothy's sister Elsie."

"So Fred and Lisa are cousins, too?"

Brandon shrugged dismissively. "Well, fourths, like you said, small towns. We aren't exactly in town, but it's the same thing."

"There do seem to be a lot of cousins about."

"You don't know the half of it."

A few minutes later Art pulled his head from the sport ute's engine. "Can't do anything for you here," he said apologetically. "You've got a small problem with your thermostat. I fixed that up no problem, but your timing belt's so worn it looks about to snap and the electrics look pretty burned too. Also, you're hea-

din' into a major oil leak there. When was the last
time you had 'er in?"

George blinked. "Two weeks ago. My mechanic
said it was all ship shape and ready to go."

"He did, huh? Well, I'd fire him if I was you; the
guy's an idiot. Anyway, you'll want that belt replaced
if nothin' else. I'd best get it back to my place, I've
got more tools there."

George squinted worriedly at him. "When did you
think it might be done?"

Art shrugged. "No time at all if you just want the
belt done. A day or two for the rest. Can you drive
a standard?"

"It's been a while, but yes I can. Why?"

"Well, I've got an old half ton you could use in the
meantime if you like."

"That would be very nice of you, if it wouldn't put
you out? I don't want to be a bother."

Art shrugged again. "No bother, you're family.
Fred, why don't you come along with me. That way
you can bring the truck back."

"Sure, Art."

George frowned. "Shouldn't we maybe follow in
case the timing belt does go."

Art shook his head. "It won't. Not while I'm drivin'
it." Hitching up his pants, he accepted the keys and
slid in behind the wheel, his eyes already wide and
dark.

"I was wondering if we might continue our conversation about the family."

George and the two brothers were sitting on what
was left of side porch sharing a beer and watching the
sun go down. In the last week they'd torn down the
roof and walls and much of the stairs. Brandon lit a
cigarette before answering.

"Sure. Whadda ya wanna know?"

"Well, I noticed something very interesting when I
went up to the archives yesterday. Hold on, I'll get my
notes." He hustled into the house, emerging with a small

laptop computer. "Most of the area residents are listed as having been born either in Mill Valley or, after the local hospital closed down, in Greenville," he said after a few moments' pecking at the keys. "But all the local Mynakers are listed as being born on Blind Duck Island, even your cousin Daryl, and he's . . . just a minute, it's here somewhere, oh, yes, he's just ten. So I dug a little deeper—I hope you don't mind—and I discovered that it's not just the Mynakers. You yourselves are listed as being born on Blind Duck Island as well, and a great many others. Four different families in fact, but that can't be right, surely."

Brandon and Fred looked over with identically neutral expressions. "How'd you figure?" Fred asked finally.

"Well, as I told you, my real estate agent said that no one's lived there for years, and the clerk at the archives agrees. He says there's no electricity no the Island, never mind any kind of medical facilities. He say's there's some kind of magnetic anomaly out in the lake that interferes with electrical equipment: generators, water pumps, telephones, you name it. So when the electricity came in, all the people on Blind Duck moved to the mainland. So I went out there . . ."

Brandon glanced over curiously, and George shrugged. "I mean, I went out to Rocky Point to have a look at it, and it seems abandoned just like they said it was.

"That's because no one's lived there for years," Fred echoed in a condescending tone.

"But what about all these birth records?"

"What about 'em?"

"Why do they list Blind Duck Island as your place of birth?"

The two men exchanged a glance, then Brandon shrugged. "Because that's where we were born. It's our island."

"How do you mean?"

"I mean its our island, ours." Brandon stubbed out his cigarette. "In 1794 a sheep farmer name of Samuel

Essen and his wife Mary settled on one hundred acres on Blind Duck Island. They had four daughters: Edith, Doris, Ruth and Agnes. They married four local fishermen: Garret Geoffries, John Frawst, Joseph Mynaker, and Roy Akorman. Between 'em they owned the entire island. We're their descendants."

"But why. . . ?"

"Because it's a family tradition, okay," Fred snapped. "That's why."

"Oh, uh, of course," George stammered, taken aback by the vehemence of the other man's reaction. "Um, do you know where Samuel and Mary Essen were from?" he asked, glancing at Brandon who shrugged.

"Dunno."

"But you do know the exact date they came to the county?"

"Sure. It's on the deed for the original hundred acres."

"But not where they're from?"

"Nope."

"Do any of the families still own land on Blind Duck Island?"

"What'd ya think, that our mothers birthed us on the beach?" Fred asked caustically.

"No, I just . . . George closed the computer. "Maybe we should talk about his another time."

"Naw, it's okay," Brandon interjected, shooting a flat look at his brother. "All the families own land on the Island, George. Our grandmother still has the original hundred acres of Essen land."

"Really?"

"Yeah," Fred answered with a grimace, helping himself to one of Brandon's cigarettes. "It'll go to Bran here eventually, the little prick."

"There's other parcels," Brandon retorted.

"Not as good."

"So fuckin' suffer."

"But nobody actually lives there now?" George interrupted.

"Nope."

"No one at all?"

"No. Why?"

"It's just that I saw a boat tied up there the other day."

Fred glanced at Brandon.

"How'd you see that, George?" he asked casually.

"Modern technology, Fred, you know, binoculars."

"Right."

"Some of the families still go over," Brandon answered. "For camping and get togethers, that sort of thing. Somethings they live there for a while in the summer."

"The winters are hard, though," Fred added.

"Right, you wouldn't want to live there in winter."

The next day they started on the floor. The concrete foundation was soft and crumbling from years of rain and, with mingled curses the two brothers went at it with sledge hammers and shovels while George and Art went into town to pick up lumber for the new porch.

That evening they accepted a beer, and covered in dust, settled back against the house. Careful to keep upwind, George opened his laptop again.

"I went back up to the archives this morning," he began. "With the information you gave me, I was able to piece together a fairly accurate family tree. You, I mean we," he amended with a slightly self-conscious smile, "are a pretty comingled group."

Fred glanced over. "Yep, that's us, the inbred hill-billy folk of the county."

"Actually the thought had occurred to me," George admitted after a careful glance assured him that Brandon, at least, hadn't taken offense. "I cross-referenced that with other statistics and came up with some rather disturbing numbers. The families all seem to have a very high percentage of birth defects and developmental and physical handicaps like Down's syndrome and cerebral palsy. Disproportionately high for the area."

Fred spat a wad of phlegm and dust onto the ground. "So?"

"So I was just curious about why?"

Brandon shrugged. "Maybe it's somethin' in the water," he said in a deadpan voice.

Fred shot him a warning glance, but George just chuckled. "Maybe." He grew thoughtful. "Maybe. Have there ever been any tests done for water quality?"

Brandon shook his head.

"None at all? Not even for *e coli* or other bacteria?"

"No."

Fred leaned forward. "No one lives there, George. Why would there be any tests?" His tone was faintly menacing, and George's eyes widened.

"Well, no reason at all, of course," he stammered. He turned to Brandon. "I'm um, I'm heading up to the library tomorrow to see if I can find anything on Samuel and Mary Essen. Would it be all right, do you think, if I studied the geography and history of the area as well?" He smiled disarmingly. "It's just the reporter in me, I can't leave a good mystery unsolved, you see."

"Plannin' to write a story on it or somethin'?"

"Um, no, I wasn't."

"Then I guess it's okay. After all," Brandon glanced over at Fred. "You are family."

The smell of frying onions permeated Brandon and Cheryl's small farmhouse. Seated on the couch by the stove, Fred leaned over to pluck one long ring from the pan before catching the beer Brandon tossed at him. At the kitchen table, Lisa was cutting up mushrooms with a worried expression.

"So how much did you tell him?" she asked.

Brandon glanced over at the small cardboard box by the woodstove to check on Cheryl's new cat before answering.

"How much should I have told him?"

Cheryl turned from the stove. "Bran?"

He grimaced. "The history. Look, he's just guy searching for his past, okay. And he's family. He has the right to know."

"But how much?"

"Everything."

Even Fred turned to stare at him. "You can't tell him everything, Bran. He's from the city. He won't get it."

"He'll get it. He's a Mynaker."

"He's a Mynaker who writes for a tabloid," Lisa added. "What if he wants to put what you tell him in his paper?"

"He won't."

"But what if he does?"

The room was quiet as Brandon lit a cigarette, blowing a long stream of smoke into the air.

Cheryl stirred. "Bran?"

"I'd stop him."

That night, lying in bed beside him, Cheryl turned. "You like him, don't you?" she asked.

Bran shrugged. "Sure. He's a good guy."

"Lisa's positive he's here to dig up dirt on the families."

"Lisa's also positive the IGA raises its prices at the end of the month to gouge everyone on pogy."

Cheryl poked him in the side. "Just be careful what you tell him, okay?"

Bran wormed his arm under her shoulders. "Worried?"

"A little."

"Then I'll be careful."

They fell silent, each thinking their own thoughts and listening to the frogs singing in the ditches. After awhile Cheryl stirred again.

"There's always one way to convince him," she said quietly.

"How?"

"Take him to the Island. If he's there long enough, it might call up his blood."

"He'd have to be there an awfully long time; he wasn't born there, remember. And I don't think he could manage without all his techno shit. He's not used to hand pumps and outhouses like we are."

"Yeah, but he'd manage better if we were there with him."

Brandon laughed. "And why would we be there with him?"

"Because I'm pregnant."

The next day they cleaned up the last of the old side porch. George leaned against the house and wiped his face with a handkerchief, looking up with dismay at the line of bees going back and forth between the spaces in the upper bricks. "I thought I heard buzzing," he said morosely. "I guess I'll need to call in the exterminators."

Fred shook his head. "Waste of money. We could probably get 'em out ourselves. I betcha they've got a shit load of honey up there."

George looked doubtful. "Well, I don't know. I doubt they'd hold off stinging me just because I'm Dorothy Mynaker's grandson," he joked.

"No, you'd have to be Edna Frawst's grandson for that."

The older man glanced over at Brandon who'd been uncharacteristically silent all morning. "So what do you think?" He asked with forced good humor. "Do we get Edna Frawst's grandson over here to help us?"

Brandon shrugged. "Why don't you just leave 'em alone."

The older man frowned uncertainly. "Well, I could, I suppose. After all, I'm not actually using the upstairs, but I should do something about them, though, shouldn't I? I mean if we're going to build the new side porch, they'll be in the way, won't they?"

"Probably," Brandon tossed his cigarette butt to the ground, crushing it with unusual violence. "Look, George. I can't help you build the new porch, okay. You'll have to get someone else."

George flushed. "Um, of course," he answered quickly. "I, uh, I know I've imposed quite a bit on you both since I came here. If it's a question of money. . . ?"

"Money's got nothin' to do with it. Cheryl and I are movin' out to the Island."

George blinked. "The Island? Blind Duck Island?"

" 'S right."

"But . . ." he glanced from one brother to the other. "Isn't it uninhabitable?"

"Not quite."

The four families began to congregate on the Island as soon as they heard the news. Most would come and go throughout the summer, using the old Essen place as the main meeting house, but Brandon and Cheryl would be staying there until after the baby was born. Standing on the shore, George watched Brandon maneuver a rowboat full of boxes to the Island's single dock, with a frown. He'd been arguing against the move for three days now with no success. The younger man had simply extended Cheryl's invitation to come along and begun packing up the farmhouse.

"It's beautiful I'll admit," he said, "but you can't honestly be thinking about living here, I mean really."

Brandon held out a box with an amused expression. "Sure looks that way, don't it?"

"But it's madness. Where does this go?"

"Leave it. Fred'll come get it."

George placed the box carefully on the crumbling dock and accepted another.

"But there's no power," he continued.

"So, who needs power? The kid'll be born in October."

"But what if something happens?"

"Nuthin's gonna happen."

"Like nothing happened to your cousin Debbie and your Cousin Anne?"

Brandon's eyes narrowed. "There's nothin' wrong with Debbie and Anne."

George just stared at him and Brandon shoved a box into his arms with more force than usual.

"Just leave it alone, okay?"

"So I hear yous don't want Cheryl and Brandon to move out here."

Seated around the woodstove in the Essen house kitchen, Janet passed George a cup of coffee before catching him in a penetrating stare. Outside they could hear the sound of children's laughter as they ran along the beach. George shrugged.

"I just think it's dangerous to give birth outside a hospital," he explained, "Especially with the medical histories I've uncovered."

"Uh-huh. You married, George?"

"I'm divorced."

"Kids?"

"One, a daughter." He gave her a challenging look. "She married a man named David Cole last summer. She's a teacher's aide, he works in computers. His family's from Campbellford, and his parents run a drug store."

Ignoring the sarcastic tone in his voice, Janet poured herself a cup of coffee. "She know you're here researching your roots?"

He glanced away. "We haven't really spoken much since the divorce. I was invited to the wedding, but . . ."

"But?"

"But her mother was there, and, well . . . I didn't want it to be awkward for them. I sent them a nice gift, though. And a card," he added.

"You lookin' forward to grandchildren?"

"Well, of course I am, what kind of a question is that?"

It was her turn to shrug. "You want what's best for them?" she asked instead of answering his question. "For the grandchildren? You want 'em to have every advantage, right?"

"Yes, certainly I do."

"Well, so do we. To do that, the children have be

born on the Island whatever the risks. If your grandmother had made it back to birth your father, you'd
understand that."

"What do you mean, made it back? My grandmother wasn't coming back."

"No?" She placed an old, yellowed envelope on the
table in front of him. "I took this from my grandmother Elsie's things. They wrote a lot of letters back
and forth during the war, and it's all there. Dorothy
Prescott was coming home to have her baby on Blind
Duck Island just like every other Mynaker woman for
generations has done. But she got sick, and she never
made it home."

George just shook his head. "That doesn't make
any sense, she was an educated woman, a nurse. Why
would she do that?"

Janet sipped her coffee. "Bran'll explain it to you."

Brandon glanced over in surprise. "I will?"

She nodded. "Art and I talked it over with your
folks. He's family. He has the right to know. But
Bran?"

"Yeah?"

"Make sure he gets it."

The two men walked silently along the Island's south
shore, Brandon's expression thoughtful, George's quizzi-
cal, almost amused. Beside an old, upside-down fishing
boat, Brandon paused to lit a cigarette, then stared
out across the water.

"They call this part of the lake the Graveyard," he
said. "More ships have gone down along here than
even in the Bermuda Triangle."

George chuckled. "Really?"

"Sure. With you bein' a tabloid writer and all, I
thought you might have known that."

The older man looked embarrassed. "I don't actually read the articles," he admitted.

"That's probably a good thing." Brandon jerked his
head toward the lake.

"It's out there, about a quarter mile away," he said.

"What its?"

"Your magnetic anomaly."

"Really?"

"Yep. Folk say that in 1794 they saw a huge shooting star hit the lake. It caused the water to boil and killed all the fish for miles. Catch was low for ten years until things sorted themselves out again."

George's eyes widened. "In 1794?"

"That's right."

The wind around them picked up suddenly as Brandon's eyes grew dark.

"They say it's still out there, whatever it was, buried in lake mud. Maybe it was a meteor, maybe it was somethin' else. All I know is that sometimes at night when the water's real clear, you can almost see somethin' glowing way down deep."

George turned to stare out at the water. Far off, he could almost see something rippling just below the waves. He swallowed.

"That's what causes the handicaps," Brandon continued. "But it causes a lot more than that. We don't talk about it in the county, but everyone around here knows the families are different. As long as we don't bother them, they don't bother us. But the kids have to be born within sight of the anomaly for their abilities to surface."

George continued to stare out at the lake.

"Abilities?"

Brandon turned, the blue of his eyes totally obliterated by darkness. "Sure, George. How'd ya figure we manage to live out here without power?"

All around him the rocks began to give off a warm, yellow glow. Brandon's eyes grew until they took up much of his upper face, his skin rippling with a silvery hue.

George left quickly, explaining that he had some packing to do if he were going to stay on Blind Duck Island for any length of time. Art went with him and, as Fred watched the two older men row back to the mainland, he helped himself to one of Brandon's cigarettes with a grimace.

"You told him we were *aliens*?" he asked incredulously.

"Not exactly. I just made him *think* I told him we were aliens."

"But why?"

" 'Cause otherwise we'd just be people with weird mutant powers, and that wouldn't be enough to protect us. Folk like George need really extreme answers to justify leavin' things alone."

"And you think that's enough to keep him away from his computer?"

"Sure. He needs family. That's why he came back here. Now that he knows we're special, that he's special, he'll keep it secret. The only way you can take the piss on a Mynaker is if he wants you to. Besides he's not gonna let his grandchildren be dissected like a bunch of lab rats. He may not read the tabloid articles, but he knows what they say."

Fred took a long drag on his cigarette.

"*Are* we aliens, Bran?" he asked quietly.

"Naw."

"So what are we?"

Brandon looked back toward the house. Above the trees a ring of children hovered in the air, Debbie in their midst. His eyes grew dark, and a fine rainbow suddenly arched over their heads. Debbie's face broke out in a huge smile.

"We're family," he answered simply.

Plucking the cigarette from his brother's fingers, he took a drag, then tossed the butt into the water, before making his way back to the house, while out on the water George Prescott watched his young cousins fly, with a wondering smile.

RITE OF PASSAGE
by Jody Lynn Nye

Jody Lynn Nye lists her main career activity as "spoiling cats." She lives northwest of Chicago with two of the above and her husband, author and packager Bill Fawcett. She has written twenty-two books, including four contemporary fantasies, three SF novels, four novels in collaboration with Anne McCaffrey, including *The Ship Who Won*, a humorous anthology about mothers, *Don't Forget Your Spacesuit, Dear!*, and over sixty short stories. Her latest books are *License Invoked,* co-authored with Robert Asprin (Phule's Company), and *Advanced Mythology,* fourth in the Mythology series.

The walls vibrated gently, but constantly, which was not surprising in an old tramp freighter of obsolete design. The world government didn't use its shiny new spaceships to get rid of a few unimportant exiles.

"So what they get you for?" the dog-faced boy asked Dimitrios Palos.

Dimitrios adjusted his dark spectacles and huddled into his collar so that most of his face was hidden by his long, black hair. It was too bright in the cargo ship's cabin. "I was breaking into Vim's warehouse. I've got a hundred people outside waiting for me to open the doors, so they could get in at the food. I can see every infrared alarm, every laser-tie. I have terrific three-dee memory, so I don't touch them even when I am in the middle of them. I miss them all. I'm within a dozen feet of the control panel. What happens? I crawl onto a pressure plate, and it sets off every siren in Cleveland. Every cop in the world zooms in."

"Bummer," said the dog-faced boy. "So you can see lasers and infrared? Cool."

"Yeah. Ultraviolet, too." What he didn't want to say aloud was that he could see through layers of skin and muscle, watch the flow of blood, even the faint electric tick of synapses firing. Dimitrios was already seeing the heat drain out of the faces of the two guards sitting across from him as their blood vessels constricted with alarm. The layers of maxilofacial muscles of the man closer to the door wrinkled. He was sneering, Dimitrios knew what he was thinking: *Mutants. Ugh.* If they knew what else he could see, they'd hold him down and pluck his eyes out. "So, what's your name and perversion?"

"Stu Trimble, sniffer. As if you couldn't tell. And you can spare me the old joke. You know? 'He's got a nose like a bloodhound, and the rest of his face isn't so good either.' I've heard it."

"I can imagine. Call me Meech," Dimitrios said in a voice that hid his anger and frustration.

"Pleased to Meech-a," Stu said, his wide nose quivering. "How about you, babe?"

This to the huddled mass of thick thermal blankets on the pallet in the corner. Meech could see the heat signature silhouetting the shape of the body within the cloth wrapping, and wondered only briefly how Stu could tell it was female. Duh.

"Co–colleen," the bundle said in a throaty soprano voice. "Can't you turn up the heat in here? I'm going to die."

The guards, a pair of crewmen wearing black uniforms piped in royal blue and visorless helmets, didn't even look her way.

"It's pretty warm already," Stu said.

"Not for her," said the motherly, dark-skinned woman on the pallet at the other end of the room with her arms around the last two transportees, a boy and girl in padded body suits. "She's Salamander Girl. She sits in a live fire all day long, blowing kisses to the punters. I'm Elastic Woman—Cindy Lumaba to you guys. This is Carmen and Bobby. We're all from Pittipat's Circus. They did a sweep last night. Found out we *weren't* fakes, and hauled us off planet before we could call a lawyer."

"Wouldn't have done you any good anyway," the first guard said, not without sympathy, to Meech's surprise. He had sallow skin and thin, dark lips and brows, and a nervous habit of grinding his back teeth that Meech found amusing to watch. "Anti-Mutant Act doesn't allow for appeals."

The bundle of cloth shivered violently.

"You can have my blanket," Meech said, pulling it out from underneath him. "Her temp's at least 20° higher than ours. She's freezing."

"You can have mine, too," Stu said.

Fellow exiles, Meech thought, sharing what little they had. In his opinion, the Anti-Mutant Act of 2166 was the most useless piece of legislation ever passed on the planet Earth. It didn't save anyone from anything. It didn't stop hunger or the chronic food shortages, which were more horrible than anything one single "enhanced" human was capable of doing, and it didn't do a single thing to address the catastrophic pollution and contamination of food, air, water, and soil that had given rise to most of the mutations in the first place. It caused innocent people to get the hell beaten out of them any time they stuck their noses out of doors, because they didn't belong.

And none of that was by accident. The bright idea EarthGov had was to get rid of the mutants, one and all. The reason Meech was stealing in the first place was because he and his fellow outcasts were forbidden to have jobs where they would have contact with the public, automatically creating an unemployed underclass reliant upon food subsidies that were not enough to nourish a sick mouse, let alone growing children or adults. It was, in fact, a deliberate action to make mutants turn themselves in for transportation off planet, where they wouldn't soil good ol' Earth with their presence.

Space exploration had uncovered a string of useful planets circling groups of contiguous stars, and some scattered ones in other systems. Some bright son-of-a-bitch figured out that one of these not very valuable worlds off the beaten trail would make a great holding pen for those people Earth never wanted to see again but didn't want to murder openly. Thanatos Planet was a fresh start, the authorities said, a new world, untouched, unsullied by technology or pollution. To the average Normal, it sounded like a pretty good deal, since they didn't have to go. To anybody a degree off beam, it was exile to hell.

"I heart it's not so bad," Stu said, voicing what they were all thinking.

"Yeah? Subsistence farming?" Meech asked, acidly.

"I'm from a farm. My family has been hiding me all these years. It wasn't until the census inspectors came around for a spot-check that they had to produce every living being on the property. They missed me the first time ten years ago because I had a cold. I couldn't hide any longer." Meech nodded. He'd heard plenty of familiar stories. I'm good with machines, but there's things I can do that machines can't. Dad used me to sniff out truffles." Stu grinned. "Dad figured take what the good Lord handed out, and make the best of it."

"Well, I like cities," Meech said. "I like technology. I don't want to live like an animal."

"No choice, freak," growled the second guard, shifting so he could put his hand on the hilt of his sidearm. It was a warning. The prisoners fell silent.

Mutants in big cities formed underground communities, but they lived as widely scattered as those new-found planets, to avoid capture and deportation. Meech knew he had it better than most. His mutation wasn't visible, as long as he kept his glasses on. His irises were a multicolored swirl, from palest blue to darkest black. "Like a Magic Eye picture," one of his girlfriends had said. So they called him Magic Eye. He liked the nickname at first, but dropped it as soon as he realized it drew the cops' attention to him. Pretty soon, it did. He had to hide out, going abroad in darkness to forage. His talent was useful, after all. If there was even a footcandle of light he could see as well as a Normal in daylight, and he could read the infrared images of people through walls, giving him time to get away when security guards making their rounds came his way.

No more of that. He missed the city already. The excitement, the flow of electrons everywhere, the energy. He knew his sight was much more than that which Normals possessed. They liked photographs. To Meech, photographs were bizarre, flat, dead images. He could see electricity, heat, wavelengths. He didn't lack an appreciation for beauty, but he knew what they thought was beautiful was the shallowest definition of the word. He found visceral interest in patterns of heat and cold, shape of muscles, pattern of blood flow. Not mere skin, but that was all the sad Normals could see. He thought that Cindy was beautiful. Guard One was beautiful. Even Stu, with his capacious sinuses and happy, cool mouth, had his measure of beauty. Meech wanted to get a better look at Colleen, but the shifting layers of mylar and fiber clouded her image.

The walls of the cabin in which they would be spending the next twenty days was lined with a thin layer of laser-resistant plastic over cold steel and aluminum plates. It was well sealed. He could feel the pulse of the ship through his feet, but he couldn't see anything through the heavy shielding. There was a single porthole, through which the unhappy transportees could watch—nothing. The ship was in its first of its daylong jumps toward the exile planet.

The Calderon Hop Drive wasn't perfected yet, which is why government officials were so happy to have the captured mutants to use as guinea pigs for transgalactic travel. If they died in the ships, who cared? The engineers would figure out what went wrong with the technology. It would be improved, for the sake of explorers and miners, who brought back important mineral wealth to benefit all of humanity. Normal humanity. The waste of talent and intelligence, not to mention the sheer indifference to the well-being of the people they were exiling, filled Meech with disgust.

"I want my video game," Bobby muttered, without lifting his head from Cindy's lap.

"Are there any toys on this vessel?" Cindy asked the guards. "Books? Videos? Anything?"

Guard Two ignored them. Guard One shook his head.

"They want you to get used to living without technology," he said. "All entertainment devices are forbidden to those going . . . where you're going."

"That's such crap!" Meech shouted, banging his fist on his bench. "This treatment is inhumane. These are kids!"

"Not human kids," Guard Two muttered.

"We are human, you son-of-a . . ."

"Kids present!" Cindy snapped. Meech shut up. "No wonder there's been so many suicides reported among exiles. You can't even show basic decency."

"If you'd give us these things, maybe we'd be more willing to go," Stu said, pleasantly.

"Look at it this way, buddy," Guard One said. "You're getting to start out afresh on a new world. There's no pollution. There's no crime. There's no crowding. It's better than Earth."

"Ironic, isn't it?" Meech said, sourly. "You're tossing us off the world where the pollution and radiation made us this way. If it's so good, why don't you Normals take it for yourselves?"

The logic of that seemed to arouse Guard Two, who hadn't thought about it that way, and didn't appreciate the humor. "If it was up to me, I'd shoot you in your mothers' wombs."

That frightened the little girl. She burst into tears. Cindy rocked her, glaring over her head at the smirking crewman. His expression was carefully bland, but Meech saw blood racing in his neck.

"Hey, honey," Cindy said, soothingly, kissing the child. "Let's play a little game. Catch my fingers. C'mon, try." She held up her big hand. Carmen raised her little hand. Meech saw webbing stretched in between the girl's fingers. "Okay . . . go!"

Carmen made a grab for Cindy's thumb. Suddenly, all the fingers stretched out like octopus tentacles. The attenuated thumb slipped easily out of the child's grasp. "Go on, you're not trying at all," the woman laughed. "Come on, now."

By then the little girl had been distracted out of her terror, and the boy was clamoring for his turn. The eyes of the guards dilated wide open, and their pulse and respiration quickened. Beside Meech, Stu grinned.

"You're scared," he said. "I can smell the sweat on you. That's the fear smell. You think we're going to reach right down your throat . . . and pull your guts out . . . and *eat them in front of you!*" He sprang up, hands extended like claws.

The guards flinched, reaching for their sidearms. Meech saw the veins in their necks throb even faster. Then Meech saw the temperature rise in their faces as blood rushed in. They were embarrassed for having reacted to a guy whose only extraordinary ability was sensing odors better than they could.

"Farm humor, huh?" Meech asked, enjoying the show.

"We told a lot of ghost stories," Stu said, dropping back easily onto his pallet. "You don't have to pay satellite bills when you make your own film. My daddy liked to save a few credits where he could."

"You think you're an improvement on us, huh?" Guard Two sneered. "You're freaks."

"I think *homo erectus* must've said that about *homo sapiens* once upon a time," Cindy said philosophically. "Because he couldn't recognize the future. What's the big brain case, for?" she asked in a moronic-sounding voice.

Meech and Stu laughed. They even heard a little chuckle coming from the mass of blankets enveloping Colleen. The guards pretended they didn't notice.

* * *

"I know," said Cindy, on shift three of the fifth day. "I'll tell your fortunes."

"Did you get to keep your tarot deck?" Colleen asked from her cocoon.

"Nope. I don't need it. I know every card by heart, and I see the truth. Choose a number between one and seventy-eight."

Meech appreciated how hard Cindy and Stu were trying to keep the group's spirits up. He vowed he'd protect them in any way he could once they reached Thanatos, though he wondered just exactly what value his street-savvy would have there, since his main talents were seeing things other people couldn't and sharing out the spoils of his raids on government buildings.

"That's easy," Stu said. "Number One, as in looking out for."

"The Fool," Cindy said, grinning. "Untapped potential, the beginning of a new road. Your life's not in your own control yet."

Stu shook his head. "I could have told you that. How much do I weigh?"

"For that, you need Kip Garland." She shot a quick glance at the guards. "He uses a concealed scale. No special talent."

Guard Six grunted. Guard Five was staring at the wall over their heads. The big, red-haired woman found it difficult even to look at the group. All their guards, with the exception of Guard One, appeared to have been chosen on a basis of total intolerance for mutations. They showed no sign of understanding their prisoners, or even caring about them. Meech felt as though they were so much ugly furniture. He didn't really care what they thought about him, so long as they didn't try to lay a hand on him. When the voyage ended, he'd never see them again.

"How about you, Meech?"

He straightened up a little. "Uh . . . twenty-eight. I was born on Twenty-eighth Street."

"Interesting," Cindy said. "Six of Rods. Rite of passage. Transition through difficulties into safe waters. Your efforts will bring you rewards. Rods are associated with fire. I think it has special meaning for you, though I don't know what."

"Uh-huh," Meech said, retiring to his corner to think about what she had said. She was right. His element was fire. All he saw was fire of one kind or another.

"Enough talking," Guard Six said, in a tone that brooked no argument. "Relief break. Her first." She stood up and pointed at Carmen. The little girl stared at the guard with fear. Cindy stood up and helped the child to her feet. Each deportee was given three meals during first shift, and two bathroom breaks each during all three shifts. One guard held the others under a drawn weapon while the other escorted a single prisoner to the facilities attached to their cell. Meech took advantage of the bathing chamber as often as he could. It was a way to pass the time. He liked to see how long he could run the vapor shower before his escort got impatient and started threatening them. Meals were served on unbreakable plastic trays with no removable parts so they had to eat with their fingers. They slept where they sat. They talked, unless told to shut up. The only other entertainment they had was to look out the porthole at the stars and try to guess where they were in between Hops.

"Look, she's got a leak in her suit," Cindy said, holding up her wet hand to show the guards. "It develops pinholes. The gauge shows she's down about two liters. Can I go with her to help refill the reservoir?"

"No," Guard Five said.

"She's got to keep her skin moist or she'll get very

sick," Cindy explained patiently as though to a toddler.

"Is she going to keep leaking all over the cell?" Guard Five asked, glaring at the girl.

"I can fix the leak." A trembling hand emerged from Colleen's cocoon. Meech was fascinated. Her skin bore a fabulous pattern of warm rings with cool, scalloped margins.

"Scales," Stu said. "Cool."

"Just the opposite," Cindy said. She brought Carmen closer to the hand, turning her so the leaking part of the plastic suit was close enough for Colleen to touch. The plastic fused at the touch of the scaled finger, melting together in a blossom of red that took Meech's breath away.

"That's the most beautiful thing I ever saw," Meech said. Before Colleen wrapped herself up again, he caught a glimpse of orbs glowing coolly inside the hood of blankets, the inrush of respiration.

"Thanks."

"What about that water?" Cindy asked.

"Not a chance," said Guard Six.

Cindy stood her ground. It took her over three hours to convince them to let her go with the child to the lavatory. By then, Carmen was red with mortification, having had an accident in her suit. Cindy took her away to bathe her and refill the shell, sacrificing her own cleanup break to make up time. At the older woman's direction, Meech and Stu helped fasten Carmen's clamps and hoses tight.

"All right, get apart," Guard Five said, gesturing at them with her laser pistol. Cindy and Carmen sat back on their bench.

"I can't stand this," Meech said, confronting them. "You've got to let us have something to do or something to read. I'm going crazy locked up here."

A laser bolt shot shocking red out of the barrel of Guard Six's gun, hitting the wall above them. "Sit down and shut up."

Carmen started crying. Bobby's blood pressure dropped.

"Cool it," Stu said, holding out his hands for peace. I'll tell some stories, and I bet Meech knows some, too."

"Yeah," Meech said, turning away from the guards. He made his breathing slow down. "Yeah, I can tell you some."

* * *

Five more days went by.

A wrenching sensation in the middle of the night that nearly threw Meech off his mattress announced the ship's emergence from Hop. A warning siren blared, as if the sudden jerk wasn't enough, but hell, procedure was procedure. So much for a decent night's sleep. The children whimpered uneasily until Cindy soothed them with her soft voice.

The lights in the cabin were dimmed for dark shift. Meech preferred it this way. He could take off his glasses and rub the bridge of his nose. Stu, asleep on the bench next to Meech, had quickly learned to ignore the sirens and humming. The guards sat in the dark, chatting in low voices. Meech got up, stretched his arms over his head, and went to look out the porthole.

Radiation, visible to no one but Meech, swirled outside as the ship displaced minute quantities of matter in the new system. He could see heat radiating in the walls in spite of the insulation. Meech studied the stars, brilliant spots of light with parabolic auras around them. They made no pictures he recognized. Perhaps he and his fellow exiles would get to name the constellations in the heavens around their new home.

There was a predominance here of red stars, old ones, like those on the verge of collapse. One of these was much bigger than Earth's sun. Either the ship was very close to that star, or it was huge. Meech thought the waves of light coming off it looked weird.

The already low lights dipped slightly, then came back up. Neither of the guards noticed, which meant the change was too slight for their limited perceptive faculties. Underneath Meech's feet, the everpresent hum of the ship changed tenor. Something was happening outside. He wished they could get out and see. There was no way he could go back to sleep. He sat back on his mattress, knees up, watching and listening. The children must have sensed it. The rise and fall of their chests had changed, and Bobby had crawled over to nestle beside Cindy. Colleen was awake, her muscles tense.

Soon, Guard Five looked at his wristcomm.

"Hey," he whispered to his partner, "our relief's late. Should have taken over an hour ago."

"Hell," the female guard snorted. "I'll report their butts. I'll go drag them back here if I have to do it bare-handed. Keep an eye on them."

She stuck her laser pistol into its holster and keyed in her code on the doorplate. "Still sealed," she said raising her wristcomm to her mouth. "Control, this is Tennant. Over." Meech realized that for the first time he knew a guard's name. The way they had acted, not knowing hadn't seemed to matter before. In ten days Tennant hadn't even met his eyes before a few minutes ago.

There was no answer. "What the hell?" asked Guard Five.

Beside Meech, Stu stirred. "Do you smell something?" he asked drowsily. "Ozone. No, burning polyurethane."

"Quiet, freaks!" Tennant growled.

"Can these kids have some food?" Cindy asked. "And I'd like some fresh water."

"No one is getting anything," Tennant said.

"We've got to get out of here," Guard Five said.

"How? The doorplate's jammed."

"We could cut the lock mechanism."

"We don't have any tools to get under the wall plate."

"Lasers?"

"No way," Tennant said. "They'll ricochet all over the place if they hit bare metal."

"I'll try, if you want," Colleen said. Holding her blankets trailing behind her like a robe, she looked to Meech's enhanced vision like a beautiful ghost gliding through a haunted house. She laid a hand on the lock mechanism and waited. The plastic bubbled around her fingers, dripping on the deck. She stepped back. The metal beneath was revealed, glowing slightly from the heat. Tennant and her partner banged on it with the butts of their laser pistols until it fell away. Tennant knelt and peered into the dark hatch.

"I can't see a damned thing," she said.

"I can," Meech spoke up. "What do you want done?"

Tennant turned toward the sound of his voice, her face scornful. "You won't help. You just want to escape."

"I will do whatever it takes right now. I want to live, too. If something's wrong I want to know. Now, what are you looking for?" He came up beside her, making her jump. In the dimness he could see the silhouette of her face more clearly than he could during bright shifts. "You need my help."

For a moment she stood silent, thinking.

"All right," she said. "We need to cut off the power source to the locking mechanism. It's a square about five centimeters across."

"Is that all?" Meech asked. He bent down to look into the hole. Streams of electrons rushed along the microcircuitry, making a neon pattern like a city at night. The lock itself was easy to reach. "It's right here."

"Guide my hand," the beautiful ghost beside him said. "I hope I don't burn you."

"I don't care," Meech said. The touch of her skin seared him, but he held on until her fingers were just touching the power supply cable. "There." She smiled as she twisted the cable loose. He smiled back at her,

wishing she could see it. Behind them, Tennant stood
over them with a curious expression on her face. The
circuit spat sparks, then died. Meech let go of Colleen's arm, watching the heat trace fade from his skin,
leaving blisters on his fingertips.

As soon as the current was cut, the door sagged
open a few inches. An astonishing burst of sound exploded on their ears. Guard Five pushed the portal
the rest of the way into its wall niche.

"Stay back," Tennant said, but without the hatred
that had colored her voice before. She sheathed her
weapon. "All hell is breaking loose out there."

The corridor was scarcely brighter than the cell. In
the light of dull red emergency beacons uniformed
crew rushed back and forth, in a flurry of frantic haste.
Something had gone very wrong.

Guard Five reached out to grab one of the passing
crewwomen and pulled her out of the stream of traffic.
"What happened?"

"The Hop terminated too sharply," the woman said.
"The computer freaked out. Captain's trying to fix it,
but we're on backup generators. The drives are okay,
but they have no power. The navigational system is
down. I've got to get back to Life Support." She shook
off Guard Five's hands and ran away.

"We need to put you somewhere until this is over,"
Tennant said. "This way."

Meech walked inbetween Cindy and Colleen, keeping them from bumping into bulkheads. Stu carried
the children, who kept their heads on his shoulders,
refusing to look around them.

"Gangway!" a couple of crewmen shouted, rolling
a heavy wheeled cart full of equipment past them.
Tennant herded them into a doorway until it passed.

"What's going on? Can't we help?" Colleen asked,
shifting to avoid colliding with a medtech in whites
escorting a limping crewwoman.

"No, freaks," Guard Five said. "We are taking you
to another cabin, one with a working lock."

"There's a storeroom near engineering," Tennant said, gesturing to Stu to keep up.

"Look, ma'am," Stu said, "I can smell burning plastic. We are heading straight toward it. Wait," he said, pausing near a ventilation grid, "we just passed it. You've got some problems. Let us do something."

"Diagnostic will fix it," Tennant said.

"Diagnostic went off line with everything else," said a man in coveralls kneeling beside the grille with a magnetic tool. "The whole system is screwed up. My computer isn't showing us where the problems are."

"What about handcomps?" Guard Five asked.

"The handcomps get their data from the same system, damn it. We don't have independent detectors. We've got circuits overloading, capacitors popping everywhere. The main generator's gone off line. If we shunt it in on top of a fault, we may cause a catastrophic crash. We can't even find everything that's breaking down." He shined his light up at Stu, and blanched, then recovered himself, necessity overcoming revulsion. "If you . . . people can do something to help, I know I would really appreciate it. I'm Vern Dugan, chief engineer."

"How about a truce? Meech and I can lead you to the breaks. I can smell the burns, and he can see radiation leaks. Right?"

"You got it," Meech said, and turned to Tennant. "Well? What about it? Truce?"

She handed her sidearm to Dugan. "They're all yours. I've got to get some food for the kids."

"What?" Guard Five exclaimed. "What are you doing?"

"If they can do something, I'm going to let them," she said, raising her chin defiantly. "Do you want to explain to the captain that we had a chance and threw it away?"

"But they're freaks!"

"If they try to jump ship, shoot them," she said, and disappeared into the crowd. Guard Five stood looking after her, his mouth hanging open.

Stu was already at work. "You've got scorched silicon back here," he said, pointing to a panel three down from the one Dugan was repairing.

"Lyle!" he shouted. A crewmember came running with her toolkit. "Follow this guy around and mark the modules he points out to you."

"Yessir," the woman said. Dugan turned to Meech. "You, with me."

Slowly, painstakingly, the repair crew went from crisis point to crisis point, fixing blown modules and components, patching conduit and replacing seals. Meech and Stu were called from side to side, pointing out faults and confirming the fixes. Colleen, given a heated suit usually used for EVAs, did quick spot welds with the tips of her fingers. She had no fear of the lasers tying systems together occasionally striking her skin.

"It's the first time I've been warm since I've been aboard," she told the astonished crew.

The corridor they were working in ran through the center of the main conduit that carried circuitry tying the ship's functions together. The strain of coming out of the last Hop had torn a lot of things loose. Meech saw dozens of places shedding heat, and radiation leaking from loosened panels. He showed the techs where the problems were, then stood back out of the way so they could do their jobs. Whether or not they liked the fact he was a mutant, they had to respect that he was always right about what needed to be fixed. He was brisk and businesslike, giving them no reason to grumble about his presence.

The chief engineer leaned into the access panel Meech had indicated. Behind it, a microgenerator that was supposed to control infrastructural systems was leaking power all over the place. It was tight quarters, and Dugan just barely fit. He was holding a portable shield over his face and upper body with one gloved hand and the spanner with the other.

"Aw, damn!" Dugan grunted, as the tool slipped out of his grasp. Meech heard it strike bottom at least one deck below them. "Somebody go get that!"

"Lose something?" Cindy said, slipping away from Guard Five. She stuck a hand into the access panel. Her arm elongated, stretching down into the cabinet, and snapped back a moment later holding the spanner. "See? There's life in the old broad yet." Dugan rocked back on his heels.

"You people are all right," he said. He turned to Tennant. "Huh?"

She shifted uneasily, not quite smiling. "I was thinking something similar myself."

When the crew and their captives reached the end of the tunnel, the overhead lights came on. The crew let out a ragged cheer.

Dugan dragged his conscripted work force to the bridge. The exiles stood in a protective huddle around the children, hanging half asleep against Cindy's legs as Dugan introduced them to Captain Patel. Tennant and Guard Five flanked them, but neither had weapons drawn. It was no longer a truce, it was an alliance. Meech, embarrassed to have such a fuss made, let his gaze wander around the room. He eyed the computers, the consoles, the wide glassteel portal looking out at the starfield underneath the blank viewscreen.

"You wouldn't believe these folks, sir," Dugan said, as he concluded the story. "Damn, they were just like regular . . . crew."

Captain Patel, a middle-aged man with large, liquid black eyes, regarded them impassively.

"You have my gratitude. Unfortunately, unless we can get systems operational again, word of your heroic exploits will perish with us, not very long from now."

"We're two jumps from the nearest repair facility," said the navigator, a thin, cool-faced woman, the tic in her cheek muscle betraying her nervousness. She gestured frustratedly at her console screen, a three-dimensional projection showing the minute points of stars. "The navicomp link's fried. We can't tie it to the helm. The best we can hope for is approximate direction. That can still put us light-years off beam."

"How's power?" Dugan asked.

"Won't last. We could make three jumps, that's all. If we are lucky. Two if not." Patel answered. "But we have no way of verifying the correct direction. One cluster of red stars looks a lot like the next one. You can see about a million stars out there, no way to tell which are which. Except for the galactic arch, we wouldn't even know which direction to guess in. If we pick the wrong one, we go off forever into the void. Without benchmarks to orient by, the navigator here might as well spin around and point."

Meech had been studying the mapping computer while the officers were talking.

"Is that thing showing the stars accurately?" he asked.

"Of course," the navigator sneered, as though she was thinking, *punk kid*. "It shows every star, artifact, nebula and energy mass in space."

"No," Meech said, struggling for the proper words, "do they show how bright the stars are compared to one another?"

"Does he mean proportional strength of astral emissions?" Dugan asked.

"Sure it does—for half a dozen types of emission," the navigator acknowledged pressing a row of buttons that caused the image on the screen to subtly change. "Why?"

"I can do it," he said. "I can guide you as to direction. You'll have to figure out how far to go, though."

Everyone burst out talking at once.

"You're out of your mind," the helm officer snapped.

"This isn't showing someone a broken power line, kid," Dugan said, astonished. "This is our lifeline. If we don't fly in the right direction, we'll end up who the hell knows where."

"I can do it. I can show you the right way." Meech insisted.

"Get these characters out of here," Captain Patel ordered, waving the guards over. Guard Five drew his weapon. Tennant crossed her arms. She looked tense, but on Meech's behalf, not against him.

"I can do it," Meech said, appealing to the circle of clenched jaws and staring eyes. It was hard to look at them in full light. He shifted his gaze to the computer. The small dots blazed, daring him. "I don't want to die in space. Look, I've been matching heat patterns to people's identities all my life. It's been my survival. If I do it wrong, you still have two chances to make it right. That's all you need." He looked at all of them, hoping for softening of their expressions. "There's fewer 'faces' out there than on any city street. I swear, if I'm wrong, I'll jump out the air lock. You won't have to push me. Give you a few days' more air that way anyhow."

The nameless guard seemed to approve of that idea.

"What can we do?" Dugan asked his captain. "Wait out here until the next ship comes along? That could be months, and they might miss us by half a system. And the salvage or tow fee will break us all."

Patel started moving so abruptly that Meech jumped back a pace. He extended a finger under Meech's nose. "All right. This ship is all I have ever owned. One try. But I can stop you at any point." He turned to the navigator. "Show him."

The thin woman nodded. Meech sat down in front of the screen. He took off his dark glasses, studying the pattern of colored lights. The navigator flinched at the sight of his eyes, then looked ashamed.

"Should I make it brighter?" she asked.

"No," he said, glancing out the wide portal for comparison. "No. I want them just the way they'll look out there. Can you turn the lights down a little?"

The captain sat down at his station in the center of the bridge, his eyes never leaving Meech, who was getting more nervous by the moment. This was the most ambitious thing he'd ever attempted. Compared to the starfield, scoping out the field of alarm signals at Vim's was an easy walk up a straight street. He knew how unlikely he was to succeed at what he'd promised, but what choice did he have? Lights, so many lights, so much alike. How could he do it? The reality was overwhelming him. The specks swam together in a mass. He found he was trembling. Time to take a moment to reorient.

The big red star was this system's sun. "This is Sherman's system." A blue dot appeared where the navigator touched the screen in the midst of one star grouping. Once Meech started studying the clusters of little dots, allowing himself to see the gradations of light going off at either end of the visible spectrum, he saw that they weren't all alike. His instincts hadn't lied to him: the patterns looked a lot like faces. He began to learn them, discovering the bright flickers of radiation that denoted solar flares, the slight wobbles of heavy planets pulling stars off center. He started to match what he saw in the screen to what was outside the port. When they were as familiar to him as the faces of the people he knew in Cleveland, he nodded to the navigator.

The better part of an hour passed, but no one spoke.

On the screen the blue dot was almost, but not quite, blocking out one small white star that was like a freckle on the cheek of one of those cosmic faces. Meech smiled involuntarily as he recognized the "constellation" he'd created in his mind earlier. Quickly he switched between displays ranging from infrared to x-ray. He compared the patterns several times, then pointed out, upward and to the left of beam. All the emissions matched. The patterns were the same.

"It's that way," he said.

"Are you sure?" the captain asked.

"I'm staking my life on it," Meech said. "If I am wrong, I'm dead, but we might be dead anyhow. Take it or leave it. If I were you, I'd take it. You have two, maybe three chances. Believe me or just flip a coin." Tennant looked at him, giving him a nod that the others might not even have seen, but he did. It helped.

Patel was still as a statue. Then he spoke. "I hope

we won't need them. Let's start out slow, make sure we've got his orientation dead straight before we Hop. Got it?"

The navigator and helm officer nodded.

"Engage subengines," Patel said.

Meech clenched the edge of the navigational computer as the helm officer swung the ship around at his spoken direction. There was that little white star. Meech oriented them until the ship was heading toward the ten o'clock point where the blue dot sat by that same star on the nav screen. His eyes were fixed on it, getting it into his head. The ship started to rotate faster and faster toward the star. He shouted directions at the navigator. "Up a little. Left a little— no, back to the right half of that. Yes. No. Yes. Yes! That's it!"

"Engines full!" Patel ordered. "Helm, prepare to Hop. On my command . . . Hop!"

The screen burst into whiteness. Meech threw up his hands to protect his eyes and fell back into his chair. His hands were trembling. He stared at them, surprised that he'd been squeezing them so hard that the blood had stopped flowing.

"It'll be hours before we know if your directions were right," Captain Patel said, rising from his seat. "Do you want to go somewhere and rest? You can have a decent cabin. It's the least I can do."

Meech looked back at his companions. Cindy beamed at him. Stu gave him an enthusiastic thumps-up. "No, thanks. If it's all right with you, I'll wait here."

"Suit yourself," Patel said.

* * *

A rough hand shook him. Meech looked up at Captain Patel's thin face.

"You're been asleep for ten hours," the man said. "You dropped off like a rock almost as soon as we left the system. We're about to come out of Hop."

Meech gathered himself cautiously, shifted to make room for the first-shift navigator, a muscular man his own age with curly hair. The helm officer was a sturdy woman with wide, dense bones.

"Twenty seconds, sir," she said, reading her gauges. "Ten seconds . . . five . . . four . . . three . . . two . . . one!"

The blackness beyond the portal blossomed suddenly to blinding yellow light, which resolved itself into a star with half-crescents of planets glinting in the void around it.

"Where are we?" Patel asked.

The navigator read his scopes. "Giant yellow star with five ringed planets, sixty-two moons. It's Sherman's system, sir."

"I'll be plucked," Patel said. "He did it."

The crew erupted into cheers. The navigator bounded out of his seat to slap Meech on the back.

"Not so fast!" Patel shouted, over the merriment. "Not so fast! Pipe down." The others stopped cheering and whistling. Meech froze. Patel turned to him, and the cool face warmed as the taut muscles relaxed. "I'm impressed, son. But can you do it again?"

Meech took a deep breath. "Yes," he said.

* * *

Forty-seven hours later the ship docked with the repair station circling a blue-white star. The crew piled off, heading for the bars with news of the human navi-computer. Meech and the others sat in their new, more comfortable cabin, worrying.

"In the end, it doesn't matter a bit," Cindy said, cuddling the sleeping children in her lap. Carmen's patched suit squeaked as she breathed. "Your fortune came true. You guided us through dangerous waters, but we're still going to that lonely planet out there with all the other sad folks." Colleen regarded Meech adoringly through the helmet of the EVA suit. "I guess we can handle it."

"They have to do something better for you," Tennant said firmly. "You did more to help us than we deserved. Especially the way we treated you all. You saved us. You're heroes."

Meech shook his head and slumped, his chin in his hands.

"She's right." The voice at the door was the captain's. You more than earned consideration." Dugan followed him in and sat down next to Colleen. "There never was such an initiation. I wish I could really give you what you deserve. I can't return you to Earth because of the law. If you don't want to go to Thanatos, I'll take you somewhere else. One of the trading planets, maybe. They're making their own laws there. You can start a new life. It'd be a shame to waste talents like yours."

The exiles looked at one another.

"We don't want that," said Meech suddenly, and knew he was speaking for all of them.

"What do you want?"

"We want jobs. Like you said, we can do more than Normals, and your crew likes us. Keep us on board. We'll be the best damned crew you ever had."

"We want to belong somewhere," Colleen added, earnestly.

Captain Patel laughed at the four serious faces staring at him with hope in their eyes. "I'll be plucked if I might not do it. Half of my crew wants to keep you already. You've won them over. If spacers were sheep like back on earth, they wouldn't be spacers. I doubt many will object, and those that do could find another berth. Still you would have a lot to learn . . ." His voice trailed off.

"It's your ship. Normals have no trouble getting jobs," Cindy said. "We got nothing else to do but learn."

"Right," added Stu, only sniffing slightly. "I mean, who would you rather have with you the next time things go blinkers? Special circumstances require special people. That's us."

Meech said nothing; his own heart raced and he could see the other mutants were equally tense.

There followed a long silence ending only when a slight smile appeared on the captain's face.

"Welcome aboard," Patel said, slapping Meech on the shoulder. "I'd be a poor master and commander if I couldn't see the advantages, not to mention increased profits."

The officer turned to Tennant, who had been there still technically guarding the prisoners. She was already leaning against a nearby wall grinning.

"We'll need to assign new berths for our new crewmembers and figure out the best way to use each of them." Then their captain looked at Meech and his smile grew wider. "Why should this young man be the only one around here with extraordinary vision?"

SENSITIVES

by Nina Kiriki Hoffman

Nina Kiriki Hoffman has been writing for almost twenty years and has sold almost two hundred stories, two short story collections, novels (*The Thread That Binds The Bones* and *The Silent Strength of Stones, A Red Heart of Memories*, and her most recent novel, *Past the Size of Dreaming*), a young adult novel with Tad Williams (*Child of an Ancient City*), a Star Trek novel with Kristine Kathryn Rusch and Dean Wesley Smith, *Star Trek Voyager 15: Echoes,* three R. L. Stine's *Ghosts of Fear Street* books, and one *Sweet Valley Junior High* book. She has cats.

You never know what story a taste will tell you till you put something in your mouth. Then it's too late not to hear it.

I spent a lot of my little kid years sucking on pennies, even though it drove Mama crazy. "Art! Don't eat that! You don't know where it's been!" "Art! Don't eat that! Want to get copper poisoning?" "Art! Don't eat that. It'll grow in your stomach and you'll have a copper forest in there so heavy you won't be able to stand up."

She didn't get it. The point was not to *eat* the pennies, it was to suck the stories off them.

I don't know what the first story I got was. I already had the penny habit in my earliest memory.

Uncle Jonah gave me a penny while Mama was back in the kitchen messing with sandwiches, and he laughed at four-year-old me when I stuck that penny in my mouth. My tongue already knew the size, weight, feel of a penny, the first flood of dirty metal taste. That wasn't the good part. The good part came a second later, a surround of images, and there I was, a penny just as a hand dropped me into a wicker basket. There I lay with quarters, dimes, nickels, pennies, crumpled dollar bills. A voice boomed over me so loud it shook the air. I felt the heat of people, the basket shaking as it passed from hand to hand, change jingling against me, more dropping from above, people chanting "Amen!" "Amen!" "Yes, Jesus!" And this hot, happy, excited feeling edged with fear, a blanket of emotion as the crowd swayed to the preacher's words.

"Art? Art? What have you got in your mouth?" Mama's eternal question was already familiar, too. She pushed my chin down with her thumb so my mouth opened, then tapped the back of my head. The penny popped out.

I didn't care. I already had a new memory off it. I already knew one story per penny was enough. Somewhere before there, so misty I couldn't really call it back, I had sucked on a penny long enough to get more stories off it than the top one, and I knew I didn't do that anymore.

"Jonah, what are you up to, giving him pennies? How many times do I have to tell you not to do that? You keep this up, you won't be welcome here anymore," Mama said.

Jonah promised he wouldn't. I remembered that from every time, too. Mom took the penny and went back to the kitchen, and Jonah said, "C'mon, Art." He slapped his leg. I went over to him and he lifted me into his lap, turned me to face him, held me loose so I knew I wouldn't fall but didn't feel trapped. His arms were strong and gentle. The grooves around his thin mouth deepened into a cheek-lifting smile, and the lids came halfway down over his dark eyes. This sequence of events, too, had the soft edges of habit. "What'd you see?" whispered my uncle.

"People," I whispered back. "Yelling."

"What were they yelling?"

"Amen." I didn't know what that meant, what most of the words I had heard meant. "They're happy and hot."

Jonah hugged me. His chest was warm and hard. His soft flannel shirt smelled good, Marlboro smoke, sweat, buttered popcorn from the movie house where he worked as a janitor. "One hundred percent, Art. Always one hundred percent with you. One of these days. One of these days." His whisper trailed away to nothing.

What he always said.

What I always felt: good. I knew Jonah loved me and was pleased with me. He always had penny memories for me.

My best friend in eighth grade, Saul, found out about my penny habit.

I usually told people about that old superstition, "See a penny, pick it up, all day long you'll have good luck" to explain why I dived on every dropped penny I saw. Not like you could actually buy anything with pennies anymore.

I usually didn't taste the pennies when anybody else was around; Mama had cured me of that habit as early as she could, then sighed and gave in to my unending desire. She bought rolls of pennies from the bank and boiled them, then doled them out to me when she needed to quiet me down. As long as I didn't taste them where anybody could see, she let me do it.

She never asked what I got from it, and I didn't tell her.

Pocket of a man going into a brothel, his sweaty hand jingling change, telegraphing his nervousness; the drop to the floor as he took off his pants, too anxious to attend to scattered coins.

Pocket of a girl going to the drugstore to buy her first Kotex. Her fingers rigid, gripping crumpled dollars.

A wooden box lined with green Contact paper where a little kid kept all her best things. The special penny with the wheat sheaves on the back that her grandpa had given her; it was from the year her father was born. It nestled in the dark with a tiny iridescent feather from a peacock she had seen at a zoo and a dried flower given her by a best friend who moved away and a silver dollar her other grandpa had given her.

That was a two-story penny. The story about the girl was strongest, because she kept the penny for a long time, took it out and looked at it, turned it over with her other things, until her dad found her stash and stole the penny and the dollar to buy beer.

I found a railroad tracks penny while Saul and I walked home from school one Friday.

"Art, sometimes you're just too weird," Saul said.

It was a late fall day, crisp and blue-skied. The section of train track between the middle school and my house led through a short stretch of pine forest. Scattered other trees between the Douglas-firs had leaves turned red and yellow from night frosts.

We walked on the tracks, teetering, balancing, practicing circus stunts. I watched the granite rocks between the tracks. You never knew what you'd find, anywhere. I always watched the ground.

"So what did I do this time?" I took a wrong step and slipped off the silver track. The crowd gasps! The gorgeous highwire partner, Lindalino the Beauteous, all shiny in red and silver spangles, lets out a shocked cry! Blood splatters everywhere as tightrope walker Arturo the Excellent dives to his doom!

"What made you say that to Linda, about her mom?"

I jumped back onto the rail. Saul never slipped. He was skinny and strong and had better balance. "She looked worried."

"She looked worried! Everybody's all the time worried! But you don't go up to them and say their mom will be all right."

I sold Linda one of my SuzyQs at lunch for twenty-six cents. She could have had it for a penny, except I figured out a long time ago people don't trust you if all you want is a penny. I hadn't found anybody else who got as much from a penny as I did. You had to ask for more or they thought you were tricking them.

Actually, since it was Linda, she could have had it for nothing. I was pretty sure she wouldn't trust that either.

So anyway, she gave me a quarter and a penny, and a little later I tasted the penny. It didn't tell me what book she was reading or who she talked to on the phone or what color her underwear was; you couldn't count on getting specific details, though sometimes you got lucky. Linda's penny told me more. There was a hospital waiting room, and Linda flipping the penny over and over, sometimes dropping it, her dad sitting in a chair across from her, his head drooping. Announcements on the P.A. A doctor came out. "She has a slight concussion. We'll keep her overnight for observation. But that's just in case."

So I didn't really know if Linda's mom would be all right. Sometimes you just say stuff and hope it makes people feel better. She smiled, anyway, but it didn't quite wipe the worry off her forehead, so maybe it was a mistake.

Bright copper gleamed among the clinker rocks between the tracks, and I dived for it.

Saul wobbled at my sudden move. "What, Art? What?"

"Sometimes kids put pennies on the tracks. A lot of the time the train wind pushes them off before they stretch." I had tasted stretched pennies. Being crushed wiped the stories right off them. "Smart kids tape the pennies on the tracks. That gets them crushed for sure. But this one—" It was a brand new penny, still bright like it had come from the mint. Probably not much of a story there—too new.

But you never knew.

I scrubbed the penny against my jeans and popped it in my mouth.

"Jeez, Art! What are you doing?"

I couldn't believe I had forgotten Saul was watching me! When was the last time that happened? Mom and Uncle Jonah had trained me to be secret about this when I was five, six max!

I knew he was there. He had been talking to me. I had been talking to him.

What was the matter with me?

I forgot Saul. Penny vision gripped me.

The flip off the ends of someone's fingers, flying through air like being shot from a cannon, arcing down over a screaming crowd, mouths wide, costumes bright, sunglasses, wild hats, bright beads glowing around their necks, a rage of noise, the air thick with excitement and half-drunken joy.

An old man snatched me out of the air, waved his fist with me inside it.

Then this rush of strange bittersweet feelings: *I've caught the treasure! The treasure is so small! In my day you could get a roll for this, but everything just gets smaller and smaller and worth less and less. I've caught the treasure! At least it shines! You catch what you can. . . .*

I let out a breath. I pushed the penny out of my mouth with my tongue, and it dropped into my hand, a practiced move. "Mardi Gras," I said, flushed with extra information the way I always was after a penny vision. I picked up lots of new things that I didn't even know I knew until awkward times later when I came up with answers I shouldn't have. What the heck was Mardi Gras? It involved a parade, and lots of people throwing things, and costumes and floats and dancing and music and crowds hot and loose. Smells of beer and wine and spicy cooking, sweat, urine, heavy perfumes, cigarette smoke, vomit, the river. Louisiana. New Orleans.

Someplace I had never been. Again. I had lots of memories of places I had never been. It was a surprise to see someone else's memory of a place I knew, like the hospital, even the waiting room where Linda and her dad had been sitting. When I was eight, Uncle

Jonah had fallen off a ladder, and I'd waited with Mom in that room to find out whether he was okay.

"Art!" Saul yelled.

He surprised me so much I fell off the rail again. Then I couldn't believe I'd been on the rail during the vision, anyway. Last thing I remembered clearly, I was rising with that penny in my hand, ready to taste it.

"What!" I yelled back.

"What on earth are you doing?"

I tried a trick Mama had taught me: turn it around. "You never ate money?"

"Not since I was five!" Saul stepped off the rail and stood on a tie between the tracks. "Come on, explain it. I've seen you do this before. What is it? How come your eyes went blank? You getting high off small change?"

"You saw me do it before?"

"At the county fair last year. Then I thought I must be nuts. That is not my best friend Art putting some filthy penny in his mouth he just picked up off the ground, I thought. Must be a piece of candy he had in his hand before. That is not my best friend Art standing there like an idiot with his eyes glazed over while other kids bump into him and laugh. Maybe it *is* my best friend Art. Maybe he's having a seizure or something. Maybe I should call somebody for help. Then you woke up and turned normal again, and I forgot about it."

I shoved the Mardi Gras penny in my pocket and walked past Saul. I felt too shook to climb up on the rail and be able to stay there, so I hopped the ties instead. They were just a little too close to each other for easy walking.

"Art," Saul said from behind. "Come on. Tell me. You some kind of sick?"

Was I? Did that explain it, this relationship I had with small metal disks?

I kept walking. His footsteps grated on the clinkers behind me.

"And that penny you found on the bottom of the pool last week. I saw you eat that one, too." Saul kicked a railroad tie. "Ouch. And how you're always selling stuff to kids and you end up with a penny every time. What is it? What is it?"

"You wouldn't believe me if I told you."

"Try me. Didn't I believe you about that goat-sucking vampire thing, huh? At least for a day. What nightmares I had. What could be weirder than that?"

We walked on, me in front and him following, for a while, till we came out of the woods and saw a forest of fences. At the first street closing I left the tracks and headed for the house where Mama and I lived. Art followed me up the walk to the front porch, and we both collapsed on the dusty old sofa there and stared at the street.

"It's sort of like a TV show," I said. That wasn't right. But how could I describe it? "My tongue hits the penny and then there's this other world."

"Like another planet?"

I narrowed my eyes and stared at him. Was he kidding, or was he going to listen? We could cancel this conversation right now.

"Come on. I don't get it." Saul sucked on his lower lip.

"It's not another planet. It's a—a stored memory. The penny has a memory on it, and I kind of fall into it for a second."

"What was on that penny from the tracks?"

"A Mardi Gras parade." I closed my eyes a second. "People dressed like things in fairy tales riding on floats, bead necklaces and fake coins flying through the air, all kinds of weird stuff. A woman on a balcony took off her shirt—" Whoa. Hadn't noticed that part of the memory before, and now that I did, I couldn't think about anything else. "Yelling, and laughing, and music, lots of different music crashing into other music."

"Wow," said Saul.

I waited for him to start mocking me.

He shook his head. He scratched his nose.

"I never know what I'm going to find out, but sometimes it's really cool like that. Linda's penny, it was about—I guess her mom went to the hospital yesterday." I shrugged.

"So you told her her mom will be okay. How do you know?"

"I don't."

Saul leaned back and dug into his pocket, pulled out a grimy penny. He handed it to me.

"I don't think so."

"You eat stuff off the ground! This you take exception to?"

"It's not that."

"I mean, I won't be insulted if you wash it. Does it work if you wash it?"

I shrugged. "What if I find out something you don't want me to know?"

"You're my best friend. What's not to know?"

I thought of penny visions I'd had in the past. Lots not to know. Some things that still troubled my dreams, or made me lie awake, too scared to sleep. Sometimes I saw things that the people who did them had no idea why anybody would be upset about them. That bothered me a lot, that people often did horrible things and didn't even realize they were horrible. But what could I do with penny knowledge? Always after the fact, often three or four people away from me. No direct line, no way to change anything.

All I could do with penny knowledge was know it.

I got up and went into the house, headed down the hall to the kitchen. Saul followed me. I washed off his penny at the kitchen sink, even though I thought it was rude. He was right. I ate things off the ground. But I knew the kinds of things he kept in his pockets. Sometimes that included small dead animals.

I dried Saul's penny off on my jeans and put it in my mouth.

Crash! Something smashed against a wall. A tinkle of broken glass followed.

Saul hunched in the shadow behind the couch. The penny lay near him on the dusty floor.

"You never listen!" yelled Saul's mother.

"If you said anything worth hearing, I'd listen to it!" yelled Saul's father.

His mother screamed, a cry of rage and frustration. Something else crashed. Saul hunched harder and snuck his hands over his ears.

I coughed out of the vision. The penny dropped from my mouth to the floor.

"So what did you see?" he stared at my face.

"Where'd you get that penny?"

"I don't know." He stuck his hand in his pocket and pulled out more change, several pennies and a couple quarters. "Where does anybody get change? Somebody gave it to me, I guess."

"It was on the floor behind the couch in your living room when your mom and dad had that fight," I said. "Maybe you picked it up then."

"Oh." He pulled out a chair and slumped in it. "Oh." This time it was a whisper. His face went red, then pale. "Oh, God, Art. You know what that means?"

"No," I said. "Divorce? Or do they always fight like that? Either way, I'm sorry."

"Huh? No, that was—" He sucked in his lip, then frowned. "It's not that. This means you can really tell stuff from pennies."

"Yeah. So?"

"Guess it's not news to you. But this is so cool! Does it work with other things? Quarters? Nickels? Bottle caps?"

"Not reliably." The summer I was eleven, Mama let me help Uncle Jonah at his job. I got to see free movies every week, I got all the popcorn I could stand, I got enough of a salary to keep me in comic books, and after the theater closed and we finished cleaning up, Jonah and I retreated to his room in the basement and tried lots of experiments. We tried every different kind of coin we could find. Other-country copper coins gave me visions I couldn't understand—different languages, for one thing, and people acting even more different than people in my regular penny visions acted. "It's got to be at least partly copper. I've figured out that much."

"Did you try wire?"

"Yeah. Not much good. Mostly it's insulated and can't pick up memories."

"How about copper jewelry?"

I shrugged. "It works. It's not any better than pennies, and it's harder to find and more expensive. Plus I cut my tongue on this brooch one time."

Saul stood up and paced around the kitchen. "But this," he said. He paced from the hall to the sink and back.

After a while I got tired of watching. I got a Coke and some cookies and sat at the table. The sizzle of carbonation on my tongue took away the taste of Saul's parents' fight.

Uncle Jonah still figured there had to be some way to use my talent. He brought me pennies from race tracks, pennies from casinos, pennies from banks. We both hoped I'd trip over a useful memory, and he would be able to figure out how to apply it so we could make some money. It had never happened.

"But we could—" Saul said. He frowned at me. His hands clenched into fists at his sides.

I shook my head. "I never know what I'm going to find. Sometimes it's useful stuff, but most of the time it's just . . . static."

That wasn't true. I never listened to static long on a radio dial, but I always wanted more penny visions—just in case. Sometimes they were the best things in the world. Sometimes I hated them and kicked out early before I tasted the whole story, but I still had the taste on my tongue afterward. Sometimes I saw nightmares and sometimes sweet dreams. I always thought the next one might be—Mardi Gras.

"How frustrating," Saul said.

* * *

It wasn't until six years later that I found what I was looking for.

Saul and I were roommates, going to community college during the day and working in a pizza parlor at night. He was working toward a teaching credential, and I—I couldn't stay away from anthropology. Under the earth and in private collections and museums there were Bronze Age artifacts—bronze, brass, copper; I had experimented with licking a few things, when I could, in museums, and I had tasted history. Not that I could understand it, but I was studying language and culture. Someday what I found in visions and what I learned in class would merge. I hoped.

"Guess where I got this one," Saul said after we'd shut down the pizza place and prepped the toppings for the next day. He handed me another penny.

I ran the penny under hot water, then put it in my mouth. This was how we ended most of our workdays, Saul presenting me with a puzzler.

"Mmm," I said after a minute. "Underwater."

"Sure," he said. "Not specific enough."

A penny itself didn't make a memory; it was contact with a person that left the stain of memory on it. Why did I have an image of underwater with no person in the picture? This penny held its secrets. It had a strange, almost electric taste.

I pressed the penny between my tongue and the roof of my mouth.

Vision of a hand around the penny, a murmur of voice, and then the penny dropped, broke the surface of dark water, teeter-tottering to the mossy bottom— not a deep distance—to land among other coins.

I pressed harder, reached for replay. What had she said when she let me go?

The hand, fingers callused at their tips. The murmur. "Wish I could find him."

Then this strange charge surged from her fingers into me, and I fell away, dropped down into the water.

I pushed the penny out of my mouth and caught it.

"So?" Saul asked.

"A wishing well."

He smiled and shook his head. "You *sure* you don't want to go into the fortune-telling business?"

He'd been bugging me about that ever since he found out about the penny visions. I just didn't see it. I could always figure out something about a penny, but it had nothing to do with peoples' futures. Often it didn't have a thing to do with whoever handed me the penny. It had to come from somebody who had felt something intense while they held the penny, and that could be sixty-three people back in the penny's past.

"Which wishing well?" I asked. I couldn't think of one nearby.

"The one in Skyview Park."

"Huh. You actually stole a penny from a wishing well?"

Red touched his cheeks. "I dropped another one in to replace it."

Saturday it was sunny again, and I went up to the park. It was on the ridgeline above the city. There was a big meadow where people could let their dogs off of leashes, and a little old wishing well with a flagstone walk around it, and picnic tables and park benches and trees around the meadow, with hiking trails below them.

I sat on a bench in the shade and watched the wishing well.

An older woman brought a golden retriever and let him loose, and he ran. Two kids threw a Frisbee back and forth. A little girl with a butterfly net stalked the edge of the forest, sweeping the net down on shrubs and crying out as butterflies escaped her. I wasn't sure how serious she was. She never caught a single one.

Some kids studied on the grass. A couple brought a picnic basket and set up not far from where I sat.

Around noon, when I was hungry and wondered why I hadn't brought a sandwich, a young woman with frizzy strawberry-blonde hair topped the stairs that led up from the base of the hill. She wore hiking boots, khaki pants, and a plain white T-shirt. Her face was flushed beneath its dusting of freckles. She pulled a water bottle out of her hip pack and took a long drink.

I felt a faint fizzing on my tongue.

She glanced around. She wiped her forehead with the back of her hand. She trudged over to the well and peered in.

I dug the wish penny out of my pocket and wandered over.

"Did you drop this?" I asked.

She straightened and stared. "Huh?"

Yeah, I guessed that sounded like a line. I felt so dumb. What was I expecting? What made me think she'd been wishing for—me?

"Let me see," she said. She held out her hand, and I dropped the penny into it.

The palm of my hand sizzled.

She rubbed the penny between her index finger and thumb. Faint frown lines appeared between her eyebrows. "Why, yes," she said. "I think this is mine. What—pizza?"

A chill walked up my spine.

Her eyelashes were light, tipped with red and gold, and her eyes, wide now, were yellow-green.

I swallowed and reached into my pocket. "Try this one," I said.

She tucked her own penny into her hip pack and held out her hand. I dropped my penny into it. she rubbed my penny between her fingers, then pressed it to her cheek. She closed her eyes.

"Mardi Gras?" she said. "Railroad tracks."

We stared at each other unmoving for what seemed like about an hour.

"Serena," I said.

"Art." She smiled and gave me back my penny.

After a second, I tossed it into the well.

FIRE AND RAIN
by Janet Pack

Originally a native of Independence, Missouri, Janet Pack now resides in the village of Williams Bay, Wisconsin, in a slightly haunted farmhouse with cats Tabirika Onyx, Syrannis Moonstone, and Baron Figaro di Shannivere. Her extensive rock collection adorns her living room. Janet's two dozen plus short stories, interviews, and nonfiction articles have been published by a number of companies. Her musical compositions can be found in Weis and Hickman's *The Death Gate Cycle*, and in *Dragonlance* sourcebooks. Janet works as the manager's assistant at Shadowlawn Stoneware Pottery in Delavan, WI, and when needed at the University of Chicago's Yerkes Observatory in Williams Bay. During free moments she sings, reads, embroiders, walks, cooks, watches good movies, plays with her companions, and does as little housework as possible.

The force that had remained hidden most of his life took over again, sprinting along his bloodstream, leaving tingling sparks and tripping mind triggers he'd thought buried beneath long years of counseling. Raw power made him tremble with the ecstasy of its being, a second shadow soul within him, waiting for the moment he mentally grasped the lightning and started the insane hot-to-cold upward mental leaps from squall line to cloud to thunderhead, centering his spirit in its whirling convection site and making him master of the storm.

Dr. Duncan Peters leaned his fevered forehead against the window of the Storm Forecasting Center where he was Director of Meteorology. Rain pelted the hi-tech protective eyes of the building, each drop a faint but insistent invitation: "Power awaits you. Come play with us, come play."

He'd just left a meeting with his so-called peers, his excuse a migraine. He needed solitude to calm down, a nook away from small-minded people and their insufferable "we know best" attitudes. Duncan clenched his fists. Lightning seared close, thunder roared response to his emotional upset.

Jack Hallberg, Director of Acquisitions for the SFC, insisted on more accurate forecasting but wouldn't approve funds for new equipment, especially not the superb systems Peters had invented and painstakingly tested himself. How could the center be expected to increase reporting accuracy on something as fractious as weather when forced to use a forecasting system installed in the 1990s? It was a government agency—they needed the best equipment to help protect people, not only in the Midwest but across the United States.

Duncan had been fighting Hallberg for more than a year to buy necessary upgrades at least, but the man's tunnelvision focused on saving money and little else. Except, Peters corrected himself grimly, Jack's obsession to undermine the meteorologist's reputation and, like a competitive sibling, either best Duncan or possess everything he had.

His lovely corner office with two windows had been the first victim. After that, peculiar small controversies had surfaced concerning how he earned his doctorate and the eccentricities of Dr. Beckwith, his mentor. Today's meeting had culminated in a subtle attack against his slightly unorthodox methods of forecasting despite years of proof collected in his lectures, his book, and SFC data.

When he'd started fighting Hallberg, storms had responded to the meteorologist's frustration, just as they had to his childhood irritations. They swirled around Kansas City, coming in from the west, southwest, and south, making this July famous for unsettled weather patterns. Peters almost choked every time he recorded the forecast, knowing his anger was their cause and unable to do anything except rail silently about the situation.

"Duncan? You all right?"

Marta Kinnison, head secretary and assistant to upper-level office personnel, stood beside him, her round maternal face all concern. She held a steaming cup of coffee in one hand. Peters regarded her through squinting, aching eyes, wondering how she'd managed to find him at an end of the little-frequented hallway.

"Yeah, thanks, Marta," he rasped, slow to offer a lie to one of the few SFC personnel he appreciated. "I'm okay."

"You don't look so good. Here." Living up to her reputation as the office "mother," the auburn-haired woman who always smelled like honey and vanilla pushed the coffee against his knuckles until his hands opened to accept it. The heat spread a sharp familiar blaze like lightning through his hand and arm. "It's decaf," she continued, now in advice mode. "Take some of your headache medicine and lie down for a while. You'll feel better soon. It's this crazy weather." She patted his arm and looked into his gray eyes. "And don't give up," she whispered. "Things'll come around."

With her typical broad-hipped sashay, Marta beamed and disappeared down the hallway. Duncan nodded thanks, immediately returning his attention outside and forgetting the coffee.

Clouds darkened, boiling. Wind lashed trees. Branches flew, bizarre birds. Golfball-sized hail hammered the window with plinks of increasing intensity. That sound finally brought Peters' attention back to the window. His unoccupied fist lay against it, knuckles white. Forcing himself to breathe deeply, he gradually unclenched his fingers. The storm loosed the last of its white missiles. The clouds settled back on their haunches, waiting for him like a pup begging to play.

Duncan sighed. It seemed as though the front which

spawned this unexpected midwestern frog-strangler fidgeted just a few feet away, eager for his next emotional crisis. It had come north to find him in Kansas City, soaring off a line of southern storms tracking through the Gulf. For some reason, probably stress from Hallberg, the conditioning he'd built up so carefully over the years had evaporated. He felt the same confusion—and might as well admit it—delight he had as a youngster when he'd noticed storms responded to his mental state. The angrier he'd been, the worse the weather.

Peters had become fascinated with meteorology during high school, hoping it held the answer to his problem. Instead, it put him more in harmony with storm fronts racing from west to east and south to north across the country. He understood the way they worked better than anyone, an insider's point of view. Duncan had written the definitive work on tornadoes for his doctoral thesis: it was published in hardback soon after he graduated. He was often called on to give lectures and seminars about weather.

Hallberg had been in place as Director of Acquisitions for the SFC for five years when Peters was hired. Jack's buddy-buddy facade concealed ravening ambition and jealousy when the younger, more handsome man whose name emblazoned a book cover was installed as Head of Meteorology. SFC policies from then on downplayed, outright ignored, or repudiated Duncan's suggestions. He didn't want to imagine what Hallberg wrote about him in semiannual reports.

The old bugaboo of Duncan's childhood now nudged his brain with a little cloud-to-cloud lightning, demanding activity—no one else he knew claimed such a powerful element as a playmate. He was a freak. He could destroy Hallberg, this building, this city, with a nod, and walk out of the devastation unsinged. No one would know except himself.

But his conscience wouldn't allow such murder and mayhem. Peters sighed and levered himself away from the window, trying to ignore the storm's entreaties.

For once in his career, he decided to take advantage of accrued sick leave. Anyway, he needed time to prepare for dinner with Amelynn Sperry.

Thought of meeting his email correspondent for the first time at a Country Club Plaza restaurant coated his backbone with sleet as he stumbled down the hallway to his office and whispered a code phrase to activate the security lock on his door. "Computer," he ordered his desktop system when he stepped inside, "this is Dr. Peters. Message to Marta, interoffice email, priority. I'm taking the rest of the afternoon off on sick leave. You can reach me at home if you need me. End e-mail. Shut down."

"Remember your meeting tomorrow morning at nine with Hallberg and Michaelson. I hope you feel better soon. Good afternoon, Dr. Peters," replied the machine's androgynous voice before the flat screen blanked and slid down into its protective housing within his desk. He pitched the cooled coffee into the building's waste disposal system. Without a backward look, Duncan slipped out of the SFC and onto the street. His shoulders bore the weight of Hallberg's scrutiny all the way down the block to the tube drop.

* * *

"Dr. Peters," Duncan nervously told the smiling hostess at the glass-walled Classic Cup Restaurant later that evening. He hoped he didn't look as shaky as his voice implied. He and Amelynn Sperry had been corresponding electronically for more than a year. Peters found himself suddenly reluctant to break the remarkable harmony he'd achieved through email by facing her across an old-fashioned wooden table over an elegant dinner.

"Oh, yes. Your dining partner has already arrived," the young lady smiled. "Right this way, sir."

Blind-date nerves sluiced his insides with more ice as he weaved between tables behind his guide. She led him to the transparent wall where a woman in fuschia silk sat watching pedestrians and cars scurry outside.

"Amelynn?"

"Duncan!" A teardrop-shaped face crowned with shoulder-length dark copper hair swiveled gracefully in his direction. "How lovely to meet you in person at last." Her intense deep brown eyes danced, their naked interest expelling the wind from his lungs. She offered a hand. He couldn't not kiss it, her warm touch melting chicken-skin goose bumps as he sat down.

She didn't appear tall or short, not fat nor thin—thoroughly striking was the only description he could summon. Other men stared enviously at her from behind their menus and laden forks.

"You know better," she reproved gently. "Call me Lynn. Things don't change just because we're finally facing each other."

"Apologies," he murmured. Several whorls of trash and desiccated leaves from honey locust trees danced in different directions in the street, kicked up by his emotions and amplified by the impending storm. He strove for equilibrium with an old meditation technique. "Uh, been here long?"

She waved the question away. "A few minutes. I caught a shuttle from the hotel. Left with plenty of time because I thought it might be late. It wasn't." She stretched with compact feline motions, bringing her arms to rest folded across each other on the tabletop and leaning toward him. "It's good to be away from those seminars. I hate being cooped up in a place without windows." She looked outside, savoring the view of the gorgeous old Spanish-style shopping district. "This is really lovely, Duncan."

"Have you ordered?"

"Of course not. I waited for you." She smiled, just for him. Energy of a type he couldn't identify played around her. Even in repose something about this woman moved, snapped, danced—in her hair, which she wore brushed back in a gently curling mane, her eyes, her expressions.

Peters reined in his imagination and gestured. For once a waiter responded immediately. "Good evening," the young man said. "I'm Charles. What may I get for you?"

"Australian Shiraz for the lady, and I'll have a . . . a chardonnay."

"Thought you preferred merlot." Lynn's eyebrows tightened as if she saw remnants of headache and storm still in his face. Her silk blouse reflected light upward, festooning her hair with elegant strawberry-garnet gems.

"I do. Just—ah, just not tonight." He sucked in a deep breath, laced with the odors of fresh bread and exotic spices wafting from the kitchen, and tried to relax. "It's been a tough day. I won't bore you with the details."

She was instantly concerned. "We could go somewhere quieter—"

"No." He looked around the dimly lit room, savoring its ambiance. Not many of the refurbished Plaza restaurants had concentrated on keeping their charm. "I don't get enough chances to come here, and I'm not about to give up this opportunity to share one of my favorite eating places with you. It's just workplace frustration." He fell silent, playing with the glass holding the unlit candle as the waiter returned and settled their drinks on napkins. Charles hovered, awaiting their orders.

"How about sharing the shrimp and giving dinner more consideration?" Lynn asked.

"Don't you have to get back?"

She smiled again. "I've scheduled the whole evening with you." Sperry looked into her wine, then back up into his cloud-gray eyes. "Anyway, I've had about enough of rather inane lectures for one week."

"Great. Hey, the waiter forgot to light our candle." Duncan turned to call the disappearing server.

"Don't bother. I always have matches. So," she

sipped wine before continuing. "You're having trouble with a coworker?" In the understated light, her dark eyes looked the same color as the shiraz. He liked that. He also liked having the complete attention of a lovely, intelligent woman. It had been a long time since he'd been so flattered.

"I—yes. I don't want to bore you . . ."

"You're not. I know that look, and that feeling. They're no fun." It was her turn to toy with the unlit candle as Peters drank his wine and tried again to unknot his shoulders. "Someone less talented than you who controls something important. Lots of workplaces are that way, including mine." She sighed, looking out the window as if the rich view of trees, statues, and fountains restored part of her soul. "Environmental science is full of such people, especially crusaders who don't know as much as they should." She hesitated. "Do you like your job?"

"Love it." He laughed softly. "I'm the youngest Head of Meteorology in the country at a prestigious government agency. I have a book out that makes me the top expert on predicting those unpredictable nuisances, tornadoes." The candle suddenly twinkled like a star between them. "I suppose one of these days I'll learn to live with the bad parts." Thunder rumbled in the distance, an echo of his irritation.

"You don't have to do that." Lynn's eyes met his, brimming with understanding and a flash of something more. "Give up defense. Take control."

"But I'm—" Duncan almost said "a freak." He caught and changed his words before they betrayed him. "I can't. He's entrenched in the good graces of everyone except me. He plays office games that give him the edge. Things I refuse to do." Duncan fell silent as the waiter served their beautifully presented appetizer and stood ready for their entree orders. Lynn chose southwestern chicken with an incendiary mole-black bean side dish, and he decided on grilled yellowfin tuna.

"I didn't know you liked hot cuisine," Duncan said in wonder as the server zigzagged away.

"Tell you a secret." Lynn leaned forward an inch, head tilted slightly. "I'm a pyromaniac. I like everything hot except the weather. Isn't that odd?" Her long tapered fingers played around the rim of the candle holder, dipping heat from its mouth and flicking it into the air conditioning. He couldn't take his eyes off them. How they moved, how they gathered warmth and dissipated it. This woman fascinated him.

"Well, at least the waiter finally lit our candle," he sighed.

"He didn't." She looked secrets at him, as if challenging him to guess. "I did."

"Of course, your matches." Duncan sipped his chardonnay, enjoying its light oaky flavor and buttery texture while watching her peel a shrimp. Peters discovered himself basking in the jealousy from male diners watching them while she savored the seafood's delicate flavor.

"I'm glad my meetings at the university gave us a chance to get to know each other beyond the messages we've traded through email." Lynn wiped her fingers on a thick cloth napkin. "I've been hoping for this chance. I think we have more in common than we've admitted. This is the time to find out." She pointed suddenly at the appetizer. "Will you please eat? I feel like I'm devouring the entire thing here. I'd rather share. With you."

Breath deserted Duncan again at the obvious hint. Was it possible she liked him as much as he liked her? That amazed him. Smiling he lifted a shrimp, peeled it, and munched the morsel, tasting only his wonder of her.

The waiter must have been watching. With perfect timing, he swept in minutes after they finished the last bite, clearing plates and depositing fragrant sourdough bread, real butter, and their salads. Duncan asked for two more glasses of wine, switching to his favorite merlot.

"You must be feeling better," Lynn observed. "I'm glad. You looked very stressed when you came in."

"I was." He related a condensed version of Hallberg's machiavellian shenanigans which poisoned Duncan's position at SFC.

Lynn laid down her fork on the tender lettuces and herbs, leaning on the table with chin in hand. "You know," she said softly, "if you quit trying to hide things and stand up for yourself, the idiot would have to back down. It works; I've done it myself."

The meteorologist spluttered. Was he so transparent she could read his soul? Her outline wavered faintly, as if a dark gold corona flared about her head. Must be fog from the air conditioning caused by high humidity outside, he explained to himself. Must be.

Their entrees arrived. Peters hoped for no more interruptions after the server left—he was determined to find the reasons behind Amelynn Sperry's mystery.

"This is really good," Lynn murmured after a forkful of the black bean concoction.

"It'll lend a bit of Mount St. Helens to your insides," he teased after a bite of succulent tuna.

"It's good for my insides," she retorted, quirking an eyebrow at him. "A little heat within tames the heat without, you know. And it is hot here. No, it's actually more humid. I have to be accurate about these things since I'm with a meteorologist."

"Stormy weather," he agreed, feeling almost brave enough to tell her his secret.

Lynn's smile infused her entire being as she met his gaze. "That's what you deal with best, isn't it? Especially tornadoes."

"Kansas City's been the victim of quite a line of thunderstorms lately. It's also within the borders of what's commonly known as Tornado Alley." He laid down his fork. Now or never. "Lynn, I—"

"Hello! Hope you don't mind the interruption. I just had to find out who this lovely creature is."

Duncan wilted as Hallberg's falsely friendly voice severed his. Of all the people he didn't want to see tonight! His voice grated as he made introductions, and his headache returned. Lightning flashed beyond the window, followed by a protracted ominous rumble of thunder emanating from hell itself.

Jack ignored the fact that Lynn didn't offer her hand and that Peters remained mute about his joining them. Swinging around to the table behind them, he swiped an empty chair with an unapologetic grin and sat down. "Heard you were sick today, Dunc." He tossed out the pleasantry carelessly, using the nickname he knew Peters hated. "Glad you're better." Hitching himself so his gray Armani-clad right shoulder excluded the meteorologist from conversation, Hallberg beamed a smile at Amelynn. "Kansas City is honored by your presence."

"If you don't mind, *Mr.* Hallberg," Lynn said in a low, pointed voice. "*Dr.* Peters and I were discussing something important. And private."

"Go right ahead. We work together very closely, you know." Jack upped the kilowatt level of his smile. It met her protective heat-banked wall and rebounded, but that only offered challenge. Hallberg accepted that challenge immediately with a flash of his blue eyes.

Lynn looked hard at Duncan. It was clear to him she was poised to do something if he didn't. A halo of dark bronze fire shot with sparks seemed to glimmer around her head. She hesitated, breath quiet, some odd feral power almost outlining her hands.

Understanding blossomed in Peters' mind. Hallberg was his problem, this was his action. Amelynn could do something, but that wouldn't enhance his image with Jack. Time to change the way things stood, and do it decisively.

The meteorologist cleared his throat with a hard hack to attract attention. "Jack, back off. We don't have to put up with your nonsense here."

Hallberg's smile hardened. "Nonsense, is it? Just wait, Dunc ol' boy." His shoulder angled Peters farther out of the conversation. "This lady doesn't deserve you. She needs a little more excitement than a bookworm writer can manage. I can't imagine an evening with you being very interesting." He pitched his voice for Lynn alone. "I propose dancing and champagne, then we'll see where that takes us, all right?"

"Is getting a woman dizzy and drunk your only method of seduction?" Lynn's tone dripped with sarcasm, finally making Hallberg blink in surprise. "Wonderful. How dull."

Duncan found himself on his feet as thunder shook the foundations of the building. His curly hair lifted from his head with static electricity and he felt clothed with the brilliance of sheet lightning. Patrons looked away from the disturbance at the table and beyond the window into the darkening sky, nervously discussing the impending storm.

"Outside, Jack."

The acquisitions director grinned, unable to see anything but Amelynn and his own victory. "The little lady hasn't made her decision. As if there's a decision to make."

"There is," the environmental scientist snapped. "I'm nobody's 'little lady,' especially not yours."

"Excuse us, Lynn." Voice hard as hail, Peters recalled his martial arts training. His left hand connected with Hallberg's right elbow, fingers seeking and finding the place he wanted.

"Hey, that hurts! What—Manager. Manager! I'm being assaulted."

Two digits jammed against the nerve between bones of his opponent's joint. Duncan pushed harder, forcing the man to rise.

"It's all right," he reassured the hovering waiter in a quiet, steady voice, steering Jack toward the door. "I'll take care of him. Only a minor disagreement, easily allayed."

"You can't do this!" Jack struggled to pull away, stopped when the meteorologist's grip sent searing pain upward through his shoulder. He snarled, "My next report will cost you your job!"

"I've been needing to do this for a long time, Hallberg. We'll take our discussion outside. I won't have other people disturbed by your boorish manners, especially not Lynn."

Peters rushed them both through heavy wooden double doors onto the walk and to the curb before he stopped. Glancing around, he made certain there was no metal near them—trash baskets, tiny computerized parking meters, the old-fashioned streetlamps which adorned the Plaza. He let Hallberg go. Hallberg cradled his painful joint as he stared hatefully at his rival.

"Don't think you can get away with anything," Jack threatened. I'll have the police on you so fast—"

"I don't think so. You've met more than your match," Duncan said evenly. He felt wonderfully calm, thoroughly in control for the first time in his life. The storm formed his backup, a formidable ally. "I'm going to teach you a lesson, and I want you to learn it well. Think about it every time you see me, and remember it can happen any time I want it to. This doctor of meteorology knows his stuff from the inside out."

Peters took one step back as Hallberg began telegraphing a swing. Duncan snapped the fingers of his left hand.

The tang of ozone abruptly overpowered the enticing smells from the restaurant. With thunder sounding as if the sky ripped asunder, a blue-white bolt seared the walk's gray-tinted plascrete just inches from Jack's designer shoe. A second responded to the snick of Peters' right fingers, singeing the Armani suit down one arm and leg. Tiny tendrils of smoke drifted up as Hallberg halted his punch and looked in disbelief at his ruined suit.

"Let's put that out immediately." Duncan's fingers fluttered. A downpour responded, dumping on Jack's head and blanketing everything to the west in gray curtains of rain. The meteorologist stood without a drop touching him or anything behind him to the east.

"Remember this lesson, Hallberg, and we'll get along just fine. You can start by authorizing funds to buy the upgrades we need tomorrow at the meeting with Michaelson. The SFC has a chance to be the best forecasting station in the world without your interference, and from now on I'm going to make sure it achieves that status." Peters turned toward the restaurant, noticing his audience for the first time. In the midst of the amazed diners sat Lynn, eyes flashing and mouth curved in a wonderful secretive smile.

"But . . . but what . . . what did . . . you . . . ?" gasped Jack.

Duncan deigned to turn only his head. "You haven't figured it out yet? Thought you were smart. I don't only forecast the weather, Hallberg. I *control* storms. That's why I understand tornadoes. That's why I can help people in this country and all over the world if idiots like you aren't constantly undermining me with dumb kid tricks to block my way." His gray eyes iced. "If you ever try and pull that childish crap again, especially if you do anything to Lynn, you better believe I'll more than toast your suit. No go home and dry off."

"But . . . but you ruined my Armani!" Jack howled.

"There's nothing you can do about it, Hallberg. It was caused by an Act of God."

Peters turned his back, stalking into the Classic Cup feeling eleven inches taller and completely in control of himself for the first time in his life. Waiters fell away from his path, expressions of awe and nervousness on their faces. When he rejoined his companion, he'd already decided to speak later about their possible future together.

"What delightful entertainment!" Lynn enthused, eyes sparkling. "I'm so glad you decided to discipline that mongrel yourself."

"Ah, Dr. Peters." The manager hovered at his shoulder. Duncan faced him, power from the storm still cloaking his shoulders.

"Yes?"

"Thank you for taking care of that . . . situation . . . so decisively, especially outside the confines of the restaurant. I appreciate your consideration for other customers." Their waiter appeared with a chilling bucket and large dark bottle. "As thanks for saving us trouble and damage, your dinners are on the Classic Cup tonight. I've taken the liberty to include a bottle of our finest champagne. Charles, clear the table and bring this couple fresh entrees."

Their waiter whisked away the cold plates as the manager popped the cork from the vintage with a flourish, pouring bubbly into fine crystal flutes he deposited on the table. "Enjoy," he said, snuggling the bottle in the chiller. "If there's anything else you desire, let me or Charles know."

"Do you still serve that wonderful hand-made cappuccino ice cream?" asked Duncan. At the manager's nod, he smiled. "Great. We'll have that for dessert."

"Very good, sir. Ma'am. Have a lovely evening."

"See?" Lynn said coyly as soon as the manager disappeared. She touched Duncan's glass with hers; the two met with a harmonious *ting*. "Good things happen when you take charge."

"Lynn, there's something I have to tell you—"

"You don't need to say anything about your ability to control storms, Duncan. I thought I recognized a fellow freak a few months after we started emailing. But you seemed to be in thorough denial, so I decided not to say anything about it then."

"A fellow freak? But . . ."

"You still don't understand?" She sighed. "And I gave you all those hints. Here, watch."

She set down her champagne and turned to the large stone fireplace which dominated the room's south wall. Logs were laid, but no flames danced behind the protective metal grating. Amelynn Sperry sucked in breath, stared at the seasoned wood, and flicked a single finger against her thumb. The corona Duncan had noticed about her head surged. In the fireplace a wisp of smoke rose, followed by ravenous golden flames. Two couples voiced delight at the restaurant's "automatic" lighter.

"That's why I'm in environmental studies," she said after Charles served their steaming dinners. "I correlate the affects of fires after storms, earthquakes, and the like, and try to find better ways for people to reestablish their lives. My specialty is flash fires. Like you, I have an insider's point of view. Also like you, I determined I could better use my talent if I kept it undeclared."

"You're giving me the benefit of a decision I don't think I ever consciously made Lynn," the meteorologist said, shaking his head. Noticing it still raining to the west and clear to the east, he changed the weather pattern to an overall fine drizzle.

"Something hidden inside you did." She poured more champagne into their flutes. "It's time for me to confess." She sighed, putting down the bottle. "You don't know how long I've searched for another person with talents comparable to mine. I found a few, but they were all somehow . . . I don't know, warped." Sperry raised her glass. "You're a real person with a real talent, Dr. Duncan Peters. You took the last step in your maturation tonight when you admitted you're exceptional and bested that Jack creature. And you're honestly working with your affinity for storms to benefit others. I think I've finally found my match." Her eyes looked straight into his soul, shaking him to his foundations with her testament. "You pass my tests, Duncan." She raised her glass to him. "Salute."

This time the thunder sounded inside his head.

Peters finished his dinner in a daze of disbelief. Lynn proved a witty and eager conversationalist, with surprising knowledge of several subjects he'd always wanted to research but hadn't yet found the chance. They lingered over the excellent ice cream, and finished the bottle of champagne before rising. With the manager's compliments ringing in their ears, the couple left the restaurant, Sperry's arm resting in the crook of Duncan's.

She looked up as the street light changed the drizzle to diamonds. "It's raining, you know," she teased as they walked the old-fashioned sidewalks through the famous early 1900s district.

"Want me to change it?"

"Heavens, no. My silk is washable, and my flame never goes out."

"Speaking of that," Duncan sucked in a huge breath before taking the plunge. "Want to create a little fog? My place isn't far."

Her laugh scintillated joy into the night. "Why, Dr. Peters, I thought you'd never ask."

TRUST

by Kristine Kathryn Rusch

Kristine Kathryn Rusch is an award-winning fiction writer. Her novella, *The Gallery of His Dreams*, won the *Locus* Award for best short fiction. Her body of fiction work won her the John W. Campbell Award, given in 1991 in Europe. She has been nominated for several dozen fiction awards, and her short work has been reprinted in six *Year's Best* collections. She has published twenty novels under her own name. She has sold forty-one total, including pseudonymous books. Her novels have been published in seven languages, and have spent several weeks on *The USA Today* bestseller list and *The Wall Street Journal* bestseller list. She has written a number of Star Trek novels with her husband, Dean Wesley Smith, including a book in this summer's crossover series called *New Earth*. She is the former editor of the prestigious *The Magazine of Fantasy and Science Fiction*. She won a Hugo for her work there. Before that, she and Dean Wesley Smith, started and ran Pulphouse Publishing, a science fiction and mystery press in Eugene. She lives and works on the Oregon Coast.

Windy, rainy, the road dark and slick through the trees. Carter was already late. He hadn't factored in the weather, the utter blackness of the Devil's Elbow in the middle of a November night.

Judy would be waiting. It seemed that women always waited for him, no matter what he did to prevent it.

His hand was on the steering wheel. He didn't trust

the car's autopilot on this dark and dangerous road.
His phone was in his pocket, but he didn't want to
take his hands off the wheel to punch her number. He
hadn't put her in the autodial yet, had a hunch she
wouldn't last any longer than the others.

He hadn't seen another pair of headlights on the
entire drive up the mountain. He was nearing the summit now—the road widened, and the reflective barrier
marked last winter's slide, the one that had rolled a
van all the way down to the ocean. Speed limit 35
here. He slowed to 20. The corners were tricky near
the top.

Then something caught in his headlights—just the
impression of the thing: fluffy white tail; wide, sad
face; a bit confused. He cursed but kept his hands on
the wheel, narrowly missing whatever it was (*it looked
like a St. Bernard-Husky mix*, his traitorous mind told
him) and started down the other side of the Elbow to
Dory Cove and Judy, and a long, luxurious dinner at
the best restaurant in town.

Dammit. He had to stop.

He made a U-turn, wheels skidding on wet leaves,
and headed back to the summit, saw the dog prowling
the side of the road like a restless ghost. It looked up
at him, big sad blue eyes—definitely Husky in there
somewhere—and sat down, as if it had known he
would come.

Dammit.

He pulled onto the shoulder, grabbed his flashlight,
and got out of the car. The rain had stopped, but the
trees were dripping—heavy, thick, cold drops that
were somehow worse than an actual shower.

"Hey, girl," he said as he crossed the road. "How're
you doing? Huh?"

The dog's tail thumped. Her head dipped down as
if she were ashamed to be in this position and relieved
at the same time.

"It's okay," he said. "I'm not going to hurt you."

Her tail continued to wag. She knew that. The reas-
surance was for him. He'd never been bit, but dogs

spooked easily, especially big dogs alone on a mountaintop on a wet November night.

He crouched beside her, fingers probing her wet fur, found a choke chain, which angered him, and an out-of-date vaccination tag, which also angered him. No ID unless she had a chip in her shoulder, and somehow he doubted that.

She whined softly, nudged at his face, and he petted her, finding lumps and scars and scratches, not all of them from being loose on this wild night.

He didn't like any of it, not in the least because he was cold and wet and frustrated. His mutant talent had snared him again. He couldn't go on a date with a big white dog in the back seat, a dog who was friendly to him but who might not like flighty women like Judy.

The dog licked his hand, feeling his hesitation, and in that moment he knew he was lost. He resigned himself to an evening of the Colonel's finest, an apologetic phone call to Judy who would now never go in the autodial, and a house that would smell of wet fur for days.

The morning wasn't going to be much better—a round of vets, first to check for the chip and to see what the lumps were, and then to study the Lost Dog notices always posted on the bulletin boards.

This time, though, would be the last. The town was too small for him to continue practicing his strange talent.

Someday soon, he would get caught.

The dog didn't want to get in the car, the first time he'd ever had an animal balk on him. All animals liked him. He was the kind of man aloof cats would cuddle with and nasty horses would never bite. But his talent, his special talent, was with dogs.

They always found him when they needed help.

It was a small enough talent that most people never noticed. The ones who did chalked it up to weird coincidence. Every once in a while, when they were with

Carter, he'd have to get a trapped dog out of the surf, or help a lost dog find its owner. He never let anyone be with him all the time for fear that the pattern would become obvious—and that played true hell on his dating life. He'd never moved in with anyone, never had a relationship that lasted longer than a month.

He didn't dare. His parents were still alive, and they would be the ones punished if he were caught.

Little mutations were the unexpected side effects of genetic alterations, the kind that were banned just after the turn of the century. Most of the mutations were obvious and somewhat threatening: incredible strength, telekinesis, and telepathy were the ones that caused the most consternation. Other mutations, like Carter's, were hard to notice.

Scientists were fascinated by these changes, claiming they weren't mutations after all, but an enhancement of abilities that already existed in the body. Carter often wondered what scientists would make of his special talent.

He had the ability to make upset animals, particularly dogs, feel better. It was as if he had a psychic bond with any canine. Perhaps, his mother once suggested, his mutation came from the human traits that were used to domesticate animals in the first place, which was why his talent was strongest on dogs, although it had some effect on cats.

Not that it mattered. If his mutation was discovered, his parents would go to jail. He would have to wear a bracelet which told the world that he was no longer considered human, if they felt he wasn't a menace to society who needed to be institutionalized for life.

The logical thing to do was the one his father had insisted on: ignore animals around him. But Carter was as unable to ignore animals as they were to ignore him. He felt compelled to help, and more than that, he wanted to help.

He couldn't have left that dog on the summit. He would have gone back no matter what.

It took him almost an hour to coax the dog into the car, but once he did, she settled into the back seat as if she were used to riding. He didn't like the way she cringed from his hands when he tried to pet her. He also didn't like the way her ribs poked against his fingers.

He had to get her to a vet, not just to check the chip, but to see what all the lumps and scratches were.

Carter had a hunch he was not going to like what he found out.

Early the next morning, he took the dog to the new vet on the outskirts of town. He arrived at the small veterinary hospital in what had once been a feed store by 7:30. He'd been around vets long enough to know that they usually scheduled their first appointments around 8:30, using that early morning hour to accept the surgery patients and the cases requiring tests or bloodwork.

Sure enough, he showed up at the same time as a woman with a Persian cat, a man with two Great Danes (one stayed in the car and the other had to be carried in), and a teenage boy with a rather scruffy-looking rabbit.

Carter waited until they were processed, then he went inside himself. There was a rattled receptionist, obviously new, and a veterinary assistant who was visible through a side door, shaving the Persian's neck.

"Hi," Carter said to the secretary. "I found this stray and I was wondering—"

"Another stray?" a woman came through the double doors. She was tall, red-haired, and sturdy, almost square. He knew without looking at her name tag on her lab coat that she was the new vet. But he did glance at her name tag. *Vanessa Simon.*

At first he thought she was directing the question to him. But the receptionist was the one who answered. "I–I–I–don't know."

But the vet was already crouching in front of the

dog. The dog leaned against Carter. He could feel her shaking.

"It's okay, honey," the vet crooned in that singsong voice which often soothed animals. "Let me see what's going on here."

"She doesn't have a nametag," Carter said, "but I thought maybe she'll have a chip. Although there are some things I don't like. That choke chain for one, and she's got scabs all over her body—"

"Improperly healed wounds. Cuts, and I think she may have a broken rib, judging by her breathing. She's also too thin for a Husky hybrid, especially if she's a Husky/St. Bernard mix like that face suggests. She's not yours?" The vet looked up as she asked the last, her expression seemingly mild.

"I found her last night on Devil's Elbow Summit."

"In the rain?"

He nodded.

"Strange place for both man and beast last night," the vet said.

"I had a date in Dory Cove. Not that I made it. This girl here prevented that."

"You got back before the winds hit, I take it."

"We were just leaving as they started."

The vet's fingers continued to probe the dog's front legs. The dog whimpered and looked at Carter. He kept his hand on her square head, not permitting her to move.

"I doubt she would have survived another day or two on the mountaintop," the vet said. "You probably saved her life."

Carter didn't respond.

The vet stood and said to the receptionist, "Tell Susan I'm going to need her help. I'm going to need to do a thorough examination of this dog. I know she needs stitches in a number of places, and I think she may be too weak to go under an anesthetic. We'll see what the bloodwork says."

The dog pressed as close to him as she could.

"She seems bonded to you, Mr.—"

"Williamson," he said.

"I don't expect you to pay for this. You're not responsible for a stray. But I'll be honest with you. This is a new practice, and I'm not easily able to float a lot of money, so . . ."

"I can handle it." His job was stable enough, even if he wasn't. He was a bartender at one of the major hotels. He managed his own money with care. Dog surgery would take a bite from his savings but not a significant one.

"I'd like to find out who did this," the vet said.

She reached over the desk and got the handheld scanner, running it over the dog's shoulders. The dog whimpered, then cringed. Carter had to crouch beside her to calm her.

Then the vet sighed. "Nothing, of course. Strays never seem to have I.D."

"There's an old vaccination tag on the choke chain," he said.

Her fingers found it. She tried to take the chain off, as he had, and made the same discovery. It was too small to go over the dog's head.

The vet cursed. "I'll cut this off soon enough."

"I didn't even think they made those any more," he said.

"They don't, but the old ones stick around somehow." The vet ran her fingers over the tag, then she turned to the receptionist. "When I get this chain off, you run the numbers on this tag. We should get an address. That's when I'll call animal control and the sheriff. No one should treat a dog like this."

"You think it was all deliberate?" Carter asked.

The vet pointed to a scar on the shoulder, parting the fur so that Carter could see it. The dog whimpered louder.

"See the edges?" the vet said. "They're clean. I'm betting that was either done with a knife or a razor blade."

"To remove the chip?" he asked.

She frowned. "Quite possibly. We see that in purebreds on occasion, but why would anyone do this to a mix? They're not worth much on the open market."

"Maybe this dog wasn't going to be resold," he said.

Her frown deepened. "I don't like the possibilities behind that."

He helped her take the dog into one of the examining rooms. The dog whined again as she walked inside, balked, and he had to urge her forward.

She leaned against him, but didn't try to leave. Nor did she growl as the vet moved her to the examining table.

"I think we can handle it from here," the vet said. "I know you're going to pay for this, but do you want her? I'll wager the place she came from wasn't home."

He would wager that, too. "I'll take her," he said, although it wasn't his custom to adopt any of the dogs he rescued.

He couldn't leave her here. She was the neediest animal he'd ever found.

"I'll be back," he said to the dog, and made sure he looked into her eyes. She seemed reassured, although that might have been his imagination.

He didn't want to think about the fear she would feel without him. Instead, he comforted himself, knowing that the vet would do everything she could.

Carter came back at four, just as the receptionist had urged him to do. He pulled up next to the only car in the lot, an ancient truck with a large cab filled with equipment he didn't recognize.

As he got out, the vet slammed one of the truck doors shut. She wasn't wearing her lab coat. She seemed very young in her blue jeans and denim shirt, with its sleeves rolled to her elbows. Her red hair was held back with a barrette, narrowing her face.

"Your dog will be fine," she said when she saw him, "but she has to stay here a few days. We found a lot more damage than we expected. Someone used a laser scalpel where a laser scalpel shouldn't have been used."

He winced.

"Listen," she said. "We traced that tag. It belonged to a pit bull treated nearly five years ago at one of the other clinics. I'm going to check the address before I call animal control. You want to come?"

He didn't, but he didn't know how to say no. "You think that's safe?"

"I think we're going to find some people who lost their dog years ago and will have no idea what happened to it, not that we'll be able to tell them. I have a hunch their dog suffered a similar fate to yours here, only didn't live through it."

He didn't like the idea of her going alone. "Maybe you should call the authorities."

"And scare some people who've been wondering what happened to their dog? Nah. I may not even stop." She pulled open the passenger side. "But I have to look."

Actually, so did he. In all his years of rescuing, he'd never seen anything quite like this.

He got in the truck. "You think she got away somehow?"

The vet nodded. "One of the links in the choke chain was broken. I think she'd been hooked onto something and broke free."

She walked to her side of the truck and got in. The automatic controls were shut off, just like in his car. She was a hands-on driver, which actually made him feel safer. These automatic controls didn't really work well on coastal roads. The controls had been designed for city driving, and they went too fast for him, took corners too sharply, and followed other cars too close.

"Where'd you learn how to drive?" he asked.

She grinned. "My father. He said one day all of us would be at the mercy of machines if we didn't learn how to do what they do. I like driving. It wouldn't bother you, will it?"

He shook his head. It actually made him feel safer.

"I'm Van, by the way," she said. "If we're going to

go snooping around other people's houses, we probably shouldn't be formal with each other."

"Carter," he said.

"Well, Carter," she said, "let's go visit a pit bull's
former home."

And they did.

The address Van had belonged to a small house on
a narrow country road, two miles away from Devil's
Elbow Summit. The house had been empty for quite
a while. Weeds grew on the driveway, and the windows were covered with dirt. Still, it was easy to see
that someone had once cared for the place. Over-
grown roses and rhododendron bushes suggested the
outlines of a large garden.

Van got out and stared at the house for a moment.
Carter got out of the car, too. The air had the pungent
odor of pine.

"Dead end," she said.

He nodded, then frowned. The breeze also carried
the scent of dog—lots of dogs. He turned toward the
scent and thought he heard a sharp, terrified bark.

"Did you hear that?" he asked her.

"What?"

Another yip, hesitant, a different dog, just as frightened. And then a wail.

Van glanced at Carter. "Where's that coming
from?"

He pointed down the road.

They walked instead of drove—it seemed more sensible. They were following their ears and noses, like
dogs did. Then he saw the tuft of white fur, coarse
mixed with gray. Husky fur. *Her* fur.

He put a finger to his mouth, pointed, and walked
into a small stand of decorative pine. A house loomed
in the distance, this one trim and beautiful, and built
within the last five years.

Van followed. She clutched her phone as if it were
a weapon.

The shed was hidden in the woods. It had been

made from a kit sold by a local hardware store, and it wasn't very sturdy. Bones littered the ground outside, most of them unattached. A pile of skulls stood at the back of the shed, and Carter recognized the distinctive narrow shape and long teeth.

Canine.

There was a rusted chain outside with the clip still attached to a broken link. The link matched his dog's choke chain.

He pointed toward it. At that moment, the wind came up, blowing in a different direction. Instantly the dogs started barking—frantic terrified barks—and they all came from the shed.

Van pulled open the door. The barks turned to growls, ferocious and still just as frightened as before, but in an attempt to defend. She backed away, her face green. She had a hand to her mouth.

He peered inside. Dogs, in various states of pain and abuse. The barking stopped and so did the growling. They whined at him. One, a puppy no more than six months old, crawled to him on its belly. It had a running sore on its shoulder—again, someone's crude attempt to remove a chip.

Van stared at him.

"Get out of here, in case whoever did this comes back." He crouched, unable to turn away from the misery before him. "Call for help. We need to get someone here, now."

"What are you going to do?" she asked.

"Wait here."

"What if the person comes back?"

Carter turned to her, fists clenched. "He's not going through that door."

Her lips thinned. "It's better if I stay. I can help them."

He shook his head. "You'll help them later. Right now, they need me."

She studied him for a moment, then dialed her phone. "We need some help," she said into it as she crouched beside Carter. "Right away."

* * *

Ten dogs. Ten living dogs who, once freed from their chains and torture racks, had circled Carter and sought his comfort.

Van had watched, unable to get close. Any time she tried, the dogs would snap at her, baring their teeth and looking feral. After a while, she didn't even try.

It was Van who protected Carter from the sheriff, who warned him to stand up when she heard footsteps in the trees. It was Van who lied for him, when the sheriff asked why the dogs didn't attack. And it was Van who figured out how to get the dogs back to her hospital so that she could start saving lives.

Carter had followed her lead numbly. The dogs had drained him, the devastation worse than anything he had ever seen, the evidence around the shed hinting at so much more. Even the sheriff had been shocked, although he had been looking for the person who had been stealing dogs from tourists. He had an entire list of dogs—including the pit bull—who had disappeared in this areas in the last five years.

The shed belonged to the neat and organized house. The woman who owned it had a friendless son, who spent most of his time in the woods.

"Hadn't you heard the dogs, ma'am?" the sheriff asked.

"The neighbor dogs," she said, shaking her head. "Sometimes those hideous creatures bark all night."

It was all Carter could do to keep from strangling her. But the sheriff had assured him strangulation wasn't necessary. It was clear, the sheriff said, that her son had a mutation. He'd obviously been tampered with on the genetic level, and what had emerged was an incredible sadistic streak that had, fortunately, only manifested on dogs.

At that moment, Carter had to turn away. He didn't trust himself, his face, his temper. He hated the assumption of mutation with no proof, the idea that whatever was wrong had to be genetic, and not plain evil. Besides, there was nothing fortunate in what had happened to those dogs, except, maybe, that he and Van had found them.

The woman and her son were arrested. The sheriff believed that the genetic tampering laws were enough to put the woman away for a long time, and to keep the son institutionalized forever.

"And what if the kid hasn't been tampered with?" Carter asked.

The sheriff studied him for a moment. Then he shrugged. "Animal cruelty, as many charges as possible. We have to put that kid away for a long time."

"Yeah," Carter said, "for the sake of the area's dogs."

"Dogs, hell," the sheriff said. "Kids like that escalate. Only'd be a matter of time before he moved on to people. And by then, he might have been good enough not to get caught."

The dogs were farmed to four different vets in the area. Van stayed up all night tending her patients. Carter found her, exhausted, sitting in front of the veterinary hospital at 7:30 the next morning.

"We lost two," she said in a ragged voice. "Eight are going to make it, but we lost two."

He sat down beside her and then, because she looked like she needed it, put his arm around her.

"We would have lost all of them and never known if it weren't for you," she said.

He shook his head. "That first dog. My dog. She got away. She's the hero."

"And you're the one who could overcome her defenses, get her into your car, get her to trust you. How do you do that?" Van looked up at him, her eyes wide.

The moment of truth. She'd seen it. She knew. She would know a lie when she heard it.

"It's innate," he said, an admission he'd never made before. To anyone.

He waited for her to pull away, to scream maybe, to run inside and call the sheriff. Carter had time to get to his car and drive out of here, stay one step ahead of if he had to.

To his surprise, Van smiled. "I thought so," she said. "What I wouldn't give to be able to do that."

"No," he said. "You don't know what responsibilities it entails."

"Yes, I do." She put a hand to his face. Her fingers were cool on his skin. "What do you do for a living?"

"Tend bar. It travels well."

"Why aren't you a vet?"

"And call attention to myself?" He shook his head. "No."

"Did I tell you my receptionist is my niece? She hates the job. She's afraid of animals."

He kept shaking his head. "It won't work, Van."

"Sure it will," she said. "People don't think about strangeness here, only about giving their animals comfort. Think how much it would calm them to know that you have a rapport with their pet. Believe me, I've seen it a lot. You're not the only one with this gift."

He stared at her for a moment. It meant risk and exposure, staying in one place long enough to be discovered. Chancing the same fate that might happen to that awful boy and his wretched mother.

Then the memory rose, of the dogs crowding around him, letting him touch their scabbed and injured bodies. The looks they had gotten of peace, of hope. Even the two who didn't make it. Van hadn't had to tell which two they were.

He knew.

"It's a gift, Carter," she said.

It was, in its way. One he used whether he wanted to or not.

She hadn't moved away from him. He still had his arm around her shoulder. He sensed no fear in her, no worry. She had been as honest with him as she could.

He leaned his head on her soft hair, felt tension drain from him for the first time in days, maybe years.

From inside the hospital his new dog barked. She

must have heard his voice. He hadn't seen her since the day before, although it felt much longer than that.

They got up, and without a word, Van let him inside. His dog lay in her cage, her tail thumping, bandages covering her fur. She smiled a doggy grin when she saw him.

"I'd be trusting you with everything," he said to Van.

"Like dogs do." She slipped her hand in his.

He nodded. "Like dogs do."

"I heal them, Carter. I don't betray them."

"I'm not a dog, Van."

"I won't betray you either," she said. "I promise."

She squeezed his hand as she said that. And his dog kept grinning her doggy grin.

Then the front door opened, and an elderly man's voice said, "Anyone here?"

"Ready to start?" Van asked.

He hesitated for a just a moment, then made his choice. "Past ready," he said, and went to greet the first patient of the day.

TRUTH
by Michelle West

Michelle West is the author of a number of novels, including *The Sacred Hunter* duology (*Hunter's Oath* and *Hunter's Death*), *The Broken Crown*, *The Uncrowned King*, *The Shining Court*, and *Sea of Sorrows*, the first four novels in *The Sun Sword* series, all published by DAW books. She reviews books for the on-line column *First Contacts*, and less frequently for *The Magazine of Fantasy & Science Fiction*. Other short fiction by her appears in *Black Cats and Broken Mirrors*, *Elf Magic*, *Olympus*, and *Alien Abductions*.

S he was alone.
Funny. Months ago she had packed a bag, stuffed money in a wallet and crept out her bedroom window, leaving her family in blissful, sleeping ignorance, just *to* be alone. But she felt it as sharply as a person feels a deadly cold now that she had achieved it.

At night, the cityscape ablaze with a hundred-thousand lights, the skyline shot through with reds and golds, pale greens and purples, and the garish blink of neon, she would wander up from her squatting place in the industrial barrens by the railroad tracks. An old switching house, windows either broken or boarded up, had become home during the warm season; she wasn't sure what they would do when the frost hit.

Was coming, soon. She could taste it in the air on the back of her tongue, stronger than diesel or automobile exhaust. Even in the city, the seasons had their rhythm.

Scrape had not come back.

He'd left before sundown, in a hunt for cigarettes, money, or the scraps of food that were left in abundance on the trays of a hundred tables in the underground complex of adjoining malls beneath the downtown core. He had to move quickly because he wasn't city clean; his coat—one of two that he owned—had the grime of spring and summer crushed into the weave of its fabric. Sweat had accumulated in layers until the smell was almost overpowering— although she marveled at the fact that she couldn't smell herself nearly as well. In the winter, it wouldn't matter as much.

They didn't sweat as much for one, and they'd have to beg, borrow or steal warmer clothing, for two, and she was pretty sure that she'd be longing for the inside of one of those malls by the time the first week of real cold had ended. People who needed the food or the shelter provided by clumps of rent-paying stores were the ones most likely to get tossed out. Didn't seem fair, after hours, no one *used* the malls, but they were havens from ice, snow, and the killing chill that came with it. People like her, Scrape, the others—they could just squat there until the doors were open to paying customers. But no. The warmth was given to fake geese and millions of dollars worth of merchandise.

No one cared.

And why should they, after all? It wasn't as if she'd cared much when she had the chance to do something—she was just as likely—more than likely—to back away, cringing at the sight of someone like Scrape. Or herself, these days.

The Sally Ann was a good walk away, but she'd been there twice; she knew what could be found, and for how much. Had even started to plan around for the winter.

Back at home—when she'd had one—planning for winter meant digging the boots, coats, and sweaters out of storage and changing the tires on the cars. Cal-

lie's father had not believed that all-season tires were
a replacement for winter radials.

Winter was for skiing, skating, arguing about whose
turn it was to shovel the drive. Family.

Not here.

Here, Scrape told her, warmth was measured in
shelters, the Y, and the vents that gusted warm air up
into the city streets in billowing clouds. People fought
for those. People fought a lot.

But no one bothered Scrape. His face would lose
its friendly expression, his muscles would go slack, his
eyes would go dark—really, *really*, dark, and they'd
practically break their backs getting out of his way.
Once or twice they started screaming.

It wasn't that he was large—he wasn't—or that he
was particularly threatening—but it was hard to look
at his face for long, almost impossible to meet his
eyes. They had that dark, hungry quality that seemed
to suggest he'd cling to you forever if you paused to
see what he was about.

No one wanted that.

Not even Callie, the time or two she'd seen it—but
she'd seen worse; in a way, the darkness, the hungri-
ness, was less threatening because it was exposed; because she *knew* that others saw exactly what she saw
when she looked at him.

Not like the voices. God, they had been so bad.

If it hadn't been for Scrape, she wouldn't be able
to think about wandering in the city now.

Scrape, damn it.

Scrape had found her wandering the streets of the
city. She'd lost her wallet two days after she'd run
away; lost her purse and her backpack about a week
later. If she'd kept the phone numbers of friends or
relatives, they had been buried in that pack; she wandered the city streets as if she'd never seen them before, increasingly hungry, tired, and afraid.

Things had gotten so bad, she'd taken to sleeping
during the day and wandering at night, like the search-

lights, when there were far fewer people around. When she was sleeping, she couldn't hear a thing. She had found that drinking helped a bit, and she drank— but only until the money was gone.

She'd been born in the vast sameness of the suburbs before the suburbs had exploded in a wild spread of growth that had eaten farm land and forest right up to the escarpment, but it was in the packed, dense buildings in the inner core that she found true wilderness; there was a terrible freedom between their windowed, concrete faces, and it was killing her quickly.

She saw—at a distance, distance was important—the girls who had chosen to turn tricks for money, and the money was important enough that she might have considered doing it herself—but she couldn't bear to be touched, because when she was touched she heard *everything*, every horrible thought. Starvation was a better choice, and she had been heading that way quickly.

She'd lost a lot of weight, and dignity had kind of gone with it that first week. But there were crazy people trapped on the outside of buildings, day in, day out. And that was where she belonged, among the crazy, dying people.

She didn't much care about dying. If she'd been less of a coward, she'd've jumped off the nearest bridge, or into the nearest subway tunnel. Some treacherous part of her, buried where nose couldn't reach it, still wanted to live, but it had been losing ground daily.

Scrape pulled that death back, grabbed her by the shoulders, make her *look* at it.

And she could bear to listen, that first time, because she was convinced he was part of the alcohol-induced delirium that made the streets bearable. After all, she couldn't *hear* him. He didn't look at her, didn't cringe with disgust, didn't think of what she might have been like if she'd been cleaned up; he didn't seem to *think* at all. When his words came, they were just that: words.

But she remembered, clearly, when he'd gone beyond words; when he'd reached out and cupped her chin in his palm; when eyes so dark she couldn't tell where the iris ended and the pupil began, reflected her face, her straggly, tangled hair, her bruised eyes. Because he hadn't thought a word.

She should have felt danger; she felt, instead, the doors of a past life open, furtive and sudden; she remembered when being touched, like this, by her father, her mother—had been simple, wordless, comforting. Comfort.

When he turned and left, she felt the world go with him, and she was sucked along in his wake because nature abhors a vacuum.

He knew the streets. Knew who to hit for money, or how to ask. Knew which of the beat cops would make them move on, and which would turn a blind eye to their presence. He knew them well enough that she could follow like a shadow in his wake.

She still heard the voices, this close to people, but they were strangers' voices, a cacophony of white noise. With Scrape by her side she could walk through the crowd and not get lost in the maze. Well, not always. Sometimes a word would stick out and jab her, catching her attention, dragging her into a stream of words that she couldn't easily escape.

When that happened, she would freeze in place, eyes wide, the city suddenly far, far too threatening, the familiarity of Scrape's back retreating.

On days like these, Scrape would stop, cocking his head to one side as if he listened for the sound of her footsteps. As if he could make out which ones were hers. As if they were distinctive amidst the fall of thousands of other feet.

He would turn, reach out for her elbow, and lead her past the voice that had trapped her, captive audience, against asphalt and concrete.

His leg had been badly broken, badly set, although he wouldn't say how or when; he walked with a terrible limp, but she learned to love this, too. Because of his loping, awkward gait, she could spot him from so far away she couldn't even see what color he was.

She didn't know much about him. She never asked.
She loved that she could be with someone for days
on end and never learn more than the words that
came out of his mouth could tell her.

She had been trapped in a house with people she'd
known all her life, and had discovered, as the voices
got louder and more intrusive, that she hadn't known
nearly as much as she thought she had. And that she
never wanted to learn any more.

"Kid," he'd said, "what they've done to you." He
shook his head. Fumbled for a match book and a half-
smoked cigarette, which was probably his most disgusting habit. He didn't spend money on cigarettes—
that was a waste. But he's search along the ground for
the leftover, half-smoked butts that people had stepped
on or put out because there was "still life in them."

"There should be laws." He'd laughed. " 'Course,
I'd just break 'em, so there's no damn point. You've
still got friends, and you've still got family; they just
forgot how to talk to you.

"But I'm Scrape, eh? And I know. I know how to
talk. You stay with me, and I'll teach you. But it won't
be easy. Come the time, it'll be harder than anything
you've ever had to learn. You listening to me?"

"I don't want to talk to my family."

He shrugged. "Doesn't mean you don't have 'em.
Some people don't, but yours are still there."

"They can stay there. I'm not going home."

"I won't make you. But I'll tell you this up front: I
want you to go back."

Scrape hadn't come home.

Home, two months or more ago—she didn't actually
know what the date was, just that it was getting colder—
had been a four-bedroom house with a garage in the
lane and a tree that caused annual arguments with the
neighbors towering above her bedroom window.

Home had been the place she left to go to school,
to see friends; it was the place she returned to, rain
or shine.

She didn't want to think about it. Didn't want to hear what her mother didn't say, her father didn't say; the angry, ugly words they kept beneath closed lips, narrowed eyes. The disgusting things that came out of nowhere, and stayed with her no matter how much she drank to forget them.

Scrape, she thought, *where the hell are you*?

During that first week, when he could tell she was still nervous—of him, of having him disappear—he started his lessons. He wasn't much in the way of a teacher, but at least he didn't stand on formality.

"You don't have to tell me anything," he said. "Because I'm sure as hell not going to tell *you* anything." He had a ratty old blanket for himself, nothing for her, but it wasn't that cold at night, and she could curl up with her knees to her chest and her cheek against the ground, preserving body warmth.

She'd been drinking; she didn't feel the cold, although she'd be stiff with it in the morning.

"You don't talk much, do you?"

She shrugged. "Words are pointless."

"Words are all you've got."

No. She stiffened. Rocked herself up into a sitting position, thighs flat against her chest.

He mumbled something rude about smoking Nazis—by which he meant anti-smoking nazis. It was a tirade she'd heard before. Scrape found it harder and harder to scrounge enough half-smoked cigarettes to support his habit, a fact he blamed on non-smokers.

"Yes." And then he'd turned and walked out of the building, looking for smoke.

It took her a minute to understand that he'd heard her. She'd almost run away, that day. Because she knew what could be heard, if someone was listening: everything. All the ugly things that no one should ever be allowed to know about anyone else.

But she hadn't run, not then. And later, it seemed pointless.

It was a week before she found the courage—a

week of sweltering humidity, of smog hazy skies and lack of rain—to ask him about it.

"You—can you hear everything I—I think?"

"Was that a question?"

"Scrape—"

"Too much muttering. Try again."

"Bastard."

He laughed. "Better, but it'd get you sent to your room."

She surprised herself. She laughed. "You don't know my family."

"No, I don't. You could tell me, though."

The laughter went wherever laughter goes when it dies. She was almost pale with the shock of it.

"Sweet sound, kid. I occurs to me you don't laugh much."

She shrugged. "Not much to laugh at." It was the first time since she'd run that she had laughed about anything to do with her family.

"Maybe, maybe not. Look at me—bum leg, no money, no food. No friends, family dead. What do I have to laugh at? But I laugh."

"So you're stupid."

"Stupid is worse than unhappy?"

"Only the people who are lucky enough to stay stupid are happy."

Scrape talked a lot. A *lot*. Sometimes talking was good. Sometimes it was confusing. He was hard to get used to. He wasn't like anyone else she'd ever met.

"What is it you think you know about people?"

She shrugged. "Nothing much."

"Must be something, kid. You avoid 'em like the plague."

"Why do people say that? There hasn't *been* a plague to avoid for a long time." She kicked a rock. There were a lot of rocks, most of them chunks of cement and concrete debris that lay scattered in and about the tracks. "Anyway, it's not like you don't avoid them."

"Me?"

"Well, you're here."

He laughed. He laughed as often as she shrugged. "I like 'em well enough, but they're more trouble than they're worth."

She shrugged. "You going to eat the rest of that?"

"Maybe. Maybe not. You going to answer my question?" He held out the half-eaten burger. It had onions and ketchup, neither of which she liked, but it was better than hunger. Her dad have been right about that.

Around a mouthful, she filled her half of the trade. "Sure. I think people are all lying hypocrites."

He lost his laugh. Fumbled in his pocket for matches. When he looked up again, she couldn't see the whites of his eyes. "Why is that?"

"Because they say one thing. They tell you it's the truth. They tell you that truth is important. But they mean something different. They—they think the exact opposite. Or worse. They hate their kids. They hate the lives they tell you you should be living. They think about sex all the time."

"Kid—"

"Never mind. I don't want to talk about it." She handed half of the food back; the rest was on its way to her stomach.

"No trade. You don't want to talk? All right. Don't talk."

She turned on heel and walked away.

But listen.

And stopped. It was the first time she could hear what she knew he wasn't saying out loud. She forgot to breathe. Turned back to face him.

Yes. You can hear me. If I want you to.

"Don't."

But you only get to hear what I want you to hear. No eavesdropping. No private stuff.

You think I don't know what you're going through.

*You think you're the only person who's ever gone
through it.*

Get real. Grow up.

Why did you run? Did they hurt you?

"Yes."

You look fine to me.

Piss off, Scrape.

He laughed again. "You learn fast, kid. You might
be okay."

Before she could run, he did—walking as quickly
and confidently as his uneven gait would allow.

Maybe he was scared, too.

*You wish. I'm out of smokes. And I'm hungry. You
want to run? Go ahead. I told you, people are more
trouble than they're worth.*

The stars above the big city were sparse. This close
to the buildings that defined the skyline, light seeped
into the edges of the night sky like a pale stain. She
could see the moon's face, the clouds that wreathed
it, and the brightest of the Northern stars; that was all.

When she'd been ten, eleven, twelve, her older
brother would climb the carport and set up his telescope on the gently sloped shingles. Then he would
flip himself up on the edge of the roof proper, slide
his way along the siding, and stop at her window.

She remembered, clearly, that the open window was
like a doorway into another country, and she would
grab her blankets and trundle out onto the rooftop,
waiting for her eyes to adjust to world by moonlight.
As they did, she would listen to her brother's voice.

It was like a lullabye infused with excitement; it
didn't make her sleep, but in an odd way it made her
feel both special and cherished. He had so loved that
telescope, those stars, that sky with its endless possibilities. Without parents as overseers, they rarely had
time for the endless bickering that seemed almost inevitable during the day; she stood by his side in silence, waiting, happy to be invited.

She was glad that the old memories couldn't be destroyed by the new ones.

New one:

Standing beside her brother when her best friend came to visit.

Listening as he noticed her breasts and wondered absently what it would be like to undress her and—

No. Enough. No. It still made her sick to her stomach.

She raised her hands to her ears, and then, almost reflexively, lifted her head from a pillow of sand and began to smash it against the ground. Pain helped.

You're loud, you know that?

She stopped instantly. Ashamed. Afraid.

What are you afraid of?

Of what her brother had been afraid of, when she'd rounded on him, shaking with fury.

Discovery.

Exposure.

She hadn't known, that day, that he hadn't said the words where anyone but she could hear them. But he knew that she had, somehow, heard him, and from then on he hated her for knowing.

Almost as much as she hated him for it.

But even though she hated him, she got up and left the building.

"Where're you going?"

"For a walk. I'll be back."

"You be careful."

"I'm always careful," she said bitterly. "I can hear them coming a mile away."

Callie, he said, when she'd gotten too far away for his words to travel, *I don't hear everything you think. I sure as hell don't listen. If I did, I'd be dead of boredom by now. But I hear you when you shout. You have to learn how to be quiet.*

No one else does. Querulous, childish words. She knew it, couldn't stop herself from thinking them anyway.

No. But they don't know any better. You do.

It was only when she started to skip in a one-two-one-two step over the train tracks that she realized that no matter how disgusted she had been, she could not bear to expose her brother to the scrutiny and contempt of a stranger.

Even though she could live with the stranger.

Morning. Breakfast provided by someone who'd taken pity on Scrape, but who was too practical to just hand him money to spend on cigarettes or booze. Instead, he handed him a bag from McDonald's. Scrape was feeling generous—it was fast food, after all—and had saved the meal until he got back to the switching station.

Most of his inquisitions took place around meals.

"Kid, you ever notice that people are good at saying what they mean?"

She shrugged. It was her first answer to almost anything he asked.

"Well, they're not, because that's not what *I* meant. Lemme try that again. You ever noticed that people are good at telling each other how they feel?"

She shrugged.

"That could get to be old real quick," he snapped. He fumbled in the lining of his coat for a cigarette, the pockets long since having disintegrated. Found the usual half-smoked castoff. She waited while he played with matches, because she knew he hadn't finished.

"The reason you haven't noticed it is because they aren't. They're no damn good at telling each other how they feel. They're no damn good at telling *themselves* how they feel. They have words, and half the time, the words get in the way."

"Why're you telling me this, Scrape?"

"I have to have a reason to be smart? I'm telling you this 'cause I *feel* like telling you this, and I'm paying your way so you're going to listen."

She shrugged.

"And I'm telling you this, girl, because all you get are words. You understand?

"You hear all the stuff they're thinking, but they only think in words. Be better all around if you could hear what they were feeling instead of what they were thinking, 'cause thoughts change faster than teen idols."

By the time the moon had crested the Manulife Building, he still hadn't come back. She didn't much like to go out into the city after him; too many people, even at night.

But she was worried.

"You ever get lonely?"

She shrugged.

Scrape couldn't find a cigarette, and he'd emptied his pockets compulsively about ten times, so she knew it would be a short conversation. "Callie, do that again, and I'll break one of your shoulders. I'm not going to be here forever. You got to pay attention."

Lonely?

"No."

He looked up from the debris he'd pulled out of his coat lining. "You will be," he told her. Something about his voice was softer than she'd ever heard it. Gentle even. "You get over this, and you will."

"How do you get over this? How do you get over the fact that you can hear everything everyone is thinking, especially when it's about you?"

If he'd been her, he would have shrugged. "That's a good place to start."

"What's a good place? Scrape, damn it, make sense!"

"Good place to start is to ask questions, no matter how pissed off they make you. Or anyone else. How do you ever get over something like this?" He gave up on the pockets. "Don't start smoking. Look at what it reduces a man to."

"I might have started, but—not those. You don't know where they've been."

"Sure I do. In someone else's mouth or under someone else's shoe. Well, both usually. Gotta run. Back soon. Try to get the dishes done, okay?" He rolled his eyes as she furrowed her brow. "That was a *joke,* girl. Joke, you know? One of those things that gets less and less funny when you have to explain it?"

"It wasn't funny to start with."

"Says the kid who doesn't know how to laugh." He got serious for a minute. "How many times have you thought about killing someone?"

She shrugged.

"Tell you, I've thought long and hard about breaking that damn shoulder."

"Killing someone? You mean seriously?"

"I mean at all."

"I don't know."

"More than once? Less than a hundred thousand times?"

"I don't know, Scrape. I wasn't counting."

"How many times have you thought about sleeping with someone? Stranger, movie star, whatever."

"I don't know."

"How many times have you wished you'd never been born, or your brother had never been born, or—"

"Scrape, *I don't know.*"

"Okay. God, I hate smoking nazis. Look, I really gotta run. But I want you to think. You don't know. You don't remember. How important can a thing be if you do it a hundred thousand times and none of them are significant?"

"Pretty damn important," she shot back. "How many times have you inhaled in your life?"

He laughed. "Touché."

But it made her think.

How many times?

If every thought counted, what did that make her?

She was waiting for him when he got back.

He handed her a paper bag—a crumpled paper bag with a half piece of pizza, assorted crusts, a salad that had probably been limp when it was made, and a half can of coke.

"Score," she said.

"Hey, I do better when you're not nattering at me."
He sat down and rubbed his leg. Winced.

She wondered what the cold would do to it.

"Not much. I ain't afraid of the cold. She and I,
we've got history."

"You're listening!"

"You're projecting."

She ate. The food was cold, but it was food; she was
hungry. Through windows opened by falling stone, she
looked up; the moon's face was shadowed. Like hers.
"Can you hear everything I think?"

"Yeah."

She didn't like the answer, but she hadn't expected
to. "Everything?"

"Yeah."

"Did you always hear everything?"

"Pretty much."

"Am I . . . am I a worse person than anyone else
you listen to?"

"I don't listen to a lot of people. They're sort of
like novels, you know? After you figure out the three
basic plots, there's not a lot left to discover."

"Then why did you listen to me?"

"Well, you're a special case."

"Special?"

"Sure. You've got a voice that's hard to ignore."
He stopped rubbing his leg, and reached into his coat
pocket. A book of matches that looked like it had
been tossed in a washer and dryer came out, followed
by a cigarette butt. He lit it and inhaled. "They ever
hit you?"

She shrugged. "Maybe when I was a kid. I don't
know. Not really."

"They ever toss you out of the house?"

"No."

"Starve you?"

"Scrape."

"Humiliate you?"

"All parents are humiliating sometimes."

"They ever do anything else?"

"Like what?"

He laughed. "Never mind. That's clear enough." Smoke wreathed his face; came out of his curved lips in a round, silent "O." "You run away because you could hear 'em?"

She shrugged.

"Kid . . ."

"Yeah."

"Sticks and stones, kid."

"Maybe. I–I could hear them all the time. *All* the time. The things they were thinking. The things they regretted, the things they didn't regret. My dad—" She fell silent. "I always thought they were decent people, you know? Normal people. But they—"

"They are normal people."

"Normal people don't think about screwing their neighbors or their kids' friends."

He laughed again. "Normal people can think about screwing almost anything. Thoughts are free."

"Not thoughts like that."

"Is that all they thought about?"

"Well—"

"Is that all they thought about, or is that all you listened to?"

"I didn't *listen*."

"Fine. Is that all you heard?"

She shrugged. Saw his lips thin. "No. That's not all I heard."

"You don't ever think about—well, maybe at your age, you don't. Never mind. You think about other things. You think bad thoughts just as much as you think good ones, and in between, you think about clothing, homework, friends, food. Stuff. The other day you wondered what it would be like to push someone in front of a train. You wondered what you would do if someone pushed you—how you'd save yourself, if you could."

She frowned. "No I didn't."

"Yeah, kid, you did."

"I'd remember that, Scrape."

"Maybe. But you don't, and I heard it. It didn't mean anything to you. You walked past the pizza place yesterday afternoon and you—"

"Which pizza place?"

"Doesn't matter. You thought that anyone who put pineapple on pizza was disgusting."

"Well, they are."

"You remember that?"

"No."

"You forget a lot for a person who expects people to suffer for random thoughts, you know? You hate yourself?"

She was silent.

He lifted his arms. Stretched them. Let them fall. "I'm pretty damn tired," he said, reclining until all of his weight was on his elbows. "And if you had any brains, you'd be tired too. Get some sleep. We can talk about this later."

"What if I don't want to talk about it?"

"Then you can listen to me. You hear like a child, and childhood's over. If you can't learn to listen, to really hear, you're never going to make it."

"Scrape—"

He closed his eyes. The gap between his name and a reply got longer and longer.

So she listened.

I've seen too many kids not make it.

What do you mean, not make it?

He smiled, but he didn't answer.

Maybe she did. Hate herself. Maybe that was the point. She *knew* the worst that she could be. And she'd spent a lot of time making sure one else did.

But she expected other people to be better. People she loved. People she trusted. What was the point of trusting someone who was just—

Just as helpless as she was.

She could usually tell when Scrape was awake because it was the only time he didn't snore.

That day, the wheezing broke up into a spate of coughing. He sat up, doubled over, and coughed until something came out of his mouth.

What are you staring at, kid?

"You don't sound so good."

Happens.

She didn't ask him why he wasn't speaking out loud; she knew. He probably couldn't get more than two syllables into a sentence without hacking his lungs out.

"Are you going to be okay?"

Sure. I'll just mosey on down to a doctor.

"You don't have to be sarcastic, I was just asking a question."

Ask smarter questions.

She fell silent. The silence was broken by coughing but not a lot else. She got up when she couldn't stand to listen to him anymore.

Where're you going?

"To get us some food. And no, I'm not crawling around the ground looking for half-smoked cigarettes. You want those? Tough. You should quit anyway— you probably wouldn't sound like that if you didn't smoke so much."

Don't you start. I'm old enough that I need a few bad habits.

"Find better ones. I'll be back."

He didn't ask her if she was going to be okay. Which was good, because she wasn't certain.

The streets weren't empty. They never were while the sun was up and office towers were open for business. She flinched and braced herself for sound, and it came, a waft of words, a cacophony of voices. She took comfort in the fact that they all belonged to strangers.

It was hard to move and listen.

It was impossible not to listen.

She forced herself forward by thinking of Scrape. She'd heard coughing like his before, but it had never come on so suddenly.

But was it sudden? She didn't see him most of the day. Maybe he'd been out here, hands out, scrounging along the concrete and the asphalt for cigarettes or money, coughing and getting sick and she'd never really noticed. He looked the same. He sounded terrible.

It was getting colder, and maybe he shouldn't be out here in the middle of car exhaust, in a ratty old coat that was more holes than material.

She looked down at what she was wearing and flinched. Hers wasn't all that much better. Certainly no cleaner. But—she wasn't sick. Not yet. She could walk without a limp. She could sit with her hands out just as well as the next person; could haunt the foot courts below the office buildings as easily as Scrape.

If she could ignore the voices.

She gave up twice; headed down to the tracks beyond Front Street before she found her courage and made her way back. Scrape wasn't much, and he was a pain, but he was all she had. She was all he had. She had to be able to do this.

Strangers' voices.

Angry voices.

Tired voices.

Frightened voices.

She stepped between them as if she were walking across a minefield with only a vague idea of where the mines actually were.

And then she heard laughter, something pleasant and light. She heard someone thinking about the color of someone else's skin in the morning, when the light through the blinds in her apartment turned everything to gold. Heard the words of a song she recognized, and realized that she could hear not only the tune, but the shadows of instruments and vocal harmonies in the background. Heard the frustrated recital of a shopping list, loitered a moment in the tangled web of someone's complicated scheme for disposing of lottery money if—well, when—they won.

She chose what she listened to with care, pausing

to let random strings of words coalesce into something that made sense before she decided whether or not to move on. It was a lot like flipping the dial on the radio; like changing the channel on the television.

Why hadn't it been like this before?

She still had to move slowly. She had to stop herself from flinching when she realized that some of the words she heard from random strangers referred to her. There was a lot of pity, a lot of contempt, a few people who thought she still had a chance if she got off drugs and cleaned up a bit. But mostly people wanted her to leave them alone; to keep her need and her desperation to herself for long enough that they could get past without having to acknowledge guilt. People were weary.

No one desired her.

Safety in that. She moved as quickly as she could, but it still took her two hours longer than it had ever taken Scrape to get to, and from, the malls, bag in hand, leftovers in bag.

He was sleeping when she arrived.

She waited until there was a break in the snoring and then nudged him gently with the tip of her foot. "Hey, Scrape."

He snuffled, turned over, covered his head with his arms.

"Scrape. Wake up."

"Go away."

"Scrape."

Bugger off. Leave me alone. I'm tired. He covered his ears with his hands and pressed them against the side of his head.

No way. You have to eat. Get up.

He rolled over, hands still pressed against the side of his, grimy elbows flapping as if he was trying to take off. He coughed a lot, and then muttered something under his breath.

She laughed. *You wanted me to learn.* Added, "Here, I went for food."

It's about time you did something useful. The hands

came off the ears; he stretched, groaned, and then shook his head in an effort to slough off sleep. "You were okay?"

"I took longer than you do—but yeah." She sounded surprised. She probably was. "I was okay."

She went out the next day, and the day after that. She never got back any earlier. Scrape spent another day and a half coughing before his body decided to save real illness for winter.

"Is it really okay?" she asked him quietly, watching while he smoked.

"What?"

"Listening. Listening to all the private stuff."

"No, not really. And they'd hate you for it, if they knew you were doing it. You'd scare the crap out of 'em. Ain't nothing as ugly as a bunch of scared people. Piss 'em off, and you're okay. Scare 'em?" He ran a finger sideways across his throat.

She shrugged. "I don't blame them. I wouldn't want anyone listening in on me."

"But you have to listen. And because you don't have a choice, there's no point in asking whether it's okay or not. God has ears, kid, and he gave 'em to you for a while." He laughed. "You ever dreamed of being God? Now's your chance to reconsider."

"You think God hears like I do?"

"Sure. But he doesn't have to ignore stuff, and it doesn't drive him crazy. Well, maybe. He hears it all. I don't think he has to pick and choose; he just takes it all in, like one giant sponge. How's that for a job?

"I wouldn't take it. Most of what he hears," he added, "is boring stuff. Hell, if I were him, I'd be happy when people thought about sex—it sure beats listening to them think about laundry."

"Scrape."

He shook his head. "All right. Seriously. People don't guard their thoughts. Everyone needs space, or they'd go nuts and start hacking each other to bits with the nearest sharp implement. City like this? No space. Thoughts are free space. Because no one can hear 'em. No one can think less of you for having 'em. No one can judge 'em."

"I can."

"Yeah, you can. But you shouldn't. The thoughts don't hurt."

"But thoughts lead to things that are—well, actions."

"Sure. Some thoughts do. Most don't. Most are just ways of marking time, of taking chances where other people won't get to watch them. It doesn't matter when we think—it's what we do that counts. I probably want to kill a person a hundred times a day. If I never do, it doesn't matter."

"Yes, it does."

"No, it doesn't."

"You can't be that angry all day long and say it doesn't matter."

He laughed. "You have a point."

"I do?"

"Yeah. But I should warn you, you won't like it."

Scrape, she thought, *where the hell are you*? She put force into it. Felt the words that she didn't speak more clearly than she had ever felt spoken ones. But if he was near, he didn't answer.

She was afraid.

Too afraid to sleep.

By morning, he hadn't come home, and she accepted, in a numb way, that he probably wouldn't. The noise of cars and distant trains were a counterpart to the silence of the tracks, the empty building. She didn't have much to pack, but she packed quietly, lingering while shadows grew shorter and shorter.

He didn't come back.

What she hated most was that she'd had no chance to say good-bye. She'd hate the rest later.

She started toward the heart of the city, listening.

*   *   *

She didn't know how to listen.

He'd told her that, a hundred times. He'd told her that she didn't understand what truth was. That she didn't have the right to judge.

She tried to remember it all.

Scrape!

A hundred voices moved like waves, like tide, rising and falling as they approached and receded. She didn't even try to catch the words; the words weren't important. What she wanted was a familiar cadence, a familiar voice.

She'd forgotten what it was like to feel this fear. The other fears—the fear of discovery, the fear of exposure, the fear of betrayal—had occupied all of her conscious time for months now. But the fear of loss?

Scrape, where are you?

She had almost given up three hours later. Daylight had given way to dusk, and dusk would fall to night; the air was cool. The streets were far from empty, but the office crowds had thinned; the malls had emptied.

She had traveled the length of the underground four or five times; had stopped in front of all the office buildings where smokers huddled; had loitered for a short time in front of the fifty-second division building before deciding that asking the police for help would be unwise; they'd take one look at her and start asking questions rather than answering them.

She had no place to go when she finished, except back to the switching station.

Maybe he'd be there.

Maybe not. She wasn't certain she wanted to go back, to wait, to give up on waiting. She walked instead.

She was exhausted. It had taken her a while to notice because what she was suffering from wasn't physical exhaustion; it was the kind of bone weariness that sets in when the ability to form a coherent thought slowly fails.

She found herself walking aimlessly, toe to heel, toe to heel, taking smaller steps as she realized that she didn't know where she was going.

Steps stopped completely when she heard—or thought she heard—something familiar.

It wasn't Scrape's voice, not exactly, because she didn't hear words. But she heard a murmuring, a rise and fall of something that might have been a voice at a distance great enough to obscure the harsh edges of distinct syllables.

Had she found him by accident? Had she heard him in some way that she hadn't known she could hear? She held her breath because breathing made noise. She lightened her step, walked more quickly; exhaustion gave way to relief, relief to something else.

Because as she drew closer to something that felt familiar, words did intrude.

Not Scrape's words.

Not Scrape's voice.

Nothing about Scrape had ever been this ugly.

She looked around and saw that she had walked her way out of the downtown core; had walked past the theatre district and the restaurants that surrounded it; had even cleared the so-called fashion district, that collection of old buildings that had once been garment sweatshops.

Height had given way to large, flat buildings, converted warehouses, small industrial refuges. Houses that might have once been beautiful cowered behind unkept lawns, their windows boarded shut, their walls covered with the broken spelling and sentiment of walk-by vandals.

Scrape?

No answer.

Not from him.

Not from the men whose voices she heard in sharp, harsh relief. They hadn't seen her. And if they had, she doubted they would pay her much attention; they were intent on different prey.

"Hey, old lady," she heard someone say. His words

and his thoughts were almost synchronized. "You look lost."

"Yeah, lost. We don't see many people lost in our neighborhood. Hey, what say we act like citizens and help you out?"

Snickering.

Old Lady. Not Scrape.

She started to back away.

Froze.

She could see the backs of four people; they were turned toward her. But it didn't matter—because she could hear the person they spoke to, even if she couldn't see her clearly.

He told me I would find my daughter. I knew—I knew I shouldn't have trusted him.

"Please let me by," she said quietly. Too quietly. "I came here with a friend, looking for someone."

There was a whoop of laughter. "Well, you sure found someone. You want friends? We're friendly."

Mom.

"Callie?"

Scrape, you bastard. I'll kill you. I'll kill you myself if anything happens to my mother.

She heard footsteps behind her, but she didn't turn to acknowledge them; they were an uneven shuffle that she recognized.

Anything happens to your mother, Scrape said, in a voice she had never heard before, *it will happen because you let it.*

You brought her here.

Yes.

Why?

She wanted to find her daughter. I told her to let it go, but she insisted.

Oh. And how the hell did she find you?

Clever girl. How do you think?

She spun round, hands clenched in fists; her whole body was shaking with rage. *How did you find her?*

Do you really want to ask that question right now?

Her mother's voice answered for her. She was praying.

Her mother.

Her mother, here. *Mom, no.* Yes. Because she had been desperate enough to take the word of a street person; had followed him here.

Listening to the four men, she was certain they intended to kill her mother. But she was certain that if they carried out half of what they dwelled so gleefully on, it would have almost the same effect.

She edged closer.

She was so far away. She couldn't breathe for fear. Of them. For her mother. For herself.

Scrape, damn you, help her. Help her!

I've done all the helping I can, he said, and she heard the sound of his steps shuffling away.

SCRAPE!

Wish I could help you, Callie, but you see—I don't have the power. You've got what you need. Use it.

Her mother said, clearly, "Let go of my arm."

"You aren't going to need that purse; you just relax and maybe that's all we'll take."

Knife. Someone had a knife. No gun. Didn't matter. She couldn't see the weapon, but she could hear it in her mother's shifting thoughts; the shock of it, the light across its side.

They didn't let go of her arm. They caught the other arm as well.

She's going to scream. Hell, let her scream. No one's going to stop us. And: *She screams, she'll get something to scream about.*

One of the empty buildings wasn't completely empty.

Callie followed.

Heard her mother's interior monologue grow wild, strained. She had never heard her mother like this. Did not want to ever hear her like this again.

"Stop!"

Four men did just that.

One of them nodded to the other. She didn't hear

the words they exchanged; she didn't have to. She could hear the thoughts that followed.

In the darkness, Callie didn't look like a victim; she looked like the person she'd become: street person. Vagabond. No fixed address.

She saw the twixt of disgust take his face as he drew closer. And heard her mother's sudden recognition of just whose voice she'd heard.

"You don't want trouble," the man in front of her was saying, "you'll leave. Now." He lashed out with a foot—because there was no way he was actually going to touch someone as dirty as she was—and sent her stumbling toward the sidewalk.

Her mother shouted something, but the words were indistinct, and quickly broken by a choked cry. Even the ability to hear thoughts failed Callie, because her mother's were too incoherent to fit into words.

Callie started to roll away from the man; he kicked her, and kicked her again, harder. She felt her side cave in, and for a moment she heard nothing at all.

But it was only a moment. He was gone; she could hear the words he left her with: *Stupid bitch. If I miss anything good, I'll go back and crush her skull.*

Scrape . . .

I'm sorry, kid.

She rolled over. Coughed. Bit her tongue. It hurt to sit up. Hurt to stand. But there were things that hurt worse.

Mom.

She screamed. She screamed so loudly she could hear no other voice but her own. There were four men. She counted them as they froze in place. She had no words to offer, none at all; they were no words that could convey her horror and her terrible, terrible fury. Words were too sophisticated. They required too great a distance.

No backs were turned toward her now; the men faced her, eyes wide, mouths open. Two carried knives in suddenly slack hands; one carried a piece of pipe.

The other had his hand shoved in balled fists into his jacket, his shiny leather jacket.

She had no idea what they saw.

She barely understood what she saw. Until she roared again.

Her lips had not moved the entire time. She was mute with fury, mute with fear.

They were mute as well, but they had words, thoughts, the things she had been so afraid of when she had run from the woman who now lay curled against the ground.

Now? Now she couldn't even understand what it was they were thinking; the words were broken, tiny things that hovered a moment before she sent them scattering back to the men from whom they'd come.

One man screamed. One man began to cry. One drove his knife into the fleshy part of his chest. One stumbled back and began to run, run, run.

She wanted them all to leave before she killed them.

But it was hard to watch them go. To watch them . . . escape.

Well done, Scrape said quietly.

Go away, Scrape.

I will. Soon.

You almost killed my mother.

Yes.

Why?

His reply? The sudden flame engulfing the head of a match. The inhalation of filtered smoke.

I killed mine.

She froze for just a second. And then she frowned. The words . . . *How?*

Does it matter? I killed her. She's never coming back.

Did you mean to kill her?

He laughed. She heard his laughter, although she knew it was as silent as the words they now spoke. *What do you think, Callie? All I've given you are the words. The truth.*

She said, instead, *I think my ribs are broken.*

Two of 'em.

You can tell?

Yes. They'll heal. I have to be going now, kid.

Where?

Don't know. Wherever it is that another kid like you comes into their power with no clue how to use it, or how not to. I killed my mother, he said again, *but I never meant to, and there's not a day goes by when I'd give back the power and bring back the dead in its place. She wasn't a bad woman. Your mother isn't a bad woman. We were just younger when were . . . came into our own. We believed in saints and angels instead of human beings.*

Scrape—

She needs you, now. You go.

But it wasn't Callie who left, it was Scrape.

The woman in her arms was older than the woman she'd run away from. Her hair was whiter, the lines across her forehead deeper. She felt a lot heavier, too, and after her ribs nearly caused her to black out, Callie decided against trying to lift her mother.

She wasn't awake. But dreaming, she began to think, and thinking she began to speak. The words made Callie flinch.

But she'd come here. She'd come here following Scrape—a madman, a cripple—looking for Callie. Her only daughter. Her baby.

The child who was never as smart as her brother, never as considerate. The child who made work impossible. The child who she sometimes hated.

Hate?

She brushed her mother's hair from her forehead.

Her mother's thoughts flew past; dream thoughts. They were as clear, as real, as any other thought her daughter had listened in on as a captive audience.

But there had to be more than those words. Could her mother really hate her and come here? Yes. Maybe. No.

Mom?

Her mother stirred.

Mom, it's okay. They're gone now. Wake up.

Eyelids moved. Eyes opened slowly, narrowed quickly.

My God, what is that smell?

Callie flinched. "Mom?"

Eyes widened again, mouth opened; her mother pulled back, out of the rough circle of her daughter's arms. She heard everything that followed shock; anger, disapproval, fear, fury, hatred—yes, even that—and she let the words spin around her as if they were moths, and she flame.

Seeing, for just a moment, rather than hearing.

"Mom?"

"C–Callie?"

"I—yeah. It's me."

Hesitation. For a moment, the silence was profound. Callie could hear no words at all.

And then she heard hundreds, a rush of sound, as her mother threw her arms wide and crushed her daughter in them.

Callie bit her lip till it bled; her ribs hurt like hell, but she—she wanted this, this hug, this welcome.

Because in it, she could see the words not as truth, and not as lie, but as facets of something larger and more complicated.

Learn to listen.

She was trying. And for just a second, before her mother pulled away and caught Callie's dirty, grimy face in clean, shaking hands, Callie could hear something that could not be contained in, or squandered by, words.

Not even her own, although she tried, would always try.

"I love you, too, Mom. Can I—can you take me home?"

Explanations were just more words, and they would come later, in their own place and time.

But she looked up, once, just past her mother's shoulder, hoping to catch a glimpse of a familiar, awkward gait.